P9-BZG-419

Had she finally found the man she longed for...or was she dreaming?

FRANCO—

High Praise for Linda Howard and Her Wonderful, Romantic Novels

"Ms. Howard never fails to entertain with a powerful and passionate story."

—*Rendezvous*

"*Angel Creek* has all the action and smoldering sensuality readers have come to expect from Ms. Howard. Once you start this spellbinding Western, you will find it impossible to put down, a fitting tribute to this talented lady. Very sensual."

—*Romantic Times*

"*Heart of Fire* is rich and compelling. . . . The strong writing and page-turning adventure will keep you up late into the night—another triumph from an already much admired historical and comtemporary writer."

—*Greeley (CO) Tribune*

Other Books by Linda Howard

A Lady of the West
Angel Creek
The Touch of Fire
Heart of Fire

For orders other than by individual consumers, Pocket Books grants a discount on the purchase of **10 or more** copies of single titles for special markets or premium use. For further details, please write to the Vice-President of Special Markets, Pocket Books, 1230 Avenue of the Americas, New York, NY 10020.

For information on how individual consumers can place orders, please write to Mail Order Department, Paramount Publishing, 200 Old Tappan Road, Old Tappan, NJ 07675.

LINDA HOWARD

Dream Man

POCKET BOOKS

New York   London   Toronto   Sydney   Tokyo   Singapore

The sale of this book without its cover is unauthorized. If you purchased this book without a cover, you should be aware that it was reported to the publisher as "unsold and destroyed." Neither the author nor the publisher has received payment for the sale of this "stripped book."

This book is a work of fiction. Names, characters, places and incidents are products of the author's imagination or are used fictitiously. Any resemblance to actual events or locales or persons, living or dead, is entirely coincidental.

An *Original* Publication of POCKET BOOKS

POCKET BOOKS, a division of Simon & Schuster Inc.
1230 Avenue of the Americas, New York, NY 10020

Copyright © 1994 by Linda Howington

All rights reserved, including the right to reproduce this book or portions thereof in any form whatsoever. For information address Pocket Books, 1230 Avenue of the Americas, New York, NY 10020

ISBN: 0-671-79935-5

First Pocket Books printing June 1995

10 9 8 7 6 5 4 3 2 1

POCKET and colophon are registered trademarks of Simon & Schuster Inc.

Stepback photo by Franco Accornero

Printed in the U.S.A.

This is dedicated to Joyce, Liz, Marilyn, Beverly, Cheri, and Kathy, for their encouragement and participation. To Gary, for taking care of me all those long months when I could barely walk. To Robin, for the pep talks. To Claire, for her patience. To Iris and Catherine and Fayrene and Kay, for the support. Thanks, guys.

Dream Man

1

I<small>T WAS ELEVEN-THIRTY WHEN</small> M<small>ARLIE</small> K<small>EEN LEFT THE</small> Cinemaplex with the rest of the Friday night moviegoers. The movie had been a good one, a lighthearted romp that had made her laugh aloud several times and left her in a cheerful mood. As she walked briskly to her car, she thought she could tell which movie people had seen by how they were acting now. It wasn't that difficult; the couples who were holding hands, or even exchanging kisses in the parking lot, had obviously seen the sexy romance. The aggressive bunch of teenage boys had seen the latest martial arts thriller. The well-dressed young professionals who were in earnest discussions had seen the latest *Thelma and Louise* imitation. Marlie was glad she had chosen the comedy.

It was as she was driving home on the brightly lit expressway that it hit her: She felt good. The best she had felt in years. Six years, to be precise.

In startled retrospect, she realized that she had been at peace for several months now, but she had been so caught up in the sedative routine of the life she had built here that she hadn't noticed. For a long time she had simply existed, going through the motions, but time had done its slow work and eventually she had healed, like an amputee recovering from the loss of a limb and learning to cope, then to enjoy life again. Her loss had been mental rather than physical, and unlike an amputee, she had prayed through dark, endless nights that she never recover that part of herself. At some point in the past six years, she had stopped living in dread that the knowing would return, and simply gotten on with her life.

She liked being normal. She liked being able to go to movies the way normal people did, liked being able to sit in a crowd; she hadn't been able to do that before. Several years ago, when she had realized it was actually possible, she had turned into a movie junkie for a while, visually gorging on the films that she thought were safe. For a long time any degree of violence was unbearable, but for the past couple of years she had been able to watch the occasional thriller, though they weren't her favorite type. To her surprise, she hadn't yet been able to watch any sex scenes; she would have thought that violence would have been immeasurably more difficult for her to handle, maybe even impossible, but instead it was the portrayal of intimacy that gave her problems. Dr. Ewell had been fond of saying that no one should ever lay bets on the human psyche, and she was amused to find he was right. The violence in her life had been traumatic, devastating, while the sex had been merely unpleasant, but it was the "love" scenes that still had her squeezing her eyes shut until it was over.

She exited off the expressway onto a four-lane street, and of course was caught by the traffic light at the bottom of the exit ramp. The radio was tuned to an easy-listening station and she inhaled deeply, feeling the slow music and the lingering lightheartedness of the movie combine in a delicious, physical sense of contentment—

—*the knife flashed down, gleaming dully. A sodden,*

muffled THUNK! as it struck. The blade rose again, dripping red—

Marlie jerked back, an unconscious physical denial of the horribly real image that had just flashed in her mind. "No," she moaned softly to herself. She could hear her own breathing, sharp and gasping.

"No," she said again, though she already knew the protest was useless. Her hands were clenched on the steering wheel, white-knuckled, and even that wasn't enough to stop the trembling that started at her feet and went all the way up. Dimly she watched her hands start shaking as the spasms intensified.

—Black, gloating pleasure. Triumph. Contempt—

It was happening again. Dear God, *it was coming back!* She had thought herself free, but she wasn't. The knowing was coming closer, growing, looming, and she knew from experience that soon it would overwhelm her. Clumsily, her coordination already deteriorating, she steered the car to the right, so she wouldn't block the exit ramp. A car horn blared as she wavered too close to the vehicle beside her, but the noise was distant, muted. Her vision was fading. Desperately she braked to a stop and shoved the gear lever into park, hoping that she had managed to get completely out of traffic, but then the nightmare image was back, hitting her full strength like a beacon that had brushed by her in search before homing in.

Her hands fell limply into her lap. She sat in the car staring straight ahead, her eyes unblinking, unseeing, everything focused inward.

Her breathing became harsher. Rough sounds began to form in her throat, but she didn't hear them. Her right hand lifted slowly from her lap and formed itself into a fist, as if she were gripping something. The fist twitched violently, three times, in a rigidly restrained stabbing motion. Then she was quiet again, her face as still and blank as a statue's, her gaze fixed and empty.

It was the sharp rapping on the window beside Marlie that brought her back. Confused and exhausted, for a terrifying moment she had no idea who she was, or where, or what was happening. An unearthly blue light was flashing in her eyes. She turned a dazed, uncomprehending look at the man who was bent over, peering into the window as he tapped on it with something shiny. She didn't know him, didn't know anything. He was a stranger, and he was trying to get into her car. Panic was sharp and acrid in her mouth.

Then identity, blessed identity, returned with a rush and brought reality with it. The shiny thing the man was using to rap against the glass transformed itself into a flashlight. A glint on his chest became recognizable as a badge, and he, frown and commanding voice and all, was a policeman. His patrol car, Mars lights flashing, was parked at an angle in front of hers.

The images of horror were still too close, too frighteningly real. She knew she had to block it out or she wouldn't be able to function at all, and she needed to get control of herself. Some vague danger was threatening, some memory that danced close to the surface but wouldn't quite crystalize. Desperately she pushed away the fog of confusion and fumbled to roll down the window, fighting for the strength to complete even that small act. The exhaustion was bone-deep, paralyzing, muscles turned to mush.

Warm, humid air poured through the open window. The officer flashed the light beam around the interior of her car. "What's the problem here, ma'am?"

She felt cotton-brained, thought processes dulled, but even so she knew better than to blurt out the truth. That would immediately get her hauled in on suspicion of being under the influence of some kind of drug, probably a hallucinogen. Yes, that was it; that was the vague danger she had sensed. A night in jail, for a normal person, would be bad enough; for her, under these circumstances, it could be catastrophic.

She had no idea how much time had passed, but she knew that she must look pale and drained. "Ah . . . I'm sorry," she said. Even her voice was shaky. Desperately she sought for a believable explanation. "I—I'm an epileptic. I began to feel dizzy and pulled over. I think I must have had a slight seizure."

The flashlight beam sought her face, played across her features. "Please step out of the car, ma'am."

The trembling was back; she didn't know if her legs would hold her. But she got out, holding to the open door for support. The blue lights stabbed her eyes, and she turned her head away from the brightness as she stood there pinned in the glare, a human aspen, visibly quaking.

"May I see your driver's license?"

Her limbs were leaden. It was an effort to retrieve her purse, and she dropped it immediately, the contents spilling half in the car, half on the ground. Innocuous contents, thank God; not even an aspirin bottle or pack of cigarettes. She was still afraid to take over-the-counter medications, even after six years, because the mental effects could be so unpredictable.

By concentrating fiercely, holding the crippling fatigue at bay, she managed to pick up her wallet and get out her license. The policeman silently examined it, then returned it to her. "Do you need help?" he finally asked.

"No, I'm feeling better now, e-except for the sh-shakes," she said. Her teeth were chattering from reaction. "I don't live far. I'll be able to make it home."

"Would you like for me to follow you, make sure you get there okay?"

"Yes, please," she said gratefully. She was willing to tell any number of lies to keep from being taken to a hospital, but that didn't mean she had lost her common sense. She was incredibly tired, the aftermath worse than she remembered. And there was still the nightmare image—knowing or memory, she couldn't tell—to be dealt with, but she pushed it out of her mind. She couldn't let herself think about it; right now she had to concentrate only on the tasks at hand, which were remaining coherent, upright, and functional, at least until she could get home.

The policeman helped her pick up her belongings, and in a few moments she was behind the wheel again, edging back onto the pavement, driving with excruciating care because every movement was such an effort. Twice she caught herself as her eyes were closing, the darkness of unconsciousness inexorably closing in.

Then she was home, turning in to the driveway. She managed to get out of the car and wave at the officer. She leaned against the car, watching him drive away, and only when he turned the corner did she set herself to the task of getting inside the house. To safety.

With weak, shaking, uncooperative hands she looped the strap of her purse around her neck, so she wouldn't drop it. After pausing for a moment to gather strength, she launched herself away from the car in the direction of the front porch. As a launch, it was spectacularly lacking in power. She staggered like a drunk, her steps wavering, her vision fading. Every movement became more and more difficult as the fatigue grew like a living thing, overwhelming her muscles and taking them from her control. She reached the two steps leading up to the porch and stopped there, swaying slowly back and forth, her blurred gaze fixed on those two steps that normally required no effort at all. She tried to lift her foot enough to take the first step, but nothing happened. She simply couldn't do it. Iron weights were dragging around her ankles, holding her back.

She began to shiver, another familiar reaction from before, in that other life. She knew she had only a few minutes to get inside before she completely collapsed.

She dropped heavily to her knees, feeling the resulting pain as only a dull, distant sensation. She could hear her own harsh, strained breathing, echoing hollowly. Slowly, torturously, she dragged herself up the steps, fighting for each inch, fighting to keep the darkness at bay.

She reached the front door. Keys. She needed the keys to get in.

She couldn't think. The black fog in her brain was paralyzing. She couldn't remember what she had done with her keys. In her purse? Still in the car? Or had she dropped them? There was no way she could retrace her steps, no way she could remain conscious much longer. She began fumbling in her purse, hoping to find the key ring. She should be able to recognize it by touch; it was one of those stretchy bracelet things, the type that could be slid onto the wrist. She could feel metal, but it eluded her grasp.

Bracelet . . . She had slipped the keys onto her wrist. It was a habit so ingrained that she seldom even thought about it. The shaking was worse; she pulled the key ring off her wrist but couldn't manage to fit the key into the lock. She couldn't see, the blackness almost complete now. Desperately she tried again, locating the lock purely by touch, concentrating with her last fierce vestige of strength on the herculean task of guiding the key into the lock . . . Got it! Panting, she turned the key until she felt the click. There. Unlocked.

She mustn't forget the keys, mustn't leave them in the lock. She slid the bracelet back onto her wrist as she twisted the doorknob and the door swung open, away from her. She had been leaning on the door, and with that support suddenly gone she sprawled in the doorway, half in and half out of the house.

Just a little more, she silently urged herself, and struggled to her hands and knees again. *Get in far enough to close the door. That's all.*

It wasn't really crawling now. She dragged herself in, whimpering with the effort, but she didn't hear the noise. The door. She had to close the door. Only then could she give herself over to the blackness.

Her arm waved feebly, but the door was out of reach. She sent a command to her leg and somehow it obeyed, slowly lifting, kicking—a very weak kick. But the door swung gently shut.

And then the darkness overwhelmed her.

She lay motionless on the floor as the clock ticked away the hours. The gray dawn light penetrated the room. The passing morning was marked by the path of sunlight, shining through a window, as it moved down the wall and across the floor to finally fall on her face. Only then did she move in a restless attempt to escape the heat, and the deep stupor changed into a more normal sleep.

It was late afternoon when she began to rouse. The floor wasn't the most comfortable of sleeping places; each shift of position brought a protest from her stiff muscles, nudging her toward consciousness. Other physical complaints gradually made themselves felt, a full bladder protesting the most insistently. She was also very thirsty.

She struggled to her hands and knees, her head hanging low like a marathon runner at the end of the race. Her knees hurt. She gasped at the sharp, puzzling pain. What was wrong with her knees? And why was she on the floor?

Dazedly she looked around, recognizing her own safe, familiar house, the cozy surroundings of the small living room. Something was tangled around her, hampering her efforts to stand—she fought the twisted straps and finally hurled the thing away from her, then frowned because it looked familiar, too. Her purse. But why had her purse straps been around her neck?

It didn't matter. She was tired, so tired. Even her bones felt hollow.

She used a nearby chair to steady herself and slowly got to her feet. Something was wrong with her coordination; she stumbled and lurched like a drunk on the way to a common destination: the john. She found the comparison faintly humorous.

After she had taken care of her most pressing need, she ran a glass of water and gulped greedily, spilling it down her chin in the process. She didn't care. She couldn't remember ever being so thirsty before. Or so tired. This was the worst it had ever been, even worse than six years ago when—

She froze, and her suddenly terrified gaze sought her own reflection in the mirror. The woman who stared back at her had her face, but it wasn't the soothingly ordinary face she had become accustomed to. It was the face from before, from six years in the past, from a life that she had thought, hoped, was finished forever.

She was pale, her skin taut with strain. Dark circles lay under her eyes, dulling the blue to a muddy shade. Her dark brown hair, normally so tidy, hung around her face in a mass of tangles. She looked older than her twenty-eight years, her expression that of someone who has seen too much, lived through too much.

She remembered the stark, bloody vision, the storm of dark, violent emotion that had taken control of her mind, that had left her empty and exhausted, just as the visions always had. She had thought they had ended, but she had been wrong. Dr. Ewell had been wrong. They were back.

Or she had had a flashback. The possibility was even more frightening, for she never wanted to relive that again. But it suddenly seemed likely, for why else would she have seen that flashing knife blade, dripping scarlet as it slashed and hacked—

"Stop it," she said aloud, still staring at herself in the mirror. "Just stop it."

Her mind was still sluggish, still grappling with what had happened, with the aftereffects of the long stupor. Evidently the results of a flashback were the same as if she had had a true vision. If the mind thought it was real, then the stress on the body was just as strong.

She thought about calling Dr. Ewell, but a gap of six years lay between them and she didn't want to bridge it. Once she had relied on him for almost everything, and though he had always supported her, protected her, she had become accustomed to taking care of herself. Independence suited her. After the encompassing, almost suffocating care of the first twenty-two years of her life, the solitude and self-reliance of the last six had been especially sweet. She would handle the flashbacks by herself.

2

THE DOORBELL RANG. DETECTIVE DANE HOLLISTER OPENED one eye, glanced at the clock, then closed it again with a muttered curse. It was seven o'clock on a Saturday morning, his first weekend off in a month, and some idiot was leaning on his doorbell. Maybe whoever it was would go away.

The bell rang again, and was followed by two hammering knocks on the door. Muttering again, Dane threw aside the tangled sheet and swung naked out of bed. He grabbed the wrinkled pants he had discarded the night before and jerked them on, zipping but not fastening. Out of habit, a habit so ingrained that he never even thought about it, he picked up his 9mm Beretta from the bedside table. He never answered the door unarmed. For that matter, he didn't even collect his mail unarmed. His last girlfriend, whose tenure had been brief because she couldn't handle a cop's erratic hours, had said caustically that he was the only man she knew who carried a weapon into the bathroom with him.

She hadn't had much of a sense of humor, so Dane had refrained from making a smart-ass remark about male weapons. Except for missing the sex, it had been a relief when she had called it quits.

He lifted one slat of the blinds to peer out, and with another curse he clicked the locks and opened the door. His friend and partner, Alejandro Trammell, stood on the small porch. Trammell lifted elegant black brows as he studied Dane's wrinkled cotton slacks. "Nice jammies," Trammell said.

"Do you know what the hell time it is?" Dane barked.

Trammell consulted his wristwatch, a wafer-thin Piaget. "Seven oh two. Why?" He strolled inside. Dane slammed the door with a resounding bang.

Trammell halted, belatedly asking, "Do you have company?"

Dane ran his hand through his hair, then rubbed his face, hearing the rasp of beard against his callused palm. "No, I'm alone." He yawned, then surveyed his partner. Trammell was perfectly groomed, as usual, but his eyes were dark-circled.

Dane yawned again. "Is this a very late night, or an early morning?"

"A little bit of both. It was just a bad night, couldn't sleep. I thought I'd come over for coffee and breakfast."

"Generous of you, to share your insomnia with me," Dane muttered, but he was already on his way to the kitchen. He had his own share of bad nights, so he understood the need for company. Trammell had never turned him away on those occasions. "I'll put on the coffee, then you're on your own while I shower and shave."

"Forget it," Trammell said. "I'll put on the coffee. I want to be able to drink it."

Dane didn't argue. He could drink his own coffee, but so far no one else could. He didn't much care for the taste of it himself, but since the caffeine kick was what he was after, the taste was secondary.

He left Trammell to the coffee and sleepily returned to the

bedroom, where he stripped off his pants, leaving them in their original location on the floor. Ten minutes in the shower, leaning with one hand propped on the tile while the water beat down on his head, made waking up seem possible; shaving made it seem desirable, but it took a nick on his jaw to convince him. Muttering again, he dabbed at the blood. He had a theory that any day that started with a shaving nick was shit from start to finish. Unfortunately, on any given day his face was likely to sport a small cut. He didn't deal well with shaving. Trammell had once lazily advised him to switch to an electric shaver, but he hated the idea of letting a razor get the best of him, so he kept at it, shedding his blood on the altar of stubbornness.

Dressing, at least, was easy. Dane simply put on whatever came to hand first. Because he sometimes forgot to put on a tie, he always kept one in his car; it might clash with whatever he was wearing, but he figured a tie was a tie, and it was the spirit rather than the style that mattered. The chief wanted detectives to wear ties, so Dane wore a tie. Trammell sometimes looked horrified, but Trammell was a clothes-horse who tended toward Italian silk suits, so Dane didn't take it to heart.

If any other cop had dressed the way Trammell did, or drove a car like Trammell's, Internal Affairs would have been all over him like stink on shit, which was an appropriate way to describe IA. But Trammell was independently wealthy, having inherited a nice little bundle from his Cuban mother as well as several successful concerns from his father, a New England businessman who had fallen in love while on a vacation in Miami and remained in Florida for the rest of his life. Trammell's house had cost a cool million, easy, and he never made any effort to tone down his way of living. His partner was such an enigmatic son of a bitch that Dane couldn't decide if Trammell lived as luxuri-ously as he did simply because he liked the life-style and had the means, or if he did it to piss off the bastards in IA. Dane suspected the latter. He approved.

He and Trammell were opposites in a lot of ways. Trammell was whipcord-lean, and as aloof as a cat. No matter what the circumstances, he always looked elegant and cultured, his clothes hanging perfectly. He liked— actually *liked*—opera and ballet. Dane was the exact opposite: he could wear the most expensive silk suit made, perfectly tailored to fit his muscled, athletic frame, and he would still look subtly unkempt. He liked sports and country music. If they had been vehicles, Trammell would have been a Jaguar, while Dane would have been a pickup truck. Four-wheel drive.

On the other hand, Dane thought as he wandered back out to the kitchen, nature had balanced itself out in their faces, in a kind of backwards way. In person, Trammell was smoothly handsome, but in photographs his face took on a sinister cast. Dane figured his own face would frighten children and small animals, assuming there was any difference between the two, but the camera loved him. All those angles, Trammell had explained. Trammell was a camera buff and took a lot of photos; he was never without his camera. Dane, being his partner and constantly in his company, was naturally in a lot of the photos. On film, the brutal lines of high, prominent cheekbones, the deep-set eyes and cleft chin, all became brooding and intriguing instead of merely brutish. Even the broken nose somehow looked right in a photograph. In person, he looked grim, his face battered, his eyes a cop's eyes, watchful and too old.

Dane got himself a cup of coffee and sat down at the table. Trammell was still cooking, and whatever it was smelled good.

"What's for breakfast?" he asked.

"Whole wheat waffles with fresh strawberries."

Dane snorted. "There's never been any whole wheat flour in *my* house."

"I know. That's why I brought it with me."

Healthy stuff. Dane didn't mind. He could be pretty damn affable when someone else was doing the cooking. When they were working they mostly lived on junk, whatever was fast and easy, so he didn't mind balancing it with low-fat, nutritious shit whenever they had the time. Hell, he'd even learned to like sprouts. They tasted like green peanuts, fresh out of the ground and not quite developed, with the hulls still soft. He'd eaten a lot of green peanuts when he was a kid, preferring them over the fully formed ones that had to be shelled.

"So what kept you awake last night?" he asked Trammell. "Anything in particular?"

"No, just one of those nights when a weird dream starts every time you doze off."

It was funny how the dreams came and went. All cops had dreams, but he and Trammell had gone through a rough patch a few years back, just after the shootout; the dreams had come every night for a while. Most cops went through their entire careers without ever firing their weapons on the job, but Dane and Trammell hadn't been that lucky.

They had been trying to find a suspect for questioning in a shooting and had been led, by the suspect's pissed-off girlfriend, right into the middle of a big-time drug operation, operated by none other than the suspect himself. That was usually the way the bad guys went down; they weren't caught by sharp detective work most of the time, but by someone dropping the dime on them.

That particular time, instead of bailing out any available window and disappearing down rat holes, the bad guys had come up with lead flying. Dane and Trammell had hit the floor, diving into another room, and for five of the longest minutes in history they had been cornered in that room. By the time backup had arrived, in the form of every cop in the vicinity, uniformed and otherwise, who had heard Dane's radio call of "officer under fire," three of the bad guys and the girlfriend were down. The girl and one of the men were dead. A slug had ricocheted, splintered, and part of it had hit Dane in the back, just missing his spine. It had still packed enough punch that it had broken a rib and torn a hole in his right lung. Things had gotten a little fuzzy there, but the one clear memory he had was of Trammell kneeling beside him and cussing a blue streak while he tried to stop the bleeding. Three days in intensive care, fifteen days total in the hospital, nine weeks before he'd been able to return to the job. Yeah, they'd both had a lot of bad dreams for a while after that.

Just as Trammell served up the waffles, the phone rang. Dane stretched to pick up the receiver, and at the same time Trammell's beeper went off. "Shit!" they both said, staring at each other.

"It's Saturday, damn it!" Dane barked into the receiver. "We're off today."

He listened while he watched Trammell hurriedly gulp a cup of coffee, then sighed. "Yeah, okay. Trammell's here. We're on our way."

"What canceled our day off?" Trammell wanted to know as they went out the door.

"Stroud and Keegan are already working another scene. Worley called in sick this morning. Freddie's in the dentist's office with an abscessed tooth." Things happened; no sense getting hot about it. "I'll drive."

"So where are we going?"

Dane gave him the address as they got into his car, and Trammell wrote it down. "A man called in and said his wife was hurt. An EMT was dispatched, but a patrol officer got there first. He took one look and canceled the EMT, and called Homicide instead."

It took them about ten minutes to reach the address, but there was no mistaking the house. The street was almost blocked with patrol cars, a paramedics van, and various other official-capacity vehicles. Uniformed officers stood around on the small lawn, while neighbors gathered in small bunches, some of the onlookers still in their nightclothes. Dane automatically studied the onlookers, looking for something that didn't fit, someone who didn't seem to belong or who was maybe just a little bit too interested. It was amazing how often a murderer would hang around.

He shrugged into a navy jacket and grabbed the spare tie out of the backseat, loosely knotting it around his neck. Somehow, he noticed, Trammell had managed to impeccably tie his own tie in the car. He looked again. Damn, he didn't believe it! The dapper bastard had chosen a double-breasted Italian suit to wear *on his day off!* He'd simply slipped into the suit jacket as they'd left the house.

Sometimes he worried about Trammell.

They showed their badges to the policeman at the door, and he stood aside to let them enter.

"Sheeit," Dane said in an undertone as he got a good look.

"And all the other bodily excretions," Trammell replied in the same disbelieving tone.

Murder scenes were nothing new. After a while, cops reached the point where violent crimes were pretty routine, in their own way. Stabbings and shootings were a dime a dozen. If anyone had asked him half an hour earlier, Dane would have said that he and Trammell had been detectives long enough that, for the most part, they were unshockable.

But this was different.

Blood was everywhere. It was splattered on the walls, on the floor, even on the ceiling. He could see into the kitchen, and the bloody path wound from there through the living room, then into a small hallway and out of sight. He tried to imagine the kind of struggle that would have sprayed blood so extensively.

Dane turned to the uniformed policeman who was guarding the door. "Have the crime lab guys showed up yet?"

"Not yet."

"Shit," he said again. The longer it took the crime lab, or forensics, team to arrive, the more the crime scene would be compromised. Some disturbance was unavoidable, unless the forensics boys were the ones to discover the victim and immediately secured the area. But forensics wasn't here, and the house was crowded with both uniformed and plainclothes policemen, milling around and inevitably muddying the evidential waters.

"Don't let anybody else in except for Ivan's guys," he told the officer. Ivan Schaffer was head of the crime lab team. He was going to be really pissed off about this.

"Lieutenant Bonness is on the way."

"You can let him in, too," Dane replied, his mouth quirking.

The house was middle-class, nothing out of the ordinary. The living room was furnished with a couch and matching chair, the required coffee table and matching lamp tables of genuine wood veneer, while a big brown recliner had the best spot in front of the television. The recliner was occupied now by a dazed-looking man in his late forties or early fifties, probably the victim's husband. He was giving mono-syllabic answers to the questions put to him by another uniformed officer.

The victim was in the bedroom. Dane and Trammell forced their way through the crowd and into the small room. The photographer had already arrived and was doing his job, but for once was noticeably lacking in his usual nonchalance.

The nude woman lay jammed in the cramped space between the bedside table and the wall. She had been stabbed repeatedly—*hacked* was a better description. She had tried to run, and when she had been cornered in the bedroom she had tried to fight, as evidenced by the deep defensive wounds on her arms. She had been nearly decapitated, her breasts mutilated by the sheer number of wounds, and all of her fingers had been severed. Dane looked around the room, but he didn't see the missing digits. The bed was still neatly made, though splattered with blood.

"Has the weapon been found?" Dane asked.

A patrolman nodded. "It was right beside the body. A

Ginsu knife from the kitchen. She had a whole set. It looks like they really do what the ads say; I think I'll get my wife some."

Another patrolman snorted. "I'd rethink that idea if I was you, Scanlon."

Dane ignored the black humor, which all cops used to help them handle the ugliness they saw on a daily basis. "What about her fingers?"

"Nope. No sign of 'em."

Trammell sighed. "I think we'd better go talk to the husband."

It was a fact that most homicides, except for the random gang drive-bys, were committed by someone who knew the victim: a friend, a neighbor, co-worker, or relative. When the victim was a woman, the usual list of suspects was narrowed down even more, because the murderer was almost invariably her husband or boyfriend. A lot of times, the murderer was the one who "discovered" the body and reported the crime.

They went back to the living room, and Dane caught the eye of the officer who was talking to the husband. The officer came over to them.

"Has he said anything?" Dane asked.

The officer shook his head. "Most of the time he won't answer the questions. He did say that his wife's name is Nadine, and his name is Vinick, Ansel Vinick. They've lived here twenty-three years. Beyond that, he ain't talking."

"Is he the one who called it in?"

"Yeah."

"Okay. We'll take it now."

He and Trammell went over to Mr. Vinick. Dane sat down on the couch, and Trammell moved the other chair closer before sitting down, effectively sandwiching Mr. Vinick between them.

"Mr. Vinick, I'm Detective Hollister and this is Detective Trammell. We'd like to talk to you, ask you a few questions."

Mr. Vinick was staring at the floor. His big hands hung loosely over the padded arms of the recliner. "Sure," he said dully.

"Are you the one who found your wife?"

He didn't answer, just continued to stare at the floor.

Trammell stepped in. "Mr. Vinick, I know it's tough, but we need your cooperation. Are you the person who called the police?"

Slowly he shook his head. "I didn't call no police. I called 911."

"What time did you call?" Dane asked. The time would be on record, but liars often tripped themselves up on the simplest details. Right now, Vinick was a suspect by virtue of being married to the victim.

"Dunno," Vinick muttered. He took a deep breath and seemed to make an effort to concentrate. "Seven-thirty or thereabouts, I guess." He rubbed his face with a trembling hand. "I got off work at seven. It takes about twenty, twenty-five minutes to drive home."

Dane caught Trammell's glance. They had seen enough death to know that Mrs. Vinick had been dead for several hours, not half an hour or so. The medical examiner would establish the time of death, and if Mr. Vinick had been at work during that time, if witnesses could reliably state that he hadn't left, then they'd have to start looking at other possibilities. Maybe she'd had a boyfriend; maybe someone had been keeping Mr. Vinick's bed warm for him while he worked third shift.

"Where do you work?"

There was no answer. Dane tried again. "Mr. Vinick, where do you work?"

Vinick stirred and named a local trucking company.

"Do you normally work third shift?"

"Yeah. I work on the dock, loading and unloading trailers. Most freight comes in at night, see, for delivery during the day."

"What time did you leave to go to work last night?"

"Usual time. Around ten."

They were on a roll, finally getting some answers. "Do you punch a time card?" Trammell asked.

"Yeah."

"Do you punch in as soon as you get there, or wait until time for your shift to start?"

"As soon as I get there. The shift starts at ten-thirty. We have half an hour to eat, and get off at seven."

"Do you have to clock in and out for lunch?"

"Yeah."

It looked like Mr. Vinick's night would be pretty much accounted for. They would check out everything he'd told them, of course, but that wouldn't be any problem.

"Did you notice anything unusual this morning?" Dane asked. "Before you came in the house, I mean."

"No. Well, the door was locked. Nadine usually gets up and unlocks it for me, then starts cooking breakfast."

"Do you usually come in the front door or the back door?"

"Back."

"What did you see when you opened the door?"

Mr. Vinick's chin trembled. "Nothing, at first. The shades were pulled and the lights weren't on. It was dark. I figured Nadine had overslept."

"What did you do?"

"Turned on the light in the kitchen."

"What did you see then?"

Mr. Vinick swallowed. He opened his mouth but couldn't speak. He put his hand to his eyes. "B-Blood," he managed. "All—all over the place. Except—it looked like ketchup, at first. I thought she'd dropped a bottle of ketchup and broken it, the way it was splattered. Then—then I knew what it was. It scared me. I thought she must have cut herself, real bad. I yelled her name and ran to the bedroom, looking for her." He stopped, unable to carry the tale any further. He began to shake, and didn't notice when Dane and Trammell got up and stepped away, leaving him alone with his grief and horror.

Ivan Schaffer and an assistant arrived with their bags and disappeared into the bedroom to gather what evidence they could salvage from the carnage. Lieutenant Gordon Bonness arrived practically on their heels. He skidded to a stop just inside the door, his expression one of shock. "Holy shit," he muttered.

"That seems to be the concensus," Trammell said in an aside to Dane as they joined the lieutenant.

Bonness wasn't a bad sort, even if he was from California and could come up with some pretty weird ideas on things. He was as fair as possible in the way he ran the unit, which Dane considered a pretty good recommendation, and he was tolerant of the different quirks and work habits of the detectives under him.

"What have you got so far?" Bonness asked.

"We have a lady who was hacked to pieces, and a husband who was at work. We'll check out his alibi, but my gut says he's in the clear," Dane answered.

Bonness sighed. "Maybe a boyfriend?"

"We haven't gotten that far yet."

"Okay. Let's move fast on this one. Jesus, look at these walls."

They went into the bedroom, and the lieutenant blanched. "Holy shit," he said again. "This is sick!"

Dane gave him a thoughtful look, and his stomach tightened. A feeling of dread went up his spine. Sick. Yeah, this was sick. And he was suddenly a lot more worried than he had been before.

He squatted beside Ivan as the tall, lanky man painstakingly searched for fibers, hair, anything that could be analyzed into giving up its secrets. "Found anything?"

"Won't know until I get it to the lab." Ivan looked around. "It would help if we could find her fingers. Maybe there'd be some skin under the nails. I've got people going through the trash in the neighborhood. No garbage disposal here, so that's out."

"Was she raped?"

"Don't know. There's no obvious semen."

Dane's feeling of dread was growing stronger. What had seemed like a fairly simple, if gruesome, murder was getting complicated. His gut feeling was seldom wrong, and he had alarm signals going off like an entire brass section.

He followed the gory trail back to its beginning, in the kitchen. Trammell came with him, and they both stood in the small, homey room, looking around. Nadine Vinick had evidently liked to cook; the kitchen was more modern than the rest of the house, with gleaming appliances, a small cooking island, and a variety of shiny but well-used pots and pans hanging over the island. A butcher's block stood at one end of the counter, and a set of Ginsu knives, with one knife missing, was arranged in a rack on top of the butcher's block.

"How did the son of a bitch get in?" Dane muttered. "Has anyone even looked for signs of forced entry, or did they just play the odds that the husband was the one who did her?"

Trammell had worked with him long enough to read him. "You getting a feeling about this?"

"Yeah. A bad one."

"You don't think maybe she had a boyfriend?"

Dane shrugged. "Maybe, maybe not. It was just something the lieutenant said, about this being sick. It is. And that makes me real uneasy. Come on, let's see if we can figure out how he got in."

It didn't take long. There was a small cut at the bottom of the screen on the window in the spare bedroom. The screen was in place but unfastened, and the latch on the window was open, not that it would have kept out even a determined ten-year-old. "I'll get Ivan," Trammell said. "Maybe he can lift a print, or find a couple of stray threads."

Dane's gut feeling was getting worse. A forced entry put a different slant on the situation, indicating a stranger. This didn't feel like a burglary that had escalated into violence when the intruder had been suddenly confronted by Mrs. Vinick. The ordinary burglar would have been more likely to run, and even if he had attacked, it would have been quick. The attack on Mrs. Vinick had been both vicious and prolonged. *Sick.*

He walked back into the kitchen. Had the first confrontation taken place here, or had Mrs. Vinick seen the intruder and tried to run out the back door, getting as far as the kitchen before he caught her? Dane stared at the appliances as if they could tell tales. A small frown knit his brows and he went over to the automatic coffee maker, the kind that was installed under the upper cabinets so it didn't take up counter space. The carafe held about five cups of coffee. Using the backs of his fingers, he touched the glass. It was cold. The coffee maker was the kind with the automatic switch that turned off the warming plate after two hours. A coffee mug, filled almost to the rim with coffee, sat on the counter. It didn't look as if it had been touched since the coffee had been poured into it. He stuck his finger into the dark liquid. Cold.

He pulled a pair of surgical gloves out of his pocket and put them on. Carefully touching only the wooden rim of the cabinet doors rather than the metal handles, he began opening them. The second door revealed a canister of decaffeinated coffee. Mrs. Vinick could drink it late at night without worrying about her sleep being disturbed.

She had made a pot of coffee and she had been in here, in the kitchen. She had just poured the first cup and replaced the carafe on the warming plate. The door from the living room was behind her and to the right. Dane went through the motions as if he had just poured the coffee himself, standing where she would have stood. According to the placement of the cup on the counter, she would have been standing slightly to the left of the coffee maker. That was when she had seen the intruder, just as she had set the carafe in place. The coffee maker had a dark, shiny surface, almost mirrorlike, behind the hands of the built-in clock. Dane bent his knees, trying to lower himself to Mrs. Vinick's general height. The open doorway was reflected in the surface of the coffee maker.

She had never even picked up her cup of fresh coffee. She had seen the intruder's reflection and turned, perhaps thinking, in that first moment, that her husband had forgotten something and returned home to get it. By the time she had realized her mistake, he had been on her.

She probably hadn't been standing naked in her kitchen, though Dane had been a cop long enough to know that anything was possible. It was just another gut feeling. But she had been naked when the killer had finished with her, and probably naked when he had started.

The odds were that she had been raped at knife point, right here in the kitchen. The lack of obvious semen didn't mean anything; after so many hours, and with the struggle that had gone on, it would take a medical examiner to make a judgment. And a lot of times, rapists didn't climax anyway. Orgasm wasn't the point of rape.

After the rape, he had started work with the knife. Until then, she had been terrified but hoping, probably, that when he was finished he would just go away. When he started cutting her, she had known that he intended to kill her and she had started fighting for her life. She had escaped from him, or maybe he had let her escape, like a cat toying with a mouse, letting her think she had gotten away before easily catching her again. How many times had he played his sick little game before finally cornering her in the bedroom?

What had she been wearing? Had the killer taken her clothing with him as a souvenir or trophy?

"What?" Trammell asked quietly from the doorway, his dark eyes intent as he watched his partner.

Dane looked up. "Where are her clothes?" he asked. "What was she wearing?"

"Maybe Mr. Vinick knows." Trammell disappeared, and returned in less than a minute. "She had already changed into her nightgown when he left for work. He said it was white, with little blue things on it."

They began looking for the missing garment. It was startlingly easy to find. Trammell opened the folding doors that hid the washer and dryer, and there it was, neatly placed on top of the pile of clothing in the laundry basket that sat on top of the dryer. The garment was splattered with blood, but certainly not soaked. No, she hadn't been wearing it when the knife attack had begun. Probably it had been lying on the floor, thrown aside, and the blood had splattered on it later.

Dane stared at it. "After raping and killing her, the son of a bitch put her nightgown in the laundry?"

"Rape?" Trammell queried.

"Bet on it."

"I didn't touch the handle. Maybe Ivan can get a print; he came up empty in the second bedroom."

Dane had another gut feeling, one he liked even less than the others. "I'm afraid we're going to come up empty all the way around," he said bleakly.

3

It hadn't been a flashback.

She knew because she had been having real flashbacks all day, frightening resurgent memories that swept over her, overwhelmed her, and left her limp and exhausted when her own reality returned.

Marlie knew the details of her own particular nightmare, was as familiar with them as she was with her face; the details that had been flashing in her brain all day were new, different. When she had awoken from her stupor the afternoon before, she had been able to remember little more than the image of the slashing knife, and she had still been so tired that she had barely been able to function. She had gone to bed early and slept deeply, dreamlessly, until almost dawn when the details began to surface.

The bouts of memory had happened all day long; she would barely recover from one when another, vivid and horrible, would surge into her consciousness. It had never happened this way before; the visions had always been overwhelming and exhausting, yes, but she had always been able to immediately recall them. These ongoing *attacks* left her bewildered, and helpless from fatigue. Several times she had been tempted to call Dr. Ewell and tell him about this frightening new development, but something in her had held back.

A woman had been murdered. It had been real. God help her, the knowing had returned, but it was different, and she didn't know what to do. The vision had been strong, stronger than any she'd ever had before, but she didn't know who the victim was and couldn't tell where it had happened. Always before she had had at least an inkling, had grasped some clues to identity and location, but not this time. She felt disoriented, her mind reaching out but unable to find the signal, like a compass needle spinning in search of a magnetic pole that wasn't there.

She had seen the murder happen over and over in her mind, and each time more details had surfaced, as if a wind were blowing away layers of fog. And each time she roused from a replay of the vision, more exhausted than before, she had been more horrified.

She was seeing it through *his* eyes.

It had been *his* mind that had caught hers, the mental force of *his* rage that had blasted through six years of blank, blessed nothingness and jolted her, once again, into extrasensory awareness. Not that he had targeted her; he hadn't. The enormous surge of mental energy had been aimless, without design; he hadn't known what he was doing. Normal people never imagined that there were people like her out there, people with minds so sensitive that they could pick up the electrical signals of thought, read the lingering energy patterns of long-ago events, even divine the forming patterns of things that hadn't yet happened. Not that this man was normal in any sense other than his lack of extrasensorial sensitivity, but Marlie had long ago made the distinction to herself: Normal people were those who didn't know. She had the knowing, and it had forever set her apart, until six years ago when she had been caught in a nightmare that still haunted her. Traumatized, that part of her brain had shut down. For six years she had lived as a normal person, and she had enjoyed it. She wanted that life to continue. She had slowly, over the years, let herself come to believe that the knowing would never return. She had been wrong. Perhaps it had taken this long for her mind to heal, but the visions were back, stronger and more exhausting than ever before.

And seen through the eyes of a murderer.

Part of her still hoped . . . what? That it hadn't been real, after all? That she was losing her mind? Would she really rather be delusional than accept that the visions had returned, that her safe, normal life had come to an end?

She had looked through the Sunday paper but hadn't been able to concentrate; the memory flashes had been too frequent, too strong. She hadn't found any mention of a murder that had triggered a response. Maybe it had been there and she had simply overlooked it; she didn't know. Maybe it hadn't happened anywhere nearby, but by some freak chance she had happened to catch the killer's mental signals. If the woman had lived in some other town, say in Tampa or Daytona, Orlando's papers wouldn't carry it. Marlie would never know the woman's identity or location.

Part of her was a coward. She didn't *want* to know, didn't want to become part of that life again. She had built something safe and solid here in Orlando, something that would be destroyed if she became involved again. She knew exactly what would happen: the disbelief, followed by derision. Then, when people were forced to accept the truth, they would become suspicious and afraid. They would be willing to use her talent, but they wouldn't want to be friends. People would avoid her; little kids would daringly peek in her windows and run, screaming, if she looked back. The older kids would call her "the witch." Inevitably some religious fanatic would start muttering about "the work of the devil," and sporadic picket lines would spring up in front of her house. No, she would have to be a fool to get involved in that again.

But she couldn't stop wondering about the woman. There was an aching need to at least know her name. When someone died, at least her name should be known, a tiny link with immortality that said: This person was here. This person existed. Without a name, there was only a blank.

So now, still shaking with fatigue, she turned on the television and waited, in a daze, for the local news to come on. She almost dozed several times, but shook herself awake.

"It's probably nothing," she mumbled aloud. "You're just losing it, that's all." Strange comfort, but there it was. Everyone's private fears were different, and she would rather be crazy than right.

The television screen flickered as the talking heads segued into another story, this time devoting an entire minute to an in-depth look at the effect of crack and gangs on inner-city neighborhoods. Marlie blinked, suddenly terrified that the visual images would overwhelm her with mental ones, as had happened in the past when she had picked up on the emotions of the people she had watched. Nothing happened. Her mind remained blank. After a minute she relaxed, sighing with relief. Nothing was there, no bleak feelings of despair and hopelessness. She began to feel a little more cheerful; if she couldn't receive those images and emotions the way she had in the past, maybe she *was* just going a little crazy.

She continued watching, and became a little drowsy again. She felt herself begin to give in to the fatigue, effortlessly sliding into a light doze even though she tried to remind herself to stay awake for the rest of the newscast—

—". . . NADINE VINICK . . ."

Marlie jerked violently as the name blared both inside and outside of her head, her inner awareness amplifying the name just spoken by the television announcer. She struggled to an upright position on the couch, unaware of having slumped over as she dozed. Her heart pounded frantically against her ribs and she heard her own panicked breathing, fast and shallow, as she stared at the screen.

"The Orlando police aren't releasing any information about the stabbing murder of Mrs. Vinick, as the slaying is still under investigation."

A photo of the victim was flashed on the screen. Nadine Vinick. That was the woman Marlie had seen in the vision. She had never heard the name before, but there was a strong sense of recognition, too strong to ignore. Just hearing the name spoken on television had been like a bullhorn sounding in her head.

So it was true, it was real. All of it.

The knowing was back.

And it would tear her life apart again if she did anything about it.

On Monday morning Dane stared at the stark photographs of the murder scene, examining each minute detail over and over as he allowed his thoughts free range, hoping that some crucial, previously unnoticed item would slip into focus, something that would give them a direction, any direction. They had nothing to go on, damn it, absolutely nothing. A neighbor across the street had heard a dog bark around eleven, she thought, but it had stopped and she hadn't thought anything else about it until they had questioned her. Mr. Vinick had definitely been at work; he had been helping another dockman unload a trailer, his time completely accounted for. The medical examiner couldn't give an exact time of death, because unless there was a witness, such a thing was impossible, and the time frame unfortunately included the half hour before Mr. Vinick had gone to work. Dane still went with his gut feeling: Vinick hadn't done it. According to his co-workers, Mr. Vinick had been completely normal when he had arrived at work, joking around. It would have taken a real monster, which Mr. Vinick had never given any indication of being, to have butchered his wife, coolly cleaned up and changed clothes, then gone to work as usual without any vestige of nervousness.

They had no semen, though the medical examiner said that vaginal bruising indicated Mrs. Vinick had been violently penetrated. They had no fibers alien to the house, except for what the Orlando Police Department had brought in themselves. They had no hair samples, pubic or otherwise. They had no fingerprints. And they hadn't found Nadine Vinick's fingers.

"We don't have shit," he muttered, tossing the photographs onto his desk.

Trammell grunted in agreement. They were both tired; they had scarcely stopped in the forty-eight hours since they had first entered the Vinick home. And with every passing hour, the chances of finding Mrs. Vinick's murderer diminished. Crimes were either solved fast, or they tended not to be solved at all. "Look at the rundown of their garbage."

He handed the itemized list over to Dane, who glanced down it. Typical garbage: food waste, empty milk cartons and cereal boxes, an assortment of uninteresting junk mail, plastic shopping bags from a couple of stores, used coffee filters, a pizza box with two remaining slices of pizza, soiled paper towels, an old shopping list, last week's *TV Guide,* a couple of scribbled phone numbers, a voided check made out to the telephone company, various empty spray cans, about a week's worth of newspapers—evidently the Vinicks hadn't been into recycling. Nothing that was out of place or unusual.

"What about the phone numbers?" he asked.

"I just called both of them." Trammell leaned back in his chair and propped his Italian-leather-clad feet on the desk. "One is the pizza delivery joint, the other is their cable company."

Dane grunted. He leaned back in his chair and propped his own feet on the desk. Dan Post instead of Gucci, and scuffed at that. What the hell. He and Trammell eyed each other across their four feet and two desks. Sometimes they did their best brainwork in this position.

"Pizza delivery would involve a stranger coming to the house, and there's a fifty-fifty chance the cable company would send out a repairman."

Trammell's lean, dark face was thoughtful. "Even if a repairman had gone out to the house, it wouldn't have been at night."

"And it would probably be too much to hope that Mrs. Vinick ordered a pizza that late at night, to pig out all by herself. The analysis of her stomach contents . . ." Dane stretched out his right arm and sifted through the scattered papers on his desk, finally plucking the one he wanted out of the mess. "Here it is. Doc says that she hadn't eaten anything for at least four or five hours. No pizza. So the pizza in the trash was from earlier, at least lunch. Maybe a day or two." For all the tantalizing possibilities, in his experience it never had been a pizza deliverer.

"We can find out from Mr. Vinick exactly when they ordered the pizza."

"And the cable company can tell us if they had to send a repairman out to the Vinick's house."

"So we have definitely one, and possibly two, strangers who have been to the house. A pizza delivery boy would have been kept outside, but he could still have seen her. A repairman might actually have been in the house."

"Women chat to repairmen," Dane said, eyes narrowed as he followed the line of reasoning. "Maybe she asked him to please be quiet, since her husband worked third shift and was asleep in the bedroom. The guy says, yeah, he used to work third, too, and it was rough. Where does her husband work? And she tells him, even throws in what time hubby leaves, when he gets home. Why should she worry? After all, would the cable company have hired him if he hadn't been an upstanding citizen? Women don't think anything about letting a repairman in and spilling their guts to him while he's working."

"Okay." Trammell got a pad and propped it on his legs. "One: We check with Mr. Vinick on when the pizza was actually delivered, and maybe a description of the delivery boy."

"Delivery person. It could've been a girl. So could a cable repairman."

"Repairperson," Trammell corrected. "Possible. If not, then we get a name from the pizza place and go from there. Two: Do the same with the cable company."

Dane felt better. At least they were working, had come up with a direction in which to start looking.

His phone rang. It was the intercom line. He punched the button and lifted the receiver. "Hollister."

"Dane," Lieutenant Bonness said. "You and Trammell come to my office."

"On our way." He hung up the phone. "LT wants to see us."

Trammell swung his feet down and stood. "What have you done now?" he complained.

Dane shrugged. "Nothing that I know of." He certainly wasn't the movie image of a rogue cop, but he did have a certain knack of stepping on toes and pissing off people. It happened. He just didn't have much patience with bullshitters.

The lieutenant's office had two big interior windows; they saw the woman with the lieutenant, sitting with her back to the door. "Who is she?" Dane murmured, and Trammell shook his head. Dane rapped once on the glass, and Lieutenant Bonness gestured them inside. "Come on in, and close the door," he said.

As soon as they were inside he said, "Marlie Keen, this is Detective Hollister and Detective Trammell. They're in charge of the Vinick case. Miss Keen has some interesting information."

Trammell took a seat on the other side of the lieutenant's desk, away from Miss Keen. Dane leaned against the wall on her other side, out of her direct line of vision but where he could still see her face. She had barely glanced at either him or Trammell; nor was she looking at the lieutenant. Instead she seemed to be concentrating on the blinds that shaded the outside windows.

A short silence fell as she seemed to be bracing herself. Dane eyed her curiously. She was so tense, he could almost see her muscles tighten. There was something vaguely intriguing about her, something that kept him looking at her. She wasn't a beauty, though she was even-featured and certainly not hard on the eyes, but she sure didn't do anything to attract attention. She wore plain black flats, a narrow black denim skirt that came down to midcalf, and a sleeveless white blouse. She had nice, clean-looking dark hair, but it had been pulled back into one of those severe French twists. About thirty years old, he guessed, his policeman's eye making an automatic assessment. Hard to tell with her sitting down, but probably average height, maybe a little less. A little slimmer than he liked, about a hundred and twenty pounds; he preferred a woman to be soft rather than bony.

Her hands were tightly clenched in her lap. He found himself watching them: slim, fine-boned hands, free of any jewelry, and a dead giveaway to her tension even if he hadn't already noticed that her posture was stiff rather than still.

"I'm psychic," she said baldly. He barely kept himself from snorting in derision. His eyes met Trammell's in a lightning-quick glance of shared thought: *Another one of the lieutenant's weird California ideas!*

"Last Friday night I was driving home from a late movie," she continued in a flat little monotone that didn't diminish the low, raspy quality of her voice. A smoker's voice, he thought, except he'd bet the farm that she didn't smoke. Uptight types like her seldom went in for the easy vices. "It was about eleven-thirty when I left the theater. I had just left the expressway when I began to have a vision of a murder that was taking place. The . . . visions are overwhelming. I managed to pull off the street."

She paused, as if reluctant to continue, and Dane watched her hands twist together until they were bloodless. She took a deep breath.

"I see it through his eyes," she said tonelessly. "He climbed in through a window."

Dane stiffened, his attention shifting to her face. He didn't have to look at Trammell to know that his partner's attention had sharpened, too.

The recitation continued in a slow, evenly spaced cadence that felt oddly hypnotic. Her eyes were wide and unfocused, as if she were looking inward. "It's dark in the room. He waits there until she's alone. He can hear her in the kitchen, talking to her husband. The husband leaves. He waits until the husband's car has pulled out of the driveway, then he opens the door and starts the stalk. He feels like a hunter after game.

"But she's easy prey. She's in the kitchen, just pouring a cup of coffee. He pulls a knife from the set that's sitting there, waiting for him. She hears him and turns. She says, 'Ansel?' but then she sees him and opens her mouth to scream.

"He's too close. He's already on her, his hand over her mouth, the knife at her throat."

Marlie Keen stopped talking. Dane kept his concentration on her face. She was pale now, he noticed, colorless except for the full bloom of her lips. He could feel the hair on the back of his neck lifting in response to that eerie present tense she was using when she spoke, as if the murder were happening right now.

"Go on," the lieutenant urged.

It was a moment before she resumed, and her tone was even flatter than before, as if she could thus distance herself from the words. "He makes her take off her nightgown. She's crying, begging him not to hurt her. He likes that. He wants her to beg him. He wants her to think that she'll be okay if she just does as he says. It's more fun that way, when she realizes—"

36

She interrupted herself, leaving the sentence unfinished. After another moment she resumed. "He uses a condom. She's grateful for that. She tells him thank you. He's easy with her, almost gentle. She starts to relax, even though she's still crying, because he isn't hurting her and she thinks he'll just leave when he's finished. He knows how the stupid bitches think.

"When he's through, he helps her to her feet. He holds her hand. He bends down and kisses her cheek. She just stands there, until she feels the knife. He keeps the first cut shallow, enough to let her know what's going to happen, so he can see the look in her eyes when she panics, but the cut shouldn't be so bad that it slows down the chase. There wouldn't be any fun in that.

"She panics; she screams and tries to run, and the rage in him is let loose. He's held it in check all this time, toying with her, enjoying her fear and humiliation, allowing her to hope, but now he can let it out. Now he can do what he came for. This is what he likes best, the complete terror he can see in her eyes, the feeling of invincibility. He can do anything he wants to her. He has total power over her, and he revels in it. He is her god; her life or death is *his* choice now, *his* decision. But it's death, of course, because that's what he enjoys most.

"She's fighting, but the pain and loss of blood have slowed her down. She makes it into the bedroom and falls down. He's disappointed; he wanted the fight to go on longer. It makes him angry that she's so weak. He bends over to slice her throat, to finish it, and the bitch turns on him. She's been faking it. She hits at him. He'd meant to make it quick, but now he'll show her, she should never have tried to trick him. The rage is like a hot red balloon, swelling up and filling him. He slashes at her over and over, until he's tired. No, not tired. He's too powerful to be tired. Bored. It was over too soon; she's learned her lesson. She hadn't been as much fun as he'd hoped."

Silence fell. After a few seconds, Dane realized that she

was finished. She still sat stiffly in the chair, her gaze locked on the window blinds.

Lieutenant Bonness seemed disappointed by Dane and Trammell's lack of reaction. "Well?" he demanded impatiently.

"Well, what?" Dane straightened away from the wall. Rage had slowly built inside him as he had listened to the flat, emotionless recital, but it was a cold, controlled anger. He didn't know what the bitch's motive was in coming here, but there was one thing he knew for certain, and he didn't have to be any sort of mindreader to figure it out: She had been there. Maybe she herself had murdered Mrs. Vinick, maybe not, but she had been in that house when it had happened. At the very least she was an accomplice, and if she thought she could waltz in here with that bullshit story and get a lot of media attention while she jerked them around, she had tangled with the wrong guy.

"What do you think?" Bonness snapped, irritated that he had to ask.

Dane shrugged. "A psychic? Get real, LT. That's the biggest load of bullshit I've ever heard."

Marlie Keen stirred, slowly unknotting her hands as if the movement were difficult. Just as slowly she turned her head and looked at Dane for the first time. Despite his icy rage, his stomach muscles contracted abruptly in reaction. *No wonder Bonness had been taken in!* Her eyes were the deep, dark, fathomless blue of the ocean, the kind of eyes a man could look into and forget what he'd been saying. There was something exotic about them, other than the richness of color: a sort of otherworldliness that he couldn't quite grasp. The expression in them, however, was easy to read, and Dane knew beyond a doubt that he hadn't exactly overwhelmed her with his charm.

She stood and faced him, squaring off with him as if they were two adversaries in the old West about to draw down on each other. Her face had gone calm and curiously remote. "I've told you what happened," she said in a clear, deliberate voice. "You can believe it or not; it doesn't make any difference to me."

"It should," he replied just as deliberately.

She didn't ask why, though he paused for her to do just that. Instead her mouth twitched into a tiny, humorless smile. "I realize that I just became your prime suspect," she murmured. "So why don't I save your time and mine by telling you that my address is 2411 Hazelwood, and my telephone number is 555-9909."

"You know the routine," he said with sarcastic admiration. "I'm not surprised." He moved a step closer to her, close enough that she had to look up to maintain eye contact, close enough to intrude into her space and subtly threaten her. "Or maybe you're just reading my mind, since you're psychic." He put an unflattering emphasis on the last word. "Maybe you can tell me what comes next, unless you need a crystal ball to tell you what I'm thinking."

"Oh, that doesn't take a mind reader, but then you aren't very original." She paused, then gave him that little smile again. "I have no intention of leaving town." She wasn't backing down, and his stomach muscles knotted again. At first glance she had looked like a drab, a nonentity afraid of making herself more attractive in any way, but the first look into her eyes had forcibly changed that opinion. The woman facing him didn't lack self-confidence, and she wasn't the least bit intimidated by him even though he was almost a foot taller. Something else stole into his awareness. Damn, he could smell her, a sweet, soft scent that had nothing to do with perfume and everything to do with female flesh. His involuntary reaction made him even angrier.

"See that you don't." His voice was low and harsh. "Is there anything else you see in your crystal ball, anything you want to tell me?"

"Of course," she purred, and the sudden glint in her blue eyes told him that he'd walked right into that one. "Go to hell, Detective."

4

D AMMIT, HOLLISTER!" BONNESS GLARED AT HIM. "DID YOU have to be such an asshole? The woman came in here trying to help, for Chrissake! She told us some amazing stuff—"

"Amazing, my ass," Dane interrupted, still aware of the fury boiling up inside, though now at least half of it was directed at himself. "If she didn't do it herself, then she was there when it was done. She did it, or she's an accomplice, and she's daring us to catch her by feeding us this loony psychic story."

"She knew details that no one but the killer, or killers, could have known," Trammell said tersely. "Hell, we've all heard the kind of crap those so-called psychics describe in their so-called visions. 'I'm getting an impression of the letter C,'" he mimicked. "'It's something to do with the letter C. And it's wet . . . Yes, yes, I'm definitely getting the impression of wetness. The body is close to water.'"

"Which narrows it down to the whole fucking state," Dane finished. "That wasn't a psychic vision she described;

40

it was an eyewitness account. The lady was there when it happened, and she just placed herself at the top of my list."

"She couldn't have done it," Bonness protested weakly, his disappointment plain.

"Not alone," Dane agreed. "She wouldn't have been strong enough."

"We definitely should check this lady out," Trammell said.

The lieutenant sighed. "I know you think it was a goofy idea, but psychics have really helped in some cases I've been involved in."

Dane snorted. "As far as I can tell, a psychic is just a psychotic with a couple of letters missing."

"All right, all right." Bonness still looked unhappy, but he flapped his hand at them in dismissal. "See what you can find out about her."

Trammell was right behind him as they walked back to their desks. "What the hell's the matter with you?" he muttered to Dane's back.

"Whaddaya mean? You think I should have pretended to believe her?"

"No, I mean you had a hard-on the size of a goddamn nightstick, and you were standing so close, you were about to poke her in the belly with it," Trammell snapped.

Dane turned and glared at his partner, but he couldn't think of any excuse to give. He didn't know what had happened, only that from the minute she had turned those dark blue eyes on him, he'd had a boner so hard a cat couldn't scratch it. He was still twitching. "Hell, I don't know," he finally said.

"If you're that horny, partner, you'd better get the itch scratched before you get around her again. Either the lady's very familiar with a knife, or she hangs out with someone who is. I wouldn't want any of *my* body parts sticking out to draw her attention."

"Stop worrying about my sex life," Dane advised grimly. "We need to find out all we can about Marlie Keen."

It had never made her angry before. Marlie was used to mingled disbelief and derision, but she had always felt an almost desperate need to *make* people believe, to convince them that she could help, that her claims were true. She felt no such need where Detective Hollister was concerned. She didn't give a damn what that Neanderthal thought, assuming he was capable of such an advanced mental process.

Maybe it was because she had dreaded going to the police so much, with the full knowledge of how this could disrupt her carefully built life. Maybe it was simply that *she* had changed. But when he had been so insultingly dismissive, she had felt nothing but anger. She certainly wasn't about to stay there and plead with him to believe her. She was already late to work, damn it, and though she had called in, she resented it that she had gone to so much trouble for nothing. She had put herself through the ordeal of recounting what she had seen, and that big jerk had called it bullshit!

Her movements were jerky as she negotiated the heavy traffic, and with sheer force of will she made herself calm down before she caused an accident. She had dealt with jerks before, many times. He was nothing new, except for the way he had moved so close to her, trying to intimidate her with his brute size. She had had to steel herself to face him, to allow him that close. He had used his masculinity as a weapon, knowing that any woman would feel threatened by a strange man looming over her like that, especially a man who looked as if he were hewn out of wood and ate nails for breakfast. In any good cop/bad cop routine, his looks would automatically make him the bad cop. No one in his right mind would expect leniency or consideration from that man.

She had almost panicked when he had moved so close. In her mind, she could still feel the heat his body had generated, overpowering the small space that had been between them. Furiously she wondered if he would have done that if she had been a man; her instinct said no. That was a tactic that men used only on women, the threat of touching. Odd that something so simple, so basic, could also be so frightening.

She shuddered. She couldn't have borne it if he *had* touched her. She would have bolted like a total coward.

As late as she was, it was difficult to find a parking space at the bank where she worked. She had to circle the lot three times before a departing customer left an open slot that she managed to get to before someone else did. Then she sat in the car for several minutes, taking deep breaths and trying to achieve some sense of calm. She stared at the bank building, finding comfort in its solidity. Her job was such a nice, safe, passionless one, in accounting. She had chosen it deliberately, when she had moved here. Numbers didn't bombard her with thoughts and feelings, didn't ask for anything from her. Their qualities never varied; a zero was always a zero. All she had to do was align them into columns, feed them into a computer, keep track of their credits and debits. Numbers were always neat, never messy like human beings were.

And it felt good to support herself, even though she knew she didn't have to. The small house she had made into a home had been bought outright for her, when she had decided that she wanted to live in Florida, on the opposite end of the country from Washington. Dr. Ewell would have arranged for her to receive a check each month, had she wanted; she hadn't, preferring to finally stand alone, without all the support systems of the Association. Even now, all she had to do was pick up the telephone and tell Dr. Ewell that she needed help, and it would be provided. Though it hadn't been his fault, hadn't been anyone's fault, Dr. Ewell was still dealing with his guilt over what had happened six years ago.

She sighed. She was paid by the hour; every minute she sat there was being deducted from her paycheck. Resolutely she pushed Detective Hollister out of her mind and got out of the car.

"Hey, doll, found anything interesting yet?" Detective Fredericka Brown, who answered only to "Freddie," patted Dane on the head as she passed behind his chair. She was a tall, lanky, endearingly plain woman, with a habitually cheerful and amused expression that invited smiles. It was tough for a woman to be a cop in general, and a detective in particular, but Freddie had fit right in. She was blissfully married to a high school football coach, size huge, who looked as if he would tear limb from limb anyone who caused his Freddie the least upset. Freddie tended to treat all of the other detectives as if they were the teenage boys on her husband's team, with a disconcerting blend of light flirtation and motherliness.

Dane scowled at her. "This should have been your case. We had the weekend off, damn it."

"Sorry," she said blithely, giving Trammell a smile of greeting when he looked up from the telephone that had been welded to his ear for most of the morning.

"How's the tooth?" Dane asked.

"Better. I'm up to my eyeteeth in antibiotics and painkillers, no pun intended. It was an abscess, so now I'm having a root canal."

"Tough." The sympathy was sincere.

"I'll live, but Worley's doing all the driving while I have to take this stuff." Worley was her partner. "Anything we can do to help, any leads we can run down? We have our own cases, but from what I've heard, the scene Saturday morning was straight out of a horror movie."

"It wasn't pretty." An understatement if he'd ever made one. Freddie patted him again, this time on the shoulder, and went about her business. Dane turned back to his.

Detective work was mostly boring; it involved a lot of talking on the telephone, going through papers, or going out to talk to people face-to-face. Dane had spent the last few hours involved in the first two activities. Usually Trammell handled this part of the job better than he did, being more patient, but this time he had set himself to it with grim determination. What had happened to Nadine Vinick should never happen to anyone, but it really pissed him off that Marlie Keen had all but rubbed his nose in her knowledge of it.

"Got anything yet?" Trammell asked, frustration plain in his voice as he hung up the telephone. "I came up empty on both the pizza delivery and the cable company. The entire street had trouble with the cable, and it was repaired on the line, over a block away. It wasn't necessary to enter any residence. And the pizza was delivered by a sixteen-year-old girl. Mr. Vinick is the one who paid her, anyway. Dead end."

"Nothing here, either," Dane muttered. "Yet." Marlie Keen had never been arrested, had never even had a parking ticket, as far as he could find. He didn't let that discourage him. Maybe "Marlie Keen" was an alias. If so, he'd eventually turn up that information. People could be tracked through Social Security numbers, tax returns, any number of means. He knew where she worked and what kind of car she drove. He'd already sent out various requests, such as for a record of calls she'd made and received; by the time he was finished, he'd even know her bra size.

He bet he could make a damn good guess at that right now: 34C. At first he would have guessed no more than a B cup, but that nunnish white blouse had been deceiving. He had noticed a tantalizing roundness—

Damn it! He had to stop thinking about sex, at least in connection with her. Every time he remembered that eerie, macabre tale she'd spun, he almost choked with rage. Nadine Vinick had endured unutterable hell before she'd died, and Marlie Keen, if that was her real name, was trying to turn it into a sideshow. He wouldn't be surprised to get a call from the local media, asking if there was any truth to the rumor that the OPD was working with a psychic to find the murderer. If Marlie Keen wanted publicity, for whatever sick reason, her next move would be to notify the media herself.

Her gall still astounded him. He totally discounted that psychic shit; the only way she could have known the things she'd known was to have been there. He didn't know if the murder had been played out exactly as she'd said, but the pertinent details of it had been dead on the money. The only way she would have had the nerve to bring herself to their attention was if she knew there was no evidence to link her to the crime. The murderer had been excruciatingly careful; forensics hadn't turned up even the tiniest shred of alien material. Therefore, she had done it for the thrill of thumbing her nose at the police department, flaunting the details before them and knowing they couldn't pin anything on her.

She hadn't handled the knife herself; he was fairly certain of that. So the actual murderer was someone she knew, someone she was close to. A brother, maybe, or a boyfriend. Someone close enough to share torture and murder. He thought of her in bed with the bastard who had carved up Mrs. Vinick, and his stomach twisted.

She had made a mistake, taunting him with her knowledge. She was the thread that would lead him to the murderer, and he wouldn't let go until he reached the end.

He stood up and reached for his jacket. "Let's go," he said to Trammell.

"Any place in particular?"

"To talk to Ms. Keen's neighbors. Find out if she has a boyfriend."

She didn't. The neighbors on the left, retirees from Ohio, were certain of that. Bill and Lou, as they introduced themselves, described Marlie as quiet, friendly, and always accommodating about collecting their newspaper and mail whenever they visited their daughter back in Massillon, and feeding their cat. Not many neighbors were so friendly.

"Have you noticed anyone coming or going from the house? Does she have many visitors?"

"Not that I've seen, though of course, we don't just sit and watch Marlie's house," Lou said with all the indignant righteousness of someone who did just that. "No, I don't think I've ever noticed any visitors over there. Have you, Bill?"

Bill scratched his jaw. "Don't think so. She's just about the perfect neighbor, you know. Always speaks when we see her, don't have her nose in the air like some. Keeps her yard neat, too."

Dane frowned as he scribbled in the small notebook that every policeman carried. "Not *any* visitors?" he stressed. "Ever?"

Lou and Bill looked at each other and shrugged helplessly, shaking their heads.

"No family? Brothers, sisters?"

More head shaking.

"Girlfriends?" he growled.

"No," Lou repeated a bit testily. "No one. She even takes care of the yard work herself, instead of hiring a neighborhood boy. I've never seen anyone over there except for the mailman."

Dead end. He was frankly puzzled by it. He glanced at Trammell and saw the small frown that said his partner was just as buffaloed. Men could be loners, but women seldom were. He tried another tack. "Does she go out much?"

"Not often, no. She sees an occasional movie, I think. I can't believe she's in any sort of trouble. Why, when Bill broke his leg two years ago, she'd stay with him whenever I had to go out." Lou glared at him. Dane noticed that she was saving it all for him, rather than including Trammell in her bad graces.

He flipped his notebook shut. "Thanks for your help." Some help.

The neighbors on the right had basically the same comments, except the lady of the house had two squalling rug rats hanging on her legs and couldn't be expected to pay a lot of attention to the comings and goings next door. No, she'd never seen anyone visiting Marlie.

They went back to the car and got in, both sitting in silence and staring at 2411 Hazelwood. It was a neat, solid little bungalow, typical of houses built in the fifties, though it had been spruced up with a cool, sand-colored paint and enlivened with the kind of touches women put on their nests, the trim done in what he thought of as ice cream colors, which only women and gays knew the names for. The front porch was decorated with a couple of ferns and some pinkish flowers, all in pots hanging from hooks. So what had they just found out? That their most likely suspect sounded like some kind of nun?

"That big thud we just heard was us, hitting a blank wall," Trammell finally said.

Dane scowled, but there was no denying it. He felt frustrated and angry, but underlying it was a certain . . . relief? Damn, what was wrong with him? He was feeling relieved because a murder case was turning into one big headache, and he couldn't come up with anything on the best lead they'd had?

"She had to have been there," he said. "She knew too much."

Trammell shrugged. "There's another possibility."

"Like what?"

"Maybe she's psychic," he suggested lightly.

"Give me a break."

"Then you explain it some other way. I can't. I've been thinking about it, and nothing that we've been able to find out about her even hints that she'd be involved in something like this. Weird as it sounds, maybe there's something to it."

"Yeah. And maybe aliens are going to land on the White House lawn."

"Face it, buddy. That neighbor lady is the type who peeps out the window every time a pizza delivery car goes down the street. If Marlie Keen went out, or had anyone over, you can bet it would have been noticed."

"We still haven't checked out her friends at work, who she has lunch with."

"Yeah, well, let me know how it goes. I for one know how to recognize a dead end when I see one."

5

SHE SAW HIM IMMEDIATELY WHEN SHE LEFT THE BANK. HE WAS alone in his car, just sitting there, watching for her. The late afternoon sunshine glinted off the windshield and prevented her from clearly seeing his face, but she knew it was him. Detective Hollister. Though she could really only discern the width of those heavy shoulders and the shape of his head, some primal sense of self-preservation, an alertness to danger, recognized him.

He didn't get out of the car, didn't call to her. Just watched her.

Marlie strode to her car, stonily refusing to react to his presence. When she pulled out of the parking lot, he pulled out right behind her.

He stayed there, tight on her rear bumper, as she threaded her way through the normal afternoon traffic. If he thought he could rattle her with this juvenile game, he was in for a surprise; her nerves had been tested in circumstances far more dire than this, and she had survived.

She had errands to run, things she would have done over the weekend if she hadn't been overwhelmed by that nightmare vision. She didn't let his presence stop her; if he wanted to see what she did after work, he was in for a real thrill. She stopped at the cleaners, leaving a few soiled garments, picking up the clean ones. Next stop was the library, where she returned two books. Then she went to the neighborhood grocery store. At every stop, he parked as close to her as possible, twice right beside her, and imperturbably waited until she returned. When she came out of the grocery store, he watched as she wheeled the cart, loaded with four bags, to the back of her car. She put her foot on the cart to keep it from rolling while she unlocked the trunk.

He was out of the car and standing beside her almost before the sound of the car door slamming could alert her. Her head jerked up and he was there, as big and grim as a thunderstorm. His eyes were hidden by a pair of very dark sunglasses. Sunglasses had always made her vaguely uneasy. As before, his physical presence was as forceful as a blow. She had to restrain herself from automatically stepping back. "What do you want?" she asked in a cool, flat voice.

He reached out one big hand and effortlessly lifted a grocery bag from the cart into the trunk. "Just helping you with the groceries."

"I've managed all my life without you, Detective, so I can manage now."

"It's no problem." The smile he gave her was both humorless and mocking. He stowed the remaining three bags in the trunk beside the first one. "Don't bother saying thank you."

Marlie shrugged. "Okay." Turning away, she unlocked the door and slid behind the wheel. The parking space in front of her was empty, meaning she didn't have to back out; she pulled out through the space in front, leaving him to park the cart or do whatever he wished with it. She wasn't in the mood to be gracious. She was tired, depressed, and angry.

Worse than that, she was frightened. Not of Detective Hollister, as unpleasant as he was. Her fears were much deeper than that.

She was afraid of the monster who had butchered Nadine Vinick.

And she was afraid of herself.

By the time she stopped at the second traffic light after leaving the grocery store parking lot, he was right behind her again. The man really had a talent for getting around in traffic.

The sight of her house wasn't as enticing as it usually was. She was wryly certain that its sanctuary was going to be violated by a big, grim man who seemed to have taken an immediate dislike to her. She was used to skepticism from people, but not actual dislike; his attitude wounded her a little, though she was surprised at herself for feeling that way. Detective Hollister wasn't anything to her, so it had to be merely that it was human nature to want others to think well of oneself.

Just as she had expected, he pulled into her driveway before she had time to cut the ignition off. He got out of the car and took off the sunglasses, tucking them into his shirt pocket. No matter how uneasy sunglasses made her, she suddenly wished he had left them on, because his hazel green eyes, caught by the last rays of the sinking sun, were hard and frighteningly intense.

"What now?" she asked. "Or did you come all this way to help me carry in my groceries?"

"You said you could manage them without my help," he pointed out. "I thought we'd have a little talk."

Someone came out next door. She looked up and saw her neighbor, Lou, standing on the porch and staring curiously at them. Marlie waved and called out a hello. Beside her, Detective Hollister also waved.

"Nice to see you again," he called.

Marlie sternly controlled her temper. Of course he had already been out questioning her neighbors; she wouldn't have expected him to do otherwise. He had made it plain this morning that he was very suspicious of her.

Despite what he had said, when she opened the trunk she plucked all four bags of groceries out, clutching two in each hand. "After you," he said politely.

She shrugged; if he was willing to carry her groceries, she was willing to let him. She unlocked the front door and held it open for him, then followed him inside and directed him back to the kitchen, where he placed the bags on the table.

"Thank you," she said.

"Why say thank you now, when you didn't before?"

She lifted her brows. "You told me not to." She began putting the groceries away. "What's on your mind, Detective?"

"Murder."

The circumstances of Nadine Vinick's death weren't something she could be flippant about. Strain tightened her face as she said simply, "Mine, too." Her eyes were wide and haunted.

He leaned against the cabinet, eyeing her thoughtfully as she moved about the kitchen, bending to stow this item here, stretching to put another on a top shelf. He hadn't missed the strain in her expression.

He looked around. He liked the kitchen, which was a rather unsettling thought; whatever he had expected the interior of her house to be like, this soothing coziness wasn't it. His own kitchen was strictly utilitarian; Trammell's was the latest in high tech, totally intimidating. Marlie Keen's kitchen was comforting. Rows of herbs in small pots grew in a rack in the window over the sink, giving the air a fresh scent. The tile under his feet was a creamy white, with patterns of soft blues and greens. The open shutters over the windows were painted the same soft blue. A white ceiling fan was positioned over the table.

"Did you find out anything interesting about me today?" she asked, keeping her back turned to him as she placed canned goods on a shelf.

He didn't reply, just broodingly watched her. He wasn't about to keep her informed of his progress, or lack of it.

"Let me tell you," she offered lightly. "Today you found that I've never been arrested, never had a traffic ticket, and that to the best of my neighbors' knowledge, I don't date or have anyone over. I pay my bills on time, don't use credit cards, and don't have any books overdue at the library, though I would have if I hadn't returned those today."

"Why don't you tell me again about Friday night," he said. His tone was sharp. She had neatly outlined his day, and he didn't like it. The anger that had simmered in him all day was under control, but just barely. The lady definitely put his back up.

He could see her shoulders tense. "What part didn't you understand?"

"I'd like to hear it all. Humor me. Just start at the beginning."

She turned around, and she was as pale as she had been that morning, when she had related the story for the first time. Her hands, he noticed, were knotted into fists at her sides.

"Does it bother you to talk about it?" he asked coolly. He hoped it did. If her conscience was bothering her, maybe she'd spill her guts. It had happened before, though usually it was sheer stupidity and a perverted sort of pride that led the perp into confession.

"Of course. Doesn't it bother you to hear about it?"

"Seeing it was a lot worse."

"I know," she murmured, and for a moment the expression in her eyes was unguarded. There was pain in those dark blue depths, and anger, but most of all he saw a desolation that punched him square in the chest.

He had to clench his own hands, to prevent himself from reaching out to support her. Suddenly she looked so frail, as if she might faint. And maybe she was just a damn good actress, he grimly reminded himself, pushing away the unwanted and uncharacteristic concern for a suspect. "Tell me about Friday night," he said. "What did you say you were doing?"

"I went to a movie, the nine-o'clock one."

"Where?"

She told him the name of the cinemaplex.

"What movie did you see?"

She told him that, too, then said, "Wait—I may still have the ticket stub. I usually put it in my pocket. I haven't done laundry since then, so it should still be there." She walked swiftly out of the room; he didn't follow but listened intently, tracing her movements through the house so she wouldn't be able to slip out without his knowledge, if that had been her intention. Of course, he had her car blocked in the driveway, and he didn't think she would try to run away. Why should she, when she was so certain he didn't have anything on her? The hell of it was, she was right.

She came back in only a minute and gave him the ticket stub, being careful not to touch him as she let the small piece of paper drop into his hand. Then she swiftly retreated a few steps; his mouth twisted as he noticed the move. She could hardly make it more plain that she didn't like being close to him. He looked down at the ticket stub in his hand; it was computer-generated, with the name of the movie, the date, and the time printed on it. It proved that she had bought a ticket; it didn't prove that she had actually watched the movie. He hadn't seen it himself, so he couldn't ask her any pertinent questions about it.

"What time did you leave the movie?"

"When it was over. About eleven-thirty." Marlie stood tensely beside the table.

"Coming home, what route did you drive?"

She told him, even the exit numbers.

"And where were you when you had this so-called vision?"

Her lips tightened, but she kept her composure, and her

voice was steady. "As I told you this morning, I had just left the expressway. The visions have always been very . . . draining, so I pulled off to the side."

"Draining? How?"

"I lost consciousness," she said flatly.

His eyebrows rose. "You lost consciousness," he repeated, disbelief so plain in his tone that her palm itched with the urge to slap him. "You mean you fainted from the stress?"

"Not exactly."

"What, *exactly?*"

She shrugged helplessly. "I'm taken over by the vision. I can't see anything else, I don't hear anything else, I don't know anything else."

"I see. So you sat there in your car until the vision ended, then calmly drove home and went to bed. If you're so certain that you're psychic, Miss Keen, why did you wait over two days before telling the police? Why didn't you call it in immediately? We might have been able to catch the guy still in the neighborhood, or maybe even in the house, if you'd called."

Marlie's face lost its last tinge of color under the lash of that deep, sarcastic voice. There was no way she could explain what had happened six years before, why some of the details had confused her until she wasn't certain if she'd had a flashback or if the knowing had returned. She couldn't expose herself to this man like that, strip her psyche naked to let him see all of her fears, her vulnerabilities. Instead she focused on the one thing he'd said that she could refute.

"N-No," she stammered, hating the unsteadiness of her voice. She took a deep breath to banish that hint of weakness. "I didn't just drive home. A patrolman noticed my car and stopped to see if there was any trouble. I don't remember anything except the vision from the time I pulled over until he knocked on my window and brought me out of it. I was pretty shaky, and I told him that I was an epileptic and must have had a mild seizure. He was a little suspicious and made me get out of the car, but finally he let me go, and followed me home to make certain I got here okay."

Dane didn't straighten away from the cabinet, but acute attention was in every line of his big body. "What time was this?"

"I don't know."

"Estimate. You left the movie at eleven-thirty; about what time did the vision start?"

"Eleven-forty, eleven forty-five. I'm not certain."

"So what time did you get home? How long did the vision last?"

"I don't know!" she shouted, whirling away from him. "I barely made it home; I collapsed afterward and didn't wake up until late Saturday afternoon."

Dane studied her rigid back. She was shaking, a very faint but visible tremor. He should have been glad that he had her rattled, but instead he had this crazy urge to comfort her.

"I'll be in touch," he said abruptly, and left before he gave in to that urge. Damn it, what was it about her? He was very aware of the heaviness in his loins, and knew that if she had looked, there was no way she could have missed it. Thank God, she seemed to want to look anywhere but at him. He'd heard of cops who got turned on by danger, but he'd never been one of them. What in hell was the matter with him?

As he got into his car he admitted that he never should have come here, at least not without Trammell. Ostensibly they had called it a day, but he hadn't been able to. Instead he'd waited for her in the parking lot where she worked, then followed her home. Stupid move; what if she called the lieutenant and complained that he was harassing her? The LT had given them the go-ahead to investigate her, but Dane knew he'd been out of bounds this afternoon.

At least she'd given him something interesting to check out. If a patrolman had stopped to investigate a suspicious vehicle, it wouldn't be difficult to verify. He had the location and date, and he knew it was on third shift. Piece of cake.

He went back to the office and started making phone calls. It took him an hour to get the name of the patrolman in question, Jim Ewan, a six-year street veteran. When he called Officer Ewan's home, there was no answer.

He waited another hour, calling Officer Ewan four more times, without results. He checked his watch; it was almost eight o'clock, and he was hungry. He supposed he could get up early in the morning and catch Officer Ewan as he was coming off his shift, but he'd never been very good at waiting when he wanted something. What the hell; Ewan would be reporting in to work in less than three hours, so Dane figured he might as well get something to eat, then come back and talk to the officer tonight. Whatever he found out, it would give him the night to think about it.

He drove home and slapped together a couple of sandwiches, then checked his messages while he munched and caught up on the scores of the new baseball season. He was still pissed at the San Francisco Giants, and wanted anyone but them to win.

Baseball couldn't hold his attention, and his thoughts kept slipping back to Marlie Keen, to deep blue eyes that held more shadows than a graveyard. Whatever scheme she was running, she wasn't entirely comfortable with it; she became visibly upset every time she talked about Friday night. Not even an Oscar-winning actress could make herself go as white as chalk, the way Marlie had been this afternoon.

He remembered how her slender frame had been shaking, and the urge welled up again to put his arms around her, cradle her close to him and tell her everything would be all right. What was with this crazy protectiveness? He accepted his natural male instinct to take care of a woman; he was bigger and stronger, so why shouldn't he put himself between a woman and any danger that might threaten her? Why shouldn't he guard her when she went up or down stairs, always ready to catch her if those treacherous high heels women wore caused her to trip? Why shouldn't he do any grunt work for her when he could, schedule permitting? When he'd been a patrolman, investigating car accidents, he had always gone first to check on any woman or child involved, without even thinking about it. But damn it, his protectiveness had never before extended to someone he suspected of murder.

He was a cop; she was a suspect. He couldn't allow himself to touch her in any way, except those necessary in his job. Cuddling her wasn't included on that list.

But he wanted to. Damn, he wanted to. He wanted to let her rest her head on his shoulder, he wanted to stroke her cheek, her neck, then let his hand drop lower to investigate her breasts, the curve of her belly, the soft notch between her legs.

He surged to his feet, cursing to himself. He'd seen her for the first time that morning, and hadn't been able to stop thinking about her since. That good old physical chemistry had sure blindsided him with this one.

He checked the time: nine-fifteen. Hell, he might as well go down to the station and wait for Officer Ewan. At least the usual bullshit going on would keep him from thinking about her so much. He paced restlessly for a moment, then got his car keys and put the plan into action.

As he had hoped, Officer Ewan came in early, as a lot of policemen did, so he would have plenty of time to change clothes and drink coffee, kind of settle into routine before the shift began. Jim Ewan was average in almost every way: average height, average weight, average features. His eyes, though, were the alert, cynical eyes of a cop, someone used to seeing everything and expecting anything.

He remembered the incident Friday night very clearly.

"It was a little spooky," he said, thinking about it. "She was just sitting there, like a statue. Her eyes were open and fixed; at first I thought I had a stiff. I turned on the flashlight, but couldn't see anything suspicious in the car, and I could tell then that she was breathing. I rapped on the window with the flash, but it took her a while to come around."

Dane felt an uneasy tingle up his spine. "Had she fainted, maybe?"

Officer Ewan shrugged. "Only people I've ever seen with their eyes fixed like that were stiffs or crazies. The eyes close when it's just a faint."

"So what happened then?"

"It was like she was real confused, and she looked scared at first. She had trouble moving, like someone coming out of anesthesia. But then she managed to get the window rolled down, and she said that she was an epileptic and must have had a seizure. I asked her to get out of the car, and she did. She was shaky, trembling all over. I couldn't smell any alcohol, and she didn't seem to be on anything; I'd already called in her plate number, and it had checked out okay, so there wasn't any reason to hold her. Like I said, she was pretty wobbly, so I followed her home to make sure she made it."

"What time was this?" Dane asked.

"Let's see. I can check my paperwork for that night to give you the exact time, if you need it, but I think it was a little after midnight, maybe twelve-fifteen."

"Thanks," Dane said. "You've helped a lot."

"My pleasure."

He drove back home, mulling over everything Officer Ewan had said. For such a brief meeting, it had given him a lot of information.

For one thing, Marlie Keen had been on the opposite side of town from the Vinick residence at about the same time Nadine Vinick was being murdered.

Officer Ewan's observations pretty much verified what Marlie had told him about how the "vision" affected her.

So what did he have now? Logically he could no longer consider her a suspect, and something inside loosened with relief. She hadn't been there; she had an alibi. There was nothing to connect her to the murder . . . except her own words. She had *seen* the murder happen. There was no other way. But how?

She knew something, something she hadn't told him. Something that put those shadows in her eyes. He was going to find out what she was hiding, find out exactly how she was tied to this murder. The only alternative was that she really was psychic, and he couldn't buy that. Not yet. Maybe not ever, but . . . not yet.

6

HE COULD FEEL THE ANGER BURNING IN HIM AS THE WOMAN marched away, and he sternly controlled it, as he controlled everything. Now wasn't the time to let his anger show; it would be inappropriate. Everything in its own time. He looked down at the complaint form the woman had filled out and smiled as he read her name: Jacqueline Sheets, 3311 Cypress Terrace. The guarantee of retribution gave him a certain peace. Then, taking care that his body blocked Annette's view of what he was doing, he slipped the complaint form into his pocket to be disposed of later. Only a stupid person would leave it lying about, perhaps for some busybody to look at and remember later, and Carroll Janes did not consider himself stupid. Quite the opposite, in fact. He prided himself on taking care of every little detail.

"I don't know how you can be so calm when people talk to you like that, Mr. Janes," Annette muttered behind him. "I wanted to punch her in the face."

His expression was perfectly calm. "Oh, someday she'll get hers," he said. He liked Annette; she had to put up with

62

the same things he did, and she was always sympathetic when someone gave him a hard time. Most people were acceptably courteous, but there were always those few who needed to be taught a lesson. Annette, however, was unfailingly polite, calling him Mister. He appreciated her perception. She was a homely little thing, short and dark and plain, but generally amiable. She didn't irritate him as so many other women did, with their silly airs and pettishness.

Carroll Janes carried himself in an erect, military posture. He had often thought he would have been perfectly suited for the military—as an officer, of course. He would have been at the top of his class in any of the academies, had he been able to attend. Unfortunately, he hadn't had the connections necessary to get into any of the military academies; connections were imperative, and those who lacked them were shut out. It was how the upper class kept their ranks closed. Joining the military as an enlisted man was unthinkable; he had likewise rejected both ROTC and OCS as being a poor second to the academies. Instead of the distinguished military career he should have had, he was stuck in this degrading job handling customer complaints in a ritzy department store, but that didn't mean he would let his personal standards slide.

He was five foot ten, but his erect carriage often fooled people into thinking he was taller. And he was generally considered a nice-looking man, he thought: in good shape, thanks to twice-weekly visits to a gym; thick, curly blond hair; even features. He enjoyed dressing well, and was always meticulous in his grooming. Attention to detail meant the difference between success and failure. He never let himself forget that.

He wondered what Annette would say if she discovered the power he kept concealed, under perfect control until it was time to be unleashed. But no one suspected, least of all Annette. Fooling them all so completely gave him immense satisfaction; the cops were so stupid, so utterly outclassed!

He was patient enough to wait until Annette took her

afternoon break before going to the computer to see if Jacqueline Sheets had a charge account with the store; to his delight, she did. It was always so much easier when he had this initial access to information. He wasn't interested in her payment record, however. The information from each customer's credit request form was at the top of each file, and that information included the spouse's name and occupation. Jacqueline Sheets was divorced. He clucked his tongue. What a pity, she couldn't maintain a relationship.

Of course, that didn't mean she lived alone. She might have children, or a live-in boyfriend, or a lesbian roommate. She might live with her mother. Any of those scenarios would make his task more difficult, but by no means impossible. He almost hoped such a complication would develop, for it was a truer test of his nerve and intelligence. It was unusual to have another transgressor so soon after the last one; he was a bit curious to see if he would be sharper, like an athlete intensifying his training, or if the opposite would be true. He hoped he would be even stronger and faster, his mind clearer, the surge of power more intense.

When he left work, he could already feel the anticipation humming in him. He ignored the pleasurable sensation and followed his normal routine, for of course, he couldn't allow it to strengthen now; it wasn't time. The pleasure would be all the more intense for having waited, once he let it go. So he drove to his apartment, read the newspaper, popped a microwave dinner into the oven. While it was heating, he set the table: place mat, napkin, everything just as it should be. Just because he lived alone was no reason to let his standards slide.

Only after it was fully dark outside did he allow himself to get out his map of the Orlando area and locate Cypress Terrace, marking the route from his apartment with a yellow highlighter, carefully memorizing the turns. It was closer than he'd expected, no more than fifteen minutes by car. Convenient.

Then he went for a pleasant, leisurely drive, enjoying the

mild spring weather. This first reconnaissance was little more than a drive-by, to locate the house and fix it in his mind. He'd also notice a few other details, such as how close the other houses were, if there were a lot of pets in the neighborhood, how many children seemed to be around. If there was a fence around the yard, how many cars were parked in the driveway, or if there was a garage. Little things like that. Details. Later he would find out more, much more, discovering more on each trip until the final reconnaissance, when he would go inside the house itself, learn the layout of the rooms. He would let the pleasure begin building then, for there was something delicious about wandering through her house when she wasn't there, touching her things, looking in her closets and bathroom cabinet. He would already be inside her, and she wouldn't even know it. It would lack only the finale.

He drove past 3311 Cypress Terrace; there was a narrow, one-slot carport instead of a garage, and a five-year-old Pontiac occupied the space. There were no other cars, no bicycles, no skateboards, nothing to indicate kids. Only one light was on in the house, indicating that there was either only one person there, or everyone was in one room. Usually it was the former.

He circled the block and drove by a second time; twice was all he allotted himself on one trip. If anyone was watching, which wasn't likely, the second pass would be attributed to someone lost, while a third pass would be suspicious. The second time he noted the fence that ran down the left side of the house, on the opposite side of the carport. Good. A fence was nice concealment. The right side was more open than he liked it, but all in all the situation was very nice. Very nice indeed. Everything was falling into place.

Marlie had been curled up on the couch, reading a book that was only mildly interesting and slowly feeling herself relax. She had felt the strain all day long, wondering if

Detective Hollister would be waiting in the parking lot when she left work as he had been the day before. She wasn't certain she could handle another of those hostile confrontations with him, but at the same time she felt curiously cast adrift when she walked out of the bank and he wasn't there. It was like waiting for the other shoe to drop, only it never did.

She leaned her head against the back of the couch and closed her eyes. His face formed behind her eyelids: the rough planes, the broken nose, the hazel green of those deep-set eyes. Not the face of a sophisticate; even if the features had been more even, the expression in those eyes would always set him apart. They were the piercing eyes of a predator, always watching. She rather thought that the people of Orlando could count themselves lucky that he had come down on the side of the law, making criminals his natural prey instead of themselves. Now, added to the force of his own nature, was the look that all cops had: that all-encompassing cynicism, the cool distance, the wall that those in law enforcement erected between themselves and those they served.

She had known a lot of cops, had seen it in all of them. Cops relaxed only with their own kind, with others who had seen the same things, done the same things. None of them went home and told their spouses about the meanness and depravity that they saw every day. What a great topic that would have been over dinner! Cops had a high divorce rate. The stress was incredible.

Cops had never known how to take her. At first, of course, they had all thought of her as a joke. After she had proved herself, though, they had all become very uneasy around her, because her psychic insight had included them. Only a cop understood another cop: That was a given. But *she* had felt their emotions, their anger and fear and disgust. They couldn't erect that wall against her, and they had felt vulnerable.

Then, six years ago, she had had to learn how to read people's emotions the way everyone else did, by picking up subtle clues of body language and voice tone, by reading expressions. She had been like a baby learning how to talk, because she had never before had to rely on visual clues. For a while she hadn't wanted to learn, all she had wanted was to be left alone in the blessed silence. But total isolation wasn't human nature; even hermits usually took up with animals. Instinctively, once she had felt safe, she had begun to watch people and read them. It was difficult to read Detective Hollister, though. Her mouth quirked with wry humor. Maybe she had such a hard time reading him because she could barely stand to look at him. It wasn't that he was repulsive, because for all his rough features, he wasn't, but rather because he was so intense. He made her uncomfortable, glaring at her the way he did, battering at her until he forced her to pull up memories she would rather forget.

She wasn't afraid of him; no matter how much he might try, he couldn't tie her to Nadine Vinick's murder, because there was no tie. He couldn't find evidence that didn't exist. The uneasiness she felt—

Marlie froze, her eyes flying open and focusing on nothing as she mentally searched the feeling that had crept over her. It wasn't a vision, or anything else that overwhelming. But she definitely sensed a vague, cold malevolence, a threat.

She got jerkily to her feet and began pacing as she tried to order her thoughts. What was happening? Was the knowing truly returning, or was she experiencing a perfectly normal reaction to a lot of stress?

She had been thinking of Hollister, and all of a sudden she had felt uneasy and threatened. Easy enough to understand that, if Hollister was the source of the threat. Most people would think so, but Marlie analyzed the feeling again and couldn't find any fear of Hollister in any way connected with his investigation.

The malevolence slapped at her, growing stronger. Marlie

gagged on a sudden rise of nausea. Something was happening. God, something was happening. What? Was it connected with Hollister? Was he in danger?

She lurched to a halt, her fists clenched. Maybe she should call him, see if he was all right. But what should she say? Nothing. She didn't have to say anything. If he answered the phone, then he was obviously all right. She could just hang up.

Childish trick. This unformed threat was sickening. She broke out in a sweat, torn with indecision, and all of a sudden the old instincts took over. Blindly she reached out with her mind, searching for Hollister, trying to pinpoint that nebulous cloud of evil. It was like groping in fog; she couldn't focus on anything.

Groaning, she sank down on the couch again. What had she expected? She hadn't been able to do that for six years, and even before, it hadn't been easy. Just because she had had one freak vision, and felt this vague threat, she thought all of the old skills had come back? She hoped they never would, damn it! But just now she needed them, needed something to calm this panic she felt.

But if he was unconscious—she banished the word *dead* before it could form—then she wouldn't be able to pick up his mental signals. Feeling even more frantic, she summoned up an image of his partner, Alex Trammell. She hadn't paid much attention to him, but she was observant enough to be able to recall his face. She closed her eyes, concentrating, hearing her own harsh, fast breathing as she tried to find one particular person. *Think!* she fiercely commanded herself. Think of Trammell.

It was no use. Nothing.

Swearing under her breath, she grabbed the phone book and ran her finger down the *H*s until she found the Hollisters. Why were there so damn many of them? Ah, there it was. Dane Hollister. She picked up the receiver and punched in the number before she could talk herself out of this.

And suddenly she knew that he was all right.

It wasn't like before. She hadn't tuned in to his emotions; there was no mental barrage. She just knew. She had a mental picture of him sitting barefoot and bare-chested in front of the television, watching a baseball game and sipping on a beer. He muttered a curse as he reached for the telephone—

—"Yeah."

Marlie jumped. The word had sounded in her ear just as she had pictured him in her mind, speaking. "Ah . . . uh. Sorry," she stammered, and dropped the receiver clattering into the cradle. She stared at the phone, so stunned she didn't know what to do. She had heard the definite sounds of a baseball game in the background.

Dane shrugged with mild irritation and hung up the telephone. He had missed an out in the game, just in that short time when he'd taken his attention off the screen. He settled back down with a grunt, his bare feet propped on the coffee table and crossed at the ankle. This was the most comfortable he'd been in a while: no shirt, no shoes, the beer in his hand so cold that it made his mouth tingle to drink it.

The caller had been a woman. He knew it instinctively, even though the voice had been low and unusually husky. A smoker's voice.

He thought of Marlie Keen. Her voice had that little rasp; just hearing it gave him a hard-on every time. Reflexively he looked down at his lap. Bingo.

He reached for the phone.

"Did you just call?" he demanded tersely, after a quick call to local Information.

"I . . . yes. I'm sorry."

"Any reason for it?"

He could hear her breathing over the line, the sounds fast and shallow. Something had upset her. "I was worried," she finally admitted.

"Worried? About what?"

"I thought you might be in some sort of trouble. I was wrong. I'm sorry," she said again.

"You were wrong," he repeated, with exaggerated disbelief. "Imagine that."

She slammed the receiver down in his ear. He winced, angrily started to punch the redial button, but hung up instead. Instead of being sarcastic, he should have tried to find out more about what had her so upset; maybe Nadine Vinick was weighing on her conscience. Maybe she'd been about to spill the beans; Officer Ewan had cleared her, though she didn't know that yet, but he'd still bet money that she knew the perp's identity. Now, because of his own big mouth, he had blown the chance to find out, because she sure as hell wasn't going to talk to him now.

Then he realized that neither of them had identified themselves. She had known who he was, just as he had known who she was.

And she had been right about one thing, damn it. He *was* in trouble. He looked down at his lap again. Big trouble.

Temptation gnawed at him. He slammed the beer down onto the table so hard that foam sloshed out of the can. Then, cussing at his own stupidity, he picked up the receiver and hit the redial.

"What?" she snapped, answering before the first ring had even completed.

"What's going on? Talk to me."

"What would you like me to say?" she asked sweetly.

"How about the real reason why you called."

"I *told* you. I thought something was wrong."

"What gave you that idea?" Try as he might, he couldn't keep the skepticism out of his tone.

She took a deep, steadying breath. "Look. I had an uneasy feeling about you and I was worried. I was wrong."

"What made you think it had anything to do with me?"

Dead silence. He waited, but she didn't say anything. It was such a complete silence, without even the sound of her breathing, that alarm chilled his spine. "Are you all right?"

he asked sharply. "Marlie?" Silence. "Come on, babe, talk to me, or I'm on my way over there."

"No!" Her voice sounded strangled. "No—don't come over."

"Are you okay?"

"Yes. Yes, I'm fine. I just . . . thought of something else."

"Such as?"

"Maybe it wasn't connected with you. Maybe it was someone else. I have to think about this. Good-bye."

"Don't hang up," he warned. "Goddamn it, Marlie, don't hang up—shit!" The dial tone buzzed in his ear. He slammed the phone down and surged to his feet. He'd go over there, check it out—

—And find what? He sincerely doubted she'd open the door to him. Nor did he have a reason, because Officer Ewan had cleared her. That had eaten at him all day; unless something else turned up, and things were looking damn hopeless in that respect, he had no reason to talk to her again. And solving Nadine Vinick's murder seemed more and more unlikely. It pissed him royally that it looked as if the case would be a real mystery, a stranger-to-stranger killing, the kind that was almost never resolved. Mrs. Vinick deserved better than that.

And he didn't want never to see Marlie Keen again. If she wasn't involved in the case, and officially he had to accept that, then he'd have to arrange something else. He didn't like what he was feeling, but it was too damn strong to ignore.

Marlie paced, alternately swearing and wiping away tears. Damn Hollister! He made her so angry, she could have cheerfully taken a swing at him, had he been there right then. But Hollister was the least of her problems. The knowing was definitely coming back, maybe a little altered from before. Maybe she wasn't as empathic as she had been; maybe there was a bit more clairvoyance. How else could she have known that Hollister was watching a baseball game? How else could she have anticipated his answer right down to the second? That had never happened before.

She had been thinking about him, unwillingly, but he had definitely been on her mind when the uneasiness, the sense of danger, had swept over her. She had automatically thought it had something to do with him, but it hadn't; he had just been so strongly in her mind that she hadn't realized the two weren't connected. That meant she had two problems; no, three. One: Her extrasensorial skills were coming back, in fits and starts. She didn't want them to, but they were, and she'd have to deal with it. She pushed that acknowledgment away, because though this problem would have the biggest effect on her life, the others were more immediate.

Two: Detective Hollister was going to be a big complication. He already was. He made her angrier than anyone else she'd ever met, and he did it without even trying. He was a big Neanderthal, sarcastic and skeptical, and she could feel his own anger blazing at her. He was so intense that she almost yielded to the impulse to hide her face every time she saw him. He burned with the sort of fierce masculinity that made women turn and go all google-eyed when they watched him. Marlie knew she didn't have much experience with men, but that didn't mean she was stupid, either. Her reactions to him were too intense, out of all proportion. The last thing she needed right now was a sexual attraction to handle, especially when nothing could come of it. Groaning, she realized that Hollister felt the same reluctant attraction. He had called her "babe." Probably the only thing that had held him back was his suspicion of her, and that couldn't last in the absence of evidence. Men like him didn't hesitate when they wanted a woman; once he admitted that she had nothing to do with Nadine Vinick's murder, she would have to fend him off.

Which brought her to problem number three, the one so distressing that she had put off thinking about it: The evil she had felt, which had made her so uneasy, had the same . . . texture, or personality, as the force she had felt the night Nadine Vinick had been murdered. It was the same man. He was still out there, and his evil was focusing on someone else. It was unformed as yet; she had caught only an echo of it. But he was going to act again, and she was the only hope the police had, and his intended victim had, to stop him in time.

She had nothing to go on. No face, no name. Eventually, though, she would be able to focus on him, stay with him, and he would make some mistake that would tell her his identity.

She would have to work with the police, and that meant working with Hollister. She had no doubt it would be an uncomfortable, difficult situation, but she had no choice. She was caught up in this and had no way of getting out.

7

$\mathbf{M}$ARLIE HAD JUST FINISHED DRESSING THE NEXT MORNING when the heavy knock at the front door made her jump, then frown with both annoyance and alarm. She had no doubt who was pounding on her door at seven-twenty in the morning, and it didn't take any special skills to figure it out.

The best way to deal with him, though, was to not let him know that she reacted to him in any way. He would see her anger as a weakness, and heaven help her if he should get even a hint of the unwilling attraction she felt. He was too aggressive to let either circumstance pass by.

She wasn't about to invite him in. She had to get to work, and she had no intention of letting him make her late. She got her purse and had her keys in hand as she marched to the front door. When she opened it, he was standing almost in her face, leaning with one muscular arm braced against the frame and the other one raised to pound on her door again. The closeness of his body made her catch her breath, a reaction she hid by stepping out and turning to close the door behind her. Unfortunately, he didn't move back, and she fetched up solidly against him, all heat and hard muscle. She was practically in his arms; all he had to do was close them around her, and she would be caught.

Grimly she concentrated on locking the door, trying to ignore the situation. The brief look she had had at his face told her that he was ill tempered this morning, but now she sensed an alarming male edginess beneath the temper. He was as fractious as a stallion scenting a mare in season.

The mental image was unfortunate, and so apt that her heart began beating wildly. With her back turned to him as she wrestled with the stubborn lock, she was suddenly acutely aware of the press of his body against her buttocks. An unmistakable ridge had formed, thick and hard, blatant in intent.

The lock finally clicked into place. She stood motionless, frozen with indecision. If she moved, she would be rubbing against him; if she didn't move, he might take it as an invitation. She closed her eyes against the insidious temptation to simply turn and face him, giving him silent permission by giving him access. Only the certainty that it wouldn't work, that she would freeze under the onslaught of a six-year-old horror, kept her from giving in. She couldn't go through that again.

She forced her voice to work. "What do you want, Detective?" Then she could have bit her tongue. Bad choice of words, under the circumstances. With his erection insistently nudging her, what he wanted was obvious.

For two seconds he didn't answer. She felt the lift of his chest as he slowly inhaled; then, thankfully, blessedly, he moved back a step. "I'm not here as a detective. I just came to see if you're all right."

The heavy sexual tension eased with the small distance between them, making her feel as if she had been freed from shackles. The relief made her light-headed, a reaction she countered with action. "I'm fine," she said briskly, and went down the steps before he could stop her. Oh, damn. His car was blocking hers in the driveway. She stopped, and her self-control had returned enough that she hesitated only briefly before turning to face him. "I have to leave or I'll be late to work."

He glanced at his wristwatch. "It's a fifteen-minute drive. You have plenty of time."

"I like to leave early, in case of trouble."

The explanation didn't budge him. His heavy-lidded hazel eyes moved over her, their expression shielded. "Anything else scare you last night?"

"I wasn't scared."

"Couldn't prove it by me."

"I wasn't scared," she repeated, this time with her teeth clenched. His obstinance was already fraying her temper. She needed to get away from him, *now*.

"Sure you were. And you're scared now." His gaze raked over her again. "Though not for the same reason," he said softly. This time when his eyelids lifted, she saw the predatory gleam of male awareness.

Marlie stiffened, a chill of apprehension touching her. He might not be psychic himself, but his male instincts were acute. It would be more difficult to evade him than she'd thought, for he sensed the response she couldn't quite mask. He came down the steps toward her, and she swiftly retreated to her car. She jerked the door open and slid behind it, using it as a barricade against him.

He regarded her over the open door, his eyes sharp now, piercingly intent. "Calm down," he murmured. "Don't get in such a snit."

She glared at him, agitated almost beyond endurance. If he didn't leave soon, she was going to lose control and say something she knew she would regret. She clutched at the door for support, her knuckles white with the effort. "Move your car, Detective. And unless you have a warrant, don't come to my house again."

Great going, Hollister. Dane felt violent as he swore at himself. He glared down at his desk, ignoring the noise around him of overlapping voices and the incessant ringing of the telephones. He was raw with frustration, both sexual and professional. There were no leads in the Vinick case, no evidence. The investigation was going nowhere, and it looked as if his interest in Marlie Keen was rapidly headed in the same direction.

What else had he expected? That she wouldn't notice his erection jammed against her ass? The wonder was that she hadn't started screaming.

He should have moved back immediately when she had stepped out of the house, but he hadn't. The first accidental touch of her body had frozen him in place, all of his senses painfully focused on the contact. It had felt so good that he had barely been able to tolerate it, but at the same time it hadn't been enough. He had wanted more. He had wanted to strip her naked, to thrust inside her. He had wanted to feel her legs wrapped around his hips, wanted to feel her quivering beneath him as she came. He wanted to dominate her, smash her resistance, bend her so thoroughly to his will that he could take her whenever he wanted . . . and he wanted to protect her from everything and everyone else. That was why he had been on her front porch this morning. He hadn't been able to rest all night, almost certain something had frightened her but totally certain that she wouldn't welcome his concern if he'd called her again. When morning came, he hadn't been able to resist. He'd had to see for himself that she was all right.

So what had he done? Alienated her even further. He had mishandled her from the very beginning, and he still had no idea what he was supposed to do about her. Officer Ewan had cleared her of being at the scene of Nadine Vinick's murder, but she obviously knew something about it, and had come to the police with it. So what was she, a suspect or a witness? Logic said the former, some uneasy instinct said the latter, and his dick frankly didn't give a damn.

"You're in a piss-poor mood," Trammell commented

lazily, all tipped back in his chair and watching Dane's expression.

He grunted. There was no denying it.

"Talked to Marlie lately?"

Annoyed, Dane shot him a glance. "This morning," he said briefly.

"And?"

"And nothing."

"Nothing? Then why did you call her?"

"I didn't." Restlessly Dane twirled a pencil. "I went over there."

"Oh, ho. Keeping secrets from your partner, huh?"

"No secrets to keep."

"So why did you go over there?"

Damn, all this interrogation was making him feel twitchy. Dane had a brief moment of sympathy for the suspects he and Trammell had questioned for hours. A very brief moment. "No reason," he replied, blatantly stonewalling and not giving a damn if Trammell knew it.

"No reason, huh?" Trammell was having fun. His dark eyes were gleeful. He had never thought he'd see the day when his good buddy Dane would be so antsy over a woman, and he intended to enjoy every minute of it. Dane *never* had woman trouble; they had always cared about him far more than he cared for them, which gave him a tremendous advantage in his relationships. He'd never mistreated a woman, but at the same time their influence on him had been very slight. If they didn't like his irregular hours, tough. If he had to miss a date, so what? He'd never given anything of himself beyond the physical to a woman, because the job had always come first. Dane was a damn good cop, one of the best. But he'd pretty much sailed unscathed through the rough seas of romance, unlike the rest of them who wrestled with the conflicts between job and relationships, so it was nice to see him squirming now.

Trammell prodded the beast again. "What did she say?"

Dane scowled, and darted another irritated look at his partner. "Why are you so curious?"

Trammell spread his hands, feigning innocence. "I thought we were working on this case together."

"It didn't have anything to do with the case."

"Then why were you over there?"

"Just checking on her."

Trammell couldn't hold back a chuckle, and the telephone rang while he was still laughing.

Dane picked up the receiver. "Detective Hollister," he barked.

"Finally turned up some stuff on the Keen woman you asked about," a laconic voice said in Dane's ear. "Interesting. Damn interesting."

Dane had stiffened at the first mention of Marlie's name, his entire body alert. "Yeah? Like what?"

"I'll let you read it for yourself, pal. I'm faxing it to you. Didn't know you went in for that kind of shit. Nice-looking woman, though."

"Yeah," he said automatically. "Thanks, Baden. I owe you one."

"I'm marking that down in my little book," Baden said cheerfully. "See ya."

Dane hung up the phone to find Trammell watching him with sharp interest, all amusement gone. "What's up?"

"Baden's faxing me some information on Marlie Keen."

"No kidding." Trammell's eyebrows lifted. "I didn't think anything would turn up on her."

"Well, it has." The fax machine in the corner began to hum and spit out paper. Dane got up and went over to it, his face grim. He wasn't sure he wanted to see this. Two days ago he would have loved to get his hands on some information about Marlie, but not now. Ever since she had called him the night before, he had stopped even trying to deny the effect she had on him. He wanted her, damn it. And he wanted her to be innocent. He wanted there to be some explanation of the things she had told them on Monday. Trammell came over to stand beside him, his dark gaze inscrutable as he watched Dane.

The first sheet came out. It was a photocopy of a newspaper article. Quickly he scanned the headline: TEENAGE PSYCHIC FINDS MISSING CHILD.

Trammell whistled, the single note almost soundless.

Page after page followed. They all had a common theme: Marlie Keen's psychic abilities. Some of the articles seemed to be from psychology magazines, or were papers on parapsychology. Several grainy photographs were printed, showing a younger, almost childish-looking Marlie. Most of them were newspaper articles, reporting how "noted psychic" Marlie Keen had worked with police to solve various cases. The articles were all from the Northwest, he noted. Oregon and Washington mostly, though there were a couple in Idaho, one in northern California, one in Nevada.

Sometimes she was described as a "youthful clairvoyant," once as "lovely," twice as "extraordinary." It was a common theme in the articles that the local police forces had been, at the beginning, both skeptical and derisive of her talents, until she had done exactly what she had said she could do. Usually it was to find a missing person, though on a couple of occasions she had helped find kidnappers. Several times it was mentioned that, when not involved in a case, Miss Keen lived in Boulder, Colorado, at the Institute of Parapsychology. A Dr. Sterling Ewell, a professor of parapsychology at the Institute, was quoted several times.

Trammell was standing right beside him, reading each sheet as he did. They were both silent. Even though they had been forewarned, by Marlie herself, reading about it in black and white was unsettling.

Then one stark headline jumped out at them: KILLER ATTACKS PSYCHIC. Dane grabbed the sheet, holding it taut as it was printed, and they began reading as it emerged from the machine.

There had been a series of child kidnappings in a remote

area of Washington; one child had been found dead, two others were still missing. Marlie had been brought in by the local sheriff, with whom she had worked before in another town, to help find the children. Just before she had arrived, another child had disappeared. A big article about her had been printed in the paper the same day.

That night Arno Gleen had kidnapped Marlie from her motel room and taken her to the same place he had taken the most recent missing child, a five-year-old boy. He had been seen, though, and the sheriff alerted. It was a small town; they were able to identify Gleen and track him down. But the little boy was already dead when they got there, and though they were in time to save Marlie's life, she had been severely beaten.

Her condition, "poor," was reported in a subsequent article. Then there was nothing else. Absolutely nothing. Dane checked the date on the last article. A little over six years ago. For six years Marlie Keen had literally disappeared from the public eye. Why had she relocated to Florida? As soon as he had the thought, he pictured a map in his mind and knew why. Florida was as far from Washington as she could get and still stay in the country. But why, after six years of anonymity and a completely normal life, had she walked into the lieutenant's office and told them about Nadine Vinick's murder?

"It couldn't have been easy," Trammell murmured, his thoughts obviously following the same path. "To have involved herself after what happened the last time."

Dane ran his hand through his hair. Part of him was elated, the last doubt demolished. There was an explanation for her knowledge. If he still couldn't quite believe, at least now he had to suspend his disbelief. There was no longer any reason at all for him to stay away from her; he could go after her the way his body had wanted right from the beginning. But another part of him, perversely, didn't want to accept what he had read. Half of it was the sheer unlikelihood of it, for it went against the grain with someone so solidly grounded in reality and facts. The other half was alarm. Shit, what if it was for real? He didn't want anyone reading his mind, though after a moment's reflection he had to admit that it would be convenient if a woman could tell how he felt and he wouldn't have to talk about it.

But it was more than that. He was a cop. He had seen things, heard things, done things, that he didn't want to have as common knowledge between him and his woman. It was something only another cop would understand. The job marked them, forever set them apart from civilians. Some cases would go with him to the grave, living in his mind. Some victims' faces, he would always see.

He didn't want anyone invading the privacy of his mind. Not even Marlie. His nightmares were his own.

He gathered up the sheets. "I'm going to check on some of this," he said. "Talk to this Dr. Ewell, find out about the past six years."

Trammell looked a little strange, a kind of amusement vying with sympathy. Dane scowled at him. Sometimes having a partner was like living with a psychic, you got to know each other so well. Trammell was sadistic enough, damn him, to enjoy seeing Dane squirm over a woman.

"What's so damn funny?" he growled.

Trammell shrugged. "It looks like we'll be working with her, and I was just picturing you trying to get on her good side, after the way you two hit it off. Or didn't hit it off, I should say."

Dane went back to his desk and got on the horn. Wryly he remembered when he had put in for detective. He had pictured a lot of fieldwork, fitting obscure pieces of evidence together like Sherlock Holmes. Instead, he had spent a lot of hours on the phone, and he'd found out that a detective was only as good as his snitches. A smart detective cultivated a lot of contacts on the street, lowlifes who were willing to drop a dime on someone else. Too bad he hadn't had any snitches in Nadine Vinick's neighborhood.

A call to Information got him the number for the Institute

of Parapsychology in Boulder. Less than a minute later he was being connected to Dr. Sterling Ewell.

"Dr. Ewell, this is Detective Dane Hollister, Orlando Police Department."

"Yes?"

Dane frowned slightly. There had been a wealth of caution in that one word. "I'd like to ask you some questions about Marlie Keen. She used to be affiliated with the Institute."

"I'm sorry, Detective," the professor said coolly. "I don't give out any information over the telephone about my colleagues."

"Ms. Keen isn't in any trouble—"

"I never thought she was."

"I simply need some background information on her."

"As I said, Detective, I'm sorry. I have no way of knowing if you are who you say you are. Tabloid reporters have often tried to get information by claiming to be with various police departments."

"Call the Orlando Police Department," Dane said tersely. "Ask for me."

"No. If you want any information about Ms. Keen, you'll have to apply for it in person. With the proper identification, of course. Good-bye, Detective."

The receiver clicked in his ear, and Dane hung up with a curse. Trammell said, "No luck?"

"He wouldn't talk to me."

"Any reason why?"

"He said he doesn't give out information over the phone. If I want to know anything about Marlie, I have to go to Boulder and talk to him in person."

Trammell shrugged. "So what's the big deal? Go to Boulder."

Dane gave him an irritated look. "The LT is going to be tickled that she's really a psychic, but there's no way he'll authorize a plane ticket just for a background check on someone who isn't a suspect."

"You won't know until you try."

Ten minutes later, he had the answer he'd expected. Bonness was indeed elated that his hunch about Marlie had turned out to be accurate, and he even gloated a bit that he must have a touch of psychic ability himself. Dane barely managed to restrain himself from rolling his eyes at that. But no way could the lieutenant justify the cost of sending Dane to Colorado to check out something that didn't really need checking out. They already had all the verification they needed, didn't they? He dismissed the six missing years as being unimportant. The budget was tight, and they needed all the resources they had to be used tracking down criminals, not snooping into the private lives of people who weren't doing anything wrong.

But those six years were important to Dane. "Do you have any objection if I take off tomorrow and go on my own?"

Bonness looked startled. "You mean pay your own way?"

"That's exactly what I mean."

"Well, no, I don't guess there's any problem, except that you're in the middle of a murder investigation."

"This is related. And the investigation isn't going anywhere. We have no evidence, no motive, no suspects."

Bonness sighed. "Take off, then. But just tomorrow. I want you back here by Friday morning."

"No problem."

Dane returned to his desk and told Trammell what was happening, then got on the phone again. He had to call three airlines before he found an available flight. After booking his ticket, he called Professor Ewell again and tersely informed him when he would be arriving.

Dane felt naked without the Beretta, but since he wasn't traveling in any official capacity, he reluctantly left it at home. He couldn't make himself travel without any weapon, though; he carried a pocketknife that was only a little larger than normal, with nothing else about its appearance that was out of the ordinary, but which had a single blade made from an alloy stronger than steel. The knife also had perfect balance, a requisite for a throwing knife. Throwing a blade was an arcane little skill he had taught himself, on the theory that it might come in handy someday. The knife wasn't the equal of a pistol, but it was better than nothing.

He was a nervous flier. It wasn't the flying itself that got to him, but the strain of being trapped in a small space with so many strangers. He couldn't leave old habits behind, couldn't draw a boundary between on-duty and off-duty. He was the same man regardless. That meant he automatically watched everyone, subconsciously noting any erratic behavior, studying appearance, constantly evaluating the situation. The situation was boring, but that didn't mean he could stop. Just as sure as he let his guard down, something bad would happen; it was an unwritten law.

He had taken the earliest flight out. Because of the two-hour time difference between Orlando and Colorado, he arrived in Denver well before lunch. He had no luggage, so all he had to do was go to the car-rental desk and lease a car for the day. Boulder was about twenty-five miles to the northwest, interstate all the way.

Once in Boulder, he stopped to look up the address of the Institute and ask for directions. With one thing and another, it was twelve-thirty when he drove up to the Institute. There were no fences, no gates; his policeman's eye noted that the security measures were skimpy, at best. There was an alarm wired to the door, but nothing any third-rate burglar couldn't disarm. INSTITUTE OF PARAPSYCHOLOGY was neatly painted in large block letters on the double glass doors. He pushed the doors open and noted that there was no tone to signal his entrance. It looked as if anyone could walk in off the street.

About twenty feet up the hallway was an office on the left, the door open. Dane approached it and stood for a moment in the doorway, silently observing a neat, middle-aged woman in front of a computer, typing a letter while she concentrated on what she was hearing through the headset plugged into her ears. Dane cleared his throat, and she glanced up, a smile breaking like sunshine. "Oh, hi. Have you been waiting long?"

"No, I just have walked up." She had a very cheerful face, and he found himself smiling back at her. This place seemed to be as short on formality as it was on security. "I'm Dane Hollister, Orlando PD. I'm here to see Professor Sterling Ewell."

"I'll give him a call to let him know you're here. He was expecting you, so he brought his lunch today instead of going out."

The artlessness of that reply made him smile again. Her brown eyes twinkled at him. "He's my husband," she confided. "I can deflate his dignity if I want to, not that he gives a hoot." She picked up a phone and punched two numbers. "Sterling, Detective Hollister is here. Okay.".

She hung up the phone. "Go on back to his office. I would take you myself, but I'm swamped today. Take the next corridor to the right, and his is the office on the right at the very end of the hall."

"Thanks," he said, winking at her as he left. To his amusement, she winked back.

Professor Ewell was a tall, barrel-chested man with thick white hair and a lined face that wore his years with grace. Like his wife, he seemed a very cheerful man, and he wasn't very big on formality either. He was wearing an ancient pair of chinos and a faded chambray shirt, and his feet were clad in scuffed boots. Dane immediately felt a sense of kinship, for the professor evidently ranked clothing fairly low on his list of priorities. His blue eyes were bright with intelligence and humor, but he regarded Dane very sharply for a long minute before some hitherto unnoticed suspicion faded away.

With a jolt, Dane understood. "All of that about tabloid

reporters was bullshit," he said. "You're . . ." He paused, unwilling to accuse the professor of being something he didn't really believe in.

"Psychic," Professor Ewell supplied benignly. He waved a large hand at a comfortable-looking chair. "Sit down, sit down." When Dane had complied, he resumed his own seat. "Not very much," he said. "Nothing like some of the people I work with. But my one small talent is that I'm very good at reading people when I meet them in person. Because of that, I don't give out any information over the telephone. My long-distance instincts are deplorable." He smiled ruefully.

"No reading minds, or anything like that?"

The professor chuckled. "No, you can relax. Telepathy definitely isn't one of my talents, as my wife will gladly tell you. Now, tell me about Marlie. How is she?"

"I'd hoped you would give *me* information about her," Dane said dryly.

"You haven't asked anything yet," the professor pointed out. "I have."

Dane was torn between impatience and humor. There was something in the good doctor that reminded him very much of an impudent six-year-old. He let humor get the upper edge, and gave in to the professor's air of expectancy. "I don't know what I can tell you. I'm not her favorite person," he admitted, rubbing his jaw. "When I saw her yesterday morning, she told me not to set foot on her property again unless I had a warrant."

The professor sighed blissfully. "That's Marlie. I was afraid the trauma might have permanently damaged her. She can be very patient, when she wants, but sometimes she can be a bit testy, too."

"Tell me about it," Dane muttered, then latched on to what had just been said. "This trauma you mentioned; was it when Gleen kidnapped her?"

"Yes. It was horrible. Marlie was in a catatonic state for a week, and didn't speak for almost two months. Everyone thought, including her, that she had lost all of her psychic abilities." Bright blue eyes studied Dane. "I assume, from your interest in her, that those abilities have returned."

"Maybe." Dane didn't want to commit himself to anything.

"Ah, I see. Skepticism. But you're intrigued enough by what she told you to take a flight to see me. It's okay, Detective; skepticism is not only expected, it's healthy. I'd worry about you if you automatically believed everything you're told. For one thing, you'd be terrible in your job."

Dane firmly returned the conversation to the subject. "About the kidnapping. There was a newspaper article saying that she'd been beaten." Ruthlessly he kept himself from imagining details; he'd seen too many results from beatings, and didn't want to picture Marlie in that condition. "There's been nothing else about her since then. Are you saying the injuries were so severe—"

"No, not that at all," Professor Ewell interrupted. "I don't mean to downplay the severity of her injuries, but she was fully recovered from them well before she started talking again. In this case, it was the mental trauma that did her the greatest harm."

"What happened, exactly?"

The professor looked thoughtful. "How much do you know about parapsychology?"

"I know how to spell it."

"I see. From that, I take it that most of your information about it is gleaned from television shows and fortune-tellers in county fairs."

"Just about."

"Well, discard all of what you think you know. I've always thought that the basis of it was very simple: electrical energy. Every action and every thought uses electrical energy. This energy is detectable. Some people are sensitive to bee stings; others are sensitive to energy. There are degrees of sensitivity, with some people being only mildly sensitive and a very few being ultrasensitive. I don't see why the issue has to be confused with hocus-pocus, though of course, there are charlatans who wouldn't know psychic ability if it bit them on the ass—" The professor broke off, and gave Dane a sheepish look. "Sorry. My wife says I get carried away."

She was right, too. Dane smiled. "I understand. Now, about Marlie—"

"Marlie is exceptional. Most people have some extrasensory ability, and call it hunches, gut instinct, mother's intuition, whatever they're comfortable with. Their degree of ability is mild. Some are a bit sharper than that. A few others are even more sensitive, to a degree that can be tested. And then there are the rare ones, like Marlie. She's the most sensitive receptor I've ever seen. To give you a comparison, most people are biplanes, some few are Cessnas, and Marlie is a high-performance fighter jet."

"You've tested her, of course?"

"My God, Marlie's been tested almost continuously since she was four years old! She could be fractious even then," he said fondly.

"What exactly are her—er, talents?"

"Mainly, she's an empath."

"A what?"

"Empath. She's empathic. She feels others' emotions, so much so that an ordinary drive on a crowded street could make her scream with frustration. All those feelings bombarding her, from all directions. She described it once as a blend of screams and static, at high volume. The biggest problem she had was controlling it, blocking it out so she could function normally."

"You said mainly. What else does she do?"

"You said that as if she's a trick pony," the professor observed, his tone disapproving.

"No offense meant. I won't lie and tell you that I'm buying all of this, but I'm interested." And that was an understatement if he'd ever made one.

"You'll come around," Professor Ewell predicted with a

certain amount of malicious satisfaction. "All of you do, once you've been around Marlie any length of time."

"Who is 'all of you'?"

"Policemen. You're the world's most cynical people, but eventually you won't be able to deny what she can do. Back to your question: She's also a bit clairvoyant, though certainly not to the same degree that she's empathic. She has to concentrate to block her empathic abilities, something she had never quite managed to completely do, while she has to concentrate to *use* her clairvoyance."

"You mean she predicts that things will happen?"

"No, that's precognitive."

Dane rubbed his forehead, feeling a headache come on. "I don't think I have all of this straight. I've always thought a clairvoyant is someone with a crystal ball, predicting the future."

Professor Ewell laughed. "No, that's a charlatan."

"Gotcha. Okay, an empathic person is someone who receives and feels the emotions of other people."

The professor nodded. "A clairvoyant senses distant objects, and is aware of events in distant places. A precognitive is someone who knows of events in the future. A telekinetic is someone who can move physical objects with the force of their minds."

"Spoon benders."

"Mostly charlatans." The spoon benders were dismissed with a wave. "I won't say that one or two don't have telekinetic talent, but for the most part it's just showmanship. None of the extrasensory abilities can be neatly categorized, because capability varies from person to person, just like reading ability."

"And Marlie's particular blend of talents made her good at finding people?"

"Mmmm. Extraordinary. Her empathy was so strong that, when she focused on one particular person, she would . . . well, she called them 'visions,' but I've observed her during the events, and I would use a stronger word than that.

A vision is something that can be easily interrupted. It was as if her mind would leave, though of course, it didn't. But she would be totally taken over by the event, so completely in empathy with the subject that she was aware of nothing else. Terribly draining for her, of course. She would virtually collapse afterward. But while she was linked, she would observe enough about the surroundings to pinpoint the location, and she always managed to fight off the exhaustion long enough to pass the details along to the local law enforcement officers."

"What else happened with Arno Gleen?"

Professor Ewell's face changed, his expression that of mingled pain and hatred. "Gleen was a monster. A pedophile, a sadist, a murderer. Little boys were his favorite. He would kidnap them, take them to a remote place, abuse them for a day or two, then kill them. Unfortunately, there are no secrets in a small town, and when the sheriff called Marlie for help, the news was all over town before sundown. The next day there was a prominent article in the local newspaper about her, mentioning her successes and when she would arrive. Gleen was waiting. As soon as he caught her alone, he grabbed her."

"But if she's as empathic as you say she is, why didn't she sense him?"

"By that time, she had learned how to block, and she automatically did it whenever she was in a town. It was the only way she could function. And there are some people who naturally block their own transmissions; maybe Gleen was one of them. Maybe he was simply a sociopath, and didn't feel anything for her to pick up. She's never said. In fact, she's never discussed it at all."

Dane was beginning to get an ugly feeling, one that was all too likely. "Did he rape her?" His voice was low and harsh.

The professor shook his head. "He couldn't."

Dane exhaled, his eyes closing briefly.

"But he tried." The professor looked down at his hands, his mouth tight. "He took her to where he had his latest victim stashed. The little boy had been horribly abused. Gleen had him tied to a bed. I believe the child was about five years old. Gleen dumped Marlie on the floor, stripped her, and tried to rape her. She wasn't a little boy, though, so he couldn't achieve the necessary erection. Every time he failed, he would hit her, working himself into a greater rage. Maybe he thought inflicting pain would arouse him enough. But it didn't, and in a frenzy he turned on the child. He stabbed the little boy to death in front of her. There were twenty-seven puncture wounds in the child's face, chest, and abdomen. And all the while Marlie was linked with the child. She felt him die."

8

DANE FELT AS IF HE HAD BEEN SCRAPED RAW ON THE INSIDE. HE didn't have to imagine what Marlie had gone through. He was a cop; he had seen too much to ever have to rely on his imagination to supply details. He knew what beatings really were. He knew what stabbings looked like. He knew how much blood there was, how it spread and spread and got all over everything, even your dreams. He knew how the little boy had sobbed and screamed, had seen in other children's faces his terror and despair, his pain, his utter helplessness.

Marlie had endured that. And when she had had the vision of Nadine Vinick's murder, what had it cost her to see those images again? The similarity was sickening.

At some point during the visit with Professor Ewell, his healthy cynicism had gone south. The germ of possibility had been planted. He didn't like it, but despite himself, he accepted that Marlie had "seen" Mrs. Vinick die. Maybe it was a one-shot deal. According to the professor, after Marlie had recovered from her injuries and the emotional trauma she had suffered, she had had no extrasensory abilities at all.

For the first time in her life, she had been able to live normally. It was something she had always wanted to be able to do, but the price had been horrendous. Even after six years, she was still paying it. Now Dane knew why there were no boyfriends.

It made him all the more determined that *he* would change that situation.

Objectively he could be a little amused at the range of conflicts that were clouding his mind and tangling his guts. He'd always been able to hold himself a little apart, unaffected by most of the worries that gnawed at other cops. Subjectively he wasn't enjoying it worth a damn. He didn't believe in paranormal stuff, had always laughed at those who did. Now he found himself not only halfway believing, but trying to figure out how he could use Marlie to find Mrs. Vinick's murderer.

That last thought tied another knot in his intestines. He wanted to protect her; he didn't want her involved with another murderer in any capacity. But he was a cop, and his job was to use whatever source he could to solve a crime, especially one as brutal as this. The bastard didn't need to be walking around, loose among the unsuspecting public. And despite the primal male instinct that told him to keep Marlie away from it, he knew that, if possible, he would use her. He would do everything he could to keep her safe, but the greatest need was to find this guy and put him away. Unless he was a certified wacko, the savagery of the murder was such that he was almost certain to be given the death penalty . . . but first he had to be caught.

Another conflict was with his own male wariness. No man he knew gladly embraced the turmoil and restrictions of an emotional relationship with a woman, and he was no exception. He liked his life; he liked not being tied down to any one woman. He didn't want to have to account for his time to anyone, didn't want to have to consider someone else when making plans for what he wanted to do. But now there was Marlie, and damn it if he didn't feel as if he'd been cornered. He'd been attracted to a lot of women before, but not like this. This was a fever, a gnawing need that never left him. It had been only four days since he'd walked into Bonness's office and seen her for the first time, and she hadn't been out of his mind since. The more he learned about her, the more involved he became. The hell of it was, *she* certainly wasn't doing anything to get him involved; he was doing it all on his own, and having to fight her every inch of the way.

She had totally avoided men, romantically and sexually speaking, since Gleen had almost destroyed her. Dane tried to tell himself to back off, to give her both time and space in order to come to trust him, but he knew it wasn't going to happen. He'd never been the type to sit and wait. He was going to make her his, and pretty damn soon, too. She would understandably be afraid of sex. He, and no one else, was going to teach her that it could be pleasurable, too. He'd never been jealous before in his life, but now he felt almost violent with it. Not jealous of Gleen, God knows, but of every other man out there who would take one look and get lost in Marlie's bottomless blue eyes. He wanted the right to pull her possessively against his side and glare a warning at any bastard who dared look too long at her.

Trammell would gloat at the irony of it. Dane had never had any trouble separating his love life from his work, because his work had always taken precedence. Now here he was, obsessed with a woman who was his best link with a killer.

It was nine-thirty when his plane landed. He was tired, having been up since before dawn, not to mention having flown most of the way across the country and back. He checked in with Trammell from a pay phone in the airport, told him he'd see him in the morning and tell him everything then.

After hanging up, he stood there for a minute, thinking. He was tired, his clothes were tired, he was grumpy. He should go home and get some sleep, think things over. He knew what he should do, but damn if he'd do it. He wanted to see Marlie. He might not like the complications, but he couldn't wait to get entangled with them, like a moth rushing giddily toward a flame.

Marlie jerked the door open on his fifth knock. She stood squarely in the doorway, her posture plainly denying him admittance. "It's ten-thirty, Detective," she said coldly. "Unless you have that warrant, get off of my porch."

"Sure," Dane replied easily, and stepped forward. She wasn't prepared for the maneuver, automatically moving back to give him room before she caught herself. She tried to recover, grabbing for the door, but it was too late; he was already over the threshold.

He didn't take his eyes off her as he shut the door behind him. She was wearing a pair of cutoffs, droopy socks, and a flimsy old T-shirt that draped over her braless breasts as faithfully as her own skin. Very pretty breasts, he noticed, making no effort to hide the direction of his gaze. High and pointed, with small dark nipples peaking the fabric. His mouth went dry and his loins tightened, the same reaction he had every time he was in her company. He was beginning to expect it, anticipate it, enjoy it.

The casualness of her clothing jolted him, making him acutely aware of the prim facade she normally projected. Behind that facade was a woman whose natural sensuality took his breath, and made him realize how successfully she had managed to hide it. He wanted to shake his head at the waste and at the same time thank God that, evidently, no other man had seen through her defenses.

She had more layers than an onion, and she was determined to keep them hidden beneath that prickly shield she had developed. The blistering glare she was giving him should have shriveled his skin. Instinctively he knew that her hostility was because of her vulnerability; she was naturally angry at his previous suspiciousness and less than gentle questioning, but most of her dismay was caused by the fact that he was seeing her like this, without the armor of her bland disguise.

Patience wouldn't work with her. She was too used to hiding, to protecting herself. He was going to have to break down her defenses, force her to let him get close to her. His blood surged hotly as he decided how to do it.

Deliberately he let his gaze roam over her. Her glossy dark hair was hanging loose on her shoulders. He liked that. Her bare legs . . . He felt another jolt of lust. Damn, her legs were great. And her breasts were so tempting that his mouth began to water, until he was all but drooling. He wasn't going to try to hide his attraction another minute; it was time to start getting her accustomed to it.

Marlie flushed angrily as he continued to stare at her breasts. She crossed her arms over them in a half-belligerent, half-defensive gesture. "If you don't have a good reason for this, I'm going to file a complaint about you," she warned.

His gaze flicked upward. "I've been to Boulder," he said abruptly. "I just got back an hour ago." He paused, watching for any flicker of expression. She didn't give much away, but he was learning to read her eyes. She hadn't quite learned how to shield the expression in them. "I talked with Dr. Ewell."

Her pupils dilated wildly, and there was no disguising her dismay. She stood stiffly, glaring at him. "So?"

He moved closer to her, so close that he knew she could feel his heat, close enough to intimidate her with his size. It was a deliberate tactic, one he had used before in interrogation, but there was a big difference this time in his own attitude. Talking to her was still important, but underlying it was the powerful sexual need to make her aware of him as a male. The closeness of his body shocked her; he saw her waver, saw the sudden color in her cheeks, saw the alarmed flicker of her eyes. She didn't allow herself to retreat, but she went very still, her nostrils flaring delicately as the hot scent of his skin reached her.

Her own feminine scent wrapped subtly about him, drawing him even closer. It was a clean, soapy odor that told him she wasn't long from her bath, mingled with the warm sweetness of woman. He wanted to lean down and nuzzle her neck, to follow that faint scent to its source, investigate all the intriguing places where it might linger.

Later. It was too soon for that.

"So the good doctor had a lot of interesting things to say," he murmured. He began to slowly circle her, letting his body brush hers, the light touches tingling through his nerves like electricity. Stallion circling mare, getting her accustomed to his touch, his smell. Gentling her. "It seems you're some kind of miracle of ESP, if you believe in that kind of stuff."

Her lips tightened. She had herself under control again, not even glancing at him as he continued to circle her, ignoring the fleeting contact of his arm, or his chest, the graze of his thigh. "You don't, of course."

"Nope," he said blithely. It wasn't a complete lie, but he wasn't about to tell her he was at least halfway convinced. He'd get a lot more reaction out of her if she was angry, and reaction was exactly what he wanted. "Unless you can prove it to me. Why don't you give it a try? Come on, Marlie, read my mind or something." Slowly, slowly, around and around. Never letting her completely escape his touch, his heat.

"I can't. There has to be something *in* your mind."

"Nice shot, but it doesn't prove anything." He kept his voice low, almost crooning. "Make me believe it."

"I don't do parlor tricks," she snapped, goaded. She was drawing more and more taut, the force of his nearness wearing on her nerves.

"Not even to prove yourself innocent of murder?" He pushed her even further. "This isn't a party, babe, in case you haven't noticed."

Her head whipped around, dark hair flying, and she gave him the full force of her glare, blue eyes narrowing like a cat's. "I suppose I *could* change you into a toad," she said speculatively, then shrugged. "But someone has already beaten me to it."

He gave a bark of laughter, startling her. "You've seen too many of the old 'Bewitched' shows; that's witchcraft, not ESP."

The slow circling finally got to her. Abruptly she bolted, toward the kitchen. He let her go, following closely behind her. "Coffee," he said blandly. "Good idea."

She hadn't planned on making coffee, of course. She had simply been fleeing. But she seized gratefully on something to do, as he had known she would. She was rattled, and fighting it every inch of the way. He was beginning to realize how important control was to her. Too bad he couldn't let her keep it.

She opened a cabinet door and took down a canister of coffee. Her hands were visibly shaking. Then she halted, her back to him as she carefully set the canister down on the countertop. "I don't read minds," she blurted. "I'm not telepathic."

"Aren't you?" That wasn't what Dr. Ewell had said, exactly. He felt a tinge of triumph. Finally she was starting to talk to him, rather than resisting him. He wanted to put his arms around her and hold her close, shelter her from the trauma of her own memories, but it was too soon. She was physically aware of him now, but she was still frightened, still hostile.

"Not—not a classic telepath." She looked down at the coffee. He could see that her hands were still shaking.

"So what are you?"

So what are you? Marlie heard the question echo in her mind. *Freak,* some people might say. *Charlatan* was the word others would use. Detective Hollister hadn't been that polite. He'd called her a fake, and possibly an accomplice to murder. It was ridiculous, of course. Even he would have had to give up on that idea by now, faced with a complete lack of evidence, opportunity, and motive. But he'd checked her out, he'd actually gone to Boulder and talked to Dr. Ewell. He knew about her now. He might not believe, but at least now he was asking instead of simply accusing. But how much did he know? Dr. Ewell could teach discretion to a diplomat, when he so chose; how much would he have told a stranger, even if that stranger was a cop? Marlie hoped desperately that he didn't know it all, because then he would ask her about it, and she didn't think she could bear to bring it all up now. She felt oddly vulnerable and exposed, her nerve endings raw. *He* had done that to her, forcing his big body so close to her that his heat had seared her skin, deliberately brushing against her, blatantly staring at her breasts.

She didn't want to be even more aware of him than she had already been. She was safe in her solitude.

"What are you?" he repeated calmly.

She turned to face him, her movements slow and deliberate. She squared her shoulders as if bracing herself for an ordeal. "I'm a clairvoyant empath. Or I was." Suddenly confused, she rubbed her forehead. "I suppose I still am."

"But you have read minds before."

"Maybe. Not exactly." It was difficult to describe being so linked with someone that you could interpret his thoughts through his emotions. Sometimes the link was so strong that it happened.

Choosing his words carefully, he said, "According to Dr. Ewell, you were the most sensitive receptor he's ever known."

She gave him a harassed look. "Receptor's as good a word as any. I pick up—I *used* to pick up things. Emotions, energy from actions. Thoughts, too, sometimes, but usually it was emotion rather than actual thoughts. The static was unbelievable."

"That's why you joined Dr. Ewell's study, for the peace of controlled surroundings."

She bit her lip. "Yes. I couldn't drive down a street, shop in a mall, go to a movie. It was like a thousand voices screaming at me at once. Most people don't make any effort to shield themselves, they just blast everything out like a shotgun, spewing their emotions in all directions."

"You didn't live at the Institute, though."

"No, I had a little place outside of Boulder. It was peaceful."

"I know about what happened six years ago."

The brusque statement was like being hit between the eyes. She reeled from the force of the blow, staggering back against the cabinet. He moved, coming toward her with that lethal, catlike grace so unusual in such a big man. Dazed, appalled, she held out a hand to ward him off. With ludicrous ease he brushed it aside and instead pulled her into his arms.

The shock of his hard body against hers was stunning. He was incredibly hot, burning her even through their layers of clothing. His muscled arms were as unyielding as steel bands; they forced her closer, until her thighs were against his, until her breasts were flattened against the hard ridges of his stomach muscles. She felt weak, disoriented, and automatically clutched his biceps in an effort to steady herself.

"Don't be scared," he murmured, bending his head down to hers. His warm breath tickled her ear as he gently nuzzled the side of her neck. He licked the small hollow beneath her ear and the sensation, as tender as a mother's kiss, made her begin to tremble. "I won't let anything like that happen to you again. I know you're skittish with men now, babe, but I'll take care of you. I'm going to take *real* good care of you."

She pulled her head back so she could look at him. Her eyes were huge, and edged with panic. "What are you talking about?" she cried thinly. She was afraid, scared by the way things had so suddenly gotten out of her control, afraid of the proximity of his big body. She didn't want this, didn't want to have to deal with the memories and unpleasantness. For whatever reason, he had decided not to ignore the wildfire of attraction that they had both been fighting, and moved with bewildering speed to change their situation. There was nothing of the detective in him now; he was purely a man, his hazel eyes glittering with sexual intent.

He pressed his mouth to her temple. "In bed, babe. When we make love."

She stiffened, pushing against his heavy shoulders as hard as she could. He didn't budge at all. "No, I don't want that. Let me go!"

"Hush," he said firmly, gathering her even closer. "I'm just holding you, Marlie. That's all. I've wanted to hold you since I first set eyes on you Monday morning."

"There has to be some sort of rule against a detective making a pass at a suspect," she blurted, searching for any weapon at all. "If you think I won't report you—"

"You're not a suspect," he interrupted. His mouth quirked. "Maybe I should have told you sooner, but the officer who saw you Friday night gave you a pretty good alibi, since you couldn't have been in two places at once."

She went still, her attention focusing on what he had just said. Her gaze locked on his. Uncomfortably he realized that there was something oddly compelling about her eyes. "When did you talk to him?"

The even tone of her voice didn't fool him. He winced inwardly. "Um . . . Tuesday night." He should have lied. He shouldn't have brought it up in the first place, at least not right now. He should have—

She bit him. He had been halfway expecting her to take a swing at him. He had to admit that he might deserve one, and he was willing to absorb a shot if it would make her feel better. Besides, the way he was holding her, he knew she wouldn't be able to put much power behind it. Evidently she realized that, too, because she simply leaned forward and sank her teeth into his chest.

"Ouch!" he bellowed, startled by the sharp pain. She hung on like a bulldog, and the pain caused by his involuntary movement quickly convinced him to stand still. "Shit! Turn loose!"

She did, and regarded him with baleful satisfaction as he hastily stepped back and rubbed his chest. A wet spot on his shirt marked where she had bitten.

Gingerly he unbuttoned his shirt and took a look, expecting to see blood. It didn't make him feel a lot better to discover that, though the indentations of her sharp little teeth were plain in his hide, there wasn't even much bruising. "The professor said you were testy," he muttered. "But he didn't mention the cannibalism."

"Serves you right," she said. "You've been hounding me for two days when you *knew* I'd been telling you the truth."

He looked a little sheepish, and continued to rub his chest. "I had to have some excuse."

"To do what?"

"See you."

"That's supposed to endear you to me?" she asked caustically, turning away to pick up the canister of coffee and return it to the cabinet. "I'm not making coffee. You can leave now."

"Will you have dinner with me tomorrow night?"

"No."

He folded his arms. "Then I'm not leaving."

She slapped the countertop in frustration and whirled to face him. "Can't you take a hint? *I don't want this.* Whatever you're offering, I don't want it."

"That's a lie."

Those hazel eyes were glittering again, this time with stubbornness. She had already noted that trait in him. It felt as if she had a bull in her kitchen, and couldn't budge him.

"You feel it the same way I do," he continued relentlessly. "You're attracted to me, and it scares the hell out of you, because of Gleen."

Her face closed up. "I don't want to talk about Gleen."

"That's understandable, but I'm not going to let you hold him between us. The bastard's dead; he can't ever hurt you again. There's too much pleasure in life to turn your back on it."

"And you're just the man who can show me what I'm missing, right?" she asked with heavy sarcasm.

"Bet on it, babe."

She crossed her arms and leaned back against the cabinet, holding herself away from him. "I've always hated being called babe or baby," she observed.

"Fine. I'll call you whatever you like."

"I don't want you to call me anything. Can't you get it through your thick head, Detective? There can't be anything between us, full stop, period."

He grinned suddenly, and her heart gave a thump at the miracle it worked on his harsh features. "There already is something between us. Can you think of anyone else who makes you as angry as I do?"

"Not right offhand," she admitted.

"See? I've been the same way. Since I saw you Monday morning, I've been in a hell of a mood, mad at you for being a suspect, mad at myself for being so attracted to you in spite of it."

"Maybe we just intensely dislike each other," she suggested.

"I don't think so." He glanced swiftly downward. "There's evidence to the contrary."

Marlie fiercely controlled the impulse to let her own gaze drift downward. After what she had felt yesterday morning on the porch, she was fairly certain what she would see. Despite herself, she was charmed by his air of slight bemusement at his body's response, and it took all of her willpower not to let it show. It just wouldn't do. He was going to be difficult enough to discourage as it was, without letting him see how very much she wished things could be different. She had always longed for a normal relationship, but she had always been set apart, first by her own talents, then by Gleen.

"It won't work," she said aloud.

He looked downward again. "You think so? I dunno," he said doubtfully, "it looks like it will work pretty well to me."

Startled, she laughed aloud, and quickly clapped her hand over her mouth to stifle the sound. He grinned at her again, making her heart do acrobatics even as she tried to control herself. He was far more dangerous than she had feared; he could make her laugh.

"I can't," she said, sobering quickly. Her voice was soft, with an undertone of regret that she couldn't hide. "Gleen—"

With two long steps he reached her, closing his hands on her waist. The humor fled his face as if it had never existed. "Gleen is dead. The only way he can hurt you anymore is if you let him."

"Do you think it's that easy?"

"Hell, no, I don't think it's easy. I'm a cop, remember. I've seen what rape victims go through."

"I wasn't—"

"Technically raped? I know. But he tried, and beat the hell out of you because he couldn't. Your reaction probably isn't any different than if he had been able to penetrate."

She laughed again, but this time the sound was harsh, tearing. "It's a little different. I wish he *had* raped me! I lie awake at night and know that if he'd been able to get an erection, maybe if I hadn't fought him so hard, that little boy would still be alive! But he got more and more frenzied, and I kept struggling, and all of a sudden he left me and attacked the little boy." She was silent for a minute. "His name was Dustin," she said. "His parents called him Dusty."

Dane's hands tightened convulsively on her waist, then relaxed. "It wasn't your fault; no one can predict what a madman will do. But that's a bad thing to have to deal with," he said quietly. His chest was tight with suppressed emotion. Gently he smoothed her hair, then slid his fingers under the warm, silky weight to cup her head in his big hand. "Have you ever told anyone everything that happened that night?"

She shook her head. "Not everything. Not the details. It was too . . . ugly."

"Have you ever told anyone else what you just told me?"

"No." She looked up, confusion in her eyes. "I don't know why I did."

"Because there's something between us, and you can't deny it any more than I can. We aren't comfortable with each other yet, but one day it will be okay. I can wait. And I can wait until you're ready to make love, too."

Frustrated at his stubbornness, at her inability to convince him, she shook her head. She didn't know whether to laugh or scream. "You're so damn sure of yourself."

"Trust me," he murmured. His hard fingers massaged her skull, relieving tension she hadn't even been aware of. "You'll think about it now, and the more you think about it, the more used to the idea you'll get. Then you'll start getting curious, wondering about how we would be together. You've done a good job putting your life back together, but you're too smart not to know that until you can trust a man in bed again, you're still letting Gleen have a hold over you. The next step is obvious. And I can promise you one thing: If anyone gets in bed with you, it's going to be me."

Before she could think of a response to that supremely self-confident statement, he took her by the hand and led her back into the living room. His palm was callused, his fingers hard and warm. His touch was consciously gentle, that of a man who was very aware of his own strength and was careful not to squeeze. There was something beguiling about his hand linked with hers, a subtle asking for, and reassurance of, trust. She felt oddly safe with him, though not safe *from* him.

"Let's sit down," he said, urging her toward the couch. Belatedly she tried to detour to a chair, but he tugged her to the couch and pulled her down beside him. He kept her hand folded in his as he settled back with a sigh of relief, stretching his long, muscular legs out before him. "Airplane seats aren't made for anyone over five and a half feet tall. I still feel cramped."

"Why don't you go home," she said tiredly. "It's late."

"Because we still need to talk."

She shook her head and tried to tug her hand free. It was a useless effort. "We don't have anything to talk about."

"I've got some more questions about what you saw Friday night."

She stiffened. She couldn't help it; every time she was reminded of that evil, something inside her froze. "I've already told you everything. Tomorrow's a workday, and I'd like to get some sleep."

"Just a few minutes," he coaxed, smiling at her. That little crook of his mouth caused another disruption in her cardiac rhythm, and she quickly looked away. Whoever would have thought that such a roughhewn face could produce such a charming smile? He shouldn't be allowed to do anything except frown, for her own protection.

"I kept thinking about it on the plane," he said, taking her silence for acquiescence. "You aren't a suspect, you're a witness. In fact, you're the only witness we have. We have no leads, no evidence, no idea who we're looking for. Two earlier possibilities turned out to be dead ends. I'm not saying I buy into this paranormal stuff, but I'm willing to investigate any leads you can give me. For instance, can you give me a description of the guy?"

She shook her head, ignoring the dismissive way he said "this paranormal stuff."

"Nothing at all? C'mon. You described the murder scene down to the smallest detail."

"But I saw it from *his* eyes. I saw . . . everything else. Not him."

"Did you see his hands?"

A memory swam into focus, that of a hand reaching for a knife, holding the knife, slashing—

"Yes." The word was a whisper of sound.

"Good." Her eyes had gone slightly unfocused. Dane made his voice as soothing as he could, not wanting to startle her. "What color was his skin? Light or dark?"

"I don't know."

"Think, Marlie."

"I don't know! He was wearing gloves. Surgical gloves. And he had long sleeves." She paused, looking inward again. "His clothes were dark."

"He didn't pull off the gloves even when he raped her?"

"No."

"Okay, then let's work on his height. We know how tall Mrs. Vinick was; how tall was he in comparison?"

Marlie silently marveled at how his cop's brain worked; she hadn't thought of height at all. Her head tilted in concentration as she tried to focus the mental images.

"When he first grabs her, in the kitchen, he holds her close, with one hand over her mouth and the other holding the knife." Marlie lifted her hands into the positions she described, pantomiming the action. "The hand over her mouth is . . . like this. Even with his shoulder."

"So that's the level of her mouth. That puts him around six feet. We can't know how long his neck is—he may be an inch shorter or taller—but at least that's something. What about his voice? Do you remember anything about it?"

She closed her eyes. "Nothing that stands out. It was just a man's voice, not particularly deep or high." His actual voice hadn't mattered; it had been overwhelmed by the raging violence, the hatred, of his emotions.

"How about an accent? Can you distinguish an accent?"

"Not southern," she said promptly, opening her eyes. "Big deal. This is Orlando; half the population, including me, is from somewhere else."

"Can you narrow it down any more than that? There are a lot of distinctive accents: New York, Boston, Ohio, Chicago, Minnesota, the western accents."

She was shaking her head even as he rattled them off.

"Nothing that I can pin down. He didn't actually *say* that much, or maybe I didn't pick it up."

"Then let's move on to something else. Did you get an impression of his body?"

Utter revulsion crossed her face.

"I mean his weight," Dane said hastily. "Was he thin, average, or heavy?"

She gave him a dirty look. "Average, I think. And strong. Very strong. Maybe it was anger, or the adrenaline, but she was helpless against him. He gloated about it. He loved it."

She leaned back, suddenly very tired, and discovered that sometime during their conversation he had draped his arm behind her, so that when she sat back she was all but in his arms. She bolted forward, only to find that heavy arm around her shoulders and herself being urged back once more, and his face was very close to hers.

"Shhh, don't panic," he murmured in a dark, soft voice. "You're still holding my hand, and the other one's behind you. You're okay."

She glared at him. "I am *not* holding your hand," she snapped. "You're holding mine!"

"Minor detail. I'm going to kiss you, Marlie—"

"I'll bite you again," she swiftly warned.

He shrugged. "I always have had more guts than sense," he said, and very gently brushed her mouth with his.

It was only a fleeting contact, lighter than a whisper, but laden with a tantalizing hint of his taste. Her pulse leaped again, but he was drawing back before the expected fear could materialize. A tiny frown drew her brows together.

He released her hand, finally, and cupped her chin in his palm. The rough pad of his thumb traced the fullness of her lower lip, his gaze focused on the movement.

"Any bad thoughts?" he asked. His voice was even darker, softer.

"No." Her response was a whisper.

"In that case . . ."

This time his mouth lingered. He wasn't holding her; she

didn't feel constrained, but was somehow helpless to move away. His lips were firm and warm, but tender in their pressure even as they moved, and shaped her own lips to accommodate him. Marlie closed both hands around his thick wrist, and her eyes fluttered shut.

The gentle pleasure of the kiss made her dizzy. She hadn't expected such tender consideration from him, or the flood of sensation that rushed through her. She made a little sound of confusion, and he lifted his head immediately.

"Are you okay?"

"Y-Yes," she stammered, her eyes blinking open.

"Good." He bent his head to her again, and resumed the kiss. His tongue slipped into her mouth, not thrusting deep but inviting her to taste him. Marlie didn't know what to do; what was happening was so opposite to what she had expected that she couldn't think. The most stunning fact was that she wasn't afraid. This was nothing like—no, she wouldn't even think his name. The shimmering pleasure she was feeling was too precious to destroy.

Hesitantly, trusting a long-unused instinct, she accepted the invitation and sucked lightly at his tongue. Instantly a shudder ran through his big body, astonishing her. She did it again, and he groaned aloud, a deep sound that reverberated through his chest. Delight in this newfound sensual power shyly bloomed inside her.

He suddenly released her mouth and sat back. His skin was flushed, and pulled taut across his cheekbones. "That's enough. That's almost too much. I'm going to leave now, before I try to push you too far."

She blinked at him, her eyes languorous and dazed, as if she wasn't quite certain what had happened. He wasn't too sure himself. He hadn't been that turned on by a simple kiss since he'd been fifteen, and lost his virginity under the stadium bleachers with a seventeen-year-old cheerleader.

He forced himself to stand up before he made a big mistake and changed his mind about leaving. He had kissed her; that wasn't enough for him, but it was probably as much as she could stand. All in all, he was extremely pleased with the evening.

"I'll call you tomorrow," he said as he walked to the door. She followed him, the awareness rushing back into her eyes. He winked at her. "Your sexy voice turns me on even over the telephone."

Like a light blinking off, all of the softness vanished from her expression. "I'm glad you like it," she said flatly. "I screamed so much when Gleen was butchering the little boy that my voice broke. It hasn't been the same since then."

9

HE WAS SO ALIVE THAT IT WAS ALMOST PAINFUL. CARROLL Janes could feel the anticipation pooling in him, the power gathering, until it felt as if he should be glowing. He was always amazed that people couldn't *see* the power, but then most people really were extraordinarily stupid.

It would be tonight. It was unusual that only a week had passed since the one last Friday, but this was so *easy,* there was no point in putting it off. And it was pleasant, this buildup of power almost as soon as the glow had faded from before. Of course, he couldn't count on this occurring every week; the really rude ones didn't happen all that often. And he normally liked to draw it out much longer, maybe even as long as a month, but that was because there were almost always difficulties to be overcome, complications to solve. Jacqueline Sheets had none. She lived alone, and her routine was suffocating in its rigidity. No, there was no reason to wait.

It was odd that it was almost always women who were rude, though there had been a man once or twice whom he had been obliged to punish. He didn't like it when it was a man. It wasn't that a man's strength made it more difficult; he was contemptuous of that concept. He was strong enough to handle almost anyone, and religiously worked out to maintain that strength. Men simply didn't offer the pleasure, the opportunity for prolonged teasing while the power built. Men were almost boring. And of course, he wasn't queer, so at least half the fun was missing. No way would he screw a man. If he was sometimes a bit more lenient with a man's rudeness—well, it was *his* decision to make, after all, not anyone else's. If he preferred women, that was no one's business but his own.

He hummed all day, causing Annette to remark that he was certainly in a good mood. "You must have big plans for the weekend," she said, and he heard the unconscious note of jealousy in her voice. He liked that. Of course, he had been aware that Annette yearned for him, for all the good it would do her. She simply wasn't his type.

"A hot date," he replied, not caring if she heard the quivering anticipation in the words. It might liven up her fantasies.

He thought of Jacqueline Sheets waiting for him. He had been inside her house, and could picture the scene exactly. He knew where she sat while watching television—which was about all she did. He knew how her bedroom looked, what she wore to sleep in: utilitarian pajamas. He hadn't been surprised. He preferred nightgowns, but pajama bottoms weren't a problem. She would pull them off for him; they all did, with a blade shining in their faces.

He had checked out the kitchen. Her knives had been in disappointing shape, with dulled edges barely capable of slicing a banana. She was obviously not a very good cook, or her knives would have been in better condition. He had selected a filleting knife and carried it home, where he had spent the past two nights painstakingly putting a razor edge on the blade. He hated having to work with inferior tools.

He could barely wait for the night, when the ritual would

begin, as his father had taught him. When you are rude, you are punished.

Dane had called Marlie at seven that morning, just to say hello and ask if she'd slept well, and the irritation in her voice had made him chuckle. She was still resisting him mentally, but physically it had gone much better than he had ever hoped. He had kissed her, and she not only hadn't been afraid, she had enjoyed it. Considering her background, that was a giant stride forward.

He grinned like an idiot all the way to work. He had kissed her! So what if it had been a kiss that would make the average teenage stud roll his eyes in boredom? What did teenage studs know? They weren't interested in anything but squeezing breasts and a few quick thrusts. He was old enough, thank God, to know that the slower it was, the better it was. He might be crazy with frustration by the time Marlie came to him, but after last night he had no doubt that it would happen. He was dizzy with delight, anticipation fizzing in him like champagne bubbles.

Trammell was already there when Dane walked in, his dark eyes sleepy as he leaned back in his chair and watched Dane approach. People moved around them, talking and swearing; telephones rang incessantly, the fax machine and photocopier hummed almost without pause. A typical day, but Dane didn't feel typical. He was still smiling as he went to the coffee machine and poured two cups of coffee. He sipped one as he returned to his desk, and gave Trammell the other. "You look like you need it. Bad night?"

"Thanks." Trammell cautiously tasted it, eyeing Dane over the rim. "It was a long night, but not a bad one. Well? Did you find out anything interesting yesterday?"

"Quite a bit. For one thing, let's say I'm not as skeptical as I was before."

Trammell rolled his eyes. "What about Marlie? What's she been doing for six years?"

"Trying to recover," Dane said briefly. "Arno Gleen beat

her, tried to rape her, and when he couldn't, he killed the kid in front of her. According to Dr. Ewell, the trauma of it severely damaged, maybe even destroyed, her paranormal abilities. Evidently this vision about the Vinick murder is the first psychic tickle she's had since then."

"So the psychic stuff is coming back to her?"

Dane shrugged. "Who knows. Nothing else has happened." *Thank God.* "I talked to her last night, asked a few more questions about what she saw in the vision, and she remembered a couple of details."

"Like what?"

"The guy is about six feet tall, he's in very good shape, and he isn't from the South."

Trammell snorted. "That really narrows it down for us."

"It beats what we had before."

"Agreed. Anything beats nothing. That's assuming we accept a psychic's vision for leads, because a court sure as hell won't accept her as evidence."

"What choice do we have? There *is* nothing else. This guy didn't leave a clue. I'll take any lead I can get, and worry about proof when we find him."

"Actually," Trammell said slowly, "we've already talked to someone who fits that description."

"Yeah, I know. Ansel Vinick. He's as strong as a bull, and even though he's lived in Florida for over twenty years, he still has a midwestern accent." He hadn't been surprised; very few people who weren't raised in the South ever managed to get the accent right. The movie and television industries never had. "But my gut says he didn't do it."

"He had opportunity."

"But no motive. No boyfriend, no insurance. Nothing."

"Maybe an argument that got out of hand?"

"The medical examiner didn't find any bruises on her that would indicate blows. She wasn't just killed, she was slaughtered."

"The textbooks say that when there are that many stab wounds, the killer was really pissed at the victim. And that if he spends a lot of time doing it, he probably lives in the neighborhood. You know the numbers as well as I do: Eighty percent of the time, when a woman's killed, it's her husband or boyfriend who does her in. And a lot of the time, the killer is the one who calls the police when he 'discovers' the body. Vinick fits into all of the categories."

"Except for the first one. If they were arguing, no one knows anything about it. The neighbors didn't hear anything, they always seemed to get along fine, and Vinick didn't act unusual in any way at work that night. And she was raped, but there wasn't any semen. Marlie says the perp wore a rubber; why would Vinick bother? She was his wife, for Pete's sake. Finding his semen in her wouldn't be incriminating. What really bothers me," he said, thinking hard, "is her fingers. Why chop off her fingers? We haven't found them. There wasn't any reason to cut off her fingers, unless—"

"—she scratched him," Trammell finished, dark eyes shining intently. "She scratched him, and he knew about DNA profiling. He cut off her fingers so forensics couldn't get a skin sample from under her nails."

"Vinick was wearing a short-sleeved shirt that morning," Dane recalled. "Do you remember any scratches?"

"No. It's possible he could have had some on his chest or upper arms, but the hands and lower arms are the most likely location."

"Don't forget the cut screen in the bedroom. If Vinick had done it himself, to make it look like a forced entry, wouldn't he have made it more obvious? He didn't strike me as a subtle type of guy, anyway. And everything that Marlie told us dovetailed with what we found at the scene. It wasn't Vinick."

"Wait a minute," Trammell said. "Marlie didn't mention the fingers, did she?"

Dane thought about it, then shook his head. "No, and it doesn't seem like the kind of detail anyone would forget."

The omission troubled him, and he made a mental note to ask her about it that night.

"All the same, I'd feel better if we talked to Vinick again," Trammell insisted.

Dane shrugged. "It's all right with me, I just feel like it's wasted time."

Trammell tried several times that day to get in touch with Mr. Vinick, between the hundred other things they had to do, but there was no answer. He called the trucking company where Mr. Vinick worked, and was told that he had been off all week, and all things considered, they really didn't expect him to return to work for at least another week.

"The funeral was yesterday," Dane said. "Maybe he's staying with friends. Hell, of course he isn't staying in the house. Forensics is finished with the scene, but would you want to sleep there?"

Trammell grimaced. "Guess not. But how are we going to get in touch with him?"

"Ask one of the neighbors. They'll know."

It was late afternoon when they pulled up in front of the Vinick house. It had a closed, unoccupied look. The yellow crime scene tape had been removed, but the house still looked set apart, made forever different from its neighbors by the violence that had happened within. A car was parked in the driveway, and Dane recognized it as the one that had been sitting there last Saturday morning. "He's here."

They knocked on the front door. There was no answer, no sound of movement inside the house. Trammell went around to the back door, with the same results. All of the curtains were pulled, so they couldn't see in any of the windows.

Both doors were locked. They banged again, identifying themselves. Nothing.

Dane walked next door. A woman came out on the porch at his knock.

"I'm Detective Hollister," he said, flipping his ID wallet

open. "Have you seen Mr. Vinick? His car is here, but we can't get anyone to the door."

She frowned, and pushed her hair out of her eyes. "No, I haven't seen him since the funeral. I went to it; just about everyone on the street did. She was such a nice lady. I don't know when he parked his car in the driveway. It wasn't there late yesterday afternoon, but was when I got up this morning."

"You haven't seen anyone over there at all?"

"No. Of course, I haven't been here all day, but no one has been there that I've seen."

"Thanks." Dane nodded in good-bye and walked back to the Vinick house. "I don't like it," he said, after telling Trammell what the neighbor had said. "How do you feel about forced entry?"

"I think we'd better," Trammell said soberly. "If we're wrong, we'll grovel and apologize and pay for the damages."

They went around back. The top half of the kitchen door was small, diamond-shaped panes of glass. Dane pulled out the Beretta and used the butt to knock out the corner pane closest to the doorknob. He was always surprised at how hard it was to actually break out a window. Shattered glass tinkled on the tile floor inside. Carefully wrapping his hand in a handkerchief, he reached inside and unlocked the door.

The house was hot, and foul with the odor of death that had been closed up inside it. The silence was almost physical.

Dane unwrapped the handkerchief from his hand and held it over his nose. "Shit," he muttered, then raised his voice. "Mr. Vinick? Detectives Hollister and Trammell."

Nothing.

The smell seeped through the cloth. It wasn't the cloying, sickeningly sweet odor of decayed flesh, but a pungent smell of human waste underlaid with the metallic scent of blood, both old and new. Dane's stomach knotted. He cursed again, quietly, and stepped inside.

The living room was empty; he had expected it to be. The walls were still splattered with Mrs. Vinick's blood, the stains turned brown.

Mr. Vinick was in the bedroom.

It hadn't been cleaned, either. Chalk still outlined the position of her body, there in the corner. Mr. Vinick lay beside the outline. There was a small pistol lying close by his head.

He hadn't taken any chances with botching the job. Anyone who jams the barrel into his mouth is serious about the attempt.

"Ah, shit," Trammell said tiredly. "I'll call it in."

Dane squatted by the body, being careful not to touch anything. Nothing he could see indicated that it was anything but a suicide, but it was habit not to disturb a scene.

He looked around, and saw a sheet of paper lying on the bed. The sheets had been stripped off, leaving only the bare mattress, and the white paper wasn't immediately noticeable against the white ticking. He could read what it said without bending down.

I don't have any family now, with Nadine gone, so I don't guess it matters much. I just don't want to go on. He had dated and signed it, even noted the time. Eleven-thirty P.M., just about the same time of night his wife had been murdered.

Dane rubbed the back of his neck, his mouth set in a grim line. Damn, this was tough. The guy had buried his wife, then returned to where she had been murdered and put a bullet in his head.

Trammell came back into the room and stood beside Dane, reading the note himself. "Was it guilt or depression?"

"Who the hell knows?"

"Shit," Trammell said. There was just something about this house of death that reduced comment to that crude, simple word. It was sad.

By the time the scene had been secured, the body taken away, and the paperwork dealt with, it was almost nine o'clock. Dane thought about calling Marlie, but decided against it. He wasn't in a good mood, and didn't feel up to any romancing. Trammell had had a date, but he was as surly as Dane, and called to cancel. Instead they went to the cops' favorite bar and slugged back a couple of beers. A lot of cops had a drink or two, or three, before they went home. It was the easiest way to wind down, and an opportunity to dump all the tension on people who knew exactly what they were talking about, before they went home to the spouse and kiddies and pretended everything was sweetness and light.

"If he *was* the perp, we'll never find out now," Trammell grunted, licking foam off his upper lip.

Dane had always liked it about Trammell that the man drank beer, instead of some hoity-toity wine. He could accept the Italian suits and silk shirts, the Gucci loafers, but he would have had a hard time connecting with a wine drinker. He didn't know why Trammell had suddenly decided that Ansel Vinick was their best bet as a suspect, but they all got maggots in their heads from time to time. "I don't think he did it. I think the poor sad son of a bitch just couldn't face living after finding his wife like that."

"I wasn't convinced he did it," Trammell denied grumpily. "I just wanted to make sure he didn't get away because we were too busy looking for phantoms."

Dane finished his beer. "Well, innocent or guilty, he didn't get away. You want another one?"

Trammell considered the level of beer in his glass. "No, this will do it." He paused, still frowning at the amber liquid. "Say, Dane . . ."

His voice trailed off, and Dane lifted his brows, waiting inquisitively. "Yeah, what?"

"These gut feelings you get. Your instincts are usually right on, and everyone knows it. Have you ever thought . . . you aren't a lot different from Marlie?"

If Dane hadn't already finished his beer, he'd have spewed it all over the table. He choked, and his outraged "What?" was just a wheeze of sound.

"Just think about it." Trammell warmed to his subject, leaning forward to prop his elbows on the table. "We all get hunches, we all go with our guts. Most of the time we don't need to, because the perp is sitting there singing like a good little birdie, but every so often we get a mystery. So how are our hunches different from what Marlie does?"

"That's a crock. Hunches are just the subconscious noticing something that consciously we haven't thought about yet."

"That's pretty much what a psychic does, isn't it?"

Dane gave him a sour look. "I think two beers is maybe one over your limit. We get hunches because of evidence we can see, and circumstances we can think about. Hell, a psychic doesn't have to be anywhere around or know anything about the situation, they just pick up these vibes, or whatever."

Trammell rubbed his head, disturbing his hair. Dane began to feel vaguely concerned; maybe two beers *was* too much for Trammell. God knows he'd never seen Trammell with so much as one hair out of place, except for that time when they'd gotten in a shootout and Dane had caught a bullet, but those were extenuating circumstances.

"I can't make up my mind what to believe," Trammell muttered. "Logic and the law of averages says that Ansel Vinick was the most likely suspect. But Marlie knew everything, except about the fingers, and how did she know unless she's for real? If she's for real, then Vinick was innocent and we're back to square one." He picked up the glass and drained it, then set it on the table with a thunk.

"That's exactly where we are. Square one. I'm beginning to feel stupid, because we sure as hell aren't accomplishing anything."

"No evidence, no witnesses, no motive. Know what?"

Trammell's lean, faunlike face was so funereal that Dane had to bite the inside of his cheek to keep from grinning. "No, what?"

"I don't metabolize alcohol very well," his dapper partner announced with grave dignity.

"No!" Dane clapped his hands to his face. "I never would have guessed." Privately he thought that anyone who could still say "metabolize" without tripping over the syllables was in damn good shape.

"I'm usually more careful than this. I . . . sip."

"You're a world-class sipper."

"Thank you. But it's probably a good thing that you're driving."

"I think so. Are you ready to go home now?"

"Any time you are. You won't have to put me to bed or anything like that, but I wouldn't want to drive."

"I wouldn't want you to drive, either, buddy. C'mon, let's go."

Trammell was steady on his feet, but he was humming under his breath, and Dane almost laughed again. Humming "My Darling Clementine" didn't fit with the image. "Will you have a hangover?" he asked curiously. A hangover from two beers would be hilarious.

"Never have," Trammell said. They were outside, and he inhaled a deep breath of smoke-free air. "This doesn't happen very often. Not since college."

"That's good."

"You won't tell anyone, will you?"

"Naw. I promise." It would be tempting, but he'd keep it to himself. Though most embarrassing things were fair game, this was something Trammell couldn't help, and the guys would rag him unmercifully for the rest of his life. On the other hand, it was nice to have something he could hold over Trammell's head occasionally. He whistled cheerfully as they got in the car, his good mood restored.

* * *

The ritual was comforting. He liked for everything to happen in exactly the same order every time, because *he* commanded it. He didn't do it often enough for it to be routine—that would weaken the power of it—but there was reassurance in the sameness of preparation. Knowing that these very preparations would make it impossible for the police to ever catch him gave him a sense of gleeful power. They caught only stupid people who made stupid mistakes, and he had never made a mistake. Not one.

Anticipation for the coming night kept rising in him, but he kept it firmly under control. He wanted to concentrate on the preparations.

First the hairpiece of blond curls came off. It was a very good hairpiece; he had paid an outrageous amount for it, but it had been worth every penny. No one had ever discovered that it was a full wig. Not only was blond his natural coloring, which meant the color wasn't jarring, but the style of blond curls was something that people remembered. It was very recognizable.

There was nothing wrong with his own hair, he thought, examining his temples for any telltale sign of a retreating hairline. But it would be stupid to let a stray hair give the police a means of identifying him. He carefully shaved his head, taking his time about it, though there was only stubble because the last time had been so recent.

He loved shaving, the wetness, the slick feel of the shaving gel, the glide of the razor over his flesh. It was almost like sex.

His beard was next. It wouldn't be gentlemanly to scratch her with a rough chin. Then his chest. He had a neat diamond of chest hair, and he was rather proud of its thickness, but it had to go.

Then his legs and arms. Slick. No wonder women shaved their legs. It really felt marvelous.

Finally, his crotch. No curlies left behind to be combed out, examined, gloated over. He was extremely careful in this area, for even a tiny nick could leave an unnoticed stain of blood behind. That simply wouldn't do. And of course, he always wore a condom, so there was no semen left behind. He even had a contingency plan in case the condom broke; so far, he hadn't had to use the plan.

Some men, he'd read, couldn't be identified by their semen; they were called "nonsecreters," and about one man in five was like that. It would have been nice to know if he was in that twenty percent, but he could hardly go to a lab and ask to have his semen classified as secreter or nonsecreter. He didn't mind wearing the condom; he didn't want his sperm inside the transgressors anyway.

Next were his clothes. Leather. No fabric fibers to be left behind, nothing to give them a clue. He kept his leathers carefully stored in a cardboard box, away from everything else. He had a vinyl seat cover that he put over his car seat, and the floorboard was covered with vinyl mats. He was always very careful not to let his feet touch anything but the mat, so his boots wouldn't pick up any fibers from the carpet. Detail. Attention to detail was everything. There was no way the police could identify him, because he left nothing behind except the object of the lesson.

Detective Hollister hadn't called, though Marlie had expected him to, or even shown up unannounced as he had a tendency to do. She had been on edge, afraid he *would* call or come by, then irritable with him for not doing so. Either way, he had managed to ruin her quiet evening at home.

She had toyed with the idea of going to a movie, partly to stymie Hollister if he did call, but had rejected the idea. She couldn't forget what had happened last Friday night. Had it only been a week? It seemed like a month. Perhaps next week she would go to a movie, but not tonight.

She went to bed earlier than normal, before ten, not even staying up to watch the late news. She was tired; the week of tension had taken a toll on her. It was a relief to close her eyes and know that she didn't have to go to work in the morning, that she could stay in bed as long as she wanted. She relaxed into the mattress, feeling her muscles go limp and her mind ease into sleep . . .

—He moved silently through the house. The television was blaring, masking his presence. He stood in the doorway for a moment, watching the woman who sat with her back to him while she watched an old movie, and contempt filled him. She was so easy. He walked forward, taking his time, enjoying the suspense. The flickering light from the television glinted on the slim, curved blade of the knife in his hand—

A grunting, animal sound tore from deep in her chest as Marlie tried to scream, tried to send a desperate warning through her closed throat. God, oh God. She whimpered, fighting the covers as she tried to throw herself out of bed. The vision was so real that she expected to see him coming at her out of the darkness, silver blade gleaming.

—He stood right behind her, looking down at her. The stupid bitch had no idea he was there. He liked that. Maybe he'd just stand here until the end of the movie, and all the time she'd never know—

She scrambled out of bed and fell, caught by the sheet tangled around her legs. She fought her way free of the sheet and stumbled to her feet, lurching wildly from side to side as she staggered for the door. Panic blinded her, froze her brain—no, it was dark, the lights were off. She careened into the wall, and the hard impact steadied her, somehow. She groped for the light switch, but it wasn't there.

—This was boring. Smiling, he reached out to touch her neck—

Marlie stumbled into another wall, a wall that wasn't supposed to be there. She stood there, trembling, totally disoriented. Where was she?

Headlights from a passing car briefly illuminated the room. The living room. How had she gotten in here? She remembered trying to get to the bedroom door, but not reaching it. But at least now she knew where a light was.

She almost knocked the lamp over as she fumbled with

the switch, and the sudden bright flare of light momentarily blinded her. The phone. The phone was right there, on the table.

His number. What was his number, damn it? She couldn't remember, couldn't think—the redial button. Had she called anyone since that night? She didn't know, didn't care. It would reach someone. She lifted the receiver, banging it painfully against her temple as she tried to hold it in place with a violently trembling hand, and punched what she hoped was the redial button. Her vision was blurring, and she wasn't certain.

The first ring buzzed in her ear. She closed her eyes, fighting to remain within herself.

The second ring. Hurry. Please, hurry hurry hurry.

The third ring cut off in midbuzz, and a deep, sleepy, grouchy voice said, "Hollister."

"D-Dane." Her voice was thin, wavering out of control.

"Marlie?" All sleepiness was gone. "Marlie, what's wrong?"

She tried to speak and couldn't; her throat was too tight. She took deep, gulping breaths.

"Marlie, goddammit, say something!" He was yelling at her now.

It was coming. She couldn't fight it off any longer. The trembling was convulsive, the light fading as her vision went. She made a desperate effort, screaming, and her voice was only a whisper. "He's . . . doing it . . . again."

10

He couldn't get her to say anything else, though the line was still open. Dane scrambled into his clothes and shoved his sockless feet into running shoes. He grabbed his shoulder holster, with the Beretta in it, but didn't take the time to slip it on. Barely a minute after answering the telephone, he was on his way out the door.

His heart was slamming painfully against his ribs. What had she said? Her last sentence had been so faint, he could barely hear; something about doing it again.

It didn't matter what she had said. Her panic had reached through the phone line to him, as real as if he could see it. She was in trouble, serious trouble.

It was raining lightly, just enough to slick the streets and make him keep the wipers on. He couldn't drive as fast as he wanted, but he was still going too fast for the road conditions. The sense of urgency kept his foot on the accelerator. He merely slowed down for stop signs, and halted at red lights only until there was a break in traffic.

An accident on the expressway forced him to cut across

the median, backtrack, and take another route, wasting valuable time. Almost twenty minutes had passed when he pulled into Marlie's driveway. Her car was in its customary place, and a light was on in the living room. He didn't bother with the two shallow steps, but leaped onto the porch with a single bound and knocked on the door.

"Marlie? It's Dane. Open up."

The silence inside was absolute, as complete as it had been that afternoon at the Vinick house, as if no living creature were inside. Dane's blood chilled, and his voice was hoarse as he called her again, banging on the door with his fist.

There were no windowpanes in this door to break, and he didn't take the time to go around back and check out the kitchen door. He backed up and lashed out with his foot. Four kicks broke the lock and splintered the frame, and the door flew open to crash against the wall. He knew he should take his time, not rush in without knowing the situation, but fear was greater than caution and he hurled himself through the opening, the Beretta in his hand.

"Marlie!"

She was just sitting there on the couch, in a pool of light from the lamp, like a statue in a niche. Her eyes were open, fixed and unseeing. She was utterly still, utterly white, and for an agonized moment he stopped breathing. The pain was like a fist, clenched around his heart.

Then he remembered what Officer Ewan had said, that at first he had thought she was dead, and he started breathing again, managed to move, though the fear hadn't released its icy hold on him. He laid the pistol aside and knelt on the floor in front of the couch, picked up one of her hands from her lap and held it against his chest while he put two fingers on her fragile wrist, pressing and finding the reassuring throb of her pulse. It was slow but steady. Her skin was cool, but the warmth of life lay just under the surface chill.

"Marlie," he said again, much calmer now. There was still no response.

Carefully he looked her over, then examined the surroundings. There was no sign of struggle, and no injuries that he could see. She seemed fine, physically.

The phone receiver was lying beside her on the couch, a beeping noise coming from it. He picked it up and replaced it in the cradle.

He swallowed as he realized what must have happened. She had had another vision, might even still be locked in it. What was it this time? Another murder? God knows, with drugs and street gangs, it was a wonder she didn't spend most of her time in a catatonic state. Did she ever pick up on the good stuff, on happy times, on people playing with their kids or groaning at a dumb joke? How could she function, if she was overloaded with all the shit in people's lives?

She was wearing only a thin tank top and panties, and her legs felt chilled to his touch. He got up and closed the ruined door, then went into her bedroom in search of a blanket. The small room, like every other room he'd seen in her house, was cozy and soothing. She had made the house her retreat, her barricade against the world. He stood in the middle of it and looked around, getting to know her in little ways. The covers on the double bed were twisted and half on the floor; she had evidently been in bed when the vision had started, and the condition of the covers was a measure of her agitation.

There was a crocheted throw lying across a rocking chair. He picked it up and returned to the living room, where he draped it over her, tucking the folds around her bare arms and legs. As far as he could tell, she hadn't moved even a centimeter, except for the barely perceptible rise and fall of her chest as she breathed.

He didn't know what else to do, except wait. He went into the kitchen and put on a pot of coffee; she might not need it when she came out of this, but he sure as hell did.

He sat on the couch beside her, watching her. Her expression was as blank and empty as that of the statue she had reminded him of earlier. There was no awareness in her;

her eyes were open, but she was either unconscious or . . . gone, somehow.

He studied her oblivious face. Seen in profile, there was an otherworldly purity to her features that he hadn't noticed before. When she was awake, the sharpness of her tongue and the cool intelligence in those bottomless blue eyes took most of his attention. Most, but not all. If she had been awake, he sure wouldn't have put a cover over her half-naked body. He looked at the tender curve of her lips, remembering how they had felt, how she had tasted. Her shape was all feminine daintiness, soft, lithe curves that made his entire body feel hot, and his skin too tight.

Ten minutes had ticked by. The mechanical thumping and spitting in the kitchen had stopped, indicating that the coffee had finished brewing.

He fetched a cup of coffee, then resumed his seat beside Marlie and placed the cup on the lamp table. Very gently he lifted her, and settled her on his lap.

"Marlie. Can you wake up now? Come on, honey, wake up." He stroked her face, then grasped her shoulder and shook her.

She made a little sound, not quite a whimper, and her lashes fluttered.

"Come back to me, Marlie. It's Dane. Wake up and tell me what happened." Her head lolled against his shoulder. He cradled her with his supporting arm and rubbed his free hand over her upper arm and shoulder, feeling the cool, sleek skin under his hard palm. He shook her again, but not hard, only enough to jar her. Her eyes were closed now, which seemed to him at least more natural, as if she were sleeping.

"Marlie!" He made his voice sharp. "Wake up and talk to me, damn it!"

She moaned and tried to push away from him, but her hand fell heavily to her lap as if she couldn't quite control it. She drew several jerky breaths, and her lashes lifted, then closed again, the effort beyond her.

"Marlie, look at me." He deliberately said her name, calling her from the far reaches of darkness, back toward the light.

Someone was insistently calling her name. Marlie's exhausted mind latched on to the familiarity, like a drowning person desperately clutching at a life ring. It gave her a center, a sense of identity in the swirling fog of nightmare. The voice was far away at first, but then came closer and closer, until it was right over her head. Reality seeped back, though there was something very *un*real about it. It felt as if she was lying against someone, as if arms were around her, and the sensation was so alien that it confused her. She didn't allow people to hold her; the mental intrusion, strengthened by physical contact, was just too disrupting. But someone *had* held her, a dim memory insisted. Oh, yes. Dane. Gently bullying, stubborn, refusing to listen to her . . . Of course. Dane.

She forced her heavy eyelids to lift, and found herself staring at that roughhewn face, the hazel eyes dark with worry. His heart thumped steadily against her, a comforting rhythm that made her want to curl against him. The heat of his big body was under her, around her, chasing away the bone-deep chill. Why was she so cold?

Hazily she looked around. She was in her living room. But why was Dane here, and why was she on his lap? Why was she so tired? She had expected him to call, but he hadn't, and she had gone to bed—

She had called him. She stiffened, memory returning in a flood of awful details that she would have given anything not to recall. Her exhausted mind struggled to cope.

"Dane." She clutched his shirt, fingers twisting in the material.

"It's all right," he murmured, smoothing back her hair. "I'm here. You had another vision, didn't you? What was it about this time? Just take your time, settle down. Do you want some coffee? Will that help?"

He was holding a cup of coffee to her lips, and she sipped

it, hoping the caffeine would buy her a few extra minutes. She had to get her thoughts ordered, tell him as much as she could, but the coffee was the worst she had ever tasted, and with a grimace she turned her head away when he tried to get her to drink again.

"He did it again," she said, the words slurred a little.

"Who did?" he asked absently, trying to get her to drink a little more coffee. She turned her head away from the cup.

"Him. He killed another woman tonight." The trembling had started again, shaking her from the inside out.

He tensed. She could feel his muscles coiling beneath her. "The same one who killed Nadine Vinick?" he asked carefully.

"Yes. I knew he was out there, looking . . . I felt him, just a hint, the night I called you." She forced the words out in a tumble, trying to get it all said.

"That's what scared you?"

She nodded, her head barely moving in the hollow of his shoulder.

Holding her securely against him, Dane picked up the telephone and called central dispatch. He identified himself and said, "Has a stabbing murder of a woman been called in?"

"No, it's been pretty quiet for a Friday night. Guess the rain's put a damper on things. You know something we don't?"

"Maybe, maybe not. Listen, if there is anything like that, give me a call on the pager. Night or day, no matter what."

"You got it."

He hung up and looked down at Marlie. "Nothing's been called in."

She was still gripping his shirt, and her eyes had taken on that faraway look they had had Monday morning, when she had recited a horror tale in a flat, emotionless voice. The trembling in her slight body had increased; he held her with both arms, trying to cushion her against the shock waves he could feel rippling through her.

"She has red hair," she said in that small, ghostly voice. "She's very pretty. She's watching television, some old movie. She doesn't know he's there. He walks up behind her and stands there, looking down. He's amused; how long will it be before she senses his presence? Too long. She's a stupid cow, and he's getting bored. He touches her neck, with his left hand, then slaps it over her mouth before she can scream. He loves that first moment of terror. The knife is in his right hand. He holds it to her throat."

"Are you sure it's the same one?" Dane asked. He desperately wanted her to say that she wasn't certain.

"Yes. The movie is still on; it masks the noise. He makes her take off her pajamas and lie down on the floor. Couches are too cramped; he doesn't like couches. He uses a condom. She doesn't deserve his sperm. Slow and easy, slow and easy . . . let her relax, not be so afraid. Don't hurt her, not yet, not yet."

Dane anchored her to him, holding her so tight he expected her to protest, but she didn't, all of her attention on her litany of terror. Chills rippled up his spine, and the hair on the back of his neck stood up. Oh, God.

"He's finished. He's on his knees beside her. She's looking up at him, eyes wide and scared, but hoping. That's good, that's real good. He smiles at her, and her stupid mouth quivers, but she smiles too. She's afraid not to, she thinks he's crazy. Too stupid to live. He's bored; this isn't as much fun as the last one. Maybe he can liven her up. He sticks her a little and she squeals like a pig, and the race is on. Around and around the mulberry bush."

"Jesus God," Dane said, his voice hoarse. "Marlie, stop it. That's enough."

She blinked and refocused on him, and the expression in her eyes made him want to cry. The pallor of exhaustion lay over her face like a clay mask.

"You have to catch him," she said in a drugged voice.

"I know. I will, honey. I promise."

She turned her face in to his shoulder and closed her eyes.

Her body went limp in his arms. He looked down at her as she began breathing in a slow, heavy rhythm that signaled deep sleep. As quickly as that, she had slipped into unconsciousness. He wasn't alarmed. After seeing her as she had been when he'd first arrived, this looked downright normal.

He sat there for several minutes, his face grim as he considered the ugly ramifications. Finally he got to his feet, with Marlie still in his arms, and carried her into the bedroom, where he carefully placed her on the bed. She didn't move when he pulled the throw away and re-covered her with the sheet.

He refilled the cup with hot coffee, then resumed his seat and thought about what had happened tonight. He didn't like any of it.

He glanced at the clock; it was after midnight. He called Trammell anyway.

The receiver was fumbled upward on the other end and he heard a very feminine "Hello?" at the same time as Trammell was saying, "Don't answer that!" Evidently two beers hadn't incapacitated him *too* much, and evidently the canceled date had been rescheduled.

Then Trammell got the phone away from his lady friend. "Yeah?"

Dane wasn't in the mood to tease him. "Marlie had another vision tonight," he said without preamble. "The same guy. She says he did another one."

Trammell was silent for a shocked two seconds as the ramifications of it hit him, too. "Where?" he asked.

"Nothing's been called in yet."

More silence. Then he said, "This will prove one way or the other if she's for real."

"Yeah. She was in pretty bad shape. I'm at her house, if you need me. Dispatch is going to call if anything's reported."

"Okay. If she's right . . . shit!"

Yeah, shit. Dane sat there drinking coffee, brooding. If Marlie was right, and the same guy who had murdered

Nadine Vinick had done another woman, in the same way, they had big-time trouble. As bad as he had wanted the bastard, he thought he had been looking for a one-timer, he had hoped it was someone who had known Mrs. Vinick. He had thought it had been personal, though he hadn't been able to find anything to indicate what that would have been. Multiple stab wounds usually meant someone was really pissed at the victim.

But another victim, killed with the same MO, meant they had a psychopath in Orlando. A serial killer. Someone without conscience, someone who acted only according to his own weird rules. Worse, it looked as if he was an intelligent serial killer, taking pains to leave no evidence behind. Serial killers were a real bitch to catch under any circumstances, and a smart one was almost impossible. Look at how long Bundy had killed before he'd finally made a mistake.

He couldn't do anything but wait. He couldn't investigate a murder that hadn't been reported, a body that hadn't been found. Until a victim turned up, all he had was a vision by a burned-out, trauma-damaged psychic. He believed her, though; his gut believed her, and that was frightening in itself. A cold corner of logic in his brain was still saying "wait and see," but logic couldn't dissipate the knot in his stomach.

He knew the terminology. Escalating sexual serial killer. He tried to remember if there had been any unsolved stabbing murders in Orlando before Nadine Vinick, but none came to mind, at least none that resembled it. Either the guy had just recently started murdering his victims, or he had moved in from another city. If a killer moved around, kept the murders spread out over different jurisdictions, cops might never figure out that it was the work of a serial killer because they wouldn't have the other murders to compare the method to.

If Mrs. Vinick was his first victim, then to have killed again so soon the guy had to have gone totally out of control, and they would soon have a bloodbath in the city. An escalating killer started out slow; there might be months between his victims. Then the killings would start getting closer and closer together, because that was the only way he could get his rocks off, and he wanted it more and more often. Only a week between victims signaled an incipient rampage.

And he couldn't do anything except wait.

When would the body, if there was a body, most likely be discovered? Maybe the husband worked third shift, like Mr. Vinick. Maybe that was the common denominator, that the husband was gone nights. If so, the discovery would be in the morning, say from six until eight. But if the lady lived alone, it could be a couple of days or longer before anyone missed her enough to check on her. Hell, he'd seen cases where people had been dead for *weeks* before anyone noticed.

Wait.

He looked at the clock again. Five after two. The coffee was gone, and he drank so much of the stuff that it only worked as long as he was pouring it in. He was tired; his eyelids felt like sandpaper.

He looked at Marlie's couch, and snorted in dismissal. He was six two, and the couch was five feet. He'd never been into masochism.

He peeked into the one room in the little house that he hadn't seen, wondering if it was a spare bedroom. It wasn't. This was where she stored odd pieces of furniture, luggage, boxes of books. It wasn't as cluttered as the main rooms in his home usually were.

The only bed in the place was the one Marlie was sleeping in. He supposed he could go home, but he didn't want to leave her alone. The lock on her door was ruined. He didn't know how long she would sleep, but he intended to be there when she woke.

He hesitated for only the barest second, wondering what she would say if she woke up with him in bed beside her, but then he shrugged and went into her bedroom. As far as he could tell, she hadn't moved at all.

He stripped down to his shorts, tossing his clothes over the rocking chair, and placed the pistol on the bedside table. His pager went right beside the pistol. There was only the one table, and Marlie was lying on that side of the bed. Dane scooted her over, then without even a twinge of conscience, slid in beside her and turned off the lamp.

It felt good. Contentment spread through him, a warm antidote to the worry of the last few hours. As big as he was, the double bed felt cramped to him, but even that had its good points because Marlie was so close to him. He put his arms around her, holding her cradled to him with her head in the hollow of his shoulder. Her slight body felt soft and fragile, and her breath moved across his chest with the lightest of touches.

He would be willing to lie awake for the rest of his life, if he could protect her from what she had gone through tonight. She had told him, Officer Ewan had told him, the professor had told him, but until he had seen it with his own eyes, he simply hadn't realized how traumatic it was for her, how it hurt her, how much it cost her.

What a price she had paid! He knew the toll it took on the human spirit to see so much ugliness, day in and day out. Some cops handled it better than others, but they all paid, and they had only normal sensitivities. What must it have been like for her, feeling everything, all the pain and rage and hate? Losing her empathic ability must have been like being rescued from torture. Now that it was evidently coming back, how must she feel? Trapped? Desperate?

Desire pulsed in his loins; he couldn't be around her and not want her. But stronger than desire was the need to hold her close and protect her, from the horrors within as well as those without.

He slept until eight, and woke instantly aware that the pager hadn't beeped at him during the night. Neither had

Marlie stirred. She lay limply against his side, her very stillness a gauge of her exhaustion. How long did this stupor normally last?

He showered, figuring she wouldn't mind the use of her bathroom and towels. Then he shaved, using her razor and swearing when he nicked himself. Then he went into the kitchen and put on another pot of coffee. He was beginning to feel as comfortable in Marlie's house as he was in his own. While he was waiting for the coffee to brew, he measured the ruined front door for a replacement. He had just finished that when the phone rang.

"Heard anything?" Trammell asked.

"Nothing."

"What does Marlie say?"

"She hasn't said anything. She's been asleep almost since she came out of the vision last night. She managed to tell me what she'd seen, then passed out."

"I thought about this for hours last night. If it's a serial killer . . ."

"We've got trouble."

"Should we tell Bonness what we think?"

"We'd better. After all, he believed Marlie before either of us did. We can't do anything until the murder is verified, but we should keep him informed."

"We're going to feel like fools if no one's found."

"I hope so," Dane said grimly. "I honest to God hope I feel like the biggest fool walking. That would be a hell of a lot better than the alternative."

Trammell sighed. "I'll talk to Bonness," he volunteered. "How long are you going to be at Marlie's?"

"I don't know. At least until she's capable of functioning on her own. All weekend, the way it looks."

"Wipes her out, huh?"

"You don't know the half of it." A thought occurred to him. "And while you're out and around today, I need you to get a door for me. Marlie's isn't very secure."

* * *

The voice pulled insistently at her, refusing to let her rest. It was a very patient voice, though relentless. On the far fringes of consciousness she knew that it was familiar, but she couldn't quite recognize it. She was tired, so tired; she just wanted to sleep, to forget. The voice had pulled her from oblivion before. Why didn't it leave her alone? Fretfully she resisted the disturbance, trying to find the comfort of nothingness again.

"Marlie. Come on, Marlie. Wake up."

It wasn't going to stop. She tried to turn away from the noise, but something was holding her down.

"That's right, honey. Open your eyes."

Surrender seemed easier; she didn't have the energy to fight. Her eyelids felt like stone, but she forced them open, and frowned in confusion at the man who was sitting on the bed beside her. His arms were braced on either side of her, holding the sheet tight; that was what was preventing her from moving.

"There you are," he said softly. "Hi, honey. I was getting worried."

She couldn't think; everything was fuzzy. Why was Dane holding her trapped like this? Her confusion must have been on her face, because he smiled and lifted one hand to smooth her tangled hair back from her face. "Everything's okay. But you've been asleep for a long time, and I didn't know if it was normal or not, so I decided to try to wake you up. It took some doing," he added wryly.

"What . . . ? Why are you here?" she mumbled, trying to sit up. He sat back, releasing the sheet, and she struggled into an upright position. It took so much effort that she ached. What was wrong? Had she been sick? The flu, maybe; her bones ached so, that could be the explanation. But why was Dane here?

"If I had to make a guess," he said, his voice pitched to a soothing rumble, "I'd say your need for the john has to be critical. Can you make it there?"

When he mentioned it, she realized that he was exactly

right. She nodded and clumsily pushed the sheet away. He stood so she could swing her legs off the bed. She didn't have many clothes on, she thought weakly as she sat on the edge looking down at her bare limbs, but she just didn't have the strength to care.

She tried to stand and sank heavily back onto the mattress. Dane bent and lifted her easily in his arms. Her head drooped into the curve of his shoulder and neck, and the position seemed so comfortable that she let it stay there.

She heard the hum of the air conditioner. The air was cold on her bare skin, and the radiant heat of his big body was heavenly as he carried her . . . somewhere. She closed her eyes.

"No you don't," he scolded, putting her on her feet. Her heavy eyelids opened and she saw that she was in her own bathroom. "Make an effort, honey. Now, can you manage by yourself or do you want me to stay in here with you?"

She wasn't so tired that she couldn't give him a "get real" look, and he chuckled. "I'm fine," she said, though she heard the fretful weakness in her own voice. She ignored it. She would manage; she always had.

"Okay, but I'll be right outside the door. Sing out if you need me."

She stood swaying in the small room after he had left, staring longingly at the bathtub and wondering if she could stand upright long enough to take a shower. It would be so embarrassing if Dane had to help her, handling her naked body as if she were a helpless infant.

First things first, though. She was very thirsty, but there was a more pressing concern. When that was taken care of, she gulped two glasses of water, then stood with the cool glass pressed against her forehead. Her mind was still so foggy, every thought such an effort. She needed to remember something, she felt the urgency, but couldn't concentrate long enough to bring it to mind. All she wanted to do was sleep. Blessed sleep. She didn't want to remember.

She really wanted that shower a lot.

Finally the simplest thing to do was to turn on the water and step under it, clothes and all, so that's what she did. She deliberately left the water not quite lukewarm, knowing that it would wake her up, not wanting to but accepting the necessity. She stood under the cool spray, her face turned up to catch the full blast, and let the fog dissipate. Let memory return. Let the water overcome and wash away the hot salty tears, the way a flood overcomes and obliterates a trickle.

Until it wasn't enough and she buried her face in her hands, sobs shaking her body.

"Marlie . . . ?" The worried, impatient tone changed at once, became quiet and steady. "I know, honey. I know it's bad. But you're not alone now. I'll take care of you."

The water was turned off, and his strong hands were on her, helping her out of the tub. She stood dripping on the mat, her eyes still closed while tears tracked down her cheeks.

"You're soaked," he said, still in that soothing, rock-steady tone. "Let's get these clothes off—"

"No," she managed, the word strangled.

"You can't keep them on."

"I'll do it."

"Are you sure?"

She nodded.

"Okay. Just open your eyes for me, honey, and tell me that you can manage, and I'll get some dry clothes for you and leave you to it. But I want to see those eyes before I do."

She swallowed, and took two deep breaths to control the tears. When she thought she could handle it, she forced herself to open her eyes and look up at him. "I can do it."

His gaze was piercing as he studied her, then he gave a short nod. "I'll get your clothes. Tell me what you want."

She tried to think, but nothing came to mind. "I don't care. Anything."

"Anything," left to his decision, was a pair of panties and her cotton robe. While he waited outside, she stripped off her wet clothes, clumsily dried herself, then dressed in what he had provided. She was rubbing her wet hair with a towel when he decided she had had enough time, and opened the door again.

"Here, I'll do it," he said, taking the towel from her and putting down the lid on the toilet for her to sit down. She did, and he carefully blotted all the excess water from her hair, then took the comb and smoothed out all the tangles. She sat there like a child, letting him minister to her, and the small attentions gave her a comfort she'd never had before. Numbly she realized that what he'd said was true: She wasn't alone this time. Dane was with her. He had been there last night, and he was still there, taking care of her, lending her his strength when she had none.

"What time is it?" she finally asked. Mundane thing, but the small and unimportant were the anchors of life, the constants that held one steady.

"Almost one. You need to eat; come on in the kitchen and I'll put on a pot of fresh coffee, then fix breakfast for you."

She remembered his coffee. She gave him an appalled look. "I can do the coffee."

He accepted the rejection of his coffee with good grace, being used to it. She was coming out of it; she could say anything she wanted about his coffee. She was more alert, though her face was utterly colorless, except for the shadows under her eyes, and tight with strain. He put his arm around her waist to support her as they slowly made their way to the kitchen.

She leaned against the cabinet while she made coffee, then sat and watched Dane competently assemble a meal of toast, bacon, and a scrambled egg. She ate a couple of bites of egg and bacon, and one slice of toast. Dane ate the rest.

When she crumpled, without a word he scooped her onto his lap and held her while she cried.

11

TRAMMELL ARRIVED ABOUT FOUR THAT AFTERNOON, DRIVING A pickup truck he had borrowed, with the replacement door in the truck bed. Dane paused for a moment to savor the incongruity of Trammell driving a truck, then went out to help him unload the door. "Whose truck is it?" he asked.

"Freddie's husband's." They each grabbed one side of the door and slid it off the bed. They didn't have to ask if anything had been reported; if it had, they both would have heard. Next door, Lou came out on her porch to watch them with open and suspicious interest. Dane took the time to wave to her. She waved back, but frowned disapprovingly. No doubt she had looked out her window first thing this morning and seen his car in Marlie's driveway; he had undoubtedly besmirched Marlie's spotless reputation.

"New lady friend?" he inquired delicately as they carried the door to the porch.

"Um, no." Trammell was being unusually reticent, and Dane was instantly suspicious. It wasn't that Trammell was the kind of guy who regaled the squad room with play-by-play details of a hot night, but he was usually forthcoming enough to at least give the lady a name.

"I thought the date was called off."

Trammell cleared his throat. "She came over anyway."

"Anything I should know about?"

"No. Maybe. But not yet."

Dane didn't get to be such a good detective by being stupid. He wondered why Trammell would feel it necessary to protect a woman's identity, and only two possibilities presented themselves. One: The lady was married. Trammell wasn't a poacher, though; married women were off limits to him. Two: The lady was a cop. That made sense; it fit. Immediately he began running through names and faces, trying to match them to the voice he'd heard last night. Everything clicked into place like three cherries in a slot machine. Ash blond hair sternly subdued to fit under her patrolman's cap, a rather austere face, quiet brown eyes. Not beautiful, but deep. She wouldn't enjoy being the butt of the raucous gossip that squad rooms specialized in, and she wasn't the kind of woman to be trifled with. "Grace Roeg," he said.

"Goddammit!" Trammell dropped his end of the door to the porch with a thump, and glared at him.

Dane set his end down with less force. "I'm good," he said, shrugging. "What can I say?"

"Nothing. Make sure you say absolutely nothing."

"No problem, but you're really getting in deep with me. That's two secrets I have to keep."

"God. All right. If you feel the need to blab about something, if you just can't stand the pressure, then tell them about the beer. I can live with that. But keep Grace out of it."

"Like I said, no problem. I like her; she's a good cop. I'd spill the beans on *you*, but I wouldn't upset *her* for anything. Watch yourself, though, pal. You could be asking for major trouble. You outrank her."

"There's no question of sexual harassment."

"Maybe not to you, maybe not to her, but the paper pushers may not look at it that way." Though the concern was a legitimate one, Dane was enjoying himself immensely. Trammell was glaring at him, black eyes as hot as coals. It was nice to get back at him, after the way he'd silently laughed at Dane's predicament with Marlie. "How long has it been going on?" Not long, he'd bet. He'd have noticed it before now.

"A couple of days," Trammell said grumpily.

"Moving a little fast there, partner."

Trammell started to say something, shut his mouth, then mumbled, *"I'm* not."

Dane started laughing at the helplessness in Trammell's tone. He knew exactly how it felt. "Another good man bites the dust."

"No! It's not that serious."

"Keep telling yourself that, buddy. It might keep you from panicking on the way to the church."

"Damn it, it isn't like that. It's—"

"Just an affair?" Dane inquired with lifted brows. "A good time in bed? It doesn't mean anything?"

Trammell looked hunted. "No, it's . . . ah, shit. But no wedding bells. I don't want to get married. I have no intention of getting married."

"Okay, I believe you. But it'll hurt my feelings if I'm not your best man." Smiling at Trammell's frustrated curse, Dane went inside to get a screwdriver, and Trammell followed him. Marlie was lying curled on the couch, asleep. Dane paused to look down at her and tuck the light coverlet around her feet. She looked small and pale, utterly defenseless as her mind recovered from the devastating exhaustion.

Trammell was watching Dane's face rather than looking at Marlie. "You have it bad yourself, partner," he said softly.

"Yeah," Dane murmured. "I do." So bad he was never going to recover.

"I thought it was just a case of the hots, but it's more than that."

"Afraid so."

"Wedding bells for you?"

"Maybe." He smiled crookedly. "I'm still not her favorite person, so I'll have to work on that. And we have a killer to catch."

He continued on into the kitchen, where he went through the cabinet drawers in search of a screwdriver. All kitchens, in his experience, contained a junk drawer, and that was the most likely place to find a screwdriver since he couldn't imagine Marlie having an actual toolbox. *Her* junk drawer, bless her neat little heart, was more organized than his flatware, and lying there in its own clear plastic holder was a set of screwdrivers. He could picture her carefully selecting the appropriate tool, using it, then sliding it back into its place in the holder, never getting them out of the order they'd been in when she'd bought them. He took the entire pack, and the small hammer lying there.

She woke as he used the hammer to tap the pin out of the second hinge, sitting up on the sofa and pushing the heavy curtain of her hair out of her face. Her eyes were heavy-lidded, her expression still showing the remoteness of mingled fatigue and shock. Dane gave her an assessing glance and decided to let her have a moment to herself. She sat quietly, watching with only mild interest as they removed the damaged door and replaced it with the new one.

It wasn't until they were finished that she said bemusedly, "Why did you change my door?"

"The other one was damaged," Dane explained briefly as he gathered up the tools.

"Damaged?" She frowned. "How?"

"I kicked it in last night."

She sat very still, slowly reconstructing the memories, putting details into place. "After I called you?"

"Yes."

There was another pause. "I'm sorry," she finally said. "I didn't intend to worry you."

"Worry" wasn't quite how Dane would have described it. He had been in a gut-twisting panic.

"Do you remember my partner, Alex Trammell?"

"Yes. Hello, Detective. Thank you for helping replace my door."

"My pleasure." Trammell's voice was more gentle than usual. It was obvious that Marlie was still struggling to get things together.

"Have you heard anything yet?" she asked.

He and Trammell exchanged a quick look. "No," he finally said.

A faraway look drifted into her eyes. "She's just lying there. Her family doesn't know, her friends don't know. They're going about their routine, happy and oblivious, and she's lying there waiting to be found. Why doesn't someone call or go by, just to check on her?"

Dane felt uncomfortable, and Trammell did, too, restlessly shifting position. They were more objective about bodies, especially bodies that might not even exist. They saw so many of them that they were hardened, for the most part thinking of the bodies as victims but not as individuals. The possibility of another murder victim had them both worried, because of the implication of a serial killer on the loose in Orlando. For Marlie, however, it was personal. She didn't have that inner wall to protect her.

"There's nothing we can do," he said. "Unless you can give us a name or a location, we have nothing to go on, nowhere to look. If it happened, someone will eventually find her. All we can do is wait."

Her smile was bitter, and not really a smile. "It happened. It's never *not* happened."

He sat down beside her. Trammell took a chair. "Can you think of any details, something you didn't tell me last night? Not about the killing, but about the location. Could you see anything that might give us a clue? Is it a house or an apartment?"

"A house," she said instantly.

"A nice-looking house, or a slum?"

"Very neat, good furnishings. One of those larger-screen televisions, on a pedestal." She frowned, rubbing her forehead as if she had a headache. Dane waited. "Cypress."

"Cypress? There's a cypress tree out front, a park with cypress trees, what?"

"I don't know. I didn't really see it. He just *thought* it."

"That's a big help," Dane muttered.

"What did you expect?" she snapped. "That he'd think, 'Now I'm breaking into this house at so-and-so number on so-and-so street, where I'm going to rape and kill Jane Doe?' *Nobody* thinks like that, everything's more automatic and subconscious. And I'm not telepathic anyway."

"Then how did you pick up on a cypress tree?"

"I don't know. It was just an impression. This guy is an unbelievably strong broadcaster," she said, trying to explain. "He's like a superpowerful radio station, overriding all the other signals."

"Can you pick him up now?" Trammell interjected, his eyes bright with interest.

"I can't pick up *any*thing now. I'm too tired. And he probably isn't broadcasting."

"Explain," Dane said briefly.

She glanced at him, then away. His attention was focused on her so intently that she almost couldn't bear it, because the lure of it was so strong and she was afraid to give in.

"His mental intensity builds as he gets closer and closer to the kill. Probably he can't maintain that level of rage for very long; he couldn't function at anything approaching normality if he did. So the only time his mental energy is strong enough for me to read is right before and during the kill, when he's at his peak. I lose him shortly after that; I don't even know how he leaves the scene."

"That explains the fingers," Dane said to Trammell, who nodded.

"Fingers?"

"Did Mrs. Vinick scratch him at any time?" Dane asked, ignoring her puzzled question.

Her eyes went blank again as she turned inward. "I'm not certain. She tried to fight, clawing at him. It's possible, but I don't think he noticed if she did."

Until afterward, Dane thought. That was why Marlie didn't know anything about Mrs. Vinick's fingers. The killer had been very calm and deliberate when he'd done it, because he hadn't noticed the scratches until his killing frenzy had cooled. That her fingers had been cut off was one of the details that hadn't been released to the press, and he didn't intend to tell Marlie about it. She had enough to bear, enough gory details to fill a thousand nightmares; he wasn't going to add to it.

"You said that you picked up a hint of him the other night."

"It wasn't a clear image; it wasn't an image at all. It was just a feeling of evil, a sense of threat. He was probably stalking her," she said, her voice trailing away as she realized that was exactly what he'd been doing. He had controlled the rage, but the hatred and contempt had leaked through, and she had felt it.

She was becoming very tired again, and her eyelids drooped. She wanted to curl up and sleep. She wanted him to leave her alone. She wanted to lose herself in the sanctuary of his arms. She wanted everything and nothing, and she was too tired to make up her mind.

But then Dane's hands were on her, strong and sure, turning her so that she was lying down, and the light blanket was arranged over her again. "Sleep," he said, his deep voice immensely reassuring. "I'll be here."

She took one slow, deep breath, and settled into oblivion.

Trammell's lean, dark face was somber as he watched her. "She's helpless," he said. "Is it like this every time?"

"Yeah. She's recovered some now. It was a lot worse last night, and earlier today."

"Then I hope the killer never finds out about her; she's

completely vulnerable to him. If his mental energy is so strong it can block hers even from a distance, think what it would do to her if *she* were the one he was after. He'd be right on her, and she wouldn't be able to protect herself in any way."

"He won't get the chance to get to her," Dane said, and in the grimness of his voice there was a promise. No matter what, he'd keep Marlie safe. "Have you talked to Bonness?"

"He wasn't thrilled with the possibility that there could be a serial killer, so he said to play it close to the vest and not mention it to anyone else until, and if, we find out there really was another murder. But he was also as thrilled as a kid at the idea of working with Marlie, because after all, it was *his* idea. I swear to God, sometimes I wonder if there isn't some weirdo juice in the water in California."

"Don't laugh," Dane advised. "Right now we're pretty involved in it ourselves."

"Yeah, but we aren't jumping up and down with joy over it."

"Bonness is a good guy; a little weird, but okay. I've seen worse."

"Haven't we all." It was a statement, not a question.

Dane's gaze wandered over Marlie's sleeping face, and his brows drew together in a frown. "Cypress," he said.

Trammell read him immediately. "You've thought of something."

"Maybe. That's all she said. Cypress. Not cypress *tree*. That was just an association I made."

"Cypress. Cypress," Trammell muttered. They looked at each other, two minds racing madly down the same track. "Maybe it's the—"

"Address," Dane finished, already on his feet. "I'll get the map." Like all cops, he had a city map in his car.

A minute later they were both bent over the map, open on the kitchen table. Dane ran down the alphabetical list of streets. "Shit! Don't developers ever think of any other word to use? Cypress Avenue, Cypress Drive, Cypress Lane, Cypress Row, Cypress Terrace, Cypress Trail—"

"It's worse than that," Trammell said, scanning the other listings. "Look at this. Old Cypress Boulevard. Bent Cypress Road. And isn't there an apartment complex called Cypress Hills?"

"Yeah." Dane folded the map in disgust. "There's no telling how many streets have cypress in the name. That's a dead end. We can't go door to door on every one of them, checking for bodies. What would we do if no one answered the door? Break in?"

Trammell shrugged. "You've done it twice in less than twenty-four hours."

"Yeah, well, there were extenuating circumstances."

"You're right, though. We're stuck. We may be fairly certain Marlie's for real, but Bonness wouldn't authorize that kind of search. People would be calling the mayor at home, screaming that Orlando wasn't a police state and we had no right to come into their homes like that. And they'd be right. We can't do that."

"So we're back to waiting."

"Looks like it."

There was no point in fretting over something they couldn't change. Dane allowed himself a moment of frustration, then changed the subject. "Would you mind going over to my place and getting some clothes for me? And my shaving kit. I had to use Marlie's razor this morning."

"I noticed," Trammell said, eyeing the nick on Dane's jaw. "Sure, no problem." He checked his watch. "I have time. I have a date tonight, but I'll be close to a phone."

"Grace?" Dane asked slyly.

Trammell scowled. "Yes, I'm seeing Grace. What about it?"

"Nothing, just asking."

"Then stop grinning like a jackass."

He left and was back within the hour with Dane's clothes

and shaving kit. "Your wardrobe is severely limited," he groused, dumping the clothes on a chair. He glanced down at Marlie, who was still asleep. "Maybe she can do something about it."

"Maybe," Dane said. "What's wrong with my clothes?" he asked innocently. If anything was certain to send Trammell into a tirade, it was that question.

"What's *right* with them?" Trammell snorted. "You have mostly jeans, very old ones. You have one suit, and it looks as if you got it from the Salvation Army store. Assorted slacks and sport coats, none of which really go together, and the most disgusting collection of ties I've ever seen. Did you actually *buy* this stuff? You paid good money for it?"

"Well, yeah. Nobody gives stuff away, you know."

"They should have paid you to take it off their hands!"

Dane hid his grin as he picked up the clothes and carried them into Marlie's bedroom, where he hung them in her closet, her very neat closet. His haphazardly hung garments looked out of place there, but he stood back and admired the sight for a minute. He liked the idea of his clothes in her closet, or her clothes in his closet. He thought about that possibility for a minute. He'd have to clean out his closet before she could, or would, put anything of hers in it.

Trammell left, and Dane watched television for a while. He couldn't find a baseball game, so he settled for a basketball playoff game. He kept the volume low, and Marlie slept undisturbed.

He'd been on a lot of stakeouts, spent a lot of time just waiting. In stakeouts, boredom and the need to piss were the two biggest problems. This reminded him of a stakeout, because the waiting seemed interminable, but the quality was different. They weren't waiting to catch a criminal, or to prevent a crime. The crime had already been done, they just didn't know where or to whom. They were waiting for a victim to surface, waiting for suspicion and worry to send someone to a quiet house somewhere in the city, to check on a friend, neighbor, or relative. Then the waiting would be over.

"You're thinking about it, aren't you?"

Marlie's voice startled him. Dane jerked his head around to look at her; she was sitting up again, her somber eyes on him. He realized that he had been staring sightlessly at the television for some time, because it was almost eight o'clock.

"It isn't something you put out of your mind," he said.

"No, it isn't." For her more than anyone else.

He got up and turned off the television. "How about calling out for a pizza? Are you hungry?"

She thought about it. "A little."

"Good, because I'm starving. What do you like? The works?"

"That's fine." She yawned. "You call it in, and I'll go take a shower while we're waiting. Maybe it will wake me up."

"Take your clothes off this time," he advised, and she smiled a little.

"I will."

The water felt good, washing away the mental cobwebs and cleansing her of the sensation of having been tainted, dirtied somehow by the evilness she had witnessed. She was tempted to linger under the cool spray, but thinking of the pizza, forced herself to briskly shower and shampoo. After blow-drying her hair to a semblance of order, she thought about clothes, but settled for the light robe Dane had selected for her.

She left the bathroom and halted, staring at her unmade bed. If she had been more alert, she would have noticed it sooner. The fact that her bed was unmade was unusual enough, but what riveted her to the spot was the sight of twin indentations in the pillows, where two people had slept. Awareness roared through her like a brushfire. Dane had slept with her, in her bed.

She had docilely accepted his presence all day, knowing

that she had talked to him the night before but never wondering about his location during the lost hours. Now she knew. He had been right there, in bed with her.

A wave of sensual heat overcame her and she closed her eyes, shuddering at the deliciousness of it. Her heart pounded, her breasts tightened, and a flooding, loosening sensation in her loins made her knees go weak. Lust. She was astounded as its presence, at its power. Instead of being outraged that he had taken advantage of the situation, she was aroused by the thought of him sleeping beside her.

He had been so gentle in his care of her that day, that iron strength and fierceness controlled so that she had felt only the protection he offered. He had combed her hair, fed her, held her while she cried, and most of all, he had given her the comfort of his presence. She hadn't been alone this time, though somehow she always had been before, even while she had still been with the Institute. Dr. Ewell and the others had always maintained a distance from her; mental privacy had been so difficult for her to attain that they had gone out of their way to let her recover in her own way, at her own pace. Until now, she hadn't realized how lonely and terrifying that had been.

Dane knocked briefly on the door and opened it without waiting for an answer. "Pizza's here."

As always, the impact of his presence was like a blow. He was so big and rugged, exuding a male vitality that made her shiver. For the first time she began to think that it might be possible, that Arno Gleen's legacy of terror was losing its power over her. Gleen had been a sick, sadistic bastard. Dane was pure, hard-edged male, too intense and grim for life around him to ever be entirely comfortable, but a woman would always feel safe with him, in bed and out.

His eyes narrowed. "Are you all right?" He reached her in two long strides, his arm sliding around her waist and pulling her into the support of his body.

"Yes," she said, not thinking about it, and slipped her hand around the back of his neck.

He didn't hesitate, didn't give her time to think about it. She wasn't certain she was extending an invitation, but he accepted it before she could decide. This time there was no careful restraint; he set his mouth over hers with open hunger, a hunger so intense and greedy that it stunned her. He caught her chin with his free hand and held her, then moved his tongue deep inside her mouth, touching her own tongue in blatant demand. She sagged against him, both frightened and tempted, and he gathered her in against his hard frame. His erection pushed against her belly. She had never been wanted before like that, so swiftly and violently. She had no experience of men like Dane Hollister, or of how he could make her feel.

But contact with that potent body was suddenly all she wanted. She put both arms around his neck, moving against him, trying to get closer. He was bruising her with the force of his kisses, and she wanted more. Her loins were tight and achingly empty, growing moist with yearning.

He put his hand on her breast, and her breath locked in her throat. His thumb rubbed over and around her nipple; at first it was a curious sensation, like a slight pricking of pins, then it suddenly intensified and pure sensation zinged from the nipple to her loins. She moaned aloud, frightened by the way her own body had so swiftly gone beyond her control.

Dane lifted his head. There was a hard, predatory expression on his face, the faint cruelty of arousal, and his lips were wet from their kisses. His hand remained on her breast, with only the very thin cotton of the robe between them. His breath was coming too fast, and she could feel the hard pounding of his heart against her. "Bed, or pizza?" he asked. His voice was so guttural, she could barely hear him. "If it's pizza, you'd better say so *now*."

She wanted to say "bed," she wanted it so much. She had never felt desire before, and the lure of it was almost irresistible. She wanted to forget the reason he was there, the murders she had seen, and simply give herself over to the physical. She had never been able to do that before, and maybe couldn't now, but for the first time it seemed possible.

"P-Pizza," she managed, and closed her eyes as she fought for control. Sick dismay filled her at her own cowardice.

She could feel him bracing himself, and he took a deep breath. "Pizza it is, then." Slowly he released her and stepped back. A huge, obvious ridge in his pants told her how difficult it had been for him to stop. Most men wouldn't even have made the offer.

He gave her a wry, crooked smile that lit his rough features. "I guess I was going too fast for you, honey. I'm sorry. It's just that I have a hair trigger where you're concerned, and I'm not talking about firearms."

Marlie stared at him, a lump in her throat and a huge knot in her chest. She felt dizzy with shock and realization. Oh, God. She had been attracted to him from the first, had recognized it and fought it, but with that smile she slipped helplessly over the edge. She had loved, but she had never been in love before, and the power of it made her actually feel faint. Swaying, she put out her hand in search of support, and he was there, solid and vital and so hot that she almost melted. His arm was around her, and her head lay against his chest.

"Shhh, it's okay," he crooned. "I didn't mean to scare you. I'm sorry."

"No," she managed to croak, alarmed that he thought he had reminded her of Gleen. He hadn't; she had been expecting it, but it simply hadn't happened. She had always assumed that sexual fear would be a constant in her life, and now that it hadn't materialized, she felt oddly adrift and off balance. "It isn't you. I was just dizzy for a minute." Somehow she formed a smile, and it was a real one for all its shakiness. "Maybe your kisses are more potent than you thought."

"You think so?" His voice rumbled under her ear. "We'll have to experiment, won't we? After the pizza."

He walked her into the living room and guided her to the couch. "Just sit; I'll get the drinks. Do you want a plate?"

"Well . . . yes. Of course."

He chuckled. "It must be a woman thing."

"I prefer a napkin, too," she said politely. "As opposed to licking my fingers."

He winked at her. "I'll be glad to lick your fingers."

She shivered in response and sat, dazed and quiescent, while he puttered around in the kitchen. He seemed to know his way around in her house. How had this happened? She was bewildered by the speed and force of it. In less than twenty-four hours he had taken over; he had spent the night with her, apparently moved in with her, and with a grin made her fall in love with him. He was a one-man SWAT team, overwhelming her defenses without effort.

He was back in a few minutes with the iced soft drinks, a plate and fork for her, and a couple of napkins. He sat beside her on the sofa, turned on the television to a sports channel, and gave a grunt of satisfaction when a baseball game filled the screen. He served her a slice of pizza, got one for himself, and settled back with obvious enjoyment. Marlie blinked at him. This was what she'd gotten herself into? She didn't know whether to laugh or cry. In the end she simply concentrated on the pizza, sitting curled beside him on the sofa, bemused that she was so content to just be close to him and watch his face as he watched the game.

Sometimes his size overwhelmed her and sometimes she was comforted by it, but this was the first time she had had the opportunity to simply sit and study him. He was definitely a big man, even bigger than she had thought, at least six two and over two hundred pounds. The feet parked on her coffee table had to be size twelves, or larger. His shoulders were so wide, he took up almost half the couch; his arms were thick and hard, sinewy with ropy layers of muscle. His chest, she knew, was rock-hard, and so was his abdomen. His long legs, stretched out before him, looked like tree trunks.

His hair was darker than hers, almost black. She eyed the blade of a nose and the brutally carved cheekbones, and wondered if there was any American Indian in his heritage. He had a heavy beard; evidently he had shaved that morning, since there was a fresh-looking nick, but already the black stubble had darkened his jaw.

He leaned forward to get another slice of pizza, and her gaze fell on his hands. Like everything else about him, they were big, easily twice the size of her own. But they weren't thick hams; though powerful, they were lean and well shaped, with short, clean nails. She felt safe with those hands on her; not safe from *him*, but from everything else. She didn't want to be safe from him. She had lost her heart about fifteen minutes ago, and she was still reeling from the shock of it.

He was a cop, a man who made his living in violence. He didn't commit the violence, as a rule, but he had to clean up after it, he was constantly surrounded by it. Close by his right hand was a big automatic pistol. At some point during the day she had become aware of it, and now she realized that it was never far from his side. A shoulder holster was slung across the back of the couch, beside him.

There was a scar across the back of his right hand. She caught a glimpse of it when he reached for a third slice of pizza, and recognition congealed in her. "That scar on your hand," she said. "How did you get it? It looks like a knife wound."

He turned his hand to look at it, then shrugged and gave his attention back to the television. "It is. A close encounter of the punk kind, when I was still working patrol."

"It looks bad."

"It wasn't any fun, but it wasn't serious. It was a shallow cut, didn't slice through any tendons. A few stitches and I was as good as new."

"Gleen cut me," she said. She didn't know why she said it; she hadn't meant to.

His head snapped around, all affability gone as if it had

never been, and the expression in those hazel eyes was scary. "What?" he asked softly, putting down the slice of pizza. His thumb moved on the remote control, and the television screen went blank. "The professor didn't say anything about that."

She set the plate aside and drew her knees tighter to her chest. "They weren't serious cuts, just little slices. He was playing with me, trying to break me down with pain and fear. He got off on that; it was what he needed. And he wasn't trying to kill me, at least not then. He wanted to keep me alive so he could play with me. He would have killed me later, of course, if the sheriff hadn't gotten there."

"Let me see." The words were a soft growl and he was already reaching for her, uncurling her, his hands opening the robe. Marlie struggled briefly for control of the robe, but then he had it open, spreading it wide as he looked down at her, naked except for thin, brief panties.

The scars, six years old, weren't disfiguring. They would, given time, probably fade completely. She had never fretted about them, because they were so unimportant compared to everything else, and she had never been vain anyway. They were just small, silvery lines, five of them: one on the inner curve of her right breast, the rest on her abdomen. There would have been more, but Gleen had swiftly lost control when the gambit hadn't worked, degenerating to the crude force of his fists to elicit the response he had wanted.

She quivered, a hot blush staining her cheeks as Dane slowly examined her. She was acutely aware of her bareness, in a way she never had been before. His mouth was a grim line as he traced the line on her breast with his fingertip, the touch as light as a breath. Her nipple tightened, though he wasn't even touching it. She heard her own ragged breathing as he slowly touched every scar. He was shaking, too, and suddenly she realized that it was with pure fury, at a man forever beyond his reach.

She put her hand on his hair, threading her fingers into the warm thickness of it. "They aren't important," she said, forgetting her embarrassment. "Of everything that he did, those little cuts amounted to the least."

"It isn't the cuts." His voice was thick with rage as he pulled her into his arms, cradling her head against his shoulder. "It's knowing what you went through, how terrified you were. You didn't *know* that he wasn't going to kill you."

"No, I expected to die. In some ways, that would have been easier."

12

Somehow she was being held on his lap, her robe still open and his hand inside it, but instead of threatened, Marlie felt utterly safe, his warmth and strength surrounding her like a citadel. It was a delicious sensation, one she had never been able to enjoy before. She wanted to sink into him, revel in this new freedom, for that's what it was, an entirely new vista opened up to her. But Dane wanted information, chapter and verse, and Detective Hollister was very good at getting his way. She could have resisted bullying, but not the waiting silence in which he held himself, a silence in which she could feel his tension. The tension wouldn't ease until he knew, and so she told him, the ugly details, the guilt that she had held inside for years.

Her head was lying on his shoulder, her face turned in to the muscled wall of his chest. Somehow it was easier that way, as if she could neither see nor be seen.

"He had knocked me out," she began. "When I came to I was naked, lying flat on my back on the floor, with my hands tied to some kind of pipe, maybe an old radiator. Gleen was naked, too, sitting astride my hips with the knife in his hand, smiling and waiting for me to wake up. Dusty was tied to a cot about five feet away, watching the whole thing. He was such a pretty little boy." Her voice was soft and distant as she remembered. "Auburn curls all over his head, and big, round blue eyes. He was so scared. He cried the whole time."

Dane looked down at his big hand lying on her belly, almost completely spanning her. The thought of Gleen seeing her like this, and using a knife on this slender, womanly soft body, was so obscene that he barely stifled the growl that began rumbling up from his chest. She seemed to have forgotten that she was all but naked now, her mind lost in the past, but Dane was very aware of it. Even in his rage, he looked at those soft, round breasts with their tender pink nipples, and felt the desire burning low in his belly. He controlled it, forcing it aside so he could hold her, and listen to her. Had anyone ever held her, given her comfort? He thought not, and that added to his anger.

"I don't know why I did it," she continued, her head lying trustingly in the hollow of his shoulder. "But something in me refused—I couldn't give in to him. I would rather have died than give him what he wanted. He wanted me to beg, but I wouldn't. He wanted me to be afraid, and I was, but I didn't let him see it. I laughed at him. Oh God, I *laughed*. He cut me, and I yelled at him that he was a pitiful excuse for a man. He pulled my legs apart and tried to put it in me." She hesitated uncomfortably. "You know—*it*, not the knife."

"I know what 'it' is," he growled.

She buried her face deeper into the curve of his neck. "He couldn't, and I laughed at him. I made fun of him, I told him what a miserable little worm he had, and what a miserable little worm he was. He was wild with it, I could feel how out of control he was, all that hate and fury pouring out, but I just kept pushing. I could feel Dusty, too, so terrified, reaching out for me, begging me not to let the bad man hurt him again.

"So I kept laughing at Gleen, and kicking at him as much as I could. Somehow I managed to kick him between the legs, not really hard because my foot slipped off his thigh, but he . . . lost it. It was like he exploded, somehow. One second he was on me and the next he was on Dusty, and Dusty was screaming. I still hear him scream. I could feel him, the absolute terror, the agony. It was like a black wave, all over me, all through my brain, and I was screaming too. I screamed and screamed and screamed. Blood was everywhere . . ." She paused, and after an interminable silence that lasted only a few seconds, said simply, "I don't remember anything else. Dusty died, and I died with him."

Dane knew what had happened after that; the professor had told him. Her screams had pinpointed Gleen's location to the sheriff and his men, and they had killed Gleen before he could turn his murderous fury on Marlie. But they hadn't been in time to save Dusty, and in a way they hadn't been in time for Marlie either. As linked to Dusty as she had been, his death had been her death, too, and it was a miracle she had survived the shock.

He smoothed her hair behind her ear, and stroked her cheek. "But you came back," he said with controlled ferocity.

"Eventually. It was a long time before I felt anything, any kind of emotion. Before, I had felt everything, everyone else's emotions, and after that I couldn't even feel my own. I didn't have any."

"You healed, Marlie. It's been a long time, but he didn't win. He couldn't break you."

"He came damn close," she said. She quietly rested against him for a minute. "If I hadn't pushed him, if I'd given him what he wanted, probably Dusty would still be alive."

Dane snorted. "Yeah, it'd be nice if we were all omnipotent." He wasn't going to waste his time babying the natural guilt she felt. He jostled her a little, forcing her to look up at him. "I'm glad you're here," he said deliberately.

She managed a fragile smile. "So am I. And sometimes that seems like the most callous thing of all, that I'm glad to be alive. I wasn't thinking beyond the moment when I was laughing at Gleen; the only thing I knew was that I absolutely couldn't bear for him to rape me. The thought of him being inside me was so revolting that I was willing to push him into killing me, rather than tolerate his touch. Of all the things that gave me nightmares, sex was the worst. I can watch some violence on television or in movies, but I still can't watch a sex scene. I can't think of it as love. I remember Gleen's face, the smell of his breath, the way saliva sprayed when he screamed at me. I remember the feel of him against me, between my legs, and I still want to gag." She took a deep breath. "Not that sex was ever good for me anyway," she said honestly.

"How so?" His voice was undemanding, and his touch almost absent as he stroked her hair back from her temple, but his hazel eyes were intense.

She had never talked about the difficulty she'd had with sex, but somehow, lying cradled in his protective arms, with the rest of the world held at bay, she could. She felt oddly dreamy, caught in a combination of fatigue and the aftermath of stress, as if nothing else were quite real. "It was awful. Mentally, I couldn't bear it. I had to work so hard to build a shield, to protect myself from everything," she explained. "It was the only way I could function, and the shield was at best only a partial protection. All my life I wanted to be *normal.* I wanted to love someone, I wanted a relationship, I wanted what normal people had. I didn't want to be alone. I wanted intimacy to be wonderful, but it wasn't. Being intimate, physically, just blew away my mental shields. I couldn't block out anything. The mental interference was enormous; all I could feel was *his* emotions, blotting out any physical enjoyment I might have felt. It wasn't very flattering, either." Her mouth quirked. "He wasn't overcome by fondness for me; all he wanted was sex.

And he was feeling proud of himself for daring to have sex with a weirdo psychic."

"The son of a bitch," Dane said softly.

She lifted one shoulder in a small shrug. "I *was* weird. I still am."

"Hell, no wonder you're skittish about sex. All you've ever seen is the ugly side of it; you've never had any romantic illusions, have you? You know about scoring, and about rape. You must think men are scum."

"No," she denied. "When you know what other people are feeling, the way I did, you know that couldn't be so. There are selfish, mean-spirited women just like there are nasty men. But when it came to sex, I couldn't close my mind and just feel. It wouldn't have been any different if I'd been madly in love with a wonderful guy who loved me just as much; I couldn't have enjoyed sex with all that mental static going on.

"I think I had accepted that I couldn't have any sort of romantic relationship," she continued. "I liked being alone, in my little cabin in the mountains. Dr. Ewell thought that moving into the cabin was good for me, a move toward normalizing my life. And it was; it was great. I worked with him on experiments and documentation, and occasionally helped find missing people, though the effort involved was such a strain that—well, you know what it's like. Once upon a time, before Gleen, I could direct the knowing. I could lock on to someone specific, and go into a vision. I can't control it at all now."

"Do you want it to be like before?"

"I never wanted to have another vision in my life," she murmured. "But if I don't have any choice about it, then yes, I'd like to be able to control them. This—this is like being ambushed." She was getting drowsy again, and her eyelids drooped.

"But except for the two visions, you haven't had any other episodes?"

She thought of the first night she had called him, and known what he was doing, what he would say, even as he answered the telephone. "There was one flash of clairvoyance, but it wasn't related to the murders, and hasn't happened again. It was just a second or two. I don't think of the visions as clairvoyant episodes; they're . . . different, more strongly grounded in emotion. Anyway—no. Nothing else."

"Good."

There was a wealth of dark satisfaction in his voice, a satisfaction she couldn't quite decipher. Then his warm hand covered her breast, and she knew, with an instinct that had nothing to do with her psychic abilities, and everything to do with being a woman. No longer sleepy, she tilted her head back on his arm to look at him.

"It seems to me that now is the perfect time to show you some of the pleasure of sex," Dane murmured. Those hazel eyes were blazingly intent, and deeply green. "You can't feel my emotions, so that takes care of one problem. If you were afraid of me, you wouldn't have been lying almost naked on my lap for half an hour, which takes care of the other problem. All you have to do is lie there and let me make you feel good."

She quivered, her gaze locked with his. Was now the time? Until Dane, she hadn't felt desire. Sex had been an experiment, a hope, and ultimately, a disappointment. She wasn't afraid of him, but rather that she would fail again. Loving him was still so new, so startling, that she didn't want to tarnish it. It was cowardly, but she would prefer to never try, and retain the frail hope that it might have been possible, than to try and fail. Might-have-been was a poor comfort, but better than nothing.

"I don't know," she said nervously. "What if—"

"Stop worrying about it," he interrupted. "Just lie back, close your eyes, and leave everything to me."

Easier said than done. Still she stared up at him with worried eyes, unable to decide yes or no. Too much had happened to her for her to be able to make that move. She hated herself for being so weak, and tears began welling.

Dane gave her approximately two seconds, then settled the issue himself. He stroked down her body and beneath the waistband of her panties, tucking his hand into the notch between her thighs. Marlie cried out in surprise, automatically grabbing his wrist. Her thighs clamped tight around his hand. Her eyes were huge, eclipsing her wan face. But even as they stared at each other, hectic color warmed her cheeks.

"Do you trust me?" he asked in a calm voice, as if it weren't taking every bit of self-control he had to keep from rolling her beneath him and sinking into her, finding blessed relief for his throbbing erection.

She chewed her lower lip, and he almost groaned aloud at the provocation. "Well, yes."

"Then relax your legs. I'm not going to hurt you. As a matter of fact, I guarantee that you'll like it."

She managed a wobbly smile. "Guarantee, huh?"

"Absolutely." He bent his head and brushed a gentle kiss across her mouth.

Marlie quivered, caught on the twin prongs of cowardice. She was afraid to try and fail, and afraid that if she didn't trust him now, she might never have another chance. In the end, the second fear proved stronger. No matter what, she wanted to know what it was like to cradle Dane within her body, to feel his incredible strength as he drove into her, to give *him* pleasure if nothing else. He was determined to bring her to pleasure first, she knew, but she also knew that afterward it would be his turn. She wasn't agreeing to just heavy petting, but to the complete sex act.

She drew a deep, shaky breath. "Okay. As long as I have your personal guarantee."

"I'll put it in writing and have it notarized," he promised, and kissed her again.

She couldn't control the fine tremors that shook her entire body, but she took another deep breath and slowly parted her thighs. He gently stroked the soft, closed folds, and Marlie released her death grip on his wrist. "Easy now," he whispered, then deftly opened her and penetrated her with one long finger.

She stiffened in his arms, her thighs locking together again in an effort to control his invading hand. It was useless, because there was nothing she could do to stop the slow probe of his finger inside her. Shock made her dizzy. Oh, God.

She wasn't dry, but she was far from being ready for penetration. The friction made his finger seem as big as a penis. She struggled briefly to contain the chaos of her rioting nerve endings, then collapsed against his chest in surrender.

"There, that's good," he crooned, and pushed another finger into her. Her hips arched, then subsided. She felt stretched, invaded, her body no longer under her control. Some dormant, primal instinct was stirring into life. Her inner muscles contracted gently in adjustment, and Dane's entire body shivered.

His voice was hoarse. "This is the most that I'm going to do to you, at least right now. You can relax because it's already happened. Am I hurting you?"

Yes. No. She hadn't realized it could feel like this. She was a little delirious with shock and pleasure, and shook her head, her hair cascading over his chest. She was stunned that her body was capable of such intense sensation.

"Then close your eyes, honey. Close your eyes and feel. Don't think, just feel."

Helplessly, she did. With her eyes shut, her concentration centered on her body and what was happening to it. Color swirled behind her eyelids. Heat surged through her, followed rapidly by a chill that wasn't really a chill, but rather a ripple of almost painful delight. Her skin felt too tight, too sensitive. Her nipples puckered and hardened, standing firmly upright.

His fingers reached deep inside her, rasping her delicate

inner tissues. Helplessly she arched her hips again, taking his touch deeper within. Her thighs fell open, giving him easier access. Her heart was thundering, and she felt as if she might fly apart. She clutched his shirt, her fingers digging into the flesh beneath as she tried to anchor herself against the storm that was buffeting her.

She heard him say something, but there was a roaring in her ears and she couldn't quite make out the words. The words weren't important; she could hear the fierce tenderness in his tone, and that was what she needed. His fingers slipped out of her, and she made a soft sound of distress, her hips rolling toward him. Swiftly he stripped her panties off and returned his hand to her body. This time she willingly parted her thighs, and felt the eager dampness between them. The intrusion, when it came, was exquisite relief, yet the relief lasted only a moment. The slow thrust of his fingers elicited a deep, powerful hunger, so that his touch wasn't an easing, but a need. Then his rough thumb searched upward in her soft folds and pressed on the small, tautly swelling nub at the top of her sex. Pure fire exploded through her nerves, and she gave a strained cry as she curled toward him.

He held her tightly against him, subduing her sensual struggles. He was talking to her, the words low and hoarse in her ear, encouraging her to greater heights while his strength kept her safely grounded. He continued to circle and rub with his thumb, tormenting the little nubbin, each touch making the fire burn hotter. A pulse began throbbing between her legs, beating in a rhythm she had never felt before. Passion was a brand, searing her flesh with its invisible mark.

"D-Dane!" It was a wail almost of anguish. He tilted her head back and set his mouth on hers, his tongue repeating the invasive movements of his fingers, the pressure hard and rough. She reveled in it, reaching up to cling to his heavy shoulders, offering her mouth more fully to him.

It built quickly, sensation spiraling into a tighter and

tighter coil, and suddenly it was too much. Her entire body clenched, then surged wildly as her climax rolled through her in waves. She shook in uncontrollable spasms, feeling as if she were flying apart. He held her close, letting her know that she wasn't alone in the tempest. She cried out in a thin, hoarse voice, and he muffled the cries with his own mouth.

The crest of sensation subsided, though small shock waves continued to ripple through her loins. She went limp, her face buried against his chest while she gasped for breath. He shifted her, then his muscles tensed beneath her and he got to his feet, holding her firmly in his arms. She gripped his shirt as he carried her swiftly into the bedroom and placed her on the bed. Her robe was hanging on her shoulders, and he pulled it completely away, then stood and began stripping off his own clothes.

He hadn't turned on the light, but the door was open, and light from the living room spilled across the bed. Marlie lay without moving, enveloped in a lassitude so complete that she thought she might never move again. In that quiet state of subconsciousness, with her physical senses so acute and her mental processes barely functioning, she could feel every slow, heavy beat of her heart as it moved blood through her veins. Her pulse throbbed in the tender places of her body.

With an effort, she lifted her heavy eyelids and watched him undress. His urgency was an almost palpable force, his movements swift and violent. In only seconds, his powerful form was bare. He crawled over her, his hard thighs pushing between hers and forcing them wide, then settled his heavy weight on her.

There was a wonderful stillness, a silence, both without and within. With incredible joy, and some trepidation, she felt the hardness of his genitals against the yielding softness of her own. He braced himself on one arm and reached between them with his other hand, guiding his shaft as he tensed his buttocks and slowly began pushing into her.

Marlie's breath tangled in her throat, and she felt herself

drowning in sensation again. She had felt stretched by his fingers probing her, but his thick sex filled her to the point of distress. Though she was damp, her delicate inner tissues were swollen by his previous attentions; her sheath was ultrasensitive, tightening convulsively on him as he inexorably thrust himself to the hilt. She gave a soft, panicked sound of discomfort that verged on real pain.

Dane paused, holding himself deep within her. His powerful body was shaking. "Are you okay?" His voice was hoarse, and barely audible.

She couldn't think what to say. She wasn't having any empathic interference; her attention was wholly focused on her body. But physically she wasn't certain she could bear it when he started thrusting. He was so big, and the slightest movement rasped along her inner nerve endings; the sensation hovered between ecstasy and pain. Her mind was a blank, and she couldn't find the words to give him the reassurance he wanted.

He was a man, not a saint. His male flesh was throbbing inside her. He held himself rigidly still for a tense moment while he waited for her answer, but when none came his control shattered. A rough sound burst from his throat and he began thrusting with heavy power, reaching deep into her. The impact shook her entire body. Now she knew her answer, and clung fiercely to him as his hips hammered. The sharp slap of their bodies coming together mingled with his harsh breathing, and her own soft moans.

She had wanted Dane, and she had wanted this. Tightly she shut her eyes, savoring every moment. She loved his roughness, the savagery of his hunger. She loved the helpless groans that escaped him, the heat and sweat as his body coiled and struck. She had always felt apart, an oddity, but with Dane she was simply, and purely, a woman. Nothing interfered with the moment; they were male and female, mating with fierce and uncomplicated passion. She wished it could go on forever.

It didn't, though. It couldn't, given the urgency of his

need. All too soon his rhythm quickened, and he reared back, pounding into her with heavy force. He pushed her legs high, lifting her ankles onto his shoulders. Gasping, she felt him getting even bigger and harder inside her. He gave a harsh cry, one last thrust, and began shuddering convulsively.

When he had stopped shaking, when the last small quake had rippled through him, she opened her arms, and he weakly let himself sink into them. His heavy weight crushed her into the mattress, but she was too tired to care. His heartbeat thudded slowly against her breast. His dark head, wet with sweat, rested beside hers on the pillow. His face was turned toward her, and his warm breath washed over her neck.

She stroked his back, loving the feel of his heated skin beneath her palms. He was becoming heavier as he drifted into sleep, but she didn't care. She was limp with utter contentment. Only heaven could be better than this, lying in the aftermath of lovemaking, the man she loved sleeping cradled in her body and her arms. She wanted time to stand still in a place where evil couldn't intrude.

It intruded with a sudden shrill beeping.

Dane reacted instantly, withdrawing from her and sitting up in the same fluid motion. He turned on the lamp and silenced his beeper, briefly glancing at the digital readout. Marlie lay frozen. Without a word he picked up the phone and punched in a number, holding the receiver cradled between his head and shoulder while he began putting on his rumpled clothes. "This is Hollister," he said tersely. He listened for a moment, then said, "I'll be there in ten minutes. Have you called Trammell? Never mind, I'll do it. Radio back to the patrol officer and tell him to make damn certain the scene is secured."

He depressed the button and got another dial tone. While he called the second number, Marlie got out of bed and fumbled for her robe. It was twisted, one of the arms turned inside out. Her hands were shaking, but she managed to straighten the garment and wrap herself in it, pulling the belt tight. Dane sat down on the side of the bed and began putting on his shoes.

"We have a victim," he said quietly into the phone. "I'll meet you there." He didn't glance at Marlie. "It's 3311 Cypress Terrace."

Cypress. Her stomach knotted into a cold lump. She had known, but this dispelled the last faint doubt.

He hung up the phone and went into the living room, shrugging into his shirt as he walked. Marlie followed him, as silent as a ghost, and stood in the doorway watching as he slipped into his shoulder holster. He tucked the big pistol into place under his left arm.

She didn't approach him, and he didn't come to her. He paused by the front door and looked back at her. "Are you all right?" he asked, but there was remoteness in his eyes and his voice, his mind already on the job awaiting him.

"Sure," she said, burying the terror and pain and loneliness deep inside her. She couldn't allow her weakness to delay him.

"I'll be back when I can," he said, and left.

She stood until the sound of his car had died away, then steadily went to the front door and locked it. Next she cleaned up the remains of their pizza, and washed the few dishes that were dirty. When she went back into the living room, she saw her panties in the corner of the couch and picked them up, wadding them in her hand.

She was very tired, but sleep seemed impossible. The delight of the night had been destroyed by a return of horror. She couldn't allow herself to think of either right now. She sat down on the couch and quietly watched the minutes of the night tick away, as she held her own vigil.

13

LIGHTNING FLASHED IN THE DISTANCE, REVEALING THE UNDER-belly of low, purplish black clouds. It would rain again before morning. Dane drove automatically, clearing his mind of everything. He couldn't let himself think about Nadine Vinick, or the expectation might lead him to see similarities that weren't there. He couldn't think about Marlie, or his concentration would be completely shot. He tried not to anticipate anything about the scene he was about to see, tried not to remember how Marlie had described it. Again, he didn't want to prejudice himself. He had to see everything clearly.

It was still early enough that traffic was fairly heavy. Anxious to reach the exit, he tucked up too close behind a semitrailer. One of the retreads on the rig chose that moment to come apart, throwing up a big road gator that slapped into the front of his car. Cursing, he backed off to a safer distance, but the distraction helped, pulled his mind away from everything he was trying not to think about.

It took a little longer than ten minutes to reach 3311 Cypress Terrace. The street was cluttered with the usual assortment of official vehicles and sightseers. Dane got out of the car, studying the bystanders with acute interest, looking for one who seemed familiar. If the same guy had done both women, he might have been at the Vinick scene, too. Nothing; not one of the gawkers triggered a memory.

Cypress Terrace was in a slightly more upscale neighborhood than the Vinicks had lived in. The houses weren't bigger, but they were about ten years newer. There was a small, attached carport, and that was where the knot of uniforms had gathered, though one patrolman was guarding the front door, and he hoped another one was at the back.

Freddie Brown and her partner, Worley, were the detectives on call that weekend, and they were already there. Freddie detached herself from the group of patrolmen as soon as she saw him. "Hi, doll," she said, tucking her hand inside his arm and drawing him to a standstill. "There's no hurry. Talk to me for a minute."

If it had been anyone but Freddie, Dane would have shrugged him off. But it was Freddie, and this was her crime scene. She wouldn't have taken him to the side without a good reason. He looked down at her and lifted an eyebrow in question.

"Word is that you asked to be notified of any female stabbing fatality," she said.

He gave a brief nod, hoping she wasn't irritated about him horning in on one of her cases.

She patted his arm, reassuring him. "I figured you wouldn't have done that without a damn good reason, so I've held the scene for you. We'll consider it a birthday present."

"Held the scene?" he repeated, stunned. "You mean no one has gone in?"

"That's what I mean. The patrolman who found the body deserves a medal. He backed out as soon as he saw her,

175

didn't touch anything except the doorknob, and secured the area. It's probably the most pristine crime scene you'll ever get. Ivan's on the way."

"We'll wait for him," Dane decided. "Thanks, Freddie. How did a patrolman happen to find the body?"

She flipped to her notes. "The victim's name is Jacqueline Sheets, divorced, no children. Her ex-husband lives in Minnesota. She worked at one of the bigger law firms as a legal secretary, very good at her work. She had made plans to meet a friend for dinner, one of the other legal secretaries. When she didn't show, the friend tried to call, but there was no answer. Evidently Sheets was normally very punctual, and had recently had some medical problems, so the friend was concerned. She drove over here to check. Sheets's car is in the carport, there's a light on, and the television is blaring, but she can't get anyone to the door. She went to a neighbor's house and called 911. Patrol Officers Charles Marbach and Perry Palmer were nearby and got here before the emergency crew. They beat on the doors and couldn't get any response. Officer Marbach forced the lock on the front door, saw the victim immediately when he opened it, and stepped right back out." She closed the notebook. "The friend's name is Elizabeth Cline. She's sitting down in the carport. She caught a glimpse of the body and she's pretty rattled."

Another car added itself to the congestion. Dane glanced at it and identified Trammell. Freddie did the same, and looked back at Dane with a wry look. "Now, how about you tell me what's going on?"

"We want to look for similarities to the Vinick case," he said quietly. "We think it might be the same perp."

Her eyes widened, and a look of horror came over her freckled face as the implications hit home. "Oh, shit," she breathed. "It's even the same day of the week."

"Don't think I haven't noticed." He could just see the headlines about the Saturday Slasher. He wondered what sensational name the newspapers would apply if the time of death was put before midnight, making it a Friday murder. The Friday Fucker?

Trammell joined them, resplendent in oatmeal linen slacks and a sky blue silk shirt. His hair was perfectly combed, his exotic face freshly shaved, and there wasn't a wrinkle in sight. Dane wondered how in the name of God he did it.

He brought Trammell up to date on what had happened so far. Freddie asked, "Do you want to question the friend?"

Dane shook his head. "This is your show. All we want is to see the scene."

"You don't have to wait for Ivan, you know."

"I know. I'd just like for him to get it as clean as possible."

"At a guess, I'd say he's never going to get one any cleaner." She patted both of them in that motherly way she had, and returned to the group in the carport.

"It's a house," Trammell said unnecessarily. "No cypress trees, but the address is Cypress Terrace. We were on the right track. It's going to be interesting to see if the television is one of the big-screen models, on a pedestal."

Dane put his hands in his pockets. "Do we really have any doubt?"

"I don't."

"I don't either. Damn it."

"I called the lieutenant. He should be here any time."

Ivan Schaffer arrived, in the crime scene van. He unfolded his long, lanky body from behind the steering wheel as Dane and Trammell walked to meet him.

Ivan wasn't in a good mood. He scowled at both of them. "I don't know why I had to personally handle this one. I have good people on duty. Why did Freddie insist that I be here?"

Evidently Freddie had sensed something unusual all the way around, bless her. Dane wondered if her husband would break his nose if he kissed her. "This one's special," he told Ivan, helping him unload his kits and equipment. "For one thing, the scene's untouched. You're the first person in."

Ivan halted. "You're shitting me." His eyes began to gleam. "That doesn't happen."

"It's happening this time. Don't expect it again in your lifetime."

"What do I look like, an optimist? Okay, what's the second thing?"

Trammell was coolly studying all the murmuring bystanders. "The second thing is, we think it was done by the same guy who did Nadine Vinick."

"Ah, jeez." Ivan sighed and shook his head. "God, I wish you hadn't told me that. That's big trouble, but I guess you already know that."

"We'd thought about it. Is this all your stuff?"

"Yeah, that's it. Okay, let's see what we have."

Dane called Officer Marbach to go in with them. A patrolman who had done that good a job deserved to be included. Marbach was young, not long out of training, and was pale under his tan. But he was steady as he detailed his actions for them, even telling them the body's approximate distance from the front door.

"Can the body be seen from the street when we open the door?" Freddie asked, she and Worley having joined them.

Marbach shook his head. "There's a little entry, with the living room to the right. I had taken one step in before I saw her."

"Okay. Ivan, it's your show."

Ivan opened the door and went in. The rest of them followed, but stopped in the small entry hall and shut the door behind them. The television, tuned to an all-movie channel, was currently showing a Fred-and-Ginger. It was too loud, as if Jacqueline Sheets had been a little hard of hearing. Either that, or the sound had been turned up to drown out her screams. Ivan punched the power button and the screen went to black, filling the room with blessed silence. Dane and Trammell, standing in the entry, looked at the television. It was a thirty-five-incher, very modern and sleek, set on a pedestal.

None of them said anything. Ivan silently began his collection ritual.

From their viewpoint, only the upper half of the body was visible. She was nude, and her torso looked as if it had been savaged by a wild animal. The pattern of blood completely circled the couch, splattering over walls and carpet, and Dane remembered the odd phrase Marlie had used: *around and around the mulberry bush.* But it hadn't been a bush, it had been the couch. Why had she used those words? Had they been something the killer had said, or thought? Had the bastard been *amused* by Jacqueline Sheets's fight for her life?

The door opened behind them and Lieutenant Bonness came in. He looked at the gore and turned white. "Oh, Jesus." The first scene had been more gruesome, but they had looked at it as a onetime deal, unconnected to anything else. This time, however, they knew better. Now they were looking at it as the work of a madman who would do this again and again, murdering innocent women and devastating the lives of their families and friends, until they could stop him. And they knew that the odds weren't in their favor; serial killers were notoriously difficult to apprehend.

But this time, Dane thought grimly, they had something the killer couldn't have anticipated. They had Marlie.

Worley said, "Dane, you and Trammell have a look around. You know what you're looking for."

"That's why you and Freddie should do it," Trammell said. His thoughts had run the same as Dane's, but then they almost always did. "Just tell us what you find, and then we'll have a look ourselves."

Worley nodded. He and Freddie briskly began their methodical search of the house. Ivan summoned the fingerprint team, and they began dusting every hard surface with black powder. Soon the house was crowded with people, most of them standing about, some of them actually working. Eventually Jacqueline Sheets's body was bagged and removed. Dane could hear the clamor of reporters' voices outside, see the glare of television lights. They wouldn't be able to keep the lid on it much longer, but he thought nothing much would be made of a second stabbing within a week. If there was a third one, though, no reporter worth his or her salt would let it pass as coincidence. Even if there were no similarities in the cases, there would be enough interest to warrant a "special segment," whatever the hell that was.

Bonness took Dane and Trammell aside. "If it looks like the same guy did it—"

"He did," Dane said.

"Everything's just the way Marlie described it," Trammell added. "Even the type of television set."

"Any way she could have had any prior knowledge? I know, I know," Bonness said, holding up his hands. "I was the one who originally thought she could help us, and you guys were the ones who thought she was an accessory, but this is a question that needs to be asked."

"No," Dane said. "We established that there was no way she could have been at the crime scene of the first murder, and I was with her last night. She called me when the vision started, and I drove straight to her house."

"Okay. I want to see everyone in my office tomorrow morning at ten. We'll go over what we have, anything new that Ivan's found, set up a task force. I'll notify the chief, and he can decide when and how much to tell city hall."

"I hope he holds off," Dane said. "Information leaks out of city hall like it's a damn sieve."

Bonness looked unhappy. "This isn't something he can keep to himself. It would cost him his job if the media break the story and he hasn't kept the head honchos informed."

"Then ask him if he can give us a couple of days, at least. Both of the murders have been on Friday night or early Saturday morning, so if the pattern holds, the guy won't hit again for almost another week. The longer we can work without him knowing that we're on to him, the better chance we have of catching him."

"I'll talk to him," was all Bonness would promise. Dane really hadn't expected any more than that.

Worley and Freddie joined them. "The murder weapon was a kitchen knife, probably belonging to the victim," Worley reported. "It matches others in the kitchen. He entered through the window in the guest bedroom, by cutting the screen."

"It rained last night," Dane said. "Any footprints beneath the window?"

Freddie shook her head. "Nothing. He was very careful."

"Or he got in before it started raining, and waited in the bedroom," Trammell suggested.

The idea made Freddie blanch. "God, that gives me the queasies, thinking of him in the house with her for hours, and her not knowing it."

"What about afterward?" Officer Marbach asked. He blushed a little when they all turned to look at him. "I mean, it should have been raining when he left. Wouldn't he have been likely to leave footprints then?"

"Only if he exited the same way he entered," Dane said. "And there was no reason for him to. All he had to do was walk out the door, making him much less conspicuous if anyone happened to see him, which I doubt. The sidewalk and driveway are concrete; no prints."

"She was evidently wearing pajamas at the time of the attack," Freddie continued, looking at her notes. "We found a pair with blood on them, dropped into the laundry basket. We're having the blood typed to make sure it's the victim's."

"How about a husband or boyfriend?" Bonness asked.

"Nope. According to her friend outside, there's an ex-husband who lives in Minnesota, but they've been divorced for twenty years, and it's been almost that long since Sheets had any contact with him. No current boyfriend, either. Okay, guys, level with me: Does this sound like the same guy did both women?"

"Afraid so," Dane replied. "Did Sheets frequent bars, gyms, anything where she'd be in contact with a lot of men?"

"I don't know. We hadn't gotten that far in questioning the friend when you guys got here. Why don't you talk to her while we finish up in here? We're all going to be pooling our notes, anyway," Worley suggested. From his tone, he would have been glad to hand the entire investigation over to Dane and Trammell.

A low wall of cement blocks, two high, enclosed the carport on the open side. Elizabeth Cline was sitting on the wall, huddled in on herself, staring numbly at the crowd of policemen milling around. She was a tall, sleek blonde, with her hair cut short in a feathery cap, and long earrings that dangled almost to her shoulders. Despite the earrings, she wasn't togged out in party clothes; she was wearing sandals, yellow leggings, and a long white tunic with a gaudy yellow and purple parrot on the front. She wore several rings, Dane noticed, but none of them was a wedding band.

He sat down beside her on the block wall, and Trammell, more aloof as always, leaned against Sheets's car a couple of feet away.

"Are you Elizabeth Cline?" Dane asked, just to make certain.

She gave him a vaguely startled look, as if she hadn't noticed him sitting beside her. "Yes. Who are you?"

"Detective Hollister." He indicated Trammell. "And Detective Trammell."

"It's nice to meet you," she said politely, then a horrified look edged into her eyes. "Oh, God, how can I say that? It *isn't* nice to meet you. It's because of Jackie that you're here—"

"Yes, ma'am, it is. I'm sorry, I know it was a shock for you. Would you mind answering a few more questions for us?"

"I've already talked to those other two detectives."

"I know, ma'am. But we thought of a couple of other things, and anything you can tell us will help us find her killer."

She inhaled shakily. She was shivering, and hugging her

arms. It was a warm, muggy night, but shock was getting to her. Dane wasn't wearing a jacket to put around her, so he asked a patrolman standing nearby to get a blanket. A few minutes later a blanket was produced, and he put it about her shoulders.

"Thanks," she said, huddling gratefully into the folds.

"You're welcome." His instincts were to put his arm around her and comfort her, but he felt constrained and settled for patting her on the back. The only woman he could hold now was Marlie; somehow, in taking her, he had forever set himself apart from other women. He was uneasily aware of the change but pushed it beneath his consciousness, to be considered later when he had the time.

"You told Detective Brown that Ms. Sheets didn't have a current boyfriend. Had she recently broken up with someone, or maybe had a casual date or two?"

She shook her head. "No."

"No one? Any steady boyfriends at all since her divorce?"

Elizabeth gathered herself enough to lift her head and give him a shaky, wintry smile. "Sure." The one word was bitter. "She had a twelve-year affair with one of the attorneys in the firm. He told her they'd be married when he divorced his wife, but the time wasn't right while he was building his career. Then the time was right, he got his divorce, and promptly married a twenty-three-year-old trophy wife. Jackie was devastated, but she'd been with the firm for a long time and couldn't afford to start over. He wanted to continue the affair, but Jackie broke it off, very quietly. At least he didn't try to get her fired, but I don't guess there was any reason for it. Their affair wasn't a secret; everyone in the office knew about it."

"When was this?"

"Let's see. About four years ago, I guess."

"Who has she dated since then?"

"I don't know that she's dated at all. Maybe once or twice, right after the affair ended, but I know she hasn't gone out with anyone for at least a year. She started having health problems, and she didn't feel well enough for the dating scene. We would eat dinner out every week or so; it helped keep her spirits up."

"What kind of health problems?"

"Several things. She had really bad endometriosis, and about a year ago finally had a hysterectomy. A stomach ulcer, high blood pressure. Nothing life-threatening, but everything seemed to hit at once, and it made her depressed. Lately she'd fainted a couple of times. That was why I was so worried when she didn't show up at the restaurant on time."

They had hit a dead end on ex-boyfriends, but Dane hadn't really expected anything different. He was just covering all the bases. "Had she mentioned anyone she'd met recently? Did she get into an argument with anyone, or had she mentioned anyone following her?"

Elizabeth shook her head. "No, Jackie was very even-tempered, got along with everyone. She didn't even lose her temper when David married his little bimbo. Actually, the closest she came to getting angry recently was when a new silk blouse came apart at the seams the first time she washed it. Jackie loved clothes, and was very particular about them."

"Did she go any place regularly, where she might have met someone?"

"Not unless it was the grocery store."

"Everyone has a routine," Dane insisted gently. They had to discover how the killer picked his victims. Nadine Vinick and Jackie Sheets had had something in common, something that had brought them to the killer's attention. They had lived in different neighborhoods, so it had to be something else, and putting his finger on that something else was vital. "Did she have her hair done regularly, go to the library, anything like that?"

"Jackie had beautiful red hair. She got it trimmed every few weeks, at a little salon close to the office. The Hairport. The stylist's name is Kathy, I think. Maybe Kathleen, or Katherine. Something like that. The library? No, Jackie wasn't much of a reader. She loved movies; she rented a lot of movies."

"Where did she rent them?"

"At the supermarket. She said they have a nice video selection, and it saved making an extra stop."

"Which supermarket did she shop at?"

"Phillips, about a mile from here."

A neighborhood market, not one where Nadine Vinick would have shopped. But Dane made notes of everything; they wouldn't know exactly what they had until they had compared every detail with the Vinick case.

"What about you?" he asked. "Are you married?"

"Widowed. Seven years ago. Jackie helped me through a rough time, and that's when we became close friends. We were friendly before that, you know, working in the same office for as long as we had, but that's when I really got to know her. She was—she was a really great friend." Tears slipped down Elizabeth's cheeks.

Dane patted her some more, aware of and ignoring Trammell's enigmatic gaze. Trammell hadn't spoken once, leaving all the questioning to him. Occasionally he did that, when for some reason he decided Dane would have better luck getting answers.

"I'm sorry," Elizabeth said, still weeping. "I know I haven't been able to help."

"But you did," Dane assured her. "You helped us eliminate several things, so we know where to concentrate and won't waste our time on dead ends." Basically it was a lie; all they had was dead ends. But she needed all the comfort she could get, lie or not.

"Do I need to come down to the station or anything? Funny," she said, wiping her eyes and trying a pathetic smile. "I know how law works on the finished end, the courthouse end, but nothing about the raw stages."

"No, there's no need for you to come to the station," he said, soothing her. "Does Detective Brown have your address and phone number?"

"I think so. Yes, I remember telling her."

"Then I don't see why you can't go home, if you like. Do you want me to have someone drive you? Or call someone, a friend or relative, to stay with you tonight?"

She looked around vaguely. "I can't leave my car here."

"If you want someone to drive you, I'll get a patrolman to drive your car and another one to follow, to bring him back. Okay?"

But she didn't seem able to make a decision, still too stunned and devastated to think clearly. Dane made the decision for her, getting her to her feet, calling a patrolman over and arranging for her to be taken home, giving instructions for her to call a friend or neighbor to stay with her that night. She nodded as docilely as a child taking homework instructions.

"I have a niece nearby," she said. "I'll call her." And she looked at him as if asking for his permission to call the niece instead of a friend. He patted her and told her that was fine, and sent her off with the patrolman, who had taken his cue from Dane and treated her as gently as he would a lost child.

When Dane turned around, Trammell was still looking as enigmatic as a cat.

"What?" he demanded testily.

Trammell raised his eyebrows. "I didn't say anything."

"You're thinking something, though. You've got that shit-eating smirk on your face."

"Why would anyone smirk while they eat shit?" Trammell asked rhetorically.

He loved the man like a brother, but honest to God, sometimes Dane felt like messing up that pretty face. But when Trammell was in one of his moods, nothing could pry information out of him. Dane thought about giving him a couple of beers to loosen his tongue, then decided to leave well enough alone. He'd save the beer for special occasions.

There was nothing left to do but assist Freddie and Worley in tying up the loose ends: make certain the trash had been sacked up, to be gone through later; search the house for personal papers such as a diary, telephone and address books, life insurance policies. In death, Jackie Sheets would lose all of her privacy. They would go through her closets and her cabinets, in search of that one snippet of coincidence and fate that linked her to Nadine Vinick. Whatever the two women had had in common was the key to the killer. If poor Ansel Vinick hadn't killed himself, he could have helped them pinpoint the crucial link, and maybe found a reason for living in helping to find his wife's killer. In Dane's opinion, the bumper sticker "Shit happens" should have the word "frequently" tacked on to the end of it.

Ivan had taken his meager findings back to the lab to begin analyzing them; the medical examiner's office had Jackie Sheets's body, though there was little to be added other than the approximate time of death. They could have saved the ME the time and trouble; Dane knew the time of death, because Marlie had called him.

Worry had settled new lines in the lieutenant's face as he glumly surveyed the outline on the floor where Sheets had lain. "Everyone be in my office at ten tomorrow morning," he said. "For now, go home and get some sleep."

Dane glanced at his watch. It was almost one, and he was suddenly aware that he hadn't had much sleep the night before.

"Are you going back to Marlie's?" Trammell asked.

He wanted to; God, did he want to. "No, I won't disturb her," he said. "She'll be asleep."

"You think so?"

He remembered the way she had looked when he'd left, that haunted expression back in her drawn face. He hadn't even kissed her, he realized. His mind had already been on the murder scene, and he had totally blocked Marlie out. He had just made love to her, had gotten off her warm body to answer the beeper's summons, and he had walked out without kissing her. "Damn," he said tiredly.

Trammell said, "See you in the morning," and got in his

car. Grace Roeg would probably still be waiting, Dane thought. She was a cop, too; she would understand that he had had to leave suddenly. But Marlie wasn't a cop; she was a woman who had been too solitary her entire life, a woman who had borne enough pain for ten lifetimes. She was strong, incredibly so; she hadn't cracked, but she wore the scars, both physically and mentally. It had taken guts for her to let him make love to her, and what had he done? Their first time, and he had turned it into a slam-bam; he hadn't even said "thank you."

If he could have reached it, he'd have kicked his own ass.

She wouldn't be asleep; she would be sitting on the couch, still and quiet, waiting for his return. He couldn't protect her by keeping her in the dark, because she knew more than he did. She was an eyewitness, inside the killer, watching through his eyes as he gleefully hacked and slashed.

Dane drove quickly, the streets much emptier now. It began raining, the slow-moving storm finally reaching the city. He felt as if it were a replay of Friday night, when he had hurried through the wet streets to reach Marlie.

As he had expected, there was a light on in the living room when he pulled into the driveway and killed the motor. Before he could get out of the car, she had opened the front door and was standing there, silhouetted against the light, waiting for him.

She was still wearing the thin robe, and he could see the outline of her body through the fabric. He ran through the rain and leaped up the two shallow steps onto the porch. She didn't say anything, just stepped back to let him in. She didn't have to ask what they had found, because she knew.

She was tired, her face wan, her eyes dark-circled. In those eyes was a weariness that went far beyond the physical, and the subtle air of distance had settled around her again.

He meant to offer comfort, if she would accept it. He meant to take care of her, give her the healing unconsciousness of sleep. She could relax, knowing that she was secure.

He meant to hold her all night long, offering her the primitive animal comfort of his closeness.

That was what he meant to do. But as they silently faced each other, with the rain pattering outside in rhythm to his suddenly racing heart, he forgot about all the noble things he meant to do. He had claimed her only a few hours before, making her his in the physical possession of mating, but they had been interrupted. The act had been completed, but the seal of the flesh hadn't been. True intimacy wasn't found in penetration and climax, but in the quiet time afterward, in the small ways that two lives meshed. He had left that undone, and his instincts were too primal and sure for him to ignore it.

He shut the door and locked it, without once looking away from her. Then, without haste, he picked her up and carried her into the bedroom, pausing on the way to turn off the lamp.

There were no angry recriminations from her, no reluctance. She lay quietly where he had placed her on the bed, waiting while he impatiently threw off his clothes. He removed the robe from her for the second time that night. Her naked body gleamed dimly in the darkness; he felt the delicious softness of her beneath him, felt her thighs opening to embrace him. He held her head between his palms and kissed her with slow hunger as he probed, found the moist yielding of her entrance, and pushed within. The heat and tightness of her enfolded him, making his shaft throb so violently that he groaned into her mouth.

"Make me forget," she pleaded, whispering in broken desperation. He forced his way in to the hilt, holding her as she arched beneath him in an effort to accommodate her body to his size and force. She made a hot little whimpering sound, and her tight nipples stabbed against his chest.

He could give her only the forgetfulness of passion, fill her senses with his body, and the pleasure he could give her. He couldn't make the night go away, but he could turn the darkness into their own private sanctuary. He could rein in his own unruly passion and make certain she was with him this time, and afterward, lying in the warm silence, he could hold her so that, all through the night, she could feel his warmth and the steady beat of his heart and know that she wasn't alone.

14

MARLIE STIRRED AND CAME ABRUPTLY AWAKE, STARTLED BY the realization that there was someone in the bed with her. She knew who he was, recalled everything, but still there was that first jarring moment when consciousness adjusted to reality. He had slept with her the night before last, too, but she hadn't been aware of it. This was the first time that she had awakened with a very hard, very warm man lying close beside her, one heavy arm thrown across her waist and anchoring her to the bed. It was a good thing he was holding her, she reflected, since he took up most of the space, and she might well have fallen off if he hadn't held her pinned.

She turned her head to look at him, enchanted by the novelty of having a naked man in her bed, of having *Dane* naked in her bed. She savored the moment, a small, quiet oasis of happiness.

The soft morning light, filtered through a light rain, gleamed on the curve of his shoulder. She lightly cupped her hand on the ball of the joint, feeling the cool resilience of his flesh, the relaxed power of the muscle beneath her palm. He stirred at her touch, tucking her more closely into the curve of his body before lapsing with a grunt back into his morning dreams.

He radiated heat like the healthy animal he was, despite the surface coolness of his skin. She felt as warm and cozy as if the bedcovers were tucked around her, rather than lying in a tangled heap on the floor.

In all her life, she had never been physically demonstrative because the mental barriers had always gotten in the way. But the psychic damage she had suffered at Gleen's hands had demolished those barriers, and last night Dane had forcefully shown her, several times, that now she could give herself over to the physical.

She felt tremulous with joy at this new world he had opened up, a world she had thought permanently closed to her. She loved him, and he had claimed her body, and given her his own. She had always been alone in the darkness, but not last night, and she had understood what he had been saying with his body, his hunger. There was death, yes, but life marched hand in hand with it. There was evil out there, but between the two of them there had been pleasure, a basic and joyful celebration of life and flesh. She had always protected herself from the world, set apart from birth by her own abilities, while he had reveled in and dominated the hot, pulsing currents. He was fierce and vital in his intensity, meeting life on its own terms and coming out the victor. Last night, with Dane, she had broken free of her self-imposed restrictions.

And now this big bruiser was lying totally, blissfully naked in her bed. She had the freedom of his powerful body, to explore and excite as she wished. She felt like a child at an amusement park, an adventurer opening the sealed door to a room of treasure. There was so much to see and do, and she quivered with excitement at the possibilities. To totally give in to the needs of her body, to find out exactly what those needs *were*—she almost couldn't bear it.

She smoothed her hand over his chest, delighting in the roughness of the thick, curly hair under her palm. Beneath the hair was a rock-solid layer of muscle, hard and warm. She found his nipples, flat brown circles with tiny points in the middle, points that hardened when she touched them. Fascinated, she rubbed her fingertip over one of the little points and watched chills roughen his skin.

A deep rumble in his chest made her look up. He was awake, the hazel eyes heavy-lidded and sleepy. Down below, his sex twitched and stretched, prodding her in the stomach. "Like what you see?" His early morning voice was like distant thunder, rough and barely audible.

"Very much." Her own voice was raspier than usual, too.

He rolled over onto his back, spreading his arms and legs wide. "Then take a good look."

The temptation was irresistible. Though they had made love several times, it had been in the dark. She hadn't been able to see her lover's body, only to feel him. Now that he had given her permission, there was no way she could deny her fascination. She got to her knees, unconscious and unheeding of her own nudity, intent on exploring this new and wondrous territory.

She put both hands on his chest and circled his nipples with her thumbs, watching in delight as they hardened again. She looked up at him, eyes luminous with discovery. "You like that, too."

He swallowed. He was breathing roughly, his deep chest expanding with the force of it. "Yeah. A lot."

His heart almost stopped at the luminous smile of discovery she gave him.

She turned her attention back to him, leaning down and circling a nipple with her tongue, then gently sucking at it. He stifled a groan as a shudder racked through him. She moved her attention to the other nipple, giving it the same tender treatment while her hands slipped around his rib cage, molding the shape and feel of him, learning the textures of his skin.

Dane sucked in his breath, digging his fingers into the mattress as he tried to control himself. Oh, God, he wanted to touch her so much, he could barely stand it. He had never felt anything as excruciatingly gentle, as exquisitely painful, as her slow exploration of his body, and he had the feeling that it was going to get much worse.

She ran her hands up to the tufts of hair under his arms, enjoying the silkiness that seemed so incongruous on so tough a man. His skin, in those hidden, protected areas, was as sleek as her own.

The crisp mat of hair on his chest narrowed to a thin line that ran down the center of his belly, circled his tight navel, then flared again at his loins. She followed the line of hair with one finger, down, down, until her hand brushed his straining erection. She paused, then turned her hand and curled her fingers around him. He gave a shaky groan, and his legs shifted restlessly, then he was still again. Marlie lifted her other hand and held him between her palms, examining him with absorbed fascination. She was entranced by the contrasts, the coolness that contained intense heat, the soft skin lying over iron hardness. He was very thick, and pulsing with arousal. She thought of taking that thickness into her body, and grew excited; she could hear herself breathing, in soft, rapid pants. Her blood was singing through her veins and she felt too warm, her skin too tight.

The sheer masculinity of him was beautiful. She cupped his heavy testicles in her hands, very gently, and his powerful body arched. He shook from head to toe. "Lord have mercy," he said in a strangled tone.

"The Lord?" she asked softly. "Or me?" The sense of her own feminine power over him was heady.

"You. Or both. I don't care."

Her secret places were damp and swollen, throbbing with need. Sex, even last night with Dane, had always been something that had been done *to* her. She wanted, needed, to be in control this time of her own body, and his. She wanted to give pleasure as well as seek it. She wanted the warm sexual confidence of a woman who had no fears, no restraints. She was tired of boundaries.

With a sigh like a soft spring breeze she mounted him, straddling his hips and holding his shaft steady as she positioned it and slowly sank down. She was sore; she bit her lip at the discomfort of her tender flesh stretching to admit him. But there was also the wonder of feeling that warmth and hardness probing deeper inside her as she slowly took him, and lingered over the taking, inch by slow inch. The sensation was so exquisite that she lifted herself almost completely off him and began again. And again.

Dane's fists knotted in the sheets, and sweat popped out on his forehead. She was only taking about half of him before sliding upward again, and he thought he was going to go howling mad for sure. He didn't dare touch her, because if he did, he would lose control. This was her show, all the way. Her face was solemn, dreamy, absorbed as she explored the pleasure she could take from his body. She was concentrating on nothing except her physical sensations as she slid up and down on him, but he didn't feel left out. Watching her learn about her own sensuality was as much a turn-on as anything in his life had been, and the way she was doing it was killing him with pleasure.

Marlie closed her eyes against the almost overwhelming surge of passion and pleasure. All that she had learned the night before was as nothing compared to this; now her body knew the sublime ecstasy awaiting, and enjoyed as well every inch of the path leading up to it. She fought against the need to rush to the finish. She wanted to savor every delicious explosion of sensation deep inside her as she lifted herself from him, feeling the drag of his sex on her acutely sensitive tissues, followed by that indescribable moment of deepening penetration as she took him again. She moaned aloud, sensing the approach of climax drawing inexorably nearer. *Not yet,* she thought dimly. She was enjoying this too much. There was no hurry.

Dane writhed on the sheet. Oh, God, if she didn't hurry,

he was going to die. The shallow way she was riding him was working the swollen head of his shaft with almost ceaseless pressure. A harsh groan tore from his chest. He wanted to thrust, deep, needed to thrust more than he had ever needed anything, but he refused to let himself do so. There would be times when his needs would take precedence. This time, however, was Marlie's. He shivered with the intensity of the pleasure. He thought his heart was going to explode; he knew for damn sure his cock was.

She was very wet now, and her rhythm had become faster. The fitted sheet came loose as he pulled at it. He arched, his body so rigid that his weight was supported only on his heels and his shoulders. A mist swam in front of his eyes.

"Marlie." The word was guttural, his voice almost unrecognizable. Despite himself, he was pleading. "Deeper . . . please. Deeper. Take . . . the rest . . . of it."

If she heard him, she didn't respond. She was lost in her own sensual whirlpool, unheeding of everything else. Her hands were braced on his chest, her eyes were closed. Her hips rocked. A breathless sob broke from her lips, and with a convulsive shudder she went down into the swirling depths, her entire body given over to the pleasure racking it.

The rhythmic tightening of her inner muscles on him blasted the last shred of his control to smithereens. With a harsh, explosive growl he released his death grip on the sheet and grabbed her surging hips, forcing her downward as his own hips slammed upward, pushing his full length into her. He came with the first stroke, his orgasm bursting from him in a powerful stream as he convulsed beneath her, clamping her to him with ruthless, implacable hands, until it was over for both of them and she lay limply on his chest. Their heartbeats pounded together, shaking them from within.

He felt as if he would never have the strength to move again. She felt as if she were warm wax, melted and poured over him. Neither of them could bear to separate their bodies.

He trailed his hand up the slender length of her spine,

feeling the way she was put together. He didn't know how many women he had made love to in his lifetime, but he did know that the way he had felt then was nothing compared to how he felt now. There had been no other woman like Marlie; everything about her was new. He had never before been so fascinated by the details of a woman's body, soft and fragrantly feminine. He had never before concentrated so intensely on a woman, so that he saw every flicker of expression and read every nuance of emotion. From the very beginning he had been aware of her slightest move, his body and senses attuned to her. He couldn't even remember the name of his last lover; there was only Marlie.

But as much as he wanted to spend the rest of the day right where he was, the red digital numbers of the clock beside the bed continued to chronicle the silent, relentless stream of time. It was eight-fifteen. He had to shower and shave, eat breakfast, and be downtown at ten.

"I have to go," he murmured.

She didn't lift her head from his chest. He continued to stroke her spine. "Where?"

"To the station. We have a meeting with the lieutenant at ten."

She didn't tense, but he felt the stillness that came over her. "About last night?"

"Yeah. It was him, all right."

"I know." She paused. "What happens now?"

"We put together all the details we have from both cases, try to find what the victims had in common. Set up a task force to concentrate on this guy. Maybe call in the FBI."

She said steadily, "If you need me to go over it again, I will."

He knew what that offer could cost her, and he knew she had already braced herself to pay it. She would be met with ridicule, disbelief, and suspicion; that was what she had gotten from him, even though he had been so attracted to her, he could barely think straight. She knew what she was letting herself in for, and was willing to do it anyway.

He squeezed her. "I don't want to put you through that."

"But you will if you have to."

"Yes."

To his relief, her feelings weren't hurt. She accepted the necessity. He smoothed her hair. "There's something I need to tell you," he said reluctantly. "I don't want you to read about it in the papers, or see it on the news."

She waited, knowing that it was going to be bad. Dane wished that he didn't have to tell her, but he'd put it off as long as possible. Yesterday she hadn't been in any shape to watch the news, but today was a different story. He didn't want her to be alone when she found out.

"Ansel Vinick killed himself Friday night."

The breath she had been holding leaked out in a sigh. So much pain, she thought sadly.

"That's three," she said. "In one week, he's killed three people."

"We'll catch him," Dane assured her, though they both knew it was far from a sure thing. He looked at the clock again. Eight-twenty.

He rolled with her until he was on top, then gently disconnected their bodies. "Want to shower with me?"

She looked at the clock, too. "No, I'll cook breakfast. It'll be ready when you're finished."

"Okay. Thanks, honey."

Amused at how quickly he had accepted her offer to cook for him, she dressed and went into the kitchen. She usually ate simply, cereal and fruit, but a man his size would probably need more than that. She put on a pot of coffee, then hauled out her seldom-used waffle iron. While it was heating she stirred up the batter from a package mix. How much would he eat? She couldn't finish one, but suspected he could put two or even three away with no trouble.

She could hear the shower running, hear him whistling. The coffee maker was hissing and popping in the manner peculiar to coffee makers. She was cooking his breakfast. The domesticity of it stunned her, and her arms dropped to her sides. She had never cooked breakfast, cooked *any* meal, for another person in her life.

For six years she had worked to build a safe, secure, ordinary, and solitary life. In one week, though, her life had been totally changed, and she was still struggling to find her balance. Safe, secure, and ordinary had gone by the wayside; now, evidently, her solitude was also gone. It wasn't something she had chafed against; she had enjoyed being able to do things at her own pace, to sit up all night reading if she chose, to eat whatever she desired at the moment. Before Gleen, she had very much wanted a relationship, marriage, children. After Gleen, however, she had wanted only to be left in peace.

Instead, there was a man in her shower. Not just any man, but Dane Hollister: grim, rough, frighteningly intense, a police detective who never went anywhere unarmed—and who was the most generous man she'd ever met. He gave of himself in a way she'd never expected, given the hostility of their first few encounters. He had come to her without hesitation, after her despairing cry for help on Friday night, and since then she had seen only tenderness in him. She had been attracted to him before, but had fallen in love with him because of his unhesitating generosity. She had needed him, so he had been there. It was as simple as that.

She heard the shower cut off, then water running in the basin as he shaved. She finished the preparations for breakfast: a dusting of powdered sugar on the waffles, fresh strawberries, and syrup that she had heated in the microwave. She was pouring the coffee when he came into the kitchen. He wore only a pair of pants, and she went weak in the knees at the sight of that broad, muscular chest. His hair was damp and his face was freshly scraped, with two small nicks decorating his jaw. She inhaled deeply, drawing in his moist, soapy, slightly musky male scent.

He smiled when he saw the meal awaiting him. "Waffles," he said appreciatively. "I was expecting cereal."

She laughed. "That's what I usually eat."

"I usually grab a doughnut, or a fast-food biscuit." He sat down and began eating with obvious relish.

She clicked her tongue reprovingly. "All that fat and cholesterol."

"That's what Trammell says."

"How long have you been partners?" She hadn't been around Trammell much, but she had liked him. He reminded her of a panther, sleek and exotic, with the same kind of supple, dangerous strength.

"Nine years. We were on patrol together before we made detective, which we did at the same time." Dane set to work on the waffles with obvious zeal.

"That's longer than a lot of marriages last."

He grinned. "Yeah, but if I'd had to sleep with him, it wouldn't have lasted a day."

"Have you ever been married?" She bit her lip as soon as the question was out. Her own privacy had been at such a premium for most of her life that she seldom asked any personal question. "Never mind. Forget I asked."

"Why?" He shrugged. "I don't care if you ask. I've never been married, never been engaged." He cleared his throat, evidently feeling that called for some explanation. "But I'm heterosexual."

"I noticed," she said dryly.

He grinned, his hazel gaze moving warmly over her. "For the record, I'm thirty-four. My folks live in Fort Lauderdale, and I have three brothers and two sisters, all of whom are married and have contributed to the population growth. Between the five of them, I have eighteen nieces and nephews, ranging in age from two to nineteen. When we all get together for holidays, it's a zoo. All of them live in Florida, though we're scattered all over the state. There are also the uncles and aunts and cousins, but we won't go into them." He watched her carefully as he outlined his large family, knowing that someone who had lived as Marlie had might find even the thought of all those relatives alarming. He had never before wanted to include any of his women friends in his private life, but everything was different with her. He hadn't yet decided *how* it was different, but he accepted that it *was*.

Marlie tried to imagine that kind of extended family, but couldn't. She had always been forced to keep relationships of any kind at a minimum, and though in the past six years that limitation hadn't been necessary, still she had clung to it, reluctant to let herself be vulnerable in any way.

"My mother died in a fire when I was three," she said. "Lightning struck our house. I don't remember anything about it except this loud crack, louder than anything you can imagine, and even the air seemed to dissolve. A white light blotted out everything. A neighbor got me out of the house, and I was only slightly burned. My mother was in the part of the house that took the direct hit."

"Thunderstorms must make you nervous," he commented.

"They should, but they don't. I've never been frightened of them, not even immediately afterwards." She had had all of her waffle that she wanted, so she laid her fork down and picked up her coffee cup. "Lightning does some funny things. Dr. Ewell theorized that the enormous jolt of electricity somehow altered or enhanced my normal mental processes, making me more sensitive to the electrical energy given off by others. I was supposedly normal before, but afterward I became difficult, easily upset."

"Maybe because you'd lost your mother."

"Maybe. Who knows? I could have had the ability before, but simply wasn't old enough to make myself understood. From what I was told, my mother was a quiet, serene sort of person, so maybe her presence kept me calm. At any rate, my father had a difficult time trying to raise me. The more frustrated and angry he became, the more I felt it. I had no idea of how to block him out. We were both very unhappy people.

"I was the area weirdo. When I started school I didn't make any friends, but that was okay with me because it was just too exhausting. Then I found some toddler who had wandered off, and it was in the newspapers, and Dr. Ewell came to talk to my father. I went to the Institute to be tested, liked the peace and quiet of it, and stayed. My father and I were both relieved."

"Where is he now?" Dane asked.

"Dead. He visited me regularly for a while, but it was uncomfortable for both of us. The visits became further and further apart. He remarried when I was fourteen, I think, and moved to South Dakota. I met his wife only once. She was nice enough, but very uneasy with me. She had two children from her first marriage, but she and Dad didn't have any. He died of a massive stroke when I was twenty."

"No other relatives?"

"A few aunts and uncles, and some cousins I've never met."

She had essentially been alone since she'd been a child, he thought. No snuggling, no hugging. No giggling sleep-overs with friends during her teen years. He wondered if she had ever really *been* a child, if she had ever played. Probably not. There was something very adult about Marlie, a mental maturity that went far beyond her years. But despite her unorthodox childhood and, by necessity, very austere lifestyle, she was amazingly normal. Almost any eccentricity could have been justified by her upbringing, but she didn't have any oddball habits or quirks.

Unless he counted picking up the thought waves of a serial killer.

He looked at the clock, and took one last sip of coffee. "I have to go, honey. This was great. What are we having for supper?"

Caught between amusement, hope, and absolute terror that he evidently planned to stay with her again, all she could do was start laughing. "You've just finished breakfast," she said between giggles.

He pinched her chin. "Even in the *Rubaiyat,* old Omar listed food first."

"I thought the wine came first."

"Tells us a lot about him, doesn't it?" He winked at her and went into the bedroom to finish dressing, and Marlie began clearing the table. She felt giddy. He was coming back that night.

She wondered how he usually conducted his affairs. Was he satisfied with spending a night together every now and then, maybe just the weekends? Or would he come by every night, spend time with her, make love, and then go home to his own house? She didn't know what to expect. There was a very satisfied air about him that led her to think he was very pleased with the personal outcome of the weekend, but perhaps that was just sexual satiation. She wasn't experienced enough to tell the difference, assuming there was one. Despite his kindness, his tenderness, even his passion, despite the fact that she had fallen headlong in love with him, she was aware that she really didn't know him.

He was shrugging into his shoulder holster as he came out of the bedroom. "I forgot that I don't have a jacket here," he said, frowning. "I'll have to stop by my house to get one, so I have to run." He bent down to kiss her. "'Bye, honey. I don't know how long this will take."

She put her hands on his chest and lifted herself on tiptoe for another kiss. "I have to do my grocery shopping, if you want anything at all to eat. If I'm not here, that's where I'll be."

He put his arms around her and pulled her close, forcing her hips against his. His mouth settled on hers for a kiss so hard and hungry that she went limp in his arms, shivering with delight. His hands sought her breasts, and rubbed between her legs. He forced her back against the cabinets and swiftly lifted her up onto them, pushing his hips between her spread thighs. She clung to his heavy shoulders, feeling the leather of the holster beneath her palms.

He tore his mouth away with a groan. "God Almighty. We can't do this. I don't have time." Sweat glistened on his forehead, and his eyes had that heavy-lidded, intent look that nearly made her beg him to stay. But she of all people knew the price of duty, and she forced herself to release him.

"Go," she said. "Now."

He stepped back, wincing as he reached down to adjust himself. "I'll be back as soon as I can, but it may take several hours. Do you have an extra house key?"

"Yes, of course."

"Let me have it."

No hesitation or uncertainty for *him,* she thought as she jumped off the countertop and hurried to her purse. She gave him the extra key, and he slipped it onto his key ring. He started to reach for her, for another kiss, but caught himself in time. "Later," he said, winking at her, and headed for the door.

When he was gone, Marlie collapsed on the couch and tried to take stock of her life. She was wary, even frightened, of what was happening, but nothing on earth could have stopped her from plunging into the experience. For the first time in her life, she was in love, and it was wonderful.

To Dane's surprise, the chief of police was present at the meeting. Rodger Champlin, tall, white-haired, and stooped from too many years behind a desk, was nevertheless a career policeman who had come up through the ranks, and he had over forty years of service under his belt. He was a sly old dog who had managed to stay abreast of the flood of new technologies involved in police work, rather than stubbornly clinging to the outmoded ways he had learned in his youth.

Bonness's cramped office wasn't big enough to hold everyone, so they went into a conference room and closed the door. Ivan was there, his lined face and bloodshot eyes evidence that he had been up all night. All the detectives were there, most of them obviously puzzled by this Sunday morning meeting, especially one that involved the chief.

Bonness was drinking coffee as if it were all that kept him going. From the looks of him, he hadn't slept much, if at all, and the hand holding the coffee cup trembled slightly from caffeine overload.

Everyone got his own cup of coffee and settled into his chosen seat. Dane decided to stand, and propped himself against the wall.

Bonness looked down at the sheaf of papers on the table before him, and sighed. He was obviously reluctant to begin, as if officially putting it in words would make it more real.

"People, we have a big problem," he said. "We only have two cases to compare, but the similarities are so overwhelming that we're pretty certain we have a serial murderer operating in Orlando."

Dead silence filled the room as the detectives exchanged glances.

"We were alerted to the possibility," he said, without going into specifics, "which is why we're able to get on it so fast." He passed some of the papers to the detective seated to his right, Mac Stroud. "Take one and pass it down. These are the files on Nadine Vinick and Jacqueline Sheets. Read both of them carefully. Mrs. Vinick was murdered a week ago Friday, Ms. Sheets was killed this past Friday night."

"So what do we have?" Mac asked.

Bonness looked at Ivan Schaffer. "Nothing," Ivan said flatly. "Not a damn thing. No fingerprints; he wears gloves. No semen, though vaginal bruising in both women indicates that they were raped. He either wears a condom or uses a foreign object. I haven't found any stray hairs, either. No footprints, no fibers from his clothing, no witnesses. We have nothing."

"Let me understand this," Chief Champlin said. His eyes flashed at the group. "I'm supposed to tell the mayor that there's a serial killer working in the city, and we don't have a shred of evidence on him? That even if, by some miracle, we managed to get our hands on him, we couldn't tie him to the crimes?"

"That's about it," Ivan said.

"How can you be so sure it's the same guy? There have

only been two murders, and stabbing deaths aren't that unusual—"

"Two stabbing deaths with absolutely no evidence left behind?" Dane interrupted. "Both of them occurred on a Friday night, at roughly the same hour. Both of the murders were done with a knife from the victim's kitchen, and both times the weapon was left behind. It's the same guy." He didn't mention Marlie, and he was betting that Bonness wouldn't, either. She would have to be brought into it sooner or later, but he wanted it to be later, when it was the right time and everything was under his control.

"Any connection between the two victims?" Mac asked.

Dane looked at Freddie and Worley, who had handled the paperwork on Jackie Sheets. Freddie shook her head. "There are still several people we need to talk to, but so far we haven't found any connection at all. They didn't look alike, they didn't live in the same neighborhood. Mrs. Vinick was a housewife, Ms. Sheets was a legal secretary. They didn't frequent the same places. As far as we've been able to find out, they never met."

"We can get a list from the telephone company of the calls made from both residences, and compare them. Maybe we'll get lucky and they have some numbers in common," Trammell said. "And there's the always interesting contents of the trash."

"And we need to get copies of their canceled checks from the banks." Dane wrote a note to himself. "Also copies of their charges on any credit cards. There's a link. There's always a link."

"I want to hold off on telling the mayor for a day or so," the chief said, glaring at all of them. "Until you can come up with a little concrete evidence so I won't feel as big of a fool as I do right now."

"The total lack of forensic evidence is a characteristic in itself," Dane pointed out. "I think we should take it to the FBI for analysis."

As he had expected, the chief's face took on a sour

expression. "Goddamn Feds," he snapped. "Are you saying you aren't good enough to handle it yourself, Hollister?"

Dane shrugged. All cops were jealous of their jurisdiction, and nobody, especially the old-timers, liked bringing the Bureau in on anything. Inevitably the federal boys got all the credit. "The Investigative Support Unit specializes in this, and I'd say we need all the help we can get. I don't have to prove that my dick's bigger than theirs."

"That's easy for you to say," Freddie remarked dryly. "But what about me?"

"What about the rest of us?" Worley countered in a plaintive tone.

The room erupted into laughter and a few coarse remarks. Bonness flushed at the lack of decorum, but couldn't keep himself from grinning. Dane winked at Freddie, and she winked back.

"If all of you are through comparing inches—or lack of them," the chief said, raising his voice, "maybe we can get back to the business at hand. Okay, maybe we take it to the FBI. But not until I say so, and not until I've talked to the mayor. Is that understood? Exhaust all the other avenues first."

"We can't afford to wait too long. Another Friday is only five days away."

"I know what day of the week it is," the chief snapped. "I'll talk to him Tuesday afternoon, and that's the absolute soonest I'll do it. That means, people, that you have two days to come up with something, so I suggest you all get to work."

15

THERE WASN'T A HELLUVA LOT THAT COULD BE DONE ON A Sunday. A call to the Hairport, where Jackie Sheets had regularly gotten her hair cut, didn't even get an answering machine but instead rang endlessly. No banks were open. The telephone company, however, was on duty and protecting the public's right to reach out and touch whomever they wanted twenty-four hours a day, seven days a week. Someone was *always* there, so Dane started the process of getting a listing of all the calls made from the Sheets residence.

Bonness organized a task force, choosing Dane, Trammell, Freddie, and Worley, since the four of them were already working on the two known cases. All of their other ongoing cases were parceled out to the other detectives, who were warned to tie up as many loose ends as they could, as fast as they could, because they would all probably be brought in on the task force soon.

What with one thing and another, it was after four when Dane and Trammell were finally able to leave the building.

Dane squinted up at the bright sky before slipping on his sunglasses. After the morning rain, the day had turned into a scorcher, with the rainfall only adding to the humidity as the heat turned the moisture to steam.

"How's Grace?" he asked.

Trammell was annoyed. "You sound as if you expect us to elope at any moment, and, old buddy, it ain't going to happen." He paused. "Grace is fine."

"Still at your place?"

Trammell checked his watch. "No."

Dane chuckled. "Not quite yet, huh? Maybe en route? You made a call right before we left; now, who could it have been to?"

"Fuck you," Trammell said mildly. "Where are *you* going?"

"Home. To my place."

Black eyebrows lifted inquiringly.

"To pick up more clothes," he enlarged, with some satisfaction.

"Why don't you just pack a suitcase and move in?"

"I would, but I still have to go by the house every day to get my mail, so that wouldn't be saving me any trouble. Most of my clothes will end up at her house eventually."

"All of your other girlfriends have moved in with you," Trammell pointed out.

"Marlie's different. She feels safe in her house; she won't willingly leave it." Besides, he didn't like the idea of Marlie moving into his own house. As Trammell had pointed out, several women over the years had taken up temporary residence there. He had liked and enjoyed them at the time, but in the end they hadn't been very important to him, certainly not as important or interesting as his job. Marlie *was* different; she didn't belong in that company of ultimately forgettable women.

Thinking of his house made him restless. It had always suited him before, but then, he had never been picky.

Suddenly he wanted to change things around. "My place needs some work done on it," he decided abruptly. "This would be a good time to have it done."

"What kind of work?"

"Maintenance stuff. New paint, the floors refinished. The bathroom needs complete renovation."

"I see." Trammell's dark eyes began to gleam. This was something he'd been itching to do for years. "How about new furniture while you're at it? That stuff you're using is about twenty years old."

"The place belonged to my grandparents. When they left it to me, the furniture came with it."

"It shows. How about it? New furniture, too?"

Dane considered it. Unlike most cops, and not counting Trammell, his bank account was healthy. He was single and had cheap tastes in food, clothes, and cars. He had inherited the house from his grandparents, so he didn't have a mortgage payment every month. He actually lived on half of his income, so the other half had been accumulating in the bank for years. Several times he'd thought about buying a boat, but when would he have time to use it? No other money-using schemes had come to mind. The house *did* need redecorating. He would like to take Marlie there occasionally, though he really couldn't imagine her living there with him, and he wanted the place to look nice for her. Unfortunately, now it looked exactly like what it was: a bachelor's home. And a bachelor who didn't pay much attention to his surroundings, at that. He wasn't the kind of slob who left food and empty beer cans everywhere, but he wasn't great on dusting or replacing things, either.

"Okay," he said. "New furniture, too."

Trammell rubbed his hands together. "I'll get started tomorrow."

Warily Dane eyed his friend. "Whaddaya mean, *you'll* get started? You're going to be busy. I'll arrange for the painters and floor refinishers, and pick out some new furniture next weekend."

"That's not quite how it's going to be, old buddy. We've already agreed that your taste in everything except women is atrocious. You have great taste in women. Just leave the rest to me."

"Hell, no! I know you. You'll put one of those little rugs that costs a fortune on the living room floor, and I'll be afraid to even walk on it. My bank account isn't yours, *old buddy.*"

"I'll take that into consideration. And no dhurrie rugs. Unlike you, I have excellent taste. It'll be a place you can be comfortable in, but it'll look a hell of a lot better. Marlie will like it," he added slyly.

Dane scowled at him, and Trammell clapped him on the shoulder. "Just relax and enjoy it."

"That sounds like I'm going to get fucked."

"I can do it for about ten thousand. How does that sound?"

"Like a damn expensive fuck. How about five?"

Trammell snorted. "Only if you want to sleep on a futon and sit on a bean bag."

Ten thousand. It was a lot of money. But Trammell was right, the self-satisfied bastard: He did have good taste. The house needed renovating, and he wanted it fresh and clean for Marlie, even if she never actually lived there. None of those other women had left much of an imprint, but he wanted even the hint of them gone. "How are you going to find time to do it?" he asked grudgingly.

"Ever hear of the telephone? It's no problem. I'll have stuff delivered, drop by to take a look at it, and if I don't like it, the store will pick it up again."

"You've been rich for too long. You need to come out of the stratosphere and live like regular folks for a change."

"Conspicuous consumers like me create jobs and keep the economy growing. It's time you did your part."

"I agreed, damn it."

"Then stop complaining about it." Trammell checked his

watch again. "Gotta go. If you have an extra house key, bring it to me in the morning."

"Sure," Dane said, wondering if his house would be recognizable as the same residence when Trammell got through with it. Still, it accomplished two things at once: The place *did* need some work, and it gave him a perfect excuse to completely move in with Marlie during the renovation. He was whistling as he got in his car.

An hour and a half later, Marlie went still with shock as she stood in the doorway and watched him unload suitcases and boxes from his car.

"What's all that?" she asked faintly. Silly question; she could see very clearly what it was. The question she really wanted to ask was "Why?" but she figured she knew the answer to that, too. Dane might enjoy very much the physical side of their relationship, but she couldn't let herself forget that, no matter what, he was always a cop. What better way to keep an eye on her than to move right in? That way he would know immediately if she had another vision.

"My stuff. My house is being renovated, and I have to clear out for a couple of weeks." He stopped on the porch, watching her intently. "I apologize for not asking, but it was a sudden decision to have the work done."

"I see." She managed an ironic smile. "Moving in is a good way to stay on top of the situation, I guess. Figuratively as well as literally."

Very carefully he set the box down on the porch. His expression was both cool and blank. "What does that mean, exactly?"

She shrugged. "Can you honestly say that moving in with me has nothing to do with the murders, with this entire situation?"

"No," he said bluntly. It was the truth. He couldn't. Marlie was his best chance of catching the bastard, but it wasn't just that. He had seen how the visions affected her, the physical and mental price she paid. For both of those reasons, in addition to the fact that he was violently attracted to her, he wanted to stay close to her.

She stood silently for a moment, considering the situation. They had become lovers, but her instinct was to take things slowly. Circumstances had decreed otherwise, throwing them together in a pressure cooker. Even though she would like to put the brakes on now, feel her way through this strange new relationship, those same circumstances were still aligned against her. He was, first and foremost, a cop, and she was his direct link to a killer. Until the murderer was caught, she couldn't expect Dane to stray far from her side. She would simply have to remember that the main reason he was there was his job; it was a sure bet that he didn't practically force his way in to live with every woman with whom he had gone to bed.

She stepped aside. "Just so we understand each other. Come on in."

Trammell gave a long, low whistle when Dane walked in the next morning, and everyone in the squad room turned to look. Never mind that there was a serial killer on the loose; cops were never too busy to harass one of their own. Freddie clutched her heart and pretended to swoon. Bonness, who had been standing beside Keegan's desk, was totally deadpan as he asked, "May we help you, sir?"

"You sure can," Dane replied good-naturedly as he dropped into his chair. "All you smart-asses can apologize for the crap you've given me for years about how I dressed."

"He said it in the past tense," Trammell noted, turning his eyes upward. "Please, God, let it stay that way."

Dane smiled at him. "Want to go for a couple of beers after work?" he asked silkily. Trammell picked up the hint and subsided, but still with an unholy gleam of amusement in his dark eyes.

"Take *me*, take *me!*" Freddie cried, waving her hand exuberantly.

"Yeah, sure, and get my legs broken?"

She shrugged. *"I* don't mind."

"Gee, thanks. I'm overwhelmed by your concern."

Bonness left Keegan's desk to perch on Dane's. "What caused the transformation?" he asked. "Were you mugged by a fashion designer on the way to work?"

Dane grinned, knowing that his answer would make Bonness choke. It wasn't something he could keep to himself, so he decided to have a little fun. "Marlie doesn't like wrinkles," he explained calmly.

Bonness looked blank. "Marlie?" Obviously he could think of only one Marlie and just as obviously he couldn't get the connection.

"Marlie Keen. You know, the psychic."

"I know who she is," Bonness said, still confused. "What does she have to do with it?"

"She doesn't like wrinkles," Dane explained again, as deadpan as Bonness had been. He could hear Trammell snickering, but didn't dare glance that way.

Poor Bonness was slow that day. "So she goes around the city zapping them out?" he demanded with heavy sarcasm.

"No." Dane smiled, a slow, very satisfied smile. "She ironed them out. At least, she ironed the shirt. She made me iron the slacks myself, because she said I had to learn."

Bonness gaped at him. Trammell was making choking sounds as he tried to keep from laughing aloud. "You—you mean . . . Marlie . . . that is, you and Marlie—"

"Marlie and I are what?"

"Um . . . dating?"

"Dating?" Dane pretended to think. "No, I wouldn't say that."

"Then what would you say?"

He gave a negligent shrug. "It's simple. When I got dressed this morning, she said that no way was I leaving the house looking like that, so she hauled out her iron and ironing board and made me take off my clothes. When I put them back on, they looked like this." He wondered why a crisply ironed shirt, neatly knotted tie, and slacks with a razor-edge crease were such a big deal, not just to Marlie but to everyone else. Not that he minded; he just hadn't cared before. He didn't care about his clothes now, but Marlie did, so therefore he would make more of an effort. Simple.

Bonness was literally sputtering, his eyes bugging out. "But you only met a week ago. You ridiculed her, accused her of being an accomplice to murder. She hated your guts on sight."

"We changed our minds," Dane said. "If you need me, you can reach me at her house."

"Shit. You're kidding me. I thought she had better taste than that."

Dane smiled peacefully. "She does. She's already improving me." And he would let her do it. If she wanted him to wear Italian loafers like Trammell's, he'd do it. If she wanted him to shave twice a day, he'd do that too. If she wanted him to stand on his head for an hour every morning, he would happily put his butt in the air. When he had returned the afternoon before, with his clothing, it had been plain that the thought of living with him made her uneasy. He knew he should have lied to her about his motives, but damn it, his interest in her *was* two-pronged. He couldn't just forget about the murders and assure her that her involvement never entered his mind. Hell, her involvement never *left* his mind.

After this was over, he would devote all of his attention to her, but right now he couldn't, and she knew it. Right away he had sensed a slight distance that hadn't been there when he'd left. She kept rebuilding that damn wall of reserve, as if she couldn't quite trust herself to let go, or trust him to catch her if she did. He would let her reform him from the ground up if it would make her feel more secure with him.

Marlie was a solitary creature who didn't easily share either her space or her time. He had carefully spent the evening not crowding her too much, but all the same establishing a tone of normalcy to his presence. They had done very ordinary things—cooked dinner, cleaned the kitchen, watched television—just as if they had been together for months instead of one stressful weekend. It had worked; she had relaxed more and more as the evening wore on. And when they had gone to bed and he had begun making love to her, the reserve had completely vanished. He didn't know if it was permanently gone; probably not. But he would deal with each reappearance as it happened, and in the meantime insinuate himself ever more deeply into the everyday fabric of her life. Besides, he had enjoyed it when she had made several acerbic remarks about his clothes. She had been too subdued and vulnerable for the past two days, and he had been delighted to see her return to her normal, sharp-tongued spirits.

Still shaking his head at Marlie's evident loss of common sense, Bonness gestured for Freddie and Worley to come over. When everyone was grouped together, they decided their course of action for the day. Freddie and Worley were going to talk to the people Jackie Sheets had worked with, including Liz Cline again, for she would be calmer now and might remember something else. They arranged to get copies of the canceled checks of both victims. Dane and Trammell went to the Hairport to talk to Jackie Sheets's hair stylist.

The Hairport was situated in a small, renovated house. There was none of the pink neon and purple-and-black decor so beloved by the trendier salons where all the clients came out looking as if they'd stuck their finger into a light socket. But there were real ferns (Dane knew because Trammell stuck his finger into the dirt to check), and comfortable waiting chairs, as well as a truly impressive selection of magazines, stacked in rickety towers on every available flat surface. There were several women in the salon, in various stages of tonsorial improvement. A sharp chemical smell hung in the air, with an undertone of hairspray and nail polish.

The Kathy who cut Ms. Sheets's hair was Kathleen McCrory, who looked as Irish as her name. She had sandy red hair that feathered around her face, a very fair complexion, and round blue eyes that widened even more when Dane and Trammell introduced themselves. She led them back to the tiny break room the stylists used, poured them each a cup of coffee, and offered them their choice of any of the varied snacks piled on the small table. They accepted the coffee, but turned down the Bugles and Twinkies.

Kathleen was a cheerful, self-confident young woman. Trammell began to ask her about Jackie Sheets, and Dane settled back to enjoy his coffee, which was pretty good. He watched Kathleen lightly flirt with Trammell, and his partner lightly flirt in return, all the while asking questions. Kathleen did stop flirting when he told her that Jackie Sheets had been killed, and her big blue eyes slowly filled with tears. She looked back and forth between Dane and Trammell, as if wanting one of them to say it was a joke. Her lips began trembling. "I—I haven't watched the news this weekend," she said, and swallowed hard. "My boyfriend and I went to Daytona."

Dane reached across the small table and covered her hand with his. She clutched his fingers, and clung tightly to him until she had fought off the tears. She gave him a small, watery, apologetic smile as she began groping for a tissue to wipe her eyes.

Yes, she had cut Jackie's hair about every three weeks. Jackie had gorgeous hair, thick and silky, with a lot of body. She could do anything she wanted with it. Trammell gently interrupted the hair analysis to get her back on track. No, Jackie hadn't mentioned seeing anyone for quite a while now. No, Kathleen couldn't remember anyone named Vinick.

Did she have any male customers? Sure. There were quite a few. Had Jackie spoken to any of them, gotten acquainted? Not that Kathleen could remember.

Another dead end, Dane thought. He was getting damn tired of them.

Tuesday was more of the same dead ends. A comparison of canceled checks and credit card receipts revealed that the Vinicks and Jackie Sheets had shopped at some of the same department stores, which told them exactly nothing. Dane imagined that almost everyone in Orlando had been in at least one of those stores at one time or another. Still, it was the only link they had come up with, so he doggedly pursued it, comparing dates to see if maybe they had been in any store at the same time.

Jackie Sheets had had several department store credit cards, but Nadine Vinick hadn't had any, usually paying for her purchases by check or charging the expense to their one credit card, a MasterCard, when she didn't have the ready funds. But Mrs. Vinick had been very frugal, and had used the card only twice in the past year. Mostly the Vinicks had operated in a pay-as-you-go household, while Jackie Sheets had regularly made charges on her cards and paid in monthly installments, always living slightly above her means. Most of her purchases had been clothes, from the best stores in the city.

Their life-styles had been different. The Vinicks had been blue-collar, and Nadine's greatest interest had been cooking. Jackie Sheets had been white-collar, a woman who had loved clothes and made an effort to always look her best. But somewhere, somehow, the two women, as different as they were, had had the bad luck to attract the attention of the same man. But *where,* and *how?*

Chief Champlin had clearly hoped they would come up with something; his disappointment that afternoon wasn't pleasant. But he was also a cop, and he had looked at the files. The same man had done both women. The very lack of forensic evidence was as much an indicator as if they had found the same fingerprints at both scenes. This was a smart bastard, and they needed help.

"All right," he said. "Call the Bureau. I'll tell the mayor."

Bonness made the call, and briefly explained the situation. The local Bureau guys knew big stuff when they heard it, and said they would like to go over the files immediately.

"Hollister and Trammell, get the files and go," Bonness said.

Dane saw Trammell check his watch, a sure sign that he had something else to do. "Why not send someone from each case?" he suggested. "They may have questions about Jackie Sheets that Trammell and I can't answer."

"Okay," Bonness agreed. "Freddie? Worley? Which one of you wants to go?"

Worley grimaced. He clearly wanted to go, but he, too, checked his watch. "It's my mother-in-law's birthday. If I'm late for the party, my wife won't speak to me for a year."

"I'm free," Freddie said. "Which one of you guys is going?"

"I am," Dane said, and Trammell flashed him a grateful smile.

FBI Agent Dennis Lowery was waiting for them. Lowery had that Ichabod Crane look to him: thin, long-legged, stoop-shouldered, his clothes always flapping about him as if they were too large. His eyes were deep-set, his nose was beaky. But he was a calm, intelligent man who was more diplomatic than some when it came to dealing with local law enforcement agencies. Dane had dealt with him before, and liked him well enough.

A second agent, Sam DiLeonardo, was a young fart barely out of training, all spit and polish. Dane wasn't as inclined to like him, because he looked like the type who would insist on going by the book even when everything was falling apart around him, but the kid redeemed himself by taking one look at Freddie and immediately falling in lust. He went absolutely still, his eyes widening a little as he stared at her. A slight blush darkened his cheeks. Freddie was always kind and could be very ladylike when she chose, so she pretended not to notice the kid's fascination. Dane and Lowery exchanged wry glances as they sat down at a long conference table.

"So what do you have?" Lowery asked, pulling a legal pad toward him and uncapping a pen.

Freddie gave copies of the files to both agents, who silently leafed through them. DiLeonardo forgot his preoccupation with the plain but remarkably fetching Detective Freddie Brown, his expression turning grim as he stared at the stark photos of the bodies, in both color and black and white.

"He probably stalks them before acting," Dane said. "He knows if they're alone or not. In both cases, we think it's possible that he was in the house for some time before they knew it, hiding out in the spare bedroom. In the Vinick case, he was probably waiting for her husband to go to work. With Jackie Sheets, we don't know why he waited."

"Maybe for the neighbors to go to bed," DiLeonardo said absently, still studying the notes.

"They would be less likely to hear anything if they were still up, with the television on. At any rate, none of the neighbors heard any screams."

Lowery's face was impassive as he looked at the photos. "You'd think, the way these women were butchered, that they would have been screaming bloody murder, but a lot of times it doesn't work that way. He chased them, didn't he? They were terrified, breathless, already traumatized by being raped. It's difficult to scream, really scream, under those conditions. The throat tightens up, restricts sound. Probably they didn't make all that much noise."

He tossed the files onto the table and rubbed his jaw. "Just two cases? That doesn't give us much to work on, but I agree, it looks like the same guy. What's the link?"

"We haven't been able to find one," Dane said. "Not looks, life-style, friends, neighborhood, anything. We compared canceled checks and credit card receipts, and except for shopping at some of the same department stores, which applies to everyone else in town, their paths never crossed. They never met each other."

"They did something to attract this guy's attention, though. Did they both buy something from the same store within, say, the last month?"

"Not that we can find. It's hard to say, because the Vinicks evidently paid cash for a lot of things." Dane wasn't irritated by Lowery's questions, though some people would have been, taking it as a suggestion that the local cops hadn't done a good job. The same questions were bound to come up over and over again, as different people grappled with the problem. There had been a lot of times when he had doggedly gone over the same file time and again, until something clicked and he saw a detail that had been there all along, but just hadn't registered.

"I'll get this up to Quantico," Lowery said. "Two murders in a week isn't a good sign. If he's escalating that fast, he's out of control."

"I'm hoping it was unusual for him to kill two so close together. Maybe Jackie Sheets was an easy opportunity that he couldn't resist."

"Maybe. But if he liked it, he won't wait long before doing it again."

"Oh, he likes it," Dane said bitterly. "He takes his time, plays with them. The son of a bitch loves his work."

16

CARROLL JANES WAS SULKY. HE HAD BEEN IN A SOUR MOOD since last Friday night. Jacqueline Sheets hadn't been as much fun as he had anticipated. The big rush of power he had expected just hadn't materialized. She had been pathetic, just whining and scrambling in circles, rather than making it interesting. And there hadn't been much press coverage about it either, which really disappointed him. Part of the fun—as it turned out, *most* of the fun—of this last one had been knowing that the cops would go crazy, with two incidences so similar, so close together, and absolutely no clues with which they could work. But evidently the cops were more stupid than he had thought, which took even more of the fun out of it. Where was the challenge? Not that they could catch him, but he had thought they would at least have *noticed*.

He wasn't sure what had interfered with his pleasure. Maybe Sheets had just been too soon after the last one. He hadn't been in the proper state of anticipation, hadn't drawn out the stalking over several weeks while the tension drew tighter and tighter, until he was at fever pitch, all of his senses almost painfully acute, all of his power focused.

Of course, he would have to try another one to make certain. He hated to waste himself on a disappointment, but it was the only way he could find out. If the next one was as boring, he would know to spend more time on the process and wouldn't let the apparent ease of a job sucker him into moving too fast, and cheating himself of his pleasure.

Every day at work he waited and watched for the slightest transgression. Which unhappy customer was going to have to pay? After all, to make it a fair test, he would have to act as soon as possible.

Marlie felt edgy, restless from an inner tension that just wouldn't let up. She couldn't pin down any one reason for it, because there were so many candidates from which to choose. The biggest reason, of course, was dread of the coming weekend. She couldn't explain to anyone, not even Dane, how she felt after touching the killer's thoughts during those bloody moments. She didn't just feel dirty, she felt permanently contaminated by his evil, as if her soul would never be free of the ugliness. More than she had ever wanted anything in her life, she wanted to run, to get far away so she wouldn't know when he killed again. That relief, unfortunately, was the one thing she couldn't allow herself, or then she would be truly contaminated by her own cravenness. She had to stay, had to stick it out, for the sake of the two women who had already died, for the others she didn't know about, for little Dusty . . . for herself.

Then there was Dane. She loved him, but having him around all the time was still disconcerting. She had spent so many years alone that it sometimes startled her to turn around and bump into him. Suddenly there was twice the amount of laundry to do, three times as much food to prepare, schedules to adjust since there was only one bathroom, and very little room in bed. Her life had been totally in control, and now everything had changed.

He knew, of course. Those sharp hazel eyes saw everything, though she struggled to hide how unsettled she was. He didn't just dump all the chores in her lap, as a lot of men would have done; he was accustomed to doing his own laundry and didn't hesitate to wash a load of clothes. The safe limits of his cooking were heating the contents of cans or slapping a sandwich together, so she did all of the cooking, and he took over the cleanup chores. He did what he could to ease the transition for her, but at the same time he refused to back off and give her more space. He was there; she had to accustom herself to him. She was happy to do so, to have this time with him no matter what his motivation, but it was still unnerving.

She couldn't escape the coming weekend, couldn't distract herself. Would the killer strike again? The thought of some other innocent woman being butchered, of herself being sucked into the sickening, evil morass of the killer's mind, was almost more than she could bear. She tried not to think of it, but it was like being tracked by a mad dog and trying not to think about that, either. With every tick of the clock, the weekend loomed closer, and there was nothing she could do to avoid it. She tried to brace herself to endure, instead, because she was Dane's only link to the killer. Sooner or later, he would give her a clue to his identity. All she had to do was wait, and endure his killing frenzies without going mad herself.

By Thursday, she was so tense that she couldn't eat the Chinese food Dane had brought for dinner, and she loved Chinese. Her throat was tight, and when she swallowed, the food seemed to form a lump halfway down her esophagus. She didn't have an appetite anyway, so finally she stopped even making an effort.

As usual, Dane hadn't missed a trick, though he was making impressive inroads on the food. "Worried?" he asked.

"How can I not be? The last two weekends haven't been a picnic."

"Are you picking up anything from him?" Dane asked the question casually, but the interest behind it was intense.

"I'm uneasy, but it's *my* feelings, not his." She rubbed her hands over her arms. "How long will it take the FBI to get a profile on him?"

"I don't know. We only had two cases, so that may make it harder for them. But they may be able to match the MO to other cases that have been brought to their attention, and that will help."

"Do you think he's killed before?" she asked tensely, looking out the back door. She could see Bill trimming the shrubbery at the rear of his lot. Her neighbors lived such nice, ordinary lives; she envied them the boredom of their security.

"Probably. He's too good at it to be a beginner. It's likely that he moves around, to keep any one area from becoming too hot for him."

"So he's moved here recently?"

"I'd say so."

"Isn't there any way you can check on recent arrivals? Wouldn't the post office have a record? Or maybe you could get a list of new customers from the utility companies."

"Do you know how many people move to central Florida every year?" he asked. "It would take a helluva lot of time. Still, it's an idea."

"You could eliminate all the women, which would cut the list in half."

"And still leave us with a cast of thousands." He stood and began clearing the table. "I'll talk to Bonness about it."

She knotted her hands together and stared at him. "Do any of the others know about me?"

"You mean, any of the other detectives?"

"Yes."

"Just Bonness, Trammell, and me. Why?"

"I've been worried about it."

"Again, why?"

"They would talk." Restlessly she got up and helped him clear the table.

"So?"

"That kind of talk would get to the media. You know how it is."

"So far, the media doesn't even know about the killer. I'm surprised, because once we told the mayor, I expected it to be blasted on the six-o'clock news that there's a serial killer loose in Orlando. No one in city hall can keep a secret. It'll leak out any day, though." He began washing their few dishes, and watched her as she paced the kitchen. "Have you had a rough time with the media before?"

She shot him an incredulous look. "Are you kidding?"

"What happened?"

"Which time?" she asked caustically. "The reporters are bad enough, every time a story breaks, with the phone ringing incessantly, and cameras and microphones pushed in my face every time I open the door. But the reporters aren't the worst of it. They're just the cause. The worst comes after they've done their stories, when the death threats start, and the crackpot evangelists hold prayer meetings in front of my house to drive out Satan, because I obviously do the devil's work. If it got out this time, I'd probably lose my job. I've never been in these circumstances before, because the Institute always supported me. But can you imagine a *bank* tolerating that kind of publicity? A weirdo psychic working in their accounting department! Some of their customers would close out their accounts, afraid I would pry into their business."

"Wonder what they have to hide," Dane said, his eyes speculative.

"Nothing, probably. Some people are paranoid enough that they think the 'authorities,' whoever that may be, watch everyone and check everything. They won't fill out their census papers because they think the information will be turned over to the IRS."

"How do you know?" he asked, sliding the question in as smooth as silk. She glanced at him to find those hazel eyes glittering with amusement.

She choked on a spurt of laughter as she realized where he had led her. "Because I used to be able to read them! *Used* to, Hollister. I can't do it anymore."

"Are you sure? Have you tried?"

"Yes, smarty, I've tried."

"When?"

"Last week. I tried to pick *him* up, but couldn't. I tried to find you. I tried to find Trammell. Nothing. I did finally see you, very briefly, but I couldn't read anything from you."

"You saw me." He didn't look pleased at the idea. "What was I doing?"

"Watching a ball game and answering the telephone," she snapped. "It was when I called you the first time. If I hadn't been so worried and frightened, I doubt if I could have seen you. That never was my strength, anyway."

He rinsed the dishes and stacked them in the drainer, then dried his hands. "But that was before we became involved. Now, maybe you could do it any time you wanted."

"Maybe. I don't know. I haven't tried again."

He turned around and propped against the sink, his arms crossed as he studied her. Marlie stood her ground, but she wasn't certain what against. He looked grim, and bigger than usual. He had removed his jacket when he'd gotten home with the cartons of takeout Chinese, but still wore his shoulder holster. A chill went through her. He had been with her for a week now, and in that short length of time she had become accustomed to his protectiveness, even to being cosseted. But a week *was* a very short time, and before that they had been adversaries.

In a flash she realized what the problem was. He wanted her, but he didn't trust her. How could he? He didn't know her well enough. Wasn't that a big part of *her* problem, too? They had been propelled together without having time to get to know each other. He was a cop; distrust and suspicion were his stock in trade. He had made love to her, moved in with her, thinking that she had lost most of her psychic abilities. He didn't at all like the idea that she could check up on him without his knowledge. He wanted to keep himself private, except for the parts he chose to share with her.

It hurt, but she couldn't blame him. She had spent a lot of effort in trying to secure privacy for herself, so she couldn't decry the same instinct in him.

"Do you want me to apologize for being what I am?" she asked steadily. "Or put my hand on a Bible and swear a sacred oath that I'll never again try to reach you?"

"You don't know that you can, except in an emergency."

She shrugged. "I won't try it even then, if you don't want me to."

"I don't like being spied on," he said, his gaze never leaving hers.

"Then I won't do it."

He shoved his hand through his hair. "Damn it," he said under his breath. "Does it work the other way around? The other time, you were worried about me. But what if you're the one in trouble? Can you call me, psychically?"

"I can place the call, Detective," she said sardonically. "But if you don't have a receiver, you can't get the signals. But I wouldn't, anyway."

"Why not?" He didn't like that. She could see his temper rising.

"That boundary you just drew. If you don't want me to cross it for my convenience, I'll be damned if I'll cross it for yours."

"Shit! I don't believe this." He closed his eyes and pinched the narrow bridge of his nose. "We're arguing about something that doesn't exist. If you can't contact me anyway, what the hell difference does it make that you wouldn't even try?"

"You tell me. You're the one with the problem about it." She turned around and headed for the living room. She had taken maybe three steps when a hard arm passed around her waist from behind and drew her back against him. She didn't try to struggle free, but neither did she relax and let him take her weight. She stood stock still, waiting. He had an erection; she could feel it pressing against her bottom. She wasn't surprised, because in the week they had been together, it seemed as if he had been hard most of the time.

"We aren't going to get this settled, are we?" His breath was warm against her temple.

"I don't see how."

"Then let's forget about it for now. Want to go for a ride?"

"Where to?"

"My place. I'm curious about what Trammell is doing to it."

She turned her head to stare incredulously at him. "You mean you don't know?"

"Nope. He told me to stay away until he's finished."

"For heaven's sake, why? It's your house."

"He said that I know as much about decorating as I know about clothes."

"In that case, I understand completely," she said wryly.

"Smart-ass. Do you want to go or not?"

"Sure." She had to admit to being curious about his house. She knew that it would be a mess while the renovation work was in progress, but houses were very personal things. Since she couldn't read Dane psychically, she had to pick up clues about him any way she could.

The drive to Dane's house took her mind off the uneasy feeling that had been her constant companion. Dismissing their quarrel for now, because there was nothing they could do about it, she prepared to enjoy prowling through his house.

Though it was late, almost seven, and long past the time when the workers would have gone home, there was another car in the driveway, and lights were on in the house. "Uh-oh," Dane said. "Caught in the act. Trammell's here."

"You don't have to stop," Marlie pointed out.

He smiled. "And miss the fun?" Deftly he pulled in behind Trammell's car.

They had barely gotten out of the car when Trammell appeared in the doorway. "I told you to stay away," he called.

"So arrest me. I've been good for four days. How long did you think it would last?"

"Three," Trammell said, stepping aside to let them in.

A tall, slim woman came forward to greet them. "Grace," Dane said, pleasure evident in his voice as he hugged her. "Marlie, this is Grace Roeg, a patrol officer with the city. Grace, Marlie Keen."

"Hello," Grace said in a slow, grave voice. Marlie swiftly evaluated her, and liked what she saw. There was something stately about Grace Roeg, and her deep brown eyes reflected the inner stillness of an unshakable serenity.

"Well, go ahead, look around," Trammell said irritably.

Dane looked around at the empty room, all the while keeping his arm around Grace. "Where's my stuff?"

"In storage," Trammell growled, forcefully removing his arm from Grace's shoulders. He glanced sharply at Marlie, as if instructing her to take Dane into custody and control him. She put an innocent look on her face, amused by watching the elegant Trammell descend to the primitive levels of jealousy.

Grace said, "Don't mind him. We're getting married, and he's still in shock." She extended her left hand to show them an exquisite marquise diamond, about three carats worth.

"I am not." Trammell turned a violent look on Dane. "Don't start."

Dane was grinning. "Start what? I'm glad for you. Congratulations, buddy. Grace is way too good for you. When are you going to do the deed?"

"About six months," Grace answered comfortably. "I thought a nice, long engagement would give him time to get used to the idea. Things have happened pretty fast, so we don't want to rush into anything and maybe make a mistake."

"I don't need time," her intended said, looking haunted. "It was my idea, wasn't it?"

"Of course it was, darling," she soothed, tucking her arm through his. "But it will take that long to plan the wedding. Now, why don't you show Dane what you're doing to his house?"

"Is it going to be a big wedding?" Marlie asked.

"Big enough," Trammell said, and turned an evil smile on Dane. "You'll have to wear a tuxedo."

"I'm tough," Dane replied, concealing his instant dread. "It might damage me, but it won't kill me. For you, old buddy, anything."

Trammell scowled, as if he had been hoping for more of a reaction, but turned and led the way through the empty rooms. Dane was frankly amazed at what had been accomplished in just four days. His grandmother had loved wallpaper, and every room in the house had sported a different pattern. The wallpaper was gone now, and in its place was fresh stucco, painted a soothing, mellow white. All of the interior doorways had been reframed into arches.

"It would look better if the exterior doors and the windows were arches," Trammell said, "but changing them would cost a lot more money than you want to spend. The floor refinishers start tomorrow."

Dane skidded to a halt, gaping at the hull of what had been his bathroom. "You've gutted it," he blurted.

"Yeah. I hadn't planned to do it, but the plumbing was fifty years old. It'll cost you probably another thousand."

"Damn it, the next time you feel the urge to spend another thousand or so of my money, ask me first!"

"If I'd asked, you'd have said no," Trammell replied calmly. "Wait until I'm finished, and you'll agree that it was worth the money."

"It had better be," Dane muttered. He sensed Trammell's

amusement, and knew his partner was getting back at him for being so gleeful about the impending marriage. He didn't mind, much. He was glad Trammell had found someone as wonderful as Grace, though he understood exactly his partner's sense of panic, as if his life had suddenly rocketed out of control.

He had felt that way himself since meeting Marlie. Things had happened too fast. Trammell and Grace had decided to get married, then set the date far enough in the future to give themselves time to settle down and be certain of their feelings. Dane hadn't mentioned marriage or even love to Marlie, preferring to give himself the time *before* the commitment. Maybe what he felt for her wouldn't last. It sure felt permanent, but maybe it wasn't; time would tell. In the meantime, they were together, and in the end that was really all that mattered. He woke up with her every morning and went to bed with her every night. As long as he had that, he could wait for the rest.

He wasn't certain how Marlie felt, either. There was passion, liking, companionship . . . maybe love. Who could tell? She had been under considerable stress from the first. When everything was settled down, then they would be able to tell more about their relationship. For the first time he considered marriage a possibility, and that in itself was a huge step for him.

It would all have to wait, though. There was a killer to catch, a plan to put into action, and he had to protect Marlie while he did it. And if he had learned anything about Marlie in the time he had been with her, it was that she wasn't going to like his plan worth a damn.

17

LOWERY CALLED FIRST THING MONDAY MORNING, ASKING them to come over immediately. He had just returned from Quantico with the character profile.

The day was hot and clear and sticky, with the temperature already in the mid-eighties, predicted to reach the high nineties, and the humidity there already. Dane hadn't slept well the entire weekend, probably because Marlie hadn't. She had been restless, able to doze for only short periods before jerking awake. The strain of the weekend, waiting for a vision of murder to appear, had left her pale and withdrawn, with dark circles of fatigue under her eyes. He had spent long hours cuddling her, letting her know that she wasn't alone even if he couldn't prevent the vision, if it came. It hadn't.

How much more of this could she take? She was under so much stress, both physically and emotionally, that he was afraid for her. A lot of people would have broken under the strain, years ago. She hadn't, which was a testimony to her strength; Marlie wasn't a delicate flower, wilting at any hardship. Despite the finely drawn lines of her too thin body, she was remarkably sturdy. But even an oak tree could be felled, and he was worried.

Trammell was showing strain, too, probably from terror of his impending nuptials. He and Dane barely spoke on the way over to the Bureau, each of them absorbed in his own worries.

Freddie and Worley were already there, as was Bonness. DiLeonardo was present, with that besotted look on his face again as he maneuvered around the conference table for a seat next to Freddie.

Lowery was freshly shaved but was more rumpled than usual, making Dane think that he had truly just arrived from Virginia, on the early-bird flight.

"The ISU really worked on this," he said quietly. "You're to be congratulated on noticing the pattern so quickly, but catching this guy isn't going to be easy. He's the worst kind of killer, the Bundy type. He's as cold as ice; he's intelligent, resourceful, and totally without a shred of guilt.

"I have a list of similar murders: slashings, no suspects, no evidence. It's possible some of them were done by the same guy. Some of them are impossible, because they took place at roughly the same time on opposite sides of the country as some of the other murders, but there's no way of telling which one to eliminate.

"The murders started approximately ten years ago. ISU puts his age in the early to mid-thirties. Most serial killers start killing in their early twenties. But ten years of successful killings means he's going to be very hard to apprehend; he's experienced, he has learned from his mistakes and perfected his crime. He knows what he's doing. He has studied forensics and police procedure, and he's very careful to leave no identifiable evidence behind."

"Could he have been a cop?" Bonness asked. "Maybe in the military?"

"Not likely," Lowery replied. "He wouldn't deal well with authority of any type, so it isn't feasible that he would have been able to complete any type of military or police training. He wouldn't even have been accepted as a candidate.

"He's white; all of the victims have been white, and serial killers seldom cross racial boundaries. He's athletic, very strong. He's an organized killer, very confident, and that's the worst kind. An unorganized killer is messy, makes mistakes, has no clear plan. This guy has everything planned, down to the last detail. He doesn't knock the victims out or tie them; he's confident that he can control the situation, and so far, he has. The weapon he uses is a knife from the victim's kitchen, which he leaves at the scene. Since there are no fingerprints, the weapon can't be connected to him. He takes no trophies. ISU thinks he stalks the victims, possibly for weeks beforehand; he enters the house when no one is home, becomes familiar with it. He's very patient.

"He rapes, but doesn't use restraints, and that's a slight aberration. Some women will fight even with a knife at their throat. For some reason, his victims haven't."

Because he soothes them, at first, Dane thought violently. He made them think that they wouldn't be hurt if they just didn't fight. He was gentle, and he used a rubber. They were paralyzed by the unexpectedness of being attacked in their own homes, and in that first terror, they believed him. But those were details Marlie had given him, so he kept quiet.

"He doesn't blindfold the victims," Lowery continued, "doesn't keep the corpses. Again, those are traits of the organized killer. It was surprising that he cut off Mrs. Vinick's fingers, because mutilation isn't one of the traits—"

"We think she scratched him," Dane interrupted.

Lowery sighed. "If so, that's even more evidence of his intelligence. He couldn't risk his skin samples being found under her fingernails. A brutal but effective solution. He doesn't panic. He thinks on his feet, and isn't a slave to a rigid plan.

"He likely holds down a full-time job, is outwardly

normal. The other murders were all done at roughly the same time for each area. In one area, the murders were committed in the daytime, meaning he was either unemployed or working nights somewhere. I suspect he was working, because there's nothing about this man that would attract attention. He's methodical, predatory, and has this down to a science. His car will be several years old, nothing flashy, the kind of car you would see hundreds of in any neighborhood. Middle-class all the way. He could walk into police headquarters and no one would think anything about it, except to ask how they could help him.

"There is the danger that he's escalating. Until now, he has kept himself under control, spacing out the murders. Killing on two successive weekends could mean that he is beginning to need the thrill of the hunt more often. I know there haven't been any slashing murders reported this weekend, but it's possible the victim simply hasn't been found."

A quick look passed between Dane, Trammell, and Bonness. They knew there hadn't been another murder, because Marlie hadn't had a vision.

"Identification at this point is impossible," Lowery said. "Unless he makes a mistake and leaves some evidence behind to link him to the crime, he'll have to be caught in the act."

It was a grim group that returned to headquarters, though Lowery hadn't told them much that they hadn't already known. The killer was a smart son of a bitch, and ordinarily they wouldn't have had a prayer of catching him. Dane was silent, thinking of Marlie. She was their secret weapon; she would be the one who caught him.

It broke on the news that afternoon. Dane was surprised that the leak had taken that long; for something to remain a secret at city hall for a week was almost unheard-of, particularly something that dramatic. It was the headline story for all the local television and radio news; he caught it on the radio while he was driving home.

"A source in city hall has confirmed that police believe a serial killer is stalking women in the Orlando area," the announcer intoned solemnly. The plummy voice continued, "Two recent murders appear to have been committed by the same man. Two weeks ago, Nadine Vinick was murdered in her home, and a week later Jacqueline Sheets was found murdered in *her* home. Chief of Police Rodger Champlin refuses to comment on the cases or say if they have any suspects. He does urge women in the city to take precautions for their safety—"

He snapped off the radio, infuriated by the knowledge that the killer was getting a real rush from this. He had expected the news to break, was prepared for it, but knowing that the bastard was laughing and soaking up all the attention was still hard to take.

Marlie was sitting curled on the couch when he got home. The television was on, though the news program had advanced to the weather portion. He tossed his jacket across a chair and sat down beside her, then lifted her onto his lap. They sat silently, watching the meteorologist point to this high-pressure system and that low one, make sweeping movements of his hand to indicate their projected movement, and finally make his prediction: hot and muggy, the way it had been all day, with the ever-present possibility of thunderstorms.

"Anything interesting happen today?" she asked.

"The local FBI gave us the character profile they had worked up; this guy has probably been moving around the country for the last ten years, leaving a string of victims behind, and nobody has a clue what he looks like, or a shred of evidence that connects to him." He hugged her to him. "But we're working on getting a list of new accounts from the utility companies. It's a long shot, but it's something."

She had changed into shorts and a T-shirt when she had gotten home from work, and he stroked his hand appreciatively over her bare thighs. "What about you? Anything interesting happen in the accounting department?"

She snorted. "Get real. The most exciting part of the day was when a man called, irate because he had been charged an overdraft fee on a bad check when he had been a customer of the bank for years."

"Bet that got the old ticker revved up."

"I almost fainted from the stress of it all." Marlie sighed and climbed from his lap. "I'd better see what's in the kitchen if we're going to eat tonight."

"Want me to go out for something?" he offered.

"No, I'm not in the mood for takeout. I'll think of something. Why don't you just sit here and read the newspaper? You look as if you need to unwind a little."

He definitely agreed with that assessment, and went into the bedroom to change out of his sticky, wrinkled clothes. Marlie poked around in the refrigerator and cabinets before deciding on chicken stir-fry. She was glad Dane had gone along with her suggestion, because she needed more time by herself. He was so intuitive that he would soon figure out that something more than the situation was upsetting her, and she didn't want to be around him until she had herself more under control.

She hadn't been paying much attention today when the head of accounting had been talking to the irate customer, trying to explain and soothe without backing down, but suddenly she had been overwhelmed by frustration and anger. Startled, she had automatically looked around for the source, and only then realized what had happened. She was picking up the department head's emotions.

She had quietly panicked, sitting frozen in her chair and trying to shut out the flow of emotion. To her surprise, it had stopped as abruptly as it had started, though the conversation behind her had continued.

She didn't know if she had succeeded in blocking it, or if her ability to read people was merely sputtering to life again. Either way, Dane wouldn't like it.

She knew that he viewed the visions differently, that he didn't see them as a threat to his privacy. But if her ability to read people returned in full force, she didn't know if Dane would be able to accept it. He hadn't liked being the target of clairvoyance, which was not, and never had been, her major talent. If he knew that she could read him at will . . . he would probably leave, even though she had promised that she wouldn't invade his privacy. She had to face that likelihood. Dane cared for her, but she doubted that he cared enough to stay under those circumstances. It wasn't anything new; people had always been uncomfortable around her.

The decision not to tell him had been easily made. She didn't know what was happening: if her abilities would return in full force, if she would recover only a portion of her former capability, or if she would be even stronger. She hoped it wasn't the last possibility, for if her empathic powers returned stronger than before, she would have to move into an underground bunker to find any peace. It was a certainty that Dane wouldn't share that bunker with her.

She felt as if she were living in limbo with him. There had been none of the customary courtship stages, no getting to know each other. They had been thrown together in a crisis, had first been adversaries, then, abruptly, lovers. They had never had a discussion about their relationship, whatever it was. He had simply moved in, and she had no idea what to expect. After the killer was caught, would he simply return to his own house with a blithe "See you around" or—or what? If circumstances had been normal, the logical step, the one she had expected, would have been for him to spend a few nights each week with her.

She needed emotional security. She could bear anything if she had a solid foundation to fall back on, but she wasn't certain she had that with Dane.

It was silly, considering that she was living and sleeping with the man, but somehow she couldn't bring herself to ask him outright what his intentions were. She admitted to herself that she was frankly afraid of hearing the answer. Dane wasn't a man who would prevaricate; he would bluntly tell her the truth, and she wasn't ready for that. Later. Everything had to wait. After this was all over, then she would be able to handle anything he said, even if it was exactly what she didn't want to hear.

She had fallen in love with him, but she didn't fool herself that she knew all about the kind of man he was. For all their physical intimacy, he kept a large part of himself private, safely secluded behind an iron wall. Sometimes he watched her with a silent, intent speculation that was almost frightening, because she couldn't read any desire in his eyes during those times.

What was he thinking? More important, what was he planning?

The media were relentless. The phones in headquarters rang endlessly. Reporters camped outside the chief's office, outside the mayor's office, outside police headquarters. Both uniformed and plainclothes officers began taking evasive action when entering or leaving the building, going to extraordinary lengths to avoid the hassle.

Even worse than the media were the crank calls that began pouring in. Hundreds of people in Orlando suddenly recalled suspicious persons skulking around Dumpsters and storefronts. People with grudges found revenge by phoning in anonymous tips, accusing the person they disliked of being the killer. Every night officers investigated panicked calls of a prowler in the house, but most times it was nothing. Several mothers-in-law turned in their daughters' despicable husbands, certain that the lazy bastards were guilty of all manner of unspeakable crimes. The hell of it was, all of it had to be investigated. No matter how wild an allegation, it had to be checked. The uniformed officers were run ragged, worn down by the sizzling heat and never-ending demands on their time.

Chief Champlin held a news conference, hoping to ease some of the intense media pressure. He explained that there wasn't a lot of information he could give them, because of the ongoing investigations. But logic was a useless weapon; it didn't satisfy the voracious appetite for facts, for stories, for airtime and column space. It didn't sell newspapers or jack up the ratings numbers. The reporters wanted juicy, gory, frightening details, and were frustrated when none were forthcoming.

Carroll Janes watched the news programs and read the newspapers, and smiled with satisfaction. The police couldn't give the media much information because they didn't have much. The stupid saps were overmatched, just as all the others had been. He was too smart for them to catch—ever.

18

ALL IN ALL, CARROLL JANES WAS PLEASED WITH THE FRENZY.
Just two punishments, and look how he had taken over as
top story. Of course, he would have to take back his
insulting thoughts about the Orlando PD; they weren't as
stupid as he had feared. Though the second punishment *had*
been rather obvious, a lot of departments wouldn't have
made the connection between the two, for after all, he had
left the fingers intact on the second one. It had irritated him
when the Vinick bitch had scratched him and he had been
obligated to go to the extra trouble of removing her fingers
and disposing of them, but at least fingers were small and
easy to get rid of. Dogs had no trouble with them at all, and
the tiny bones, if any remained, were unidentifiable.

There was no way the cops could catch him, but at least
they *knew* about him; it added an extra fillip to the process.
It was nice to be appreciated, rather like the difference
between an actor performing in an empty theater and one
performing before an awestruck, standing-room-only

crowd. He enjoyed the details so much more, knowing that the police would be amazed at his intelligence, his inventiveness, his absolute perfection, even while they cursed it. How gratifying it was to know one's opponents were properly respectful of one's talents.

He had been frustrated in his attempt to find another transgressor, for experimental purposes, but Janes considered himself a patient man. What would be, would be. It would be cheating to rush things; it would take away from the power of the moment. He had been more content since the news had broken, for of course, it was always exhilarating to read about oneself, to be the topic of conversation on everyone's lips. Even Annette, at work, had talked of little else. She had told him about all the elaborate precautions she was taking, as if he would ever be challenged by her, the little sow. But it amused him to commiserate with her, to feed her fear and drive her to even more ridiculous safety measures. She refused to even walk to her car by herself, as if he had ever dragged anyone off the streets. How pedestrian that was—he chuckled at his own wit—when the real challenge was to take them in their own homes, where they felt safest.

Annette was at lunch on Wednesday when a tall, buxom brunette sailed up to the counter, her face tight with anger. "I want to speak to someone about the service in this store," she snapped.

Janes gave her his best smile. "May I be of assistance, ma'am?"

The crux of the problem was that she was on her lunch hour and had stood for fifteen minutes in the clothing department trying to get someone to exchange a blouse for her. She still hadn't been waited on, and now she wouldn't have time to eat lunch. Janes controlled a thrill of anticipation as she ranted on, fury in every line of her body.

"I'll call the clothing department and make certain you're taken care of immediately," he said. "Your name is . . . ?"

"Farley," she said. "Joyce Farley."

He glanced at her hands. No wedding ring. "Do you have an account with us, Miss Farley?"

"That's *Ms.* Farley," she snapped. "What difference does that make? Does a customer have to have a charge account before this store is interested in her?"

"Not at all," he said politely. It was simply easier to get vital information if she was in the computer bank. She was one of those prickly, man-hating feminists. The anticipation grew stronger; he would enjoy punishing her. He slid a form toward her. "If you don't mind, would you fill out this complaint form? We like to follow through on all complaints, and make certain the customer is satisfied with our action."

"I really don't have time for this. I'm going to be late back to work already."

"Then just your name and address will do. I'll pencil in the details myself."

Hastily she scribbled her name and address at the top of the form while he phoned the clothing department and spoke with the head clerk. He smiled again as he hung up. "Mrs. Washburn will be waiting personally to make the exchange."

"This shouldn't have been necessary."

"I completely agree." He slid the form off the top of the counter.

She turned to go, took a step, then abruptly stopped and turned back. "I'm sorry," she said. "I have a terrible headache and I'm angry, but I shouldn't have taken it out on you. It wasn't your fault, and you've done everything you can to help me. I apologize for being so nasty to you."

He was so taken aback that it was a moment before he could say, "Think nothing of it. I'm glad I could be of service." Conventional reply, one that was mouthed thousands of times a day by thousands of bored salespeople, because it would mean their jobs if they said what they really wanted to say. Ms. Farley gave him a brief, hesitant smile and walked away.

Janes stared after her, fury rising in him. Viciously he crumpled the complaint form and threw it in the trash. How dare she apologize! She had ruined everything. That wasn't the point. Punishment was the point. He felt cheated, as if a ripe prize had been dangled in front of him and then snatched away. He had already begun to feel the flow of vitality, and known the hunger to let his power have free rein. Now he was left with nothing! He should kill the bitch anyway, to teach her that she couldn't act any way she wanted and then escape the consequences by whining an apology.

No. Rules were rules. He had to obey them; it would ruin everything if he didn't. There were certain criteria to be met, standards to be upheld. If he couldn't maintain those standards, then he would *deserve* to be caught. No matter how much he wanted to discipline her, he had to save himself for the true lessons.

Marlie sat very still at her desk, trying to control her trembling. Thank God it was lunchtime, and almost everyone had gone out to eat. She had brought her lunch and a book, intending to spend a quiet hour reading. She had been happily engrossed in the book, absently munching an apple, when a dark sense of mingled anger and anticipation had filled her. It hadn't been as overwhelming as a full vision, but she had recognized the source. There was no mistaking the cold evilness at the core. And then, suddenly, the anger had intensified, but the anticipation was gone, and she sensed disappointment instead.

She had come to know him. His mental force hadn't been strong enough for her to "see" the events, but she knew without seeing. He had selected his next victim, and something had happened to deprive him of his sadistic pleasure.

He was out there. And he was hunting.

* * *

"He's looking for someone," she told Dane that night. She prowled restlessly around the room. "I felt him today."

He put aside the newspaper he had been reading—which was full of slightly hysterical and mostly erroneous stories about the Orlando Slasher—and focused the full intensity of his attention on her. Even the planes of his face hardened; she had grown accustomed to that roughhewn face, seeing it through the eyes of love, but abruptly she perceived him again as she had seen him the first time they had met: Dane Hollister the cop, the Dane Hollister who was dangerous.

"What happened?" he asked, a bite in his tone. *"When* did it happen? Why didn't you call me?"

She shot him a brief glance and resumed her aimless pacing. "What could you have done?"

The answer was "nothing," and she saw he didn't like that. "It was during my lunch, about twelve-thirty. All of a sudden he was there. I could feel his anger, but he was excited, too, like a kid anticipating a treat. He had picked her out, I know he had. Then something happened, I don't know what, but she got away and he was disappointed."

"And then?"

"Nothing. I couldn't feel him anymore."

He was watching her closely. "But you can tell when he's choosing his victim?"

She shrugged. "I did this time."

"Anything else? Could you tell anything about the victim?"

"No."

"The slightest detail would help—"

"I told you, no!" she suddenly shouted, wheeling toward the bedroom. "Don't you think I've tried?"

He moved like a tiger pouncing, springing up from the couch and catching her before she could reach the bedroom and close the door between them. He wrapped his arms around her from behind, pulling her tightly against him. Now he could feel the slight tremors running through her, the shaking that hadn't completely left her since lunch. "I'm sorry," he murmured, rubbing his rough chin against her temple. "I know how hard this is for you. Are you okay?"

She hesitated, then reluctantly admitted, "I'm a little spooked."

He rocked her back and forth for a minute, letting her absorb the security of his presence. She had been living with the stress for almost a month now, and it had to be much worse for her than for him. She needed a break. He brushed her hair back from her face, thinking hard. "Want to go see a movie?"

"That was your solution last time," she said tautly. "Going somewhere."

"Did it work?"

Involuntarily she relaxed a little. She was so tired; it felt good to lean on him. "You know it did."

"Then let's go to a movie. Isn't there something you'd like to see?"

"I don't know." She was hesitant. "I haven't been to a movie since the first murder."

"Then it's time. I haven't seen a movie in a couple of years. What interests you?"

"I don't know what's playing." She turned to face him, and managed a smile. "I'd rather just go for a drive, I think."

He was relieved to feel the tension easing out of her. He would have preferred to take her to bed, but knew she was too tense to enjoy it. "Then that's what we'll do," he said.

The twilight air was thick and heavy when they left the house, the heat lingering even though the sun had gone down, and thunder rumbled dully in the distance. Dane rolled down his window, hit the interstate highway, and turned the car's nose toward the Gulf Coast, straight into the approaching storm. The cloud bank loomed overhead like a great beast, streaks of lightning darting across its purplish black underbelly.

The air blasting in through the open window became

cooler, almost cold, and carried with it the sweet, dusty scent of rain. Marlie sat silently beside him, her eyes on the storm. The first raindrops splatted on his windshield. He had time to roll up his window and turn on the wipers, and then they were plunging headlong into the torrent sweeping toward them.

He had to slow down to almost a crawl, while the thunder boomed around them and lightning cracked. Other, more prudent drivers pulled off the highway completely, seeking shelter under overpasses or simply getting out of traffic. A few daring souls continued into the heart of the storm, as darkness crashed down and the puny efforts of headlights could illuminate only a short distance in front of them.

Marlie was motionless. The fierceness of the storm emptied her, sucked out all sense of self and filled her instead with its own raw power. She knew she should have been afraid of electrical storms, but she wasn't. The magnificence of it filled her with awe, and the energy unleashed somehow replenished her.

Dane always drove with his interior lights extinguished, and the car was a dark cave. He didn't speak, and neither did she. She felt no need for words. She was safe and dry while the fury thrashed around them, battering the car with sheets of rain and gusts of wind that rocked it from side to side. Dane held it steady, his powerful forearms rippling with muscles as he fought to counteract the storm's fury. Marlie didn't feel even a second of uneasiness; she was safe and she knew it.

Eventually they drove out of the storm, leaving it flashing and rumbling sulkily in the distance. It continued to rain, but it was a light, steady, ordinary rain. They rolled their windows down a couple of inches and let the sweet air flow around them.

He looped around on the next exit and headed back toward Orlando, this time chasing the storm.

She leaned her head back. The storm had intensified

everything; she had never felt quite like this before. Her heartbeat was slow and heavy, a silent drum; her body felt heavy and ripe, pulsing with life. She wanted him, wanted his hardness and passion inside her. She could feel him beside her, taut with sexual awareness. His eyes were on the road, but his attention was focused on her; she knew that he was acutely aware of every movement she made, of the slight rustling of her breathing, the warm, faint scent of her body.

"Dane," she said. The one word vibrated in the darkness.

He was sweating; she could see the sheen on his face whenever they met an oncoming vehicle. Heat was rolling off him in waves. Excitement coiled in her belly; he was almost out of control, in a way she hadn't experienced before. Always before, even the first time, no matter how aroused he was, he had managed to hold himself back until she had been satisfied. He had wanted her before they had left the house, and the primal fury of the storm had only fed his hunger, just as it had awakened hers.

She wanted to ask him if he loved her, but the words wouldn't come. He was with her here and now, and if sexual attraction was all he felt, she would find out all too soon. Since the present was all the time she was guaranteed, she decided to stop fretting and make the most of it. Wasn't that what life was about anyway? Hadn't she learned anything from all the pain, her own and others, she had experienced? No one made it through life without suffering. The trick was to make the most of the present, and enjoy the gifts of life as they were offered.

She reached out and gently trailed one finger along the crease between thigh and groin, feeling his muscles harden beneath her touch. His erection was like iron, pushing against the constraint of his pants. She stroked her finger up and down the length of it.

His breath hissed out between his teeth. "Stop teasing me."

"I'm not teasing," she murmured, almost purring the words. "I'm very serious." She delved her hand between his legs, and he groaned as involuntarily he shifted them apart. The car slowed, then he gathered himself and increased speed again.

"I can't stop now," he said with stifled violence. "There's too much traffic."

"See any interesting motels?" she asked, her tone absent as she concentrated on unbuckling his belt.

He shuddered, sucking in his breath to give her hands more room. He wanted her to stop, but at the same time he was helpless against the pleasure. "I don't have any rubbers with me." Except for their first night together, he had used a condom every time they made love. That first night, he hadn't been able to think of anything except getting inside her. Privately he had been shocked at his own carelessness, which had never happened before, and since then had made damn sure it hadn't happened again.

The solution of stopping at a drugstore occurred to her, but she dismissed it. She didn't want the distraction, and he wasn't in any shape to go shopping. "You'd better drive faster," she said, just as she eased down his zipper and worked her hand inside his pants to close her fingers around his naked shaft.

A rough moan burst out of him. She savored the sound of it, just as she savored the feel of him throbbing in her hand. She knew that a few quick, hard pumps would finish it for him, so she deliberately kept her touch light, slow, and lingering. His face was set in taut lines as she snuggled closer and kissed the underside of his jaw. Her breasts were pressed against his muscled arm, and she could feel the fine tremor shaking it.

"You're going to pay for this," he warned.

She bit his earlobe. "Sounds interesting. Got any ideas?"

He had several, but none that could be enacted in the car. He only hoped he wasn't stopped for speeding, because he didn't think there was any way in hell he could get his pants fastened. She continued to gently caress him, keeping him achingly hard. "Are you having fun?" His lungs were constricted, preventing him from speaking above a growl.

"Oodles." Her tongue dipped briefly into his ear, and he shivered convulsively. "I'm not ready to stop, either. You just keep on driving."

He did. He drove as he had never driven before, with a desperate concentration that still wasn't enough to block out what she was doing to him. A rough laugh escaped his throat. "You little witch, you're enjoying this."

She gave him a slow, satisfied smile. "Of course I am. You usually drive *me* crazy. How does it feel to be on the receiving end?"

"Like I'm going to die," he gasped.

She looked around and pinpointed their location. "We'll be home in another five minutes. You can hold out that long, can't you?" She continued caressing him, using every bit of knowledge she had about his body to enflame him further. She licked him very delicately.

He gasped again, his body going rigid. "Maybe."

By the time they got home he was wild, his hips surging upward with every lingering stroke of her hand. He literally dragged her out of the car and into the house, where they stumbled into the bedroom, tearing and pulling at each other's clothes. They were still half-clothed when they fell onto the bed. Dane managed to delay until he got a condom on, then he flipped her onto her stomach, kneed her legs apart, and drove into her with battering force.

Marlie dug her fingers into the bedcovers, her body shuddering under the force of his thrusts. She was as excited as if she had been the one so deliciously tormented. She lifted her buttocks, wriggling against him to take him deeper, though that didn't seem possible. He groaned with every thrust, wild, guttural sounds that hung in the darkness of the night. And then his entire body tensed and he shoved violently into her and held himself there, shuddering, hoarsely crying out his satisfaction as his climax shook him to the core.

Afterward he eased down to lie half beside her and half on her, his movements blind and uncoordinated, his big body trembling. His chest heaved as he struggled to get enough oxygen, and she could feel the force of his heartbeats thudding through his body. "Oh, God," he wheezed. "That damn near killed me."

"Really?" she murmured. "I thought you enjoyed it. But if you didn't like it, I won't do it again—"

He thrust his hand into her hair and turned her head so he could stop the words with a hard, forceful kiss. "I'll try to bear up under the strain."

"My hero," she said, nipping at his lower lip, then returning for a deeper kiss.

A bass purr rumbled in his chest. He turned her in his arms and lifted himself to loom over her. "Now, lady, let's see about you."

He took care of that very well, leaving her exhausted, limp, and satiated. Afterward they lay together in the darkness, listening to the rain. She absently played with the curly hair on his chest. After a while she yawned and said, "Did you close the car door?"

He went still, thinking very hard. Then he said, "Oh, hell," and heaved himself out of bed. She lay there giggling while he pulled on his pants and stumbled through the dark house. She heard the front door open, then close again a couple of seconds later. In another minute he came back into the bedroom. "Yes, I did, smart-ass," he rumbled.

"Well, I didn't remember."

He chuckled. "I didn't either." He shucked his pants and crawled back into bed. He yawned as he gathered her close to him again, tucking her protectively into his embrace. "When this is over," he murmured into her hair, "we're both going to need a vacation. Which do you like, the mountains or the beach?"

Her heart gave a little skip of happiness. It was the first time he had said anything about a mutual future, even if it was something as casual as planning a vacation. "This is Florida," she replied. "We can go to the beach anytime."

"Mountains it is, then. We'll rent a cabin with a hot tub, get naked, unwind, and shock the squirrels."

"It's a deal."

The phone rang, and Dane stretched out his arm to get it. "Hollister," he said lazily. Lying against him as she was, Marlie felt him tense. He sat up and swung his feet to the floor. "Okay, okay, I'll be there in about fifteen minutes. Try to keep the media from driving everyone into hysterics."

He hung up the phone and turned on the lamp. "There's been another slashing murder," he said, hastily pulling on his clothes.

Marlie sat up, fear consuming her as she remembered earlier in the day when she had felt the killer searching for another victim. She and Dane had gone for that drive out of town; had they been so far away that she wouldn't have been able to pick up the killer's energy? Had he acted, after all, and somehow she hadn't felt him?

19

WHAT'S THE VICTIM'S NAME?" DANE ASKED, LOOKING AT THE body as the police photographer snapped pictures from different angles.

It was a typical murder scene, if there was such a thing. The place was working like a beehive, and most of the people weren't doing a damn thing except standing around. The house was crawling with policemen, and the neighborhood was crawling with reporters, who ignored the light rain in favor of getting comments from anyone who would talk to them. Bonness was there, Trammell was there, Freddie and Worley were there—hell, it looked as if every detective on the squad was there—and the chief was reportedly on the way. The fingerprint guys were dusting their black powder over everything, the forensic evidence people were vacuuming—it was a zoo.

"Felicia Alden," Freddie said. "Her husband, Gene, found her. He's a sales rep for a pharmaceutical firm and had been away on business."

"And he just happened to come home right after his wife

was murdered," Dane said wearily. They all looked at one another. They had seen the other scenes, and this was nothing like them, except for the fact that a woman had died from knife wounds. For one thing, the victim was still clothed, and she was lying on the bed as if she had been arranged there. There was no indication of sexual attack.

Dane sighed with relief. Marlie hadn't failed; they all knew, and it was just a matter of proving it, that Gene Alden had probably murdered his wife and tried to set it up so that it looked like one of the serial murders. Alden had likely thought that, since the media had reported there was no evidence left behind, he would be safe when investigation turned up only forensic material that could be linked to him; after all, he *lived* there.

"Take him in for questioning, and find out about any life insurance policies he had on her," Bonness said. "Or maybe if he caught her fooling around. I'll try to calm the reporters down, but I can't say much until we actually charge the guy, so they won't believe me." He looked depressed at the thought of facing the horde of shouting reporters.

"At least we'll be able to do something about this one," Freddie said.

Trammell walked over to join Dane, and they went outside. Reporters were mobbing Bonness, shouting questions at him. He was trying to talk, but they kept interrupting him. "I guess Marlie didn't have a vision with this one," Trammell said.

"Not even a glimmer, but it was scary anyway; it wasn't a vision, but this afternoon she sort of locked on to him. He had picked out his next victim, but something happened and he lost her."

Trammell whistled. "How's Marlie?"

"On edge. It's wearing her down."

"No wonder. I wish there was some way to make it easier for her."

"I'll make damn sure she's okay," Dane said grimly. "By the way, how's the work going on my house?"

"The floors are almost finished, and the furniture will be delivered this weekend. You can move back in on Monday, if you want."

Dane snorted as he got in his car. "Get real, buddy."

Trammell laughed. "Yeah, that's what I thought. See you in the morning."

As Dane had expected, Marlie was still awake when he got there. "It wasn't him," he said, and watched the tension ease out of her face. She looked very small, curled up in a corner of the couch with her robe pulled tightly around her. "Probably the woman's husband did it, and tried to make it look like the other murders." He held out his hand to her. "Come on, honey, let's go back to bed."

Janes carefully controlled his elation Friday afternoon as he watched the indignant customer stalk away. Annette was there, so it wouldn't do to let even a hint of his emotions show. At last! He was going to savor this one; too much time had passed, three weeks, for him to accurately compare it with the last one. Besides, he had concluded that it was the haste of the last punishment that had ruined it for him. He would do this one the way it should be done, with slow and careful planning, letting the anticipation build. He needed at least a week to do it properly.

He checked the calendar, though of course, he didn't need to. It was just a part of his incredible precision. Yes, the earliest possible date would be next Friday night. The weekends were the best because those were his off days, and he could sleep late the next day. Let the media hoopla, satisfying as it was, die down a bit. The frenzy had nothing to feed on, though there had been that silly burst of hysteria the other night when some salesman had offed his wife and tried to blame it on him. It hadn't worked, of course; the stupid bastard hadn't had the same attention to detail. The cops had immediately seen through him. The television reports had sounded a tad disappointed.

Yes, this one would be good, maybe the best yet. The

woman had been a complete bitch, the kind he had always despised on sight: lean, tanned, brittle, overloaded with jewelry of questionable taste. She flaunted her money. She might have a security system, or even guard dogs. The possibility was intriguing. It would be a real test of his genius, if she did. He disregarded the probability of a husband; that had never stopped him before.

He looked down at the name she had scribbled, repeating it in his mind, savoring the syllables. Marilyn Elrod. Anticipation was already flooding his body with energy. Marilyn Elrod. He hummed a few bars of a song, substituting her name. Mar-uh-lynn, O Mar-uh-lynn, ta dum de dum something. It was played before the Preakness race. The joke was, she didn't know she should be running.

Friday night, Marlie asked him how work was coming along on his house. Dane lied without hesitation. "It's almost finished," he said. "There's been a delay on the furniture Trammell ordered."

The furniture was in place, and everything looked great, but he had no intention of moving out of Marlie's house until the killer was caught. Another weekend had come and gone without a murder. A few sarcastic reporters were beginning to ask if the police were *certain* there was a serial killer, or had they just been spooked by a similarity between the murders of Nadine Vinick and Jackie Sheets?

"Feel anything today?" he asked.

She shook her head. "Nothing concrete. Just kind of uneasy." And when she had been driving home, she had passed a young couple so engrossed with each other that they had been passionately kissing there on the sidewalk. She had been in that automatic state that takes over when driving, her guard down, and suddenly she had been reading the young man. Again, it had been such a shock that she had immediately shut down, withdrawing from the emotional contact. She had had the wry thought that she hoped they would find somewhere private soon, given the intensity of the young man's arousal, or she wouldn't be the only one shocked.

Then the realization dawned that twice now she had been able to control the contact, to break it off. Even before, at the height of her abilities, she hadn't been able to do that. She had learned how to partially shield herself, but had never managed complete protection. Okay, so the initial contact had slipped in, when she had been relaxed; she had still been able to immediately sever the connection.

She hadn't wanted the return of her abilities, but suddenly she was filled with a sense of triumph, and contentment. Gleen hadn't won, after all. The healing process had taken a long time, but in the end, she was the victor. She had emerged from the trauma even stronger than before, better able to control the gift that had been given her. She had even, with Dane, gotten past the physical terror and learned the joy of sexual pleasure. She couldn't have done it two years ago, even a year ago, but her healing had finally progressed to the point that she had won.

"Is he hunting?" Dane asked.

"Who knows? Like I said, it wasn't anything concrete. Maybe it's just that I dread tonight so much."

"Maybe I can do something about that," he said in a slow, deep tone. He was leaning against the cabinets while she threw together a quick meal, getting in her way as usual. She looked at him and went weak in the knees. He looked so thoroughly male that every cell in her body responded. Dane was always slightly rough-edged, even when his clothes were freshly ironed, but even more so now with his shirt wrinkled, his dark hair disheveled, and his jaw showing both the mark of this morning's assault with a razor and the need for another shave. As always, he still wore his shoulder holster, the butt of the big pistol sticking out under his armpit; he was so accustomed to being armed that he no longer noticed it. Those sharp hazel eyes were greener than usual, and held a predatory gleam as he watched her.

"Maybe you can," she agreed, her own voice huskier than usual. Maybe, nothing; she was certain of it. His sexual power over her was so strong that the only thing that kept her from panicking was the knowledge that, when she chose, she could drive him just as crazy. She might have doubts about his emotional involvement, but there was no mistaking his physical response. All she had to do was brush against him, or give him a certain look, or even do nothing, and he would get aroused.

It sometimes startled her, for she was certainly not a sex kitten by any stretch of the imagination. She had always deliberately dressed to downplay her femininity, because she had never wanted to attract attention of any kind. None of that mattered with Dane; it was as if he never saw the clothes, but looked straight through to the woman. She still dressed the same, out of habit and convenience—after all, the clothes were *there*—but now, a bit surprised at herself, she realized that she didn't feel the need to continue the camouflage. Things had changed. She didn't have to hide herself away to protect her mental privacy, nor did she have to worry about the sickening intrusion of sexual advances. Dane intruded with sexual advances quite often, and there wasn't anything the least sickening about them.

She was stronger. Her abilities had changed. She had healed, and was in control. She felt another little jolt as she truly realized, for the first time, that she was no longer at the mercy of her own mental powers.

She could dress any way she wanted. She could buy the trim, stylish clothes she had always admired, or even something downright sexy.

"What are you thinking?" Dane asked uneasily. "You've been staring at me like I'm Tweetie Bird, and you're a hungry cat."

She let her gaze drop lower, and delicately licked her lips.

His face changed. He straightened away from the cabinet, every muscle in his powerful body growing taut. Then he reached out and deliberately turned off the stove. She raised her eyebrows at him. "This may take a while," he explained, his eyes heavy-lidded as he pulled her close.

Nothing happened that weekend, though Marlie couldn't shake the uneasy anticipation. She was beginning to think she would feel that way until the man was caught. But she managed the tension better than she had the weekend before, perhaps because of her newfound confidence. She tested her control when she stood talking to Lou for a while on Saturday, deliberately opening herself up; she immediately read her neighbor's emotions, and when she decided to stop, the flow was blocked. It was like opening a door and closing it again. She could do it!

It wasn't an entirely satisfying experience, however; she found that Lou was extremely disapproving of the situation next door, with that man, even if he was a police officer, just blatantly moving in. Lou felt it set a bad example. Marlie wondered who she was setting a bad example *for,* since she was the youngest person in the neighborhood anyway. Most of her neighbors were retirees.

It didn't help when Dane chose that moment to come out on the front porch, wearing only a pair of disreputable jeans. Because they had spent a lazy day around the house, he hadn't shaved. He looked big, rough, slightly dangerous, and wholly masculine, with his powerful chest bare. "Hi, Lou," he called. "Sorry to interrupt. Honey, do you know where I put my gun oil?"

"You didn't," she replied. "You left it out. *I* put it in the kitchen, second drawer from the right."

He flashed a grin at her. "Sorry." Then he disappeared back into the house.

Lou's face was stiff, her eyes wide as she stared at the spot where he had stood. Marlie shifted uncomfortably. This was one time she definitely didn't want to open that door and feel what Lou was feeling.

Then Lou exhaled in a long sigh. "Holy cow," she said.

Her cheeks looked a little flushed. She gave Marlie a slightly embarrassed look. "I may be old-fashioned," she admitted, "but I'm a long way from blind."

Marlie entered the kitchen a few minutes later to find Dane calmly reassembling his pistol. There was no way he could have cleaned the weapon in the time that had elapsed. "You did that deliberately," she accused, keeping her voice level with an effort. Lou had still been a little giddy when she had gone inside.

He grinned, not pausing in his brisk, practiced actions. "I like ruffling her feathers," he admitted. "I thought about unsnapping my jeans, but I decided against it. Overkill."

"It's a good thing. You might not have made it back into the house unscathed, if you had."

"Really pissed her off, huh?"

"Not exactly."

He glanced up, his expression quizzical. Marlie smiled sweetly at him. "Lou fell in lust with your manly form, big boy."

After a startled moment, he began laughing. He was too heavy for her to budge his chair, so she shoved the table away and planted her hands on his shoulders as she straddled the chair and sat down on his lap. His laughter stopped, that familiar tenseness hardening his features. "I know how she feels," Marlie whispered, nuzzling his jaw. Her heart pounded at the scent of him, all hot, musky male mingled with the sharp odor of gun oil. She moved slowly against the ridge in his jeans.

"Wait." His protest was feeble. "I have oil on my hands."

"So? I'm washable," she murmured, and that was all he needed to hear.

The weekend was wonderful. She ignored the frisson of alarm that was always there, never quite allowing her nerves to settle down, and enjoyed what she had. There were no visions, no false alarms of copycat murders. She suggested going over to his house to see how everything looked, but he was in a lazy mood and didn't seem interested. They watched television and read. They tried out recipes . . . or rather, Marlie tried them out, while Dane kept her company and sampled the results. And they made love, often. It was exactly the type of life Marlie had always wanted, and always thought impossible.

By Monday, with nothing happening over the weekend, the press reports were scathing. The Orlando PD had overreacted, like Chicken Little squawking about the sky falling. One columnist suggested that not only had they made fools of themselves on the basis of two similar murders, but the hoopla might even have triggered the copycat murder of Felicia Alden.

"They forget," Dane said sarcastically, "that the department isn't responsible for all the publicity; the media did that. We've been trying to keep everything as low-key and under wraps as possible."

Marlie gave him a troubled look. "But now, with them calling it a false alarm, people will stop being as careful. It's giving him a greater opportunity of success."

"Tell that to the press. All they'll give you is the smart-ass answer that they don't make the news, they just report it."

"If reporting was all they did, that would be fine. But they angle it, they slant it, they 'interpret' it."

He saw how truly upset she was; he was pissed off, but the press reports bothered Marlie on a deeper level. He remembered that her experiences with the media generally weren't pleasant, and he swiftly changed the subject.

Janes was pleased with what he had accomplished over the weekend. He had made several casual trips by the Elrod house, and been delighted by what he had discovered so far. The house was large and upscale, set in the middle of a big lot with an excess of landscaping that would provide plenty of cover. Six-foot-high fences marked the boundary lines of almost every lot in the neighborhood, which further restricted any nosy neighbor's observation.

He hadn't seen Mr. Elrod, though the city directory listed

one. Was he out of town? It was a concern that had been laughably easy to answer, though the answer had come from an unexpected source. Marilyn Elrod had conveniently left the house not five minutes before her mail was delivered, and Janes had simply used the opportunity to collect the mail and go through it. Some of the usual assortment of junk mail had been addressed to a Mr. James Elrod, confirming his existence. A more interesting envelope bore the imprint of an Orlando law firm. Janes didn't hesitate to open it, and what he read greatly pleased him. It seemed Mr. and Mrs. Elrod were currently embroiled in divorce proceedings, and Mr. Elrod had recently moved out. What a pity.

He kept the letter, since it had been opened, and shoved the remainder of the mail back into the box. A quick look around the house revealed that there was no dog—if there had been, it would have been barking like mad by then— but there was an alarm system. Not particularly sophisticated, he saw, but a problem. Still, every system had a weakness, and he had no doubt that he would be able to find a means of entry. All in good time, though, all in good time. He wouldn't make the mistake of hurrying as he had the last time.

"We're being made to look like fools," Chief Champlin growled. He wasn't in a good mood. The mayor had raked him over the coals for jumping the gun and driving old women all over the city into hysteria. Not only that, the bad publicity had cost the city money. Orlando relied heavily on the tourist trade, with visitors from all over the world coming to the Mouse House. The rate of occupancy at the local motels and hotels had fallen off since the news had broken.

"I can't believe this," Bonness said plaintively. "Everyone is bitching because someone *hasn't* been murdered!"

"There were just two murders. Granted, the details were eerie in their similarity—"

"The FBI agrees that it's the same man," Dane broke in.

"We didn't go out on a limb in this, Chief. He's out there. With the Bureau's help, we think we've identified at least seventeen other killings that he's done."

"So maybe he left the city when the news broke!" the chief snapped.

Dane shook his head. "We think he's still here."

"On the basis of what information?"

"Marlie," he wanted to say, but he didn't. He contented himself with replying, "He never left an area so soon before. We're going with his established pattern."

"The mayor wants to know, and so do I, just what you're doing with your time. If there is no evidence, just what in hell are you doing?"

Dane's face had taken on a stony look. Trammell saw the signs of an incipient loss of temper and stepped in. "We've received lists of names from the utility companies on new customers for the past year, and we're working our way down the list, investigating all the men on it. With the profile the FBI gave us, we'll be able to narrow it down to a few possibilities."

Chief Champlin was from the old school. He didn't like Trammell's slick sophistication, his money, his snappy clothes, or his exotic looks. He did, however, respect the political ties that Trammell had in the city, courtesy of that same money. He growled a reply along the lines of "They'd better come up with something soon, or else," and left Bonness's office.

Bonness sighed and pulled out a handkerchief to blot his forehead. "Shit. Anything on those names we're running?"

"Nothing that sets off any alarms, but we still have a lot of names to go."

"Okay. Let me know the minute you hear bells."

"Will do."

"Son of a bitch," Dane said between his teeth as they returned to their desks.

"Calm down, partner. He doesn't know what we know,

because we can't tell him about Marlie. I don't think he'd understand."

"Bonness was right." Cold fury was still in Dane's voice and eyes. "These bastards won't be satisfied until another woman is killed."

Janes made good use of his time at night. He found a secure place to leave his car, he checked out the situation with the neighbor's dogs. There were two, but one of them tended to bark at everything, and the other, across the street, would join him. The barking usually elicited no more than a few irritable "Shut ups."

Marilyn Elrod was a party girl. She was out hitting the bars almost every night, which may have been the reason Mr. Elrod was no longer living there. So far, though, she hadn't brought anyone home with her. Her active night life gave him plenty of opportunity to make sure things were perfect.

Her night life also gave him a means of getting into the house. Thick shrubbery grew all along the house, right up to the garage. She had a habit of backing into the garage, so she could just drive right out whenever she left; since she was facing ahead, it was child's play for him to slip from his hiding place in the shrubbery into the garage, before the automatic door closed. She never looked back.

The door leading from the garage into the utility room wasn't wired into the security system, though the door from outside into the garage was. It was locked, but locks weren't a problem for him. It was another skill he had taught himself, with the aid of a mail-order locksmithing course that he had taken under an alias, just as a precaution. Another little detail he had foreseen and taken care of.

The first time he entered the house he had simply walked around and familiarized himself with it. He kept himself calm, not letting anticipation trick him into acting before he was really ready, as he had the last time.

The second time, he explored more. He opened her closets and went through her clothes, deciding that her taste seemed frozen in the eighties singles-bar style. She spent a fortune on makeup, he noticed, prowling through her bathroom vanity.

He satisfied himself that there were no guns in the house. Guns could be a big problem.

Then, humming to himself, he explored the kitchen. She wasn't much on cooking; the refrigerator held mostly microwave stuff. But she had catered to the fashion of having a large rack of butcher's knives standing on the shiny black countertop, something he had counted on. Since she cooked so little, it wasn't likely that she would miss a knife. He examined each knife, *tsk*ing at the dulled edges on the stainless steel blades. Most women no longer had any pride in the domestic skills, which he deplored. If she had kept her knives in good condition, he wouldn't have to take the slight but admitted risk of removing one of them so he could put a proper edge on it.

All in all, he severely disapproved of Marilyn Elrod.

"Come to the house for dinner with Grace and me tonight," Trammell said on Friday.

Dane leaned back in his chair. He was so sick of the damn lists on his desk that he wanted to cram them all into the trash. He never would have believed that so many people had moved into the Orlando area in the past year. What really pissed him off was that they weren't turning up a damn thing. He was glad the weekend had come, though he and Trammell were on call.

"It's Friday," he reminded Trammell.

"So? You have to eat on Fridays the same as any other day, don't you?"

"Marlie gets pretty tense on Fridays."

"Then it will do her good to take her mind off things. If she has a vision, she can have it just as well at my house as at hers."

"Okay, let me call her."

Marlie advanced the same arguments that he had, and he gave her the same answers Trammell had given him. She really didn't need much convincing, because she had spent the week dreading the approaching weekend. Dinner with Trammell and Grace would be a welcome distraction.

She had spent a few of her lunch hours shopping this past week, and for the first time wore one of her new outfits that evening. Trammell had said to dress casually, and she did, but the slim, white cotton pants and sleeveless white vest were very fetching, if she did say so herself. Dane shared the opinion. When she came out of the bedroom, his gaze settled on her bare shoulders and the deep vee of the neckline. "Are you wearing a bra?" he asked in a strained voice.

She looked down at herself. "Why?"

"I just want to know. Are you?"

"Can you see anything?" she asked, returning to the bedroom to examine herself in the mirror.

Dane followed. "Damn it, Marlie, are you wearing a bra or aren't you?"

"Do I need one?"

"I'll find out for myself," he said in frustration, reaching for her.

She slipped away, giving him a roguish smile. "Down, boy. You'll have to wait until later to find out. We're going to be late if we don't leave right now."

"I haven't seen that outfit before," he said as he followed her out the door.

"It's new. I bought it this week."

He studied her back, trying to decide if he could make out the outline of a bra beneath the white vest that bared a disconcerting amount of her. It wasn't that it was indecent, just that he wasn't used to seeing her dress like that. He liked the hell out of it, but he didn't want anyone else to appreciate the view.

Trammell's house was large and airy, with sleek furnishings in light, soft colors that opened up the rooms even more. His taste, Marlie admitted, was wonderful. There was a sense of space, serenity, and coolness, enhanced by lush indoor plants and overhead fans gently stirring the air.

Dinner was relaxed, with a lot of joking and teasing. Marlie asked Trammell when Dane's house would be finished, and he lied without turning a hair. More delays, he said solemnly.

Grace told Marlie all about the wedding plans she was making, and how lucky it was that they had planned on a long engagement because she would need all the time to plan a large, formal wedding. Trammell broke out in a slight sweat as he listened to the discussion, but the look of wild panic was gone; he was adjusting to the idea of marriage in connection with himself.

A series of thunderstorms, normal during the hot summer nights, popped up and entertained them with dramatic flashes of lightning and booms of thunder. After dinner, Trammell took several photographs of them all, and that led him into showing the thick albums of shots he had taken over the years.

Dane figured prominently in a good many of them, and Marlie studied his face with interest. He looked different, somehow, in the stark black-and-white photos Trammell had taken. Seeing her interest, Trammell settled beside her to tell her all about every shot.

It was earlier than usual when Marilyn Elrod arrived home, but the passing storms had knocked out the electricity at the bar, and the patrons had been politely but firmly invited to leave. She was also tipsier than usual, and when the garage door didn't lift, she pressed the button on the opener again. Still nothing happened.

"Damn it," she muttered, pointing the opener directly at the doors and holding her thumb on the button. Nothing. She threw it onto the car seat beside her. "Stupid batteries."

She tottered in her high heels up the walk to the front

door, then stood weaving as she tried to remember the code for the security alarm. She only had a few seconds after unlocking the door, she didn't remember how long, to punch in the code and prevent the alarm from sounding. She hated that damn alarm, so shrill it hurt her eardrums. The security system had been James's idea, not hers. Men and their gadgets.

It took her a minute to notice that the little red light above the lock wasn't shining. Damn, was everything in the house malfunctioning?

Then she laughed softly to herself. Of course! The electricity was off here, too. She should have noticed how dark the neighborhood was.

She fumbled the key into the lock and opened it, stumbling a bit over the threshold as she went inside. Damn, it was dark as a tomb! How was she supposed to see?

Candles, she thought. She had candles. She had bought an assortment of incense candles, thinking of the sexy atmosphere they would make when she brought a lover home. There hadn't been any lovers yet, but she was prepared just in case. James had probably had some flashlights around, but she didn't know where they were. It was likely he had taken them with him, the bastard. He wouldn't want his little dolly to be caught in the dark.

But where had she put them? The kitchen? That didn't seem like the right place to put incense candles.

On the other hand, that's where the matches were, and maybe she had put them there. She slipped out of her heels as she felt her way through the dark house to the kitchen. She found the matches first and struck one, relieved by the small flare of light. Three of them burned down before she located the incense candles.

She lit one immediately, to give herself light. Well, this was a fine end to a boring evening, she thought in disgust. She might as well go to bed, since she couldn't even watch television.

She carried the sack of candles in one hand and the

lighted candle in the other as she went upstairs, only stumbling once. "Oops," she whispered. "Have to be careful. I'm carrying fire." The thought made her giggle.

In her bedroom, which she had changed completely after James had left—she had burned all the sheets the bastard had slept on—she lit the candles one by one and set them on her dresser, so she could see the effect when they were reflected in the mirror. Yeah, she thought. Pretty damn sexy. The thick aroma of incense rose, and she coughed a little. Maybe she should go for unscented candles.

She began to undress, leaving her clothes were they fell. The incense grew stronger, and she coughed again.

She halted, her head tilted a little to the side. Had she heard something? She waited, but the house remained silent. Too silent, she thought. Yeah, that was the problem. She was accustomed to hearing the quiet hum of the refrigerator, the clocks, the ceiling fans. Without them, she was too aware of the sounds outside.

When she was naked, she pulled on a robe and belted it loosely at her waist. She was suddenly too sleepy to do the complete cleansing cream routine, so she simply wet a washcloth in the dark bathroom and scrubbed it over her face, then dropped it in the basin.

She yawned as she went back into the bedroom. The candle flames flickered, sending up sickening waves of incense. She leaned over to blow them out, and a face appeared in the mirror.

She whirled around, a scream lodging in her throat.

"Hellooo," the man said softly.

20

THE ALBUM WENT SKIDDING ACROSS THE FLOOR, STARTLING everyone. Marlie was on her feet, swaying, her face utterly white. Her pupils were so constricted that only tiny black dots remained, the intense blue of the irises dominating her stricken face.

"Dane," she said. Her voice was thin and almost soundless.

"Oh, hell." He lunged out of his chair and caught her weight against him as her knees began to buckle.

"What's wrong?" Grace cried in alarm.

Both Dane and Trammell ignored her, their attention focused on Marlie. She was breathing in heavy, jerky gasps, her eyes wide and fixed as she stared at something they couldn't see.

"Dane?" she said again, pleading despair in her voice. Her hands clutched his shirt, twisting the fabric.

Dane gently eased her down onto the couch. "I'm here, baby," he said, hoping she could hear him. "Is it happening again?" She didn't answer. He shook her insistently. "Marlie!"

The jerky breaths roughened into dry sobs. "He's looking at me," she said in a voice that was no longer hers.

Dane couldn't get her to respond again. She sat motionless, her breathing evening out until it was barely perceptible. Her eyes were open and unseeing, unblinking.

"Shit," Trammell said softly, crouched beside Dane. "When I said she could have a vision here as well as at home, I was joking."

"Alex," Grace said in a very clear, determined voice. "What is going on?" Her lack of understanding proved that Trammell had been his usual closemouthed self, not telling even Grace about Marlie's abilities.

Dane didn't take his worried gaze off Marlie's face. She was beyond his reach and he didn't like it, didn't like knowing that she was going through hell and there was nothing he could do. The waiting was over.

"Alex." Grace sounded as if she were about to resort to violence.

"Go ahead," Dane murmured absently to Trammell. "You might as well tell her."

"Tell me what? What's wrong with Marlie?"

Trammell stood up and put his hand on Grace's arm. "Marlie's psychic," he explained softly. "She has visions of the murders while they're happening."

"Psychic?" Grace glared at him. "I'm warning you, Alex Trammell—"

"It's true," Dane said. Violently he wished that it weren't. "She's having a vision now. Another murder is happening right now."

"If this is a joke—"

"It isn't," he said flatly.

"Don't tell anyone," Trammell instructed. "Other than the three of us, and Lieutenant Bonness, no one else knows."

She looked uneasily at Marlie. "How long does this last?"

Dane checked his watch. It was 10:36, earlier than the other two murders had happened. "I don't know. Half an hour, maybe." The last time, when Jackie Sheets was killed, it had taken him longer than that to bring her out of it. Somewhere in the city, at this very moment, another woman was dying a horrible death; Marlie was gone from him until it was finished.

At 10:54, her right hand twitched convulsively several times, in an abbreviated stabbing motion. Both Dane and Trammell understood the significance of the small movement. Sweat rolled down Dane's face despite the chill of the air conditioning. He caught her hand and held it, hoping that the contact would comfort her on some unconscious level. Trammell paced restlessly, his dark eyes hooded and dangerous.

"Make some coffee," Dane murmured. "Or tea. She'll need it." Grace moved toward the kitchen, but Trammell waved her back to her seat and went to do it himself.

At eleven, Dane sat down beside her and eased her against his shoulder. Her arms felt icy to his touch. He shook her gently. "Marlie? Can you come back to me now, honey?"

Her eyes didn't even flicker.

He waited a couple of minutes and shook her again, calling her name. He saw some small movement in her eyelids.

He began stroking her hands and arms, trying to rub some warmth back into her skin. "Wake up and talk to me, honey. Come on, pull out of it."

Slowly her eyes began to close, and she drooped in his arms as the rigidity began to leave her muscles. He shook her again, not wanting her to slide into that deep, unconscious sleep. "You have to talk to me, Marlie. You can't go to sleep yet."

With visible effort she lifted her eyelids and looked at him. She was dazed, incomprehension in her eyes. Panic edged into the blue depths as she fought for consciousness, for her sense of self. It was another moment before recognition flared, followed closely by horror and anguish.

"Shhh, shhh," he whispered, holding her close. "I'm here, baby." He could feel the tremor that started in her legs and worked upward, becoming stronger and more violent with every passing second. He reached out, and Trammell put the coffee cup in his hand. Carefully he held it to Marlie's trembling lips, forcing her to sip. She was gray now, as the shock worsened.

"Please," she begged, her voice shaking and barely audible. "Let me lie down."

"Not yet. Drink some more coffee." He wanted to carry her to bed and let her sleep, while he held her close against the terrors of the night, but ruthlessly he pushed that impulse away. He had to get the details before he could allow her to rest.

"Tell me about it," he demanded, putting force in his voice. "Tell me what you saw."

She closed her eyes, trying to pull away from him.

"Damn it, Marlie!" He wasn't gentle when he shook her this time. "Tell me!"

Her mouth trembled wildly, and tears seeped out from under her lashes. "It's dark," she said. She took a deep breath and let it out with a shuddering sigh. She opened her eyes. "The electricity is out. The storm knocked it out."

That flat, expressionless tone entered her voice, as she let herself sink into the horror again. She stared straight ahead, and Dane braced himself. "She came home earlier than expected. She's drunk. She puts some candles on the dresser, lights them. Incense candles, in little glass holders. They stink. She takes off her clothes, puts on a robe. Nice of her; saves him some trouble. She goes into the bathroom and washes her face. When she comes out, he's waiting for her."

"Dear God," Grace said quietly, as the horror of what she was hearing, of what Marlie had endured, began to come home to her.

"He comes up behind her when she bends down to blow out the stinking candles. She sees him, turns around. She doesn't scream; they almost never do. He's already too close, the knife already at her throat. Even though she's drunk, the stupid bitch, he can see that she knows what's happening. Good. There's no point in punishment if they don't understand the lesson.

"He makes her take off the robe. She's too skinny; he can see her ribs. He doesn't like that. She's terrified. She doesn't argue when he tells her to lie down. Not on the bed—the floor. He prefers the floor. He's gentle with her, but he can see in her eyes that she knows who he is, knows his power. That's nice, but it takes away the element of surprise.

"Afterward, he helps her to her feet. He kisses her cheek, strokes her hair. He pulls on her hair a little to make her tilt her head back, and she looks up at him. Please, she says, begging already. No pride. They never have any pride. He smiles at her, and watches her eyes as she feels the first sting of the blade. Then he lets her go, so the race can start."

Trammell swung away, muttering a curse.

Marlie wasn't looking at any of them, wasn't seeing any of them. "She doesn't run. She just looks at him. He cuts her again. Says, *Run bitch*. She doesn't. She swings at him, hits him in the face. Then she's all over him, hitting, kicking, screaming at him. He's furious; this isn't the way he wanted it to work. Stupid bitch. If that's the way she wants it, he'll give it to her. He slices deep, again and again, to get it over with. He hates her. She was stupid, she ruined it for him. It was supposed to be a race, like the Preakness. Maryland, O Maryland." Marlie sang the last little bit.

"She's down. His arm is tired. She isn't even grunting now when the knife goes in. He gets up . . ." Her voice suddenly wavered. Dane felt her jerk, then begin to tremble again.

"What?" he asked softly.

Her face was colorless, her eyes stark. "He looked in the mirror," she said. When Dane merely stared at her, puzzled, she said it again. "He looked in the mirror! He saw himself—and *I* saw him!"

"Jesus Christ." Every hair on his body stood upright, and a chill chased down his spine. Trammell and Grace were utterly silent, their attention riveted on her.

"He's completely bald," she whispered. "He shaves his head. A square jawline. H-His eyes are a little too small, a little too close together."

Dane couldn't contain himself. He was on his feet, his powerful body tense and ready for action. "We'll get a police artist in," he said. "He'll work with you on the sketch, and then we'll get it to all the television stations and newspapers in the area." It was their first break, and it was a huge one. "Call Bonness," he told Trammell. "Fill him in on what's happened. We need to find the woman, too, one way or another. Marlie, what did she look like—" He turned back to her, and broke off in midsentence. Her head had fallen back against the couch and her eyes were closed, her hands lying limply in her lap.

"Ah, honey," he said softly. She had given in to the debilitating exhaustion. For a moment he had forgotten the physical price she paid in this. He wanted to kick himself. Immediately he pushed all other concerns aside; others could take care of the details in finding the victim, but only he could take care of Marlie. "You handle everything," he told Trammell as he bent over her to lift her in his arms. "I'm taking her home."

"You can both stay here," Trammell said, but Dane shook his head.

"She's confused when she first wakes up, and it takes her a while to get her bearings again. It'll be easier for her if she's in her own home."

"How long will it be before she'll be able to talk to an artist? Bonness will want to know."

"Noon, at the very earliest. More likely two or three in the afternoon."

"He won't like waiting that long."

"He'll have to." With Trammell and Grace flanking him, and cradling Marlie gently in his arms, he carried her to the car. Trammell opened the door for him, and he placed her on the seat, let the back down into a reclining position, and buckled her seat belt.

"Do you need me?" Grace asked. She eyed Marlie's pale, unconscious face worriedly. "I'll be glad to sit up with her."

"I can handle it. She'll sleep for at least twelve hours."

"Well, all right. Call me if you need me."

"I will," he said, and kissed her cheek. "Thanks for the offer, though."

Marlie didn't move during the drive through the misty, foggy night. Having seen it before, he wasn't as worried as he had been the first time, but on the other hand, now he knew how exhausted she would be, and how long it would take her to recover. This had to be the last one. He couldn't let her go through this time and again. As soon as they got a police sketch ready and to the media, he would put his plan into action.

He had barely gotten Marlie home and placed her on the bed before the phone began ringing. Irritably he snatched it up. "Hollister."

It was Bonness. "We can't wait until tomorrow to get started on that sketch. This is information that needs to be in newspapers tomorrow."

"It'll have to wait," Dane said harshly. "She can't do it now."

"She *has* to."

"She can't," he snapped. "This isn't a choice she has, or that you have. She's unconscious with exhaustion, and it takes hours for her to recover."

"Maybe a doctor can give her adrenaline or something, to snap her out of it—"

Dane ground his teeth together to control a flare of fury. "I'll break anyone's arm who comes near her with a needle," he said, his voice hard and crisp.

Bonness paused, taken aback more by the warning implicit in his tone than the actual words. The words were bad enough, but the tone was deadly. Nevertheless, he tried again. "Damn it, Hollister, you need to get your priorities straight—"

"They're as straight as they're going to get," Dane interrupted again. "No one is touching her. I'm turning off the phone here, so she won't be disturbed. If you need me, call the beeper number, but don't waste my time trying to change my mind. Talk to Trammell if you have any doubts about her condition."

"I already have," Bonness said reluctantly.

"Then why the hell did you call?"

"I thought maybe there was something we could do—"

"I've already pushed her as far as possible, to get what information we did. This hit her harder than the last time, harder and faster. Just leave her alone and let her sleep. I promise that I'll call as soon as she wakes up."

"Well, all right." Bonness was still reluctant. "But the chief is going to be pissed. Obviously, for us to have a sketch, there has to be a witness. He's going to want to know who and how."

"You can keep it quiet about the sketch until we actually have one. Until then, just say that a street informant gave us the word on another murder."

"That's a good idea. Okay. But when he finds out—"

"Blame it on me," Dane said impatiently. "I can take the heat. But make it damn plain that if anyone gets to her, he'll have to go through me."

"I'll do that."

Hanging up the phone, Dane first cut off the ringer, then turned his attention back to Marlie. She lay limply where he had placed her, her chest barely moving. She had lost weight during these past few weeks, he realized, and she hadn't had a lot to spare. When this was over, he was definitely taking her away on that vacation he had promised her, someplace quiet and serene, with nothing to do but eat, sleep, and make love.

Gently he removed her clothes and placed her, naked, between the sheets. Since he had moved in, she hadn't worn anything to bed anyway. He checked the time: fifteen after midnight. Time for him to be in bed, too. He doubted he would sleep for quite a while yet, but at least he could hold her. He threw off his own clothes and got into bed beside her, then gathered her thin, silky body against his sheltering warmth. The faint, sweet scent of her skin soothed him. He buried his face against the thick swath of straight, dark hair. "Sleep, baby," he whispered. "I'll take care of you."

He began trying to rouse her at eleven the next morning, but she was totally unresponsive. His beeper had been driving him crazy all morning. Bonness had called every half hour. Trammell had called twice. Grace had called three times, demanding to know if there was anything she could do, if she needed her to spell him so he could rest.

Trammell had hit on the idea of having the television and radio stations broadcast the information that there had been another murder, but that so far no victim had been found, and asking that people check on their neighbors and call their relatives to account for everyone. It was a tactic likely to drive some people into hysterics if a family member was unreachable for any reason, and Chief Champlin had gone through the roof when he heard it on the radio. The mayor was apoplectic. Didn't they realize the risk they were running with lawsuits? He envisioned thousands of people suing over emotional distress. Bonness covered his ass by blaming it all on Trammell, even though he had given his approval. When the chief called him, screaming in fury, Trammell coolly pointed out that the tactic had precedence, that during natural disasters and emergencies, such as heat alerts, people were often urged to check on their friends and relatives. That calmed the chief down somewhat, but he still wasn't happy.

All over the city, telephones and doorbells rang.

Carroll Janes, indulging in a lazy morning in bed, was

puzzled when he turned on the television at noon and heard the news. If the cops hadn't found the victim, how did they know there was one? He wasn't alarmed, though; he was almost certain no one had seen him, even at a distance, but even if someone had, he couldn't be identified. He yawned and turned off the television set. Let them look.

By twelve-thirty, Dane had gotten Marlie roused enough to visit the bathroom and drink some water, but she had gone to sleep again as soon as he helped her back into bed.

At 12:55, his beeper went off again. The number displayed was Trammell's. Impatiently Dane dialed it.

"We found her," Trammell said, his voice cool and expressionless. "Her name is Marilyn Elrod. Her estranged husband heard the bulletin and called from his girlfriend's house to check up on her. When he didn't get an answer, he drove over. Her car was in the driveway, and she always put it in the garage, so that bothered him right away. He still had keys to the house and let himself in, and found her upstairs in her bedroom."

"Marilyn," Dane said. "Not Maryland. Marilyn."

"Yeah. Look, do you want Grace to come over and stay with Marlie so you can go to the scene?"

He didn't like leaving Marlie, but it was his job, his weekend on call. "Send her over," he said gruffly.

"She's on her way," Trammell said. "I gave her directions. She should be there in five minutes or less."

"You think you're smart, don't you?"

"I just know you, pal."

Grace proved that she drove faster than Trammell by knocking on the door right then. Her normally serene face was troubled when Dane let her in. "How is she?" she asked immediately.

"Still sleeping. I managed to rouse her for a few minutes about half an hour ago, but she was still too groggy to think. She conked out again as soon as I got her back to bed." As he talked, Dane was slipping into his shoulder holster and putting on his jacket.

"I'm on second shift tonight," Grace said, following him to the door. "I brought my uniform so I can stay until the last possible minute, but I can't stay much past two-thirty. I know it isn't enough time," she said apologetically.

Dane swore under his breath, but didn't see anything else he could do. "It's okay. She'll be more alert next time. Let her sleep until two, then *make* her respond to you. Tell her where I am, and that I'll be back as soon as possible."

Grace nodded in understanding. As he started down the steps, she said hesitantly, "Dane? Um . . . I was wondering. That is . . . Marlie . . . Can she . . . ? Oh, damn," she said in frustration. "I don't know how to say this."

Dane turned back. It was unusual for Grace to lose her composure. He saw how uncomfortable she looked, and took a guess. "Can she read your mind?"

Grace bit her lip. "Alex said you were good at doing that yourself," she muttered. "But . . . yes. Can she read my mind?"

"She says she doesn't." Let Grace see if she could find any more reassurance in that than he did. "And I didn't read your mind. It was a lucky guess, because the idea makes *me* uncomfortable too."

Grace nodded, understanding completely. Dane went to his car, and she stepped back inside, closing the door against the heat.

She followed his instructions and at two began shaking Marlie and talking to her. To Grace's relief, Marlie blinked her eyes open after only a minute. "Grace?" she asked, the word as blurred as if she had been drinking.

Grace sighed with relief. "Yes, it's me. I've made some fresh coffee. Would you like some?"

Marlie swallowed, trying to push aside the thick fog in her brain so she could think. "Yes," she finally said.

"I'll get it. Don't go back to sleep."

"I won't." It was difficult. Marlie fought it, struggling to understand. Grace was here . . . Where was Dane? Had something happened to him? Sudden panic dissipated the fog even more, and she managed to sit up. She was nude under the sheet; she clutched the bedcovers to her, looking around, trying to gather some clue about what was going on.

Grace returned with a cup only half-full of coffee, making it easier for Marlie to hold without spilling any. "Where's Dane?" she blurted, her eyes dark with distress. "Has something happened to him?"

"No, of course not!" Seeing her distress, Grace sat down on the bed and patted her arm. "Dane's fine. He left just an hour ago."

"Left?" Confused, Marlie closed her eyes. Behind her lids flashed a nightmare image, surrounded with what seemed like a hundred candles, reflected in a darkened mirror. She caught her breath as part of her memory returned. "What day is this?"

"Saturday," Grace replied.

"Then it was just last night that it happened." She inhaled deeply, shoring up her fragile control, and opened her eyes.

"The victim's been found. Dane's at the scene now." Grace knew, from talking to Trammell, that the scene was exactly as Marlie had described it. If she hadn't been there herself last night, and listened to Marlie talking, she would never have thought it possible. Being an eyewitness, however, tended to make one a believer. "He didn't want to leave you alone, so I came over."

"Thank you," Marlie said. "I'm so foggy when I first wake up that it's easier if someone is here to explain things." She had always gotten through it alone until Dane, but still, it was nice to have someone there.

"I can't stay much longer. I'm on second shift," Grace explained. "Will you be okay by yourself?"

"I'll probably go back to sleep." Marlie sipped the coffee. "Does Trammell mind that you work nights?"

"Of course. If I were on first shift and he worked nights, I wouldn't like it either," Grace said, her eyes twinkling. "However, being an intelligent man, he hasn't made the mistake of demanding that I quit work or try to arrange my hours around his."

"He's doing better. We mentioned the word 'marriage' several times last night, and you couldn't see the white around his eyes."

Grace considered the matter. "His eyes did look rather like those of a panicked horse, didn't they?" she said judiciously. "I keep reminding him that it was his idea, and he can change his mind any time he wants. Then he thinks that I must not be sold on the idea myself, so he tries to convince me it's the right thing to do and convinces himself instead."

"Dane may have to prop him up at the altar."

"I expect he'll be steadier by then. I hope so, anyway. It's just that it happened so fast between us. Things were out of control from the first time we went out together. Alex likes to be in control, so it's driving him crazy."

Tactfully Grace didn't ask about Marlie's relationship with Dane, and Marlie was grateful. There was nothing settled between them, no hint of permanence despite their living together, and she was too tired to try to explain. She liked Grace a lot, but she had never had the comfort of a confidante, nor had she grown up spending long hours giggling with other girls her age while they dissected every detail of their lives. Until Dane, she hadn't really spent a lot of time just talking with anyone.

"Do you want to shower while I'm here?" Grace asked. "That will clear out a few of the cobwebs. Trammell said that they'll want you to work with a police sketch artist as soon as possible, to get the killer's description out."

Marlie shoved aside the memory of his face. She couldn't let herself dwell on it right now. "I'd love a shower. I'll hurry, so you won't be late."

Grace left her alone, and Marlie got out of bed. She felt stiff and uncoordinated, her muscles weak. She had made an effort with Grace, but things still hadn't quite clicked back into their proper places for her. She would have to make an even greater effort to concentrate, later on, so the sketch would be accurate.

She kept the shower brief, and as cold as she could stand it. After dressing and drinking more coffee, she felt more in control. Grace was reluctant to leave, but Marlie shooed her on her way, then forced herself to walk around rather than lying down as she wanted.

How long would Dane be gone? Would he immediately take her to headquarters, so they could get started on the sketch? She paced until she was dragging, then stretched out on the couch. Sleep came almost immediately, but right before the dark curtain dropped, she had one last, very clear thought:

How long would it be before she no longer saw that face every time she closed her eyes?

21

THE SKETCH ARTIST WAS A SHORT, PLUMP REDHEAD NAMED
Esther. Esther had small, quick, ink-stained fingers, shrewd
eyes, and a voice like Tinkerbell's. Her age could have been
anywhere between thirty and fifty; her hair was liberally
salted, but her skin was smooth and fresh. Like most artists,
she wore whatever was at hand. In this case, it was a pair of
cutoff sweatpants, one of her husband's shirts, and sneakers
but no socks.

With a cup of coffee in her hand to sustain her, Marlie sat
beside Esther and worked through the details of the killer's
appearance. It was a painstaking chore, involving endless
variations of eyebrows and noses, size of eyes, width and
thickness of lips, slant of jaw, jut of chin. She could close her
eyes and picture the face, but duplicating it on paper wasn't
easy.

Dane didn't interrupt but was always close by, frequently
refilling Marlie's coffee cup. It had been close to six when he
had gotten home and roused her from the couch, where
she had been sleeping. Though he had been solicitous of her,

his mood had been grim as he drove her to police headquarters.

"The bridge of the nose should be higher," Marlie said thoughtfully, examining the latest effort. She'd done work with police artists so many times in the past, she knew what they needed from her. "And his eyes were a bit closer together."

With a few deft strokes of her pencil, Esther made the changes. "Is this better?"

"Better, but still not quite right. It's the eyes. They're small, hard, and close together. Sort of deep-set, with a straight browridge."

"Sounds like an ugly son of a bitch to me," Esther drawled, making more minute adjustments.

Marlie frowned. She was very tired, but forced herself to concentrate. "No, he really wasn't, not physically. I suppose he could have been called attractive, even with a bald head."

"Bundy was a handsome devil, but he wasn't anyone's dream man. Just shows that you can't tell by looks."

Marlie leaned forward. This time Esther's corrections had brought the sketch closer to the face in her memory. "That's good. Make the forehead a little wider, and taper the skull more. His head wasn't that round."

"More like Kojak, huh?" Deft pencil strokes changed the shape of the head.

"Stop. That's good." Seeing the face on paper made her feel a little queasy. "It's him."

Dane came over to stand behind Marlie and look at the finished sketch, staring hard at it. So that was the bastard. Now he had a face. Now he would be hunted.

"Thanks, Esther," he said.

"Any time."

Marlie stood and stretched, vaguely surprised at how stiff she felt. Trammell, who had been waiting patiently in the background, came forward to stand beside Dane and examine the sketch. "I'll get this circulated," he said. "Take Marlie home and put her to bed before she collapses."

"I'm okay," she said, but the flesh around her eyes was dark with fatigue, and her face was drawn.

Dane didn't argue. "I'll call later tonight," he said, putting his arm around Marlie and urging her toward the door. Once they were in the car, she tried to stay awake, but her eyes drifted shut before they had reached the second traffic light.

As he had the night before, Dane carried her inside, put her on the bed, and efficiently stripped her. "Good night, honey," he whispered, bending over to kiss her.

She put her arms around his neck and clung. "Hold me tonight," she said.

"I will. Go to sleep now. You'll feel better in the morning."

She was in his arms when she awoke the next morning. Seeing her eyes open, Dane turned her to her back and moved on top of her, pushing her thighs apart and settling himself between them. Gently he penetrated, and rocked them both to climax.

His lovemaking made her feel alive again, pushed the ugliness into the background. They lay together for a long time, each finding comfort in the other's embrace. Finally she said, "Tell me about her."

Dane kissed her temple, and held her closer as if his nearness would keep the horror at bay. "Her name was Marilyn Elrod," he said. "Recently separated from her husband, but he was concerned enough to check on her, and went to the house when he couldn't get her on the phone. He seems pretty broken up about it now, when it's too late."

"Marilyn," she said, making the connection. "Not Maryland, then. Marilyn."

"The storm had knocked out the electricity in the neighborhood. She lit candles on her dressing table. Everything else was the way you saw it."

"She fought him?"

"Looks like it. Her knuckles were bruised. Pity she didn't

manage to scratch his face; that would have given us an identifying mark." Though it probably would have gotten her fingers cut off like Nadine Vinick's, but he had never told Marlie that little detail. If she didn't see it in the vision, he certainly wasn't going to add to her burden of knowledge.

"Won't his face be marked? Maybe she cut his lip. Was there any blood other than hers?"

"Not that we've been able to identify," he said carefully. He tried not to think about the savage butchery, the vast amount of blood that soaked the room. Finding a few alien drops of blood wouldn't have been feasible; it would have taken pure dumb, blind luck, and luck hadn't been their best friend so far. If it hadn't been for Marlie, they wouldn't have a clue even now.

"But there should be a bruise, or a fat lip."

"That was Friday night. A cut lip heals quickly, and isn't all that noticeable anyway. A bruise can be minimized with ice, and covered with makeup. This is a smart guy. He'll know all the tricks."

"But you'll catch him anyway."

"Yes," Dane said grimly. "I will."

Carroll Janes stared at the Sunday morning newspaper in infuriated disbelief. The police sketch was eerily accurate, though of course, it showed him completely bald rather than with thick blond curls. He crushed the paper and threw it aside. For the first time, he felt a twinge of alarm, and that made him even angrier. The police weren't supposed to get this close to him! Oh, they wouldn't catch him, but they shouldn't even know this much. Who had seen him? He would have sworn he had been unobserved. Had that stupid bitch had a security camera somewhere? He couldn't believe it, for if she had, it would have shown him the first two times he had entered the house, unless, of course, she had been so stupid that she never checked the tape. The police would have, even if she hadn't. No, there hadn't been a camera. He would have discovered it, had there been.

How had this happened? What had gone wrong?

He took comfort in the fact that, as usual, he hadn't left any forensic evidence behind. No hair, no skin, no fingerprints, no footprints. The knife belonged to the victim, and had been left at the scene. He had taken no trophies, nothing that could link him to the scene. He was safe.

But someone had seen him. He had slipped up—totally unacceptable—and someone had seen him. To atone for his error, he would have to correct it. He would have to find this person, and eliminate him—or her.

"Will you go with me over to the Elrod house?" Dane asked.

Marlie stared at him, so stunned for a moment that she couldn't believe what he'd asked. To actually go into the house . . . Her mind reeled away from the idea. It was bad enough to see it in her mind; to walk into that blood-soaked room was more than she thought she could bear.

Dane's mouth set in a hard line as he saw her sudden loss of color. He clasped her shoulders so she couldn't turn away. "I know what I'm asking," he said harshly. "I know how much it will cost you. I wouldn't ask if I didn't need your help. We're all stumbling around in the dark here, and you're the only light we have. It's a long shot, but maybe, if you were at the actual scene, you'd be able to pick up more about him."

The last scene she'd been at had been when Dusty had been murdered, when she had lain helplessly and watched as Gleen butchered a terrified, equally helpless little boy. She had lived with the memories ever since; it wasn't fair of Dane to ask her to add to those memories. He knew what she'd been through, but he hadn't lived it, so he didn't know the torment as intimately as she did.

She stared up into those fiercely determined hazel eyes, feeling the force of his will batter at her. She could withstand him, she thought dimly. It was much more difficult to withstand the silent entreaties of Nadine Vinick, of Jackie

Sheets, of Marilyn Elrod. She could see all of them, their shades crying out for justice.

Why hadn't she been able to get into *their* minds, instead of his? He had to select them in some manner; maybe one or all of them had known his name. But instead it was his mental energy that had reached out and tapped into hers, forcing her to feel his evil. But she had once before been in the victim's mind, had felt Dusty's death, and it had nearly killed her too. What would it have done to her to have mentally endured that pain and terror again?

"Marlie?" Dane shook her lightly, forcing her to focus on him.

She squared her shoulders, bracing herself. She couldn't turn her back on this now any more than she could have at the beginning. "All right," she said steadily. "I'll go with you."

Once she had agreed, he didn't waste any time. Within five minutes they were on their way. It was just after noon; churches had let out, and children were swarming as they drove through the upscale neighborhood where the Elrods had lived. She sat silently, her eyes on her hands as she tried to prepare herself. She didn't know what to expect; maybe nothing, maybe she would relive the vision, maybe she really would sense something new.

And maybe she would look in the mirror and come face-to-face with a killer.

She knew him, knew that he killed without remorse. He enjoyed it. He gloated over his victims' pain and terror. He wore a human form, but he was a depraved monster who would keep killing until someone stopped him.

Dane pulled into a driveway. The house was sealed with yellow crime scene tape. Though it had been twenty-four hours since the body had been found, neighbors stood in small knots pointing and gawking, rehashing the few details they had gleaned from television and newspaper reports, and adding new gory ones from the multitude of rumors that raced through the neighborhood.

"We think he entered through the garage, when she went out early in the evening," Dane said, keeping a firm hand on Marlie's elbow as they went up the walk to the front door. He held up the crime scene tape for them to duck under. "Because the power was off when she got home, the electric garage door opener wouldn't work. She left the car in the driveway and entered through the front door. The alarm system didn't work, either, because of the power outage, but it wouldn't have helped in any case: It wasn't connected to the door from the garage into the house. People can make some of the dumbest decisions, for the dumbest reasons. Mr. Elrod said that particular door wasn't connected so they would have a way of entering without having to fool with the alarm code. They might as well have put a sign on it saying 'Criminals Enter Here.'"

He talked steadily as he unlocked the front door and ushered her inside. The alarm system had been turned off, because there had been so many people coming and going the day before.

Marlie took a deep breath. The house looked deceptively normal, except for the black powder dusting every slick surface. It had been a very nice, upscale home at one time. She wondered if anyone would ever live here again, if Mr. Elrod would be able to sleep in this house, or be able to sell it if he couldn't. Perhaps it could be unloaded on some unsuspecting snowbird newly migrated from the North. In her opinion, it should be razed.

She looked around at the spacious, open, high-ceilinged rooms. There was a sense of airy coolness; it must have been a wonderful place to live. The downstairs floors were either polished hardwood or designer tile. She wandered silently through the rooms, trying to force herself to relax and let her mind open, but she couldn't lock out the dread of going upstairs. She didn't want to, but knew that she would have to.

Maybe if they waited another day; she wasn't fully recovered from the vision. Maybe that was why she couldn't open the mental door that would allow the impressions to enter. She glanced at Dane, then abandoned the suggestion that had been on her tongue. He hadn't been following her every step, but remained in the doorway of each room while she prowled it. His face was grim, his expression shuttered as she had never seen it before. There was something curiously remote about him, as if he had shut himself off from any appeal she might make.

"Anything?" he asked, seeing her look at him.

She shook her head.

He didn't push her. He didn't urge her to try harder. He didn't try to hurry her, or tell her to go upstairs to the scene. He was just there, waiting, implacable.

But when she put her hand on the railing and her foot on that first step of the staircase, he caught her arm. His gaze bored into hers, an expression she couldn't quite read flickering in his eyes. "Are you all right?"

"Yes." She took a deep breath. "I'm not enjoying this, but I'll make it."

"Just remember," he muttered. "I'm not enjoying it either."

She looked at him questioningly. "I never thought you were."

Then she went upstairs. He was right behind her, his tread silent, his presence as solid as a wall.

Where had the killer waited for Marilyn to come home? Her vision hadn't quite picked up on that; it had begun when he had begun trailing her through the dark house. Maybe, when the electricity had gone off, he had left his hiding place and made himself comfortable where he could see if anyone drove up. She stopped in the hallway and closed her eyes, concentrating, trying to read any leftover energy. Cautiously she opened that mental door, and a buzz of static assaulted her. She slammed the door shut and opened her eyes. She had gotten an impression of many people, of much activity; too many people had been here since the murder, blurring the image.

The door at the end of the hall stood open. That was Marilyn's bedroom. Marlie walked steadily toward it, and once more Dane caught her arm. "I've changed my mind," he said abruptly. "You don't need to go in there."

"Marilyn Elrod didn't need to die, either," she replied. "Neither did Nadine Vinick or Jackie Sheets, or any of the other women he killed before moving here." She gave him a wintry smile and tugged her arm free. "Besides, I've already been in there, remember? I was there when it happened."

Four quick steps carried her into the room. She stopped. She couldn't go any farther without stepping on dark brown bloodstains. There was no way to avoid them; the blood was spattered all over the carpet, the walls, the bed, though the largest stain by far was the huge one beside the bed, where Marilyn Elrod's life had finally ended. But she had fought him all over this room, and left her own blood as her witness. About ten incense candles in their tiny glass pots still sat on the dresser; it was in that mirror that Marlie had seen the killer, looking at him through his own eyes.

She had to open that mental door again, to perhaps glean some other snippet of information. Marilyn deserved that she at least try.

"Don't talk to me for a minute, okay?" she said to Dane, her voice soft, almost soundless. "I want to think."

Maybe the energy was in layers, with the most recent on top. She closed her eyes, picturing the layers, giving them different colors so she could more easily tell them apart. She had to block out that top layer, the one peopled with detectives, uniformed officers, photographers, forensic squads, the multitude who had swarmed the house after Marilyn's death. They had been trying to help, but they got in the way. Mr. Elrod had been here, too, adding another level of energy.

She assigned blue to the policemen and related others, and red to Mr. Elrod. The killer's color was black, the density evil and thick, resisting any penetration of light.

Marilyn . . . Marilyn's color would be a pure, translucent white.

She formed the picture in her mind, seeing the layers, concentrating on them so all else was forgotten. She existed only inside herself, pulling inward so her ability wouldn't be diluted. Very delicately she peeled off the blue layer and put it to the side. Next came the red layer, very thin because Mr. Elrod hadn't contributed much, harder to handle. It, too, went to the side.

Only black and white were left, but the layers were so entwined that she didn't know if she could separate them. Killer and victim, locked together in a life-and-death struggle. Marilyn had lost that fight.

Very clearly she saw that if she tried to pull the layers apart, she might damage them, damage the information they held. She would have to leave them as they were.

Now was the time to open the door. She mentally stepped into the layers, like stepping into a mist, wrapping the energies around her. She let them surround her, soak into her pores. And then she opened the door.

The blast of evil was suffocating, but nothing she hadn't felt before. She forced herself not to retreat from it, to examine it, while fighting to keep it from overwhelming her as it had the first time. She couldn't let herself be sucked into reliving the murder, or the effects would be so debilitating, she wouldn't be able to continue.

The evil layer writhed around her, but bits of white kept touching her, distracting her. She pushed the contact away, intent on reading every black energy wave.

There was nothing new, no mental clue about how he had selected Marilyn as his victim. A touch of white jolted her again. There was something compelling about it, an insistence on gaining her attention.

Marlie held back. She couldn't experience Marilyn's death. She simply couldn't.

But the white layer pressed more strongly. The evil of the killer was pushed aside. Marlie saw it clearly in her mind, and was astonished, for she hadn't done it. She looked back to the whiteness, and that break in concentration was enough to let the white energy in.

Panic squeezed her heart as sheer terror seized her. And then a sense of calm seeped in, a quiet soothing.

She stood bathed in the translucent whiteness. This wasn't the energy of Marilyn's last moments, of her terrified, pain-filled struggle for life. This was the energy of afterward, and it wasn't in the past. It was here. It was now.

There were no spoken sentences, no actual words. Marilyn wasn't suffering anymore. She seemed peaceful. But there was a sense of inconclusiveness; she was reluctant to leave. Justice had not been done, the scale was still unbalanced, and Marilyn couldn't leave until her killer no longer stalked innocent women in the night.

Don't worry, Marlie whispered in her mind. *He made a mistake. Dane will catch him now.*

Though the reassurance was welcome, it made no difference. Marilyn would linger until a resolution.

A noise tugged at Marlie's consciousness. It was irritating, but insistent. Instinctively she recognized its source, and her automatic response.

I have to go now. He's calling.

Still she was reluctant to leave that serenity. She hesitated, and felt one last touch of the white energy.

"—Marlie! Goddamn it, answer me!"

She opened her eyes to Dane's furious, worried face. He was shaking her, and her head wobbled back and forth. She squeezed her eyes shut against the dizziness. "Stop," she gasped.

He did, and hauled her into his arms. She could feel his heart pounding against his ribs like thunder, hard and frantic. He held her head pressed to his chest, and his grip was so tight that it compressed her rib cage.

"What were you doing?" he raged. "What happened? You've been standing there like a damn doll for half an hour. You wouldn't answer me, wouldn't even open your eyes!"

She put her arms around him. "I'm sorry," she whispered. "I didn't hear you. I was concentrating."

"I don't call that mere concentration, babe. You put yourself into a goddamn trance, and I don't like it. Don't you ever do that again, do you hear me?"

She had frightened him, she realized, and like all strong men, he didn't take kindly to it. In his anger he had even called her "babe," something he hadn't done since she'd told him how much she disliked it.

He bent his head down to hers, pressing his forehead against her hair. "This was a bad idea," he muttered. "Let's get the hell out of here."

But because he was a cop, when they were halfway down the stairs he reluctantly asked, "Did you pick up on anything?"

"No," she said softly. "Nothing that would help." She didn't tell him about Marilyn's presence, peaceful but resolute, patiently waiting. That had nothing to do with the investigation. It was private, between herself and Marilyn, both of them victims, in different ways, of the same evil.

Dane opened the door, and she stepped out. The bright sun glared directly into her eyes, momentarily blinding her, and she paused. She didn't see the people rushing toward her until they were right on her.

"I'm Cheri Vaughn with WVTM-TV," a young woman said. "We have learned that the Orlando Police Department is using a psychic named Marlie Keen to aid in apprehending the Orlando Slasher. Are you Marlie Keen?" Then she thrust a fat black microphone in Marlie's face.

Stunned, she stared at the lean, fashionably dressed young woman, and at the burly, shorts-clad man who stood behind her with a camera balanced on his shoulder. A van with the station's insignia blazoned on the side was parked at the curb, and the crowd of neighbors had drastically increased, drawn by the television camera. Roughly Dane shouldered in front of her. "I'm Detective Hollister," he snapped. "You're behind the police line. You have to leave—*now.*"

But the tenacious Ms. Vaughn neatly sidestepped him and once more pushed the microphone at Marlie. "Are you the psychic?"

A confusing flurry of impressions hit Marlie broadside. She couldn't read Dane; his mental shields were too strong. But Cheri Vaughn, ambitious and slightly nervous, was no match for Marlie's abilities. Marlie didn't even have to try; the truth was broadcast at her in deafening waves.

Shock hit her in the pit of her stomach, and she almost choked as the bile of betrayal rose to her throat. It was possible that someone else had leaked the news of her involvement—but no one else had. And only one person had known where she would be at this exact moment.

She felt cold, icy cold, and suddenly alone. Slowly, her face very still, she looked at Dane. He still wore that grim expression, his eyes as narrow and fierce as a hawk's as he watched her. She could barely breathe. Accusation and betrayal were in her expression as she put her hand over the microphone.

"You set me up," she said to the man she loved, the man who had used her.

22

MARLIE TURNED BACK TO THE TELEVISION REPORTER. "YES, I'm Marlie Keen," she said coldly.

"Ms. Keen, have you been working with the Orlando Police Department to help them locate the killer?"

"Yes." The one word was clipped. She could barely contain her fury, her sense of betrayal.

Dane put his hand out, as if to block the camera, but Marlie knocked it aside. Cheri Vaughn plunged ahead. "In what way have you aided them, Ms. Keen?"

"I gave them the killer's description."

"How did you know what he looked like? Did you have a psychic vision?"

Again Dane moved in front of her, his rough face furious. Marlie sidestepped. This was what he'd wanted, wasn't it? She was going to deliver, in spades. "Something like that. I know the killer the way no one else does. He's not a dream man, unless you're into nightmares," she said, borrowing Esther's words. "He's a worm, a coward who gets his jollies by attacking women—"

"That's enough!" Dane roared, pushing the camera down and grabbing Marlie's arm with his other hand, his fingers biting into her soft flesh. "You people leave this scene, *now.*"

Cheri Vaughn blinked at him, looking both frightened and elated. Marlie didn't have to guess how the reporter felt; she knew. She had come here to act a part, with the promise of some news, but she had walked into a sensational gold mine. Her stock at the station had just gone stratospheric.

Still gripping her arm, Dane hustled Marlie to the car, putting her in on the driver's side and shoving her over to make room for himself. He slammed the door and turned the key in the ignition. "What the hell were you doing?" he said from between clenched teeth.

She could feel the white heat of his rage, but she wasn't impressed. "What you wanted me to do," she replied bitterly. "Attracting the killer's attention. Wasn't that the whole point of the exercise?"

Dane thought of denying it, but realized there wasn't any point in it. She wouldn't believe any denials he could come up with, and he was so angry right now that he wasn't inclined to try. "Attract his attention, yes, not drive him into a killing rage!"

"But now you can be certain he'll come after me. He won't forgive an attack on his ego." She was facing forward, not even glancing at him as he drove.

Dane took a firm grip on his temper. He had known she wouldn't like being exposed as a psychic, but he hadn't expected her to immediately realize he had set up the entire situation, or to react by goading and taunting the killer.

"How did you know?" he asked a moment later, his voice as grim as his face. "Did you read my mind?"

"You can't get over your fear of that, can you?" she gibed. "You can relax; your head's too thick for me to get even a glimmer from you. But the reporter was a different story. She might as well have been carrying a sign. Why didn't you call her anonymously?"

"She knows me, knows my voice. Besides, I owed her a

favor for some information she got for me last year. Breaking a story would help her at the station."

"Then by all means, if it will help her, throw me to the wolves," she said, her voice flat. Now that the first shock of betrayal and exposure had passed, several likelihoods had presented themselves, none of them pleasant. She had fretted over his lack of commitment, over the way they had never even discussed their relationship, and now she knew why. For Dane, there *was* no commitment; he had simply been marking time until the killer struck again, so he could put his plan into action. He had played her perfectly, setting her up for that scene. She thought of what it had cost her to go to that house, and got even angrier.

"I haven't thrown you to the wolves!" he snapped.

"Haven't you? You've set me up as bait."

"Damn it, he's not going to get anywhere near you! Do you think I'd take a chance on something like that happening? I've arranged for a policewoman to take your place. She's already at your house. All you have to do is pack some clothes, and I'll take you to a safe house until it's over."

"No," she said, just as flatly as before.

He slammed his fist onto the steering wheel. "Don't fight me on this, Marlie. You don't have a choice."

"I'm not going to a safe house." She thought of being confined for days, perhaps weeks, with shifts of officers to guard her, and knew she couldn't tolerate it. Her nerves were already raw; that would simply be too much.

Very evenly he said, "I can take you into protective custody and lock you in a cell, if you'd prefer. I don't think you'd like it."

She whirled on him, incensed by the threat. "I don't think you would either, Hollister. I can't stop you from doing it, but I promise you that I'll make your life miserable if you do."

"For God's sake, use your common sense! You can't stay in your house. Or do you think I'd planned to actually use you as a tethered goat?"

"Why not? Why stop short of that? Using me has been your plan all along, hasn't it? Personally, I think you carried it a little far by moving in with me, but I suppose you needed to be on hand when I had another vision, so you could get the ball rolling."

His head snapped around. "Just what you are saying?"

"That if you'd bothered to *ask* me, Detective, I'd have gone along with your plan if it would help flush out the killer. I hate being exposed by the media, because this will wreck my life again, but I'd have done it. You didn't have to sacrifice your body for the cause."

Furiously he slammed on the brakes, stopping the car with a force that jerked her forward in her seat. Luckily there was no one behind them or they'd have been rear-ended. He was as infuriated as she. "Getting involved with you has nothing to do with this!"

"Doesn't it? I've been puzzled by the situation from the very beginning. Can you honestly say that you didn't have this plan in mind *before* you moved in?"

His jaw worked. "No." Damn if he'd lie.

"I didn't think so."

"Moving in wasn't part of the plan."

"It was just too much to resist, wasn't it?" she taunted.

Roughly he seized her shoulders. "You're damn right it was. I wanted you, and when I got the opportunity to move in, I took it. Or maybe you think I've been faking all those hard-ons?"

"That doesn't prove anything. I think you'd get an erection if a fly landed on you." She tried to jerk away, but he tightened his grip.

Dane took another grip on his temper; the first one hadn't lasted very long. "Our relationship has nothing to do with this. They're two totally separate things."

"If you say so," she drawled, mimicking his accent.

"Damn it, Marlie—" An angry blast of a horn interrupted him, and he darted a furious glance into the rearview mirror. Several cars were lined up behind him. He stomped the accelerator. "We'll finish this at the house, while you pack."

"I'm not going to a safe house." The words were stony, implacable. "I'm going to work tomorrow just like always. You've probably wrecked that, too. They'll probably fire me, but I'm still going to try."

"You aren't going to be fired!"

She stared out the window. So he thought he could just use her to bait his trap, and afterward everything would return to normal? "You can pack, too."

He slanted a look at her. "What?" He couldn't stay at the safe house with her.

"I want your stuff out of my house."

For the first time, the conviction in her voice pierced his impatient anger. Marlie wasn't just upset; she was deeply, coldly furious, and she hadn't believed a word he'd said. His stomach knotted. He inhaled deeply, reaching for control. "Okay. Maybe it's for the best, for now. I'll see you as often as I can at the safe house—"

"I am not going to a safe house. Can't you understand English?"

"Maybe you don't," he said slowly. "Honey, I'm not giving you a choice in this. You can't stay in your house."

"Then I'll stay in a motel, or rent an apartment. I am not going to be locked up because of your schemes. As much as I can, I'm going to live a normal life. I'm going to work, if I have a job, and I'm going to do normal things, like laundry and shopping and going to movies. I lived like a virtual prisoner for the first twenty-two years of my life. I'll be damned if I let you lock me up again."

He thrust his hand through his hair. God Almighty, he hadn't expected her to dig in her heels like this. This was a Marlie he hadn't seen since the first week he'd known her, and somehow he had let himself forget about her temper. The woman sitting beside him was seething like a volcano, and wasn't likely to cooperate with him in anything he suggested. He decided to shut his mouth, for now, and cut his losses.

The remainder of the drive was accomplished in silence. When they reached her house, there was a strange car in her driveway, and Trammell's sports car was parked out front. Marlie got out and went inside without looking at Dane.

Trammell and Grace were both there, as well as a young policewoman who resembled Marlie in size and general coloring. Trammell stood when Marlie entered, took one look at her face, and said, "Uh-oh."

Coming in behind her, Dane sharply drew a finger across his throat, silencing any other comments.

Marlie turned in time to see the gesture. She gave Trammell a cool look. "Were you in on it too?"

He shifted uneasily. "Not until yesterday." He had become accustomed to thinking of Marlie as someone who was vulnerable and needed protecting, but there was a look in those deep blue eyes that suddenly made him wary. Dane had told him about Gleen, but until this moment he really hadn't seen her as a woman who, tied and helpless, had nevertheless spat defiance at a crazed killer. "I take it you're unhappy."

"A mite disturbed," she said, her tone heavy with irony. "I barely lived through one attack from a maniac with a knife, so it bothers me to be set up as bait for another one."

Dane flinched. He hadn't thought of it that way. "You'll be safe," he said. "Do you think I'd have done it if there were any risk to you?"

She tilted her head, considering him. "Yes," she finally said, and went into her bedroom.

Trammell whistled through his teeth. "I sense trouble in paradise."

Grace gave Dane a dirty look. "I would think so," she said, and followed Marlie into the bedroom.

The policewoman, Beverly Beaver, sat watching them uncomfortably. "Is the stakeout canceled?"

"No," Dane answered. "You're still on. As soon as I get Marlie settled, I'll be back to help set up everything. We have time; the bit won't be on until the evening news."

Beverly said, "How are you going to keep the reporters away? The guy can't get to me if a hundred reporters and photographers are camped on the front yard."

"The television station is going to play it as a joke. The department will take a lot of heat for it, and the chief is going to say they've investigated Marlie and there isn't anything to her claims. But the killer will know the truth, and he'll come after her." He paused. "Are you sure you want to do this, Bev?"

"I'm sure. I'm closest to her in size and coloring, and I've had advanced self-defense training. I'm the best choice." Her voice was philosophical. Dane wasn't fooled; Beverly had the reputation of being a tiger. She was chomping at the bit to be in on the stakeout, even though she knew she would have to let the killer get far too close for comfort, so they would have enough on him to make the charges stick.

"Okay." He cast a harried glance toward the bedroom. "She's refusing to go to a safe house."

"We already have it set up," Trammell said.

"Tell it to her. She's agreed to leave, but she says she's going to stay in a motel, or rent an apartment. She's so mad at me that she won't go along with anything I suggest."

"I've got an idea. Maybe she'll listen to me."

"Give it a try."

Marlie looked up from the bags she was packing when Trammell sauntered lazily into the bedroom. Grace was helping, taking garments out of the closet and placing them on the bed for Marlie to fold and pack in the suitcases. Dane leaned against the doorway, his face like a thundercloud as he watched her.

"Dane says you don't want to go to a safe house," Trammell began.

"That's right."

Grace gave her a quick, concerned look. "Marlie, it's the best place for you."

"Would you like being confined, possibly for weeks? It would drive me crazy. I've done whatever I can to help, and I refuse to be punished for it."

"But it isn't punishment," Grace tried to explain. "It's to keep you safe."

"The best judge of whether or not something is punishment is the one on the receiving end," Marlie replied. "I don't mind being secluded; I even like it. But I can't bear being confined."

"A motel won't be very comfortable," Trammell said. "I have an idea. You'll still need protection, so why don't you move into Dane's house? I've finished with the renovations, and got the furniture delivered yesterday. That way you'll be more comfortable, and he'll be with you at night."

She gave him an icy glare. "That's *not* a very good suggestion."

"It's the only workable solution." Trammell countered her glare with a gentle smile. "I know it isn't ideal, but it's a compromise that will work, if you'll let it. Dane won't take you into protective custody, but I can tell you right now that the chief will order it and not blink an eye."

Frustrated fury welled up in her, almost choking her. She didn't want to stay in Dane's house, didn't want to be forced into intimacy with him. But Trammell, unfortunately, was right; the chief didn't know her, and wouldn't think twice about ordering her detained, for her own good.

"Trammell's wrong," Dane said softly, breaking into the silence. He met her angry gaze without blinking. "I *will* take you into custody. You might hate my guts for it, but I'll do it if I have to. It's better than risking your life. So, honey, it's my house or jail."

Stated like that, she accepted that she had no choice. The move was swiftly accomplished. Marlie took the time to thank Beverly for the risk she was taking, and to show her around the house, then she was hustled out. She insisted on taking her car, so it was a caravan of three that parked at Dane's house not long afterward.

Dane had seen the completed changes Trammell had wrought in his house, and considered the money well spent. The new furniture was both comfortable and chic; his living room now felt like a patio, with the same sense of freshness and space. His bed was the one thing in the house that had been fairly new; he'd replaced his grandparents' standard double with a king-size when he inherited the house. The only reason he had endured the double bed at Marlie's these past weeks was the fact that she had been in it. For that, he had been content to have his feet hang off the end.

If he had had any hope of sharing that big bed with her now, it disappeared when she resolutely carried her clothes into the second bedroom, which had also received Trammell's sprucing up. Still he was fiercely elated. She was here; that was what mattered. She obviously wanted to make a complete break with him, but circumstances had conspired against her, and she was forced to stay with him. He would have the chance to break down that wall of anger.

Again Grace helped Marlie with her clothes. They worked quietly together for several minutes before Grace said, "You're really angry at him, aren't you?"

"Anger doesn't begin to describe it. Not only did he set me up, that was his reason from the beginning for getting involved with me."

Grace looked shocked. "That can't be so!"

"Can't it? He didn't deny planning it before he moved in with me."

"But Alex has been positively gleeful because Dane is so obviously crazy about you. Surely you know that he loves you!"

"If he does, he's never even come close to saying it. In fact, we've never discussed our relationship at all, except for sex. I'm beginning to think that's all it ever was, just sex. He had this plan of his, and as a side benefit I happened to be acceptable in bed."

Grace thought about it. "You've never talked about your feelings at all?"

"Not one word. I called him when a vision started, he came over and took care of me, and simply never left. The next thing I knew, he was hanging up his clothes in my closet."

"I see. Even on our first date, Alex admitted that emotionally he was in deep water," Grace murmured. "And Alex is the most skittish man in the world." She thought about it some more, then pronounced: "You're right. On the evidence, you have to assume that Dane deliberately became involved with you to gain your trust, and moved in with you to stay close to the action, so to speak."

"In a nutshell, he used me."

When Grace left the bedroom, she gave Dane a frosty glare. Trammell caught his partner's eye and shrugged in amusement. Dane didn't think it was a damn bit funny. He didn't protest when they left; the sooner he and Marlie were alone, the sooner he could begin mending fences. God, what if he couldn't change her mind?

At the thought of losing her forever, he felt a cold knot of panic form in the pit of his stomach.

Marlie finally came out of the bedroom to watch the local evening news. As she had expected, she was the lead story.

"WVTM learned today that the Orlando Police Department has been using the services of a local psychic, Marlie Keen, to aid them in their search for the Orlando Slasher WVTM reporter Cheri Vaughn talked to Ms. Keen earlier today, when she and a city detective were seen leaving the house of the latest victim, Marilyn Elrod, who lived in Wildwood Estates."

The picture switched from the studio to the tape shot earlier. Marlie watched in silence for a minute, then said,

"You played it perfectly. The way you told them to leave, and kept stepping in front of me, looked exactly as if you were trying to keep me under wraps. Do you think I came across as a publicity-hungry kook?"

"Not quite," he muttered. At least she was talking to him. He had been worried that she would give him the silent treatment for the rest of his life. No, she hadn't come across as a kook, at least not to anyone with an ounce of perception. There had been too much controlled anger in her face, too much disgust when she had described the killer.

The next scene featured Lieutenant Bonness, sweating in the heat, looking properly embarrassed. Dane had briefed him on how to play it. Bonness wasn't comfortable with what he was doing, but his discomfort fit in with what he wanted to project. Yes, Marlie Keen had contacted them. They were willing to listen to anyone who might be able to help them with the investigation. Ms. Keen's allegations hadn't panned out, though, and the Orlando PD would no longer be working with her.

Back to the studio. The evening anchors had a few pithy remarks to make about the police department wasting tax dollars chasing down wild ideas from the loony fringe. The spot ended with the information that Ms. Keen, the alleged psychic, worked in the accounting department of a local bank, and named the bank.

"There goes my job," Marlie drawled.

Dane's hand tightened on the can of beer he was holding. "I told you—"

"I know what you told me. I also know you don't know what you're talking about."

His teeth ground together. "For the last time, I didn't get involved with you just to set you up as bait."

"No? Just exactly when did you come up with this brilliant plan? And I'm not being sarcastic. It's a damn good idea. It'll probably work. But when did you think of it?"

He didn't have to think, he knew exactly when the plan

had occurred to him. Again he chose not to lie. "On the plane coming back from Denver."

Her eyebrows lifted. "You mean right before you came to my house and made a heavy-duty pass?"

"Yes," he growled.

"The timing's a mite suspicious, isn't it?"

"I wanted you before that, damn it!" he yelled. "But you were a suspect, and I couldn't get involved with you. As soon as I cleared you of all suspicion, I was knocking on your door."

She smiled. "And it was just pure luck that I could be used in this way, wasn't it? I don't mind that part of it, Dane, I really don't. What I hate is the way you used a personal relationship to set it up—though it wasn't very personal for you, was it?"

Red mist swam in front of his eyes. He was so angry that he could feel himself losing control. He got up and walked out of the house, to keep himself from doing something he would regret later.

Damn, this wasn't looking good at all. How could she doubt what they'd had together? He'd never felt like this about any other woman, and she thought it meant less than nothing to him. He walked around the yard, the lingering evening heat making him sweat. When he thought he had himself under control, he went back inside, but Marlie had gone back into the bedroom.

Probably that was for the best. Both their emotions were too raw for them to talk about this sensibly. Tomorrow, when they both had calmed down, would be better.

Carroll Janes watched the evening news telecast. So that was how they had known! A damn psychic. Whoever would have thought? That certainly wasn't something for which he could have planned.

The cops didn't seem to have much faith in her, but just looking at her had given him chills. And what she had said;

how could she have been so vicious? She had called him a worm and a coward. After a moment of hurt, he began to get angry. So he wasn't anyone's dream man, was he? What did that little bitch know?

Actually, he realized, she knew quite a lot. The cops didn't believe her—for now—but the fact was, she was a real danger to him. As no one else had, she had gotten close to him. The only way she could have seen him was in a psychic vision, and the thought made him feel maddeningly vulnerable.

It was intolerable. How ignominious it would be for his downfall to come about because of some kook psychic! The trouble was that she *wasn't* a kook. She was for real. It was the only way she could know what he looked like.

He wasn't safe as long as she lived.

The solution was obvious. The psychic would have to die.

23

Janes called in sick the next morning. Marlie Keen had been listed in the phone book, and he had looked up her address on a city map. He didn't have any time to waste; he had to get rid of her as soon as possible. And then perhaps he would think about leaving Orlando; he usually remained in an area longer than this, but the psychic bitch had loused things up for him here. They had that sketch of him. They might discount it now, but when the bitch turned up dead, they would give it a lot more credence.

He smelled setup, but he didn't dare ignore the situation. It was simply too dangerous for him. But he didn't take any chances; he switched license plates with a car belonging to an old lady in the apartment building who seldom drove anymore. He would switch them back when he returned, so that if any suspicious cop was watching the traffic on Marlie Keen's street, when they traced that tag, it would come back as belonging to a Mrs. Velma Fisher, whose car was nothing like the one that had been sporting the plate. But when they checked Mrs. Fisher's car, the license plate would be there, convincing them that they had made an error in writing down the number.

His blond curls were snugly in place when he set out. Such an extravagant head of hair was a brilliant disguise, if he did say so himself. They were looking for a bald guy. It was an ingenious way of changing his appearance, because either way, his head was what people noticed: They would look at the blond curls, and not the face beneath it, or, if he was seen during one of his nights, they would notice the slick skull and nothing else. Simply brilliant.

He rolled down his car window and turned up the radio. That was another piece of psychological subterfuge: Cops wouldn't expect him to draw attention to himself with a loud radio. If this was a trap, they wouldn't expect him to boldly drive by, where they could get a good look at him. That was why they never had been able to catch him. He could predict their actions and reactions, but they didn't have a clue how his mind worked. After all, how could anyone without an imagination begin to understand what it was like to have one?

So he casually drove by the bitch's house, and just as casually glanced at it. There was a car in the driveway; why wasn't she working? The newscast had plainly said that she was employed at a bank. There seemed to be a lot of cars parked along the street. That chill went down his spine again. He didn't actually see anything, but he hadn't escaped for so long by being stupid; quite the opposite. This definitely felt like a setup.

He didn't risk another drive-by. He drove back to his apartment, switched the license plates again, and thought. If it was a setup, then the cops wouldn't let the bitch stay at her house. They would have her salted away somewhere they thought was safe. It would be impossible for him to locate her, much less get at her.

Or would they? The trap would look much more realistic if she appeared to be going about her normal routine.

There was only one way to check. He looked up the

telephone number of the bank where she worked and punched in the numbers. It was answered on the first ring, by a bored-sounding young woman with a breathy voice.

"Marlie Keen, in accounting, please," Janes said briskly.

"Just one moment."

Another ring, and a click. "Accounting." Another female voice.

"Marlie Keen, please."

"Hold on." He heard the woman say, in a more distant voice that indicated she had taken the receiver away from her mouth, "Marlie, line two."

Janes hung up the phone. She was at work.

He laughed to himself as he went back out to his car. What simpletons they all were, if that was the best they could do! He would follow her when she left work, though of course, if she went to her house, he would break off contact rather than take the risk of driving down her street again.

His biggest problem, he told himself, was finding some shade to park in while waiting for her to leave the bank.

He picked her out when she went to lunch; he remembered that thick dark hair and slender build. His heart pounded with excitement, then he sternly brought himself under control. He couldn't allow himself to make a mistake out of haste.

He snickered as he followed her. She wasn't much of a psychic if she couldn't tell that he was only two cars behind her. But she was still a danger to him, and that couldn't be tolerated.

She picked up lunch at a drive-through fast-food window, and returned to the bank. He had no chance to get at her. So he patiently settled down to wait once more.

She left work at four. He had carefully watched the parking lot. There hadn't been any suspicious lingerers—other than himself, of course. He hummed as he pulled out a few cars behind her, and kept about the same distance behind her.

She didn't make any stops. She drove straight to a

smallish house in an older neighborhood. He noted the address and kept on driving. He went to the library and looked up the address in the city directory; the house was listed as the residence of Dane Hollister. Janes's eyebrows shot up, and he grinned. He knew that name; it had been in the papers quite a bit lately. Detective Dane Hollister was investigating the Slasher murders. Now, wasn't that a coincidence?

The bank president hadn't done it; not even the vice president had done it. But the head of accounting had been called into a meeting with them, and this was one of those occasions when Marlie didn't need to be psychic to know what was happening. She wasn't surprised when the department head returned, looking unhappy, and asked Marlie into her office. They regretted the necessity, but their first responsibility was to their depositors, et cetera, et cetera. The bottom line was that Friday was her last day. They felt magnanimous in allowing her to stay that long.

She thought about being magnanimous in turn and quitting right then, which was obviously what they wanted, but the impulse didn't last long. She wasn't in the best of moods.

She was still angry when she drove to Dane's house, so angry that there wasn't much room for anything else. She had been angry since the moment she had realized how Dane had betrayed her, and expected to be angry for the foreseeable future.

She had been home just long enough to change into comfortable clothes when she heard a car drive up. She looked out the window expecting to see Dane, but instead watched Trammell unfold his long form from his low-slung car. She went to the door to let him in.

"Hi, sweetie." He twirled his sunglasses from one long finger and bent down to kiss her cheek.

She lifted a sardonic brow at the display of affection. "What's with the sweet talk?"

He grinned and raised his hands. "Don't shoot, I'm unarmed. I see you haven't cooled down much."

"Are you the symbolic hat through the door, to see if I attack?"

"Not exactly. Dane got delayed for a few minutes, and we don't think you should be alone."

"Thanks for the concern."

"You don't sound sincere," he teased, but his lazy dark eyes were watchful.

"I was fired today," she retorted. "I don't feel like celebrating. Out of the goodness of their hearts, I'll be allowed to finish out the week."

He snorted. "I'd have walked out on them today."

"So would I, if that hadn't been exactly what they wanted. Do you want something cold to drink?"

"Only if it isn't alcoholic."

"I can manage that. Lemonade, fruit juice, tea, or soft drink?"

"Tea."

"Coming up. Smart man, not to drink and drive."

"I don't drink much anyway. It upsets my system," he drawled. He followed her into the kitchen. "Did you get settled in last night?"

"I wouldn't go that far. I got my things put away." She took two glasses out of the cabinet, dropped ice cubes in them, and filled them up with the tea she had brewed that morning before going to work. "Lemon?"

"No, thanks. I drink my tea straight."

She chuckled as they clinked glasses.

Trammell eyed her as he sipped the cold liquid. "Are you going to forgive him?"

She shrugged. "It wasn't the media ploy that upset me as much as realizing he 'trifled with my affections,' to use an old southern phrase."

"You really think he doesn't care anything for you?"

"If he does, he's never mentioned it. What hurts is that he

deliberately cultivated my feelings for him, and then used them to manipulate me."

"He can have tunnel vision when it comes to his work," Trammell said delicately. "Let's sit down."

"Are you going to plead his case?" she asked as they took chairs at the table.

"Not really, but I know Dane better than anyone else on earth, including you, including anyone in his family. They only grew up with him; you've only slept with him. I've risked my life with him. I know him from the ground up."

"Do you think he's capable of cold-bloodedly using someone in an investigation?"

"Of course he is. He's a cop. So am I. But he's never been cold-blooded where you're concerned. How can I put this without being crude?" he mused, looking at the ceiling. "Do you remember when you came to Bonness's office, and you and Dane all but went to war right then?"

She nodded.

"Well, to put it delicately, he had a boner so hard a cat couldn't scratch it."

Marlie choked on her tea, then fell back in the chair, shrieking with laughter. Trammell stretched out his long legs, as languorous as a cat, looking pleased with himself while he waited for her to calm down.

"He's my hero," he continued lazily after a moment. He wasn't looking at her now, but a tiny, rather self-mocking smile lurked around his mouth as he stared at the ice in his glass. "I didn't join the force out of idealism or anything like that; I was bored, and it seemed like an interesting job. Dane and I were paired after the first year, and we've been together ever since. I don't believe in much, or trust much, but Dane is a rock I can rely on no matter what. Not that he's idealistic, either. He's even more cynical than I am.

"But he's got a sense of right and wrong that he's never lost touch with. All I see are shades of gray, but Dane can see the black and white. He knows that there are certain things worth fighting for, and he's willing to put himself in the front line. He's a gallant, heroic bastard, and he's never even conscious of it. He's an old-fashioned southern good old boy, the salt of the earth. He's street-smart, woods-savvy, and sly as a fox. A real throwback. Mean, too. Damn, can he be mean! But he turns to putty where women are concerned. We used to laugh at him, when he was still on patrol and had to work an accident. If there was a woman involved, it didn't matter if she was just holding her arm and a man was lying there bleeding from a dozen places; it was as if Dane never saw the guy. He'd go straight to the woman, make certain she was all right, so tender they'd be melting at his feet within a few minutes. It would embarrass him when he realized he'd left another man lying in the street, and we were all laughing at him."

"You don't have to tell me he has a good bedside manner," she said dryly.

"No, I don't suppose I do. But I've never before seen him the way he is with you. He's always had women, and not one of them ever meant enough to him to interfere with the job. Until you. He couldn't get you off his mind. You drove him crazy; you made him so angry he couldn't think. It was the most amusing thing I've seen in a couple of years. *He* may not know he's in love with you, but trust me, he won't let you go. I know him. If you walk out that door, he'll be right behind you."

She gave him an incredulous look. "How can a man not know if he's in love? Give me a break."

"Well, it's never happened to him before."

"Had it happened to *you,* before Grace?"

He looked uncomfortable. He swallowed, hard. "Uh, no."

"Did you recognize it?"

"Let's just say that I fought it."

"But you knew it was there. *I'd* never been in love before, either, but I knew what it was."

"Dane's more hardheaded than most."

"You're telling me," she muttered. "I can't read a thing from him."

Trammell gave a shout of laughter, but quickly sobered. He gave her an uneasy look. "Can you read me?"

She smirked at him, happy to see him squirm. "I haven't tried since I regained the ability."

"How about Grace?"

"I don't intrude on my friends," she said sternly.

"Psychic's Code of Honor, huh?"

"It wouldn't be polite. I've always had to try to block people out, rather than try to receive their feelings."

They heard a car door slam outside. "There's Dane," Trammell said, and drained his glass. "Think about it, Marlie. Give the guy a break, and save our sanity. It's been dangerous to talk to the man today."

"I'll consider your view of things," she said. "But my final decision depends on him." Until ten minutes ago, she had thought that she had already made her final decision, but Trammell's explanation that Dane was hardheaded had made her pause.

Dane walked in, looking hot and irritable. His gaze settled first on Marlie, with a sort of bad-tempered yearning, then on the tea they were drinking. He prepared a glass of tea for himself and sat down with a sigh. "It's been a bitch of a day."

"Tell me about it," Marlie said sweetly. "I got fired."

He stared at her for a moment, then dropped his head to the table in despair. "Shit."

"I'm out of here," Trammell said, smiling at Marlie. "See you in the morning, partner."

Dane didn't reply. Marlie sipped her tea. Trammell let himself out.

The silence in the kitchen became thick. Marlie said, "When this is over, I think I'll move back to Colorado."

Dane lifted his head. There was a pale cast to his tanned skin, and his mouth was compressed to a thin line. "No," he said, very softly.

She leaned back and crossed her arms. "What are you

going to do, threaten me with protective custody again? I don't think you can get away with that." She pushed her chair back and got up, then carried her glass to the sink.

She had just rinsed it out and placed it in the drainer when two hard hands closed on her arms and whirled her around. She drew back as far as she could, but the cabinets halted her retreat. He leaned heavily into her, his hips grinding against hers. His face was stark.

"I won't let you go," he muttered. "Damn it, Marlie, how can you even talk about leaving when we have this between us?"

"This?" she flared, wriggling her hips and feeling him get hard. "It's just sex."

"It's more than just sex, damn it!"

"Is it? From where I stand, that's all it's ever been," she taunted him, feeling him quiver with rage and enjoying it. Something fierce and hurt inside her wanted him to feel the pain as she had.

His hazel eyes went green as his control broke. "By God, if sex is all it is, then we might as well enjoy it," he said thickly as he swooped her into his arms.

Dizzily off balance, Marlie clung to him as he strode toward the bedroom. Her heartbeat was thundering wildly, blood surging through her veins. She wanted to hit him. She wanted to bite him. She wanted to tear his clothes off and hurl herself onto him. Love and anger and lust swirled together in a volatile mixture. Maybe they couldn't communicate with words just yet, the anger was too strong, but maybe their bodies could bridge the gap. When he roughly placed her on the bed, she reached up and grabbed his shirt and tugged, pulling him down on top of her.

In fierce silence they struggled together. His hard mouth bruised hers with the force of his kisses; she bit his lower lip, making him curse, then gently sucked at it. He tore the button off her shorts in his need to get her out of her clothes. She fought with his zipper, finally got it down, and hungrily shoved her hand down the front of his briefs. His shaft filled her hand, hard and throbbing. The head of it was already wet.

He was breathing roughly, audibly, as he stripped her panties off and in the same movement rolled on top of her, kneeing her thighs apart. He drove into her with savage need, and she cried out at the rough penetration even as she coiled her legs around him.

Supper was forgotten in the long, heated hours that followed. The heat of sunset dimmed into twilight. At first, Dane made love to her with a furious intensity that held anger and resentment at the tension he had been under. Marlie was as fierce, biting him, digging her nails into him, slamming her hips upward to take him.

They didn't talk. That first wild lovemaking didn't allow room, or thought, for words. Afterward they lay together in silent exhaustion, their bodies still linked. The bond they had just reforged felt too new, too fragile, to allow for separation just yet. They dozed, and Marlie awoke some undetermined time later when he began making love to her again.

This time he was tender, lingering over her. He kissed the bruises his fierce grip had left on her silky skin, silently apologizing. She licked the crescents her nails had made on him. He rode her for a long time, slowing down whenever he felt his climax approaching, not yet ready to release the pleasure.

Both of them were acutely aware that he wasn't wearing a condom. He supported his weight on his forearms as he moved in and out of her, their gazes locked, and the knowledge was in their eyes. When he couldn't hold off his climax any longer, when she had already convulsed twice, she gripped his buttocks and pulled him deeper into her as he let it overtake him. He shuddered and bucked with the force of his pleasure as he jetted his semen into her.

Again, it wasn't time for words. Not yet. They slept again, entwined together, and twilight became dark.

Marlie woke first. Her body ached deliciously, and she felt the hunger growing for more of what had caused the ache. Dane still slept, but when she began caressing his shaft, both he and it stirred immediately. He rolled over onto his back and closed his arms around her as she slid on top of him.

"Stay with me," he whispered, and closed his eyes in delight at the way the hot silk of her body so snugly enveloped him.

She hesitated, then felt him throb within her. "All right," she whispered in return, and gently began to move. It wasn't much, but after the ferocity of their lovemaking, she didn't doubt his sincerity. He hadn't been a cop, trying to catch a killer; he had been simply a man, wild with need for his woman. He hadn't committed himself yet, at least not with words, but the bond of the flesh had reassured her. She could wait for the rest of it.

Carroll Janes had thought it over very carefully. He had to get the bitch alone, so that meant he had to get Detective Hollister to leave.

He didn't call 911, which would give the dispatcher the telephone number he'd called from. He called police head-quarters directly.

He knew himself to be a very good actor. He was proud of the frantic tone of his voice when he said, "There's been a woman killed! There's been another—it's him! I swear to God it had to be him. Blood—she's cut everywhere! Butchered! I saw him leaving, bald head just like in that sketch!"

"Slow down, slow down," the authoritative voice said. "I can't understand you. Repeat that, please."

Janes drew in deep, audible breaths. "Another woman's been killed. I saw a bald man run. She's cut all to pieces, there's blood—" He made gagging noises in the phone.

"Calm down, sir. Where are you? Can you give me an address?"

Janes rattled off an address he had looked up, on the opposite side of town. He stumbled over the street and numbers a couple of times to make it realistic. Then he hung up and waited.

He was at a phone booth two blocks from Detective Hollister's house.

The telephone rang. Dane snatched it up. After listening a minute, he said, "I'm on my way." He rolled out of bed and began pulling on his clothes.

Marlie raised herself on her elbow. "What?"

"Another murder," he said tersely. "They think it was him."

She shook her head. "No."

He paused, remembering. "That's right. You didn't feel anything, did you?"

"Not a thing. It wasn't him." She got out of bed and began dressing, too.

He sighed. "It's probably another copycat, damn it. I'm sorry, baby."

"It isn't your fault," she said. "You're on the task force; you have to go."

He pulled her into his arms, holding her tight against him. "I don't know how long I'll be gone."

She rubbed her face against his chest, enjoying the heated scent of him. "I'll watch television and wait up for you."

He tilted her face up and leaned down to kiss her. "If you happen to go to sleep, I'll wake you up."

"It's a deal."

"We have a lot to talk about," he said, determination in his voice.

"I know. Go!"

He started toward the door, then turned back. He pulled open the top drawer of the bedside table and took out a pistol. He checked it, made certain the chamber was full and that the safety was on. "Keep this handy. Do you know how to use it?"

She nodded. She wasn't exactly experienced, but she knew how a pistol worked. After all, she had lived alone in the mountains; it had seemed only smart to teach herself the basics.

He kissed her again. "Okay. Be careful, keep the pistol with you, and don't open the door to strangers. I'll radio in and have a patrolman over to watch the house; one should be outside within five minutes. I'll call you when I'm on the way home, so you won't shoot me by mistake."

"I said I'll wait up for you," she said, smiling.

"A man can't be too careful. Or a woman," he added sternly.

"Gotcha."

He left, and she turned on the television, settling down on the couch to run through the channels and look for something interesting.

Dane had been gone for less than five minutes when she sat bolt upright, her heart pounding. A cold chill chased over her skin, roughening it. A powerful sense of alarm filled her.

She felt the blow of recognition as an image flashed through her mind, blotting out her own thought: black-gloved hands, one of them holding wire cutters, tugging at a group of wires.

She panted, trying to draw in enough oxygen from air that suddenly seemed to suffocate. Dear God, so he was striking after all! And Dane had left. Had the call been a false alarm, to draw them away, so the killer could get at Beverly? The policewoman would be all alone.

Marlie stumbled toward the phone. A vision flashed, halting her. In her mind, she saw the wire cutters biting through plastic and wire.

And the lights went out.

24

Marlie froze, blinded by the sudden darkness, paralyzed by terror and the crashing knowledge. He wasn't after Beverly, he was after her—*and he was right outside.*

She closed her eyes, squeezing them tight, trying to hurry her night vision. She should try to get out, but by which door, front or back? Or was he at a window? Which one? *Which one?*

—Gently he cut a screen, snipping the tiny strands one by one—

Desperately she fought off the vision. Oh, God, she wouldn't let herself be swamped by the vision. She would be helpless. But she had never been able to resist one for long, never been able to block it, or control it. They rolled over her like tidal waves.

—He knew she was in there. He could *feel* her, the bitch. He could already taste the triumph, the power—

"No," Marlie moaned in a whisper. Desperately she summoned up an image of the mental door she had learned how to open and close. All she had to do was close it, and keep him on the other side.

—He'd see how smart she was when she felt the blade biting into her—

It was washing over her in black waves. The evil was so strong, she couldn't breathe. He was so close, the power of it was crushing her. She couldn't fight him off.

—The damn lock on the window wouldn't budge. White-hot fury roared through him at this delay. Snarling, he smashed his gloved fist into the glass—

She heard the crash and tinkle of breaking glass, but the vision was roaring through her, blotting out everything else, and she couldn't tell where it was coming from. It could have been right behind her, but he was sucking all the strength out of her, and she couldn't even turn around.

Dane. Oh, God, Dane! She didn't want him to have to see this.

As soon as he got into his car, Dane radioed in and told the dispatcher to send a patrol car to his house immediately.

"Ten-four," said the dispatcher. "It'll take ten, fifteen minutes, though. It's a busy night."

"Do it faster than that," Dane said, iron in his voice.

"I'll try. Depends on when a patrolman gets free."

Dane hesitated, reluctant to leave Marlie alone for that long, but his job was to be on the crime scene, copycat or not. The detectives who had worked the other scenes had to make the call, decide if it was the same perp. He had given her his pistol, and a patrolman would be there soon. She would be okay.

He told himself that for several miles, but finally pulled to the side of the street and stopped. This didn't feel right, damn it. Something was wrong. He felt a sense of dread that had grown stronger with each passing mile and minute, but he couldn't pin down the cause.

It was a copycat killing, no doubt about that. It wasn't

unusual; they had already had one. But something was *wrong*.

He keyed the mike. "Dispatch, this is Hollister. Has a patrolman gotten to my house yet?"

"Not yet. A car is on its way."

Frustration welled in him. "Any further information on that knifing that was just called in?"

"No further—wait." Dane listened to static, then dispatch came back on the air. "That's affirmative. A squad car is on the scene, and the patrolman just radioed in. It looks like a false alarm."

Dane's sense of dread increased. His mind raced as he went through the angles. "Dispatch, was it a male or a female who called in the initial report?"

"A male."

"Shit!" He keyed the mike again. "Dispatch, contact the stakeout immediately! Verify that everything is okay. The false alarm may have been deliberate."

"Affirmative. Stand by."

Dane waited tensely in the dark car, sweat rolling down his face. Within a minute his radio crackled. "No problems at the stakeout, Dane. Everything's as quiet as a graveyard."

He shook his head. There was trouble and he knew it. But where? *Where?*

The false alarm had been deliberate, in an effort to draw off Marlie's protection. But Beverly had taken Marlie's place, and the ploy hadn't worked—

He froze, horror exploding in his brain. It had worked all too well. Marlie!

More glass shattered as he punched the window again. Desperately Marlie pictured the door, pictured the vision pressing against it, all black, loathsome evil. She pictured herself shoving against the door, forcing it shut, closing out the vision. She had to control it; she would die if she didn't. Her only chance was to control it, as she had the knowing.

She was stronger now than she had been before. She could do it.

The pistol. It had been beside her on the couch. She opened her eyes and lurched in the direction of the couch, but the vision had already sapped her strength, and her legs gave way beneath her. She fell heavily to the floor, but her outstretched hand brushed the couch, and she forced herself to her hands and knees, crawling to it and groping along the cushions for the pistol.

There it was, cold and heavy, reassuring in her hand. With wildly trembling fingers she fumbled the safety off.

—He was in. It wouldn't be long now. The knife glinted in his hand, long and lethal, the blade honed to a razor's edge—

The door! Mentally she slammed it shut once more. Keep him out. She had to keep him out.

She could hear her own breath coming in strangled sobs. Quiet. She had to be quiet. Weakly she crawled toward the corner, to put a wall at her back so he couldn't come at her from behind. The darkness in the house was almost total, with the blinds closed. She had the advantage there; she knew the house, knew where she was. He had to hunt her. She had to be very, very quiet.

Keep the door closed.

But where was he? She couldn't hear over the roaring in her ears, deafened by the thunder of her own blood racing through her veins.

She used both hands to steady the heavy pistol. Dane. Dane, who never went anywhere unarmed. *Thank you, Dane, for this chance. I love you.*

Where was he?

She closed her eyes and mentally opened the door a crack.

—Where was she, the bitch? He could turn on the flashlight, but not yet, not yet. So she thought she could hide, did she? Didn't she know how much he enjoyed the chase? Of course she did. Sweet bitch. Was she in the bathroom? He pushed the door open. The white fixtures gleamed in the darkness like enamel ghosts. No bitch here—

She slammed the door. She could feel the pressure of his mental energy, pushing against her. She opened her eyes and forced herself to look toward the hall where the bathroom was. *Don't stare, Marlie. Don't let yourself stare. You won't see him if you do. Keep your eyes moving, don't let them fix. You'll see his movement.*

Was that him? Was that a darker shadow, coming toward her? She didn't dare open the door again, not now. If it was him, he was too close. He would be on her before she could react. But was he really there, or was it her imagination?

A bright light exploded in her face, blinding her, and a ghastly voice crooned, "Well, hellooo there."

She pulled the trigger.

Several cars converged on the house almost simultaneously. Dane had given orders for them to go in with lights flashing and siren blaring, hoping against hope that they would be in time and scare him off. He drove like a maniac, praying as he had never prayed before. He didn't care if they missed this chance to catch him. *Please, God, let them scare him off. Don't let him be in the house. Don't let him have already been and gone. God, please. Not Marlie.*

He slammed the gear into park, the car rocking violently on its springs. He was out and running before the motion stopped. The house was dark. *God, no.*

Something heavy hit Dane in the back, sending him sprawling on the ground. He rolled to his feet with a savage snarl, his fist drawn back. Trammell picked himself up, as fast as Dane, and grabbed his arm. "Get control of yourself!" Trammell roared, his face as savage as Dane's. "You won't help her by going in blind! Do it the way you know it's supposed to be done!"

Uniformed officers were swarming around the house, surrounding it. All Dane could think of was Marlie inside. He shook Trammell off and plunged at the door. It was locked. He threw himself at it like a maddened animal, the force of his weight making it shudder in the frame. It was a solid door, reinforced with steel. The dead-bolt lock was one of the best made. It held. The hinges didn't. The screws ripped out of the wood with a tortured shriek, metal twisting.

Seeing he couldn't stop Dane, Trammell added his considerable strength to the task, and helped him wrench the door out of the frame. Hoarsely screaming Marlie's name, Dane pitched himself into the dark bowels of the house.

He stumbled over something soft and heavy, and crashed to the floor. His heart stopped beating, for a long, agonized moment that froze in time.

"Oh, God," he said, the voice not recognizable as his. "Get a light."

One of the patrol officers took his long, heavy flashlight out of his belt and thumbed the switch. The powerful beam illuminated Dane, crouched on the floor with a look of frozen horror on his face, and Trammell, who looked almost as bad. In the center of the beam sprawled a black-clad figure, the shaven skull gleaming dully. He was on his back, and his sightless eyes stared upward. The stench of blood and death was overpowering. A black pool of blood had gathered around the body.

"Dane." The almost soundless whisper raised the hairs on their arms. "Dane, I'm here."

The flashlight beam swung wildly toward the corner, and Marlie flinched from the light, closing her eyes and turning her head away. Dark wetness glistened on the white of her shirt. She still held the pistol, both hands clasped around it.

Dane couldn't manage to get to his feet. He crawled to her, his mind still unable to believe that she was alive. He cupped her cheek in a shaking hand, and smoothed her hair back from her face. "Baby. Oh, God, honey."

"He cut me," she said, as if apologizing. "I shot him, but he didn't stop. He just kept coming. So I kept shooting."

"Good," he said with barely restrained savagery. His

hands were trembling wildly, but with the utmost tenderness he lowered her to the floor. "Just lie down, honey. Let me see how bad you're hurt."

"I don't think it's serious," she said judiciously. "It's the top of my shoulder, and my left side. But it's just cuts; he didn't stab me."

He was barely holding himself together. Only the knowledge that she needed him now kept him from throwing himself on the body and tearing it to pieces. God! This was the second time in her life a madman had attacked her with a knife. How could she be so calm, when he was shaking apart?

"He cut the wiring," she was saying. Suddenly she sounded exhausted. "I'm very tired. If you don't mind, I'll tell you all about it later."

"Sure, baby." He pressed the heel of his palm over the oozing cut in her side. "Go to sleep. I'll be with you when you wake up."

She gave a little sigh, and her heavy eyelids closed. Dane was aware of the house filling with people, but he didn't look up.

"Dane." It was Trammell, kneeling beside him. "The medics are here, buddy. You need to move back so they can help her."

"I'm stopping the bleeding," he said in a hoarse voice.

"I know. It's almost stopped. She's going to be all right, partner. Everything's going to be okay." Trammell wrapped his arms around him, easing him away from Marlie. The medics moved to take his place. "We'll go to the hospital with her, but she's going to be fine. I promise."

Dane closed his eyes and let Trammell lead him away.

"I really do feel well enough to go home," Marlie said the next morning. She yawned. "It's just that I'm tired from fighting off the vision."

"And from loss of blood," Dane said. "Maybe tomorrow."

She was propped up in bed, and except for the thickness of the bandages on top of her shoulder and at her waist, it was difficult to tell there was anything wrong with her, though to Dane's critical eye she was still far too pale.

He had been at the hospital with her all night. If he lived to be a hundred and fifty, he'd never forget the absolute, bone-chilling terror of those minutes when he had realized that he had been lured away, and left Marlie unprotected. It had taken him a lifetime to get back to her, and cost him another lifetime in the effort to get into the house. The hospital had been a zoo, with cops everywhere and reporters fighting to get in to talk to Marlie, and Dane had been totally unable to cope with it. All he had been able to do, once the doctors had let him get to her again, was hold her hand and try to reassure himself that she was really all right.

Trammell had taken over; he had handled the reporters, categorically denying them access to Marlie's room but promising a news conference later in the morning. He had deflected Bonness and Chief Champlin away from Dane. He had called Grace, who had brought fresh clothes and toiletries for both Dane and Marlie. Dane had showered and shaved, but the haggard lines in his face revealed the toll the night had taken on him. If it hadn't been for Trammell, he wouldn't have made it through the night.

Trammell had been there for most of the night, too, but he had left around dawn and just returned. He was impeccably dressed, as always, though he, too, showed the signs of a sleepless night. Grace had remained with them.

Marlie pressed the button that moved the head of the bed to a more upright position. She truly did feel well enough to go home; the cuts were sore, and she had to be careful when she moved, but all in all she wasn't in any undue pain. She was alive. The heavy sense of evilness that had been pressing down on her for weeks was gone. The sun seemed brighter, the air fresher.

"I've told you everything that happened last night," she

said. "Now I want to know what you've found out this morning."

Dane smiled at her reassuringly normal tone. "Don't look at me. I haven't left this place. I don't know anything."

Grace stretched out her long legs. "Yes, Alex, spill your guts."

Trammell propped himself against the windowsill. "We found his car about two blocks away, and ran the license plate. His name was Carroll Janes; he moved here from Pittsburgh about five months ago. Pittsburgh PD have several unsolved murders that fit the bill. We searched his apartment and found a blond wig he evidently wore all the time, except when he was killing. He worked at Danworth's department store, in customer service. Evidently that's how he picked his victims. If anyone gave him a hard time— bingo."

"That was the tie," Dane murmured. "They all shopped at Danworth's. I remember Jackie Sheets's friend saying that she had been upset about a blouse that came apart, or something like that. God, it was right there in front of me. I even thought that they shopped at the same place, but that just about everyone in the city did, too."

"Don't beat yourself up over it," Marlie advised tartly. "You aren't clairvoyant, you know." After a startled second, he chuckled. He was looking better, she decided, that stark look fading as he recovered from the shock.

"Carroll Janes," Grace said. "That's a strange name for a man."

"No joke. That's why we didn't turn him up on those lists we were running. His name was crossed out because it looked like a woman's name." Trammell sounded disgusted at that oversight. "We don't have much background on him yet. We may never know what made him tick. I don't know if it even matters. A subhuman son of a bitch like that doesn't deserve to live."

Marlie saw Dane flinch. He was having a harder time handling the night's events than she was. He deeply regretted that she had been touched by such ugly violence, but in an odd way she felt stronger. She wasn't elated that she had killed a man, but neither was she consumed by guilt. She had done what was necessary. If she had hesitated, she would be dead now. She had controlled the vision, and this time she had won. Carroll Janes was dead; Marilyn Elrod and Nadine Vinick and Jackie Sheets, and all of the other women he had killed, finally had their justice.

Dane picked up her hand and played with her fingers, his eyes closing as he felt again the overwhelming relief that she was all right.

Grace elbowed Trammell. "We have to go now," she said. "I have to get ready for work."

"I'll be back this afternoon," Trammell added. "Call me if you need me before then."

"Okay," Dane agreed. After they left, he walked to the door and leaned out to get the attention of the uniformed officer who stood guard there. "No visitors," he said. "Not even the mayor. No one."

"I may have trouble keeping the docs out, Hollister," the officer warned.

"Well, maybe them. But knock first." He closed the door and went back to Marlie's bedside. He stroked her face, smoothed her hair.

She reached up and touched his cheek. "I really am all right. And I'd much rather be at home than here."

He turned his head to kiss her fingers. "Just be patient, okay? If the doctor wants to watch you for another twenty-four hours, he must have a reason. Let me be certain you're okay before you leave. I need that."

There was naked emotion in his face. Dane was wide open, not bothering to guard himself. After what he had been through, he would never again try to control his feelings for her. He had almost lost her the night before; life was too short, too uncertain, to do anything but live it to the fullest.

His expression was serious as he smoothed her hair away

from her face. "We didn't finish getting things ironed out between us last night."

"No, everything got a little hectic there, didn't it?"

"Are you still mad at me?"

A little smile curved her mouth. "No."

"I swear to God I didn't string you along just to stay on top of the situation. The only thing I thought about being on top of was you."

She snorted. "Gosh, that's romantic." But the smile remained.

"I don't know how to be romantic. All I know is I want you, and I can't let you go. I've never run into this type of situation before, so I probably messed up in the way I handled it. I wanted to take my time, see how things developed. I didn't want to rush you, or put pressure on you while all of this other mess was going on. You had enough to worry about."

She bit her lip, bemused by his words. Ye gods, maybe Trammell was right; maybe Dane really was too hardheaded to know when he was in love, or that a woman would reasonably expect him to say so. She took a deep breath, conscious of how much she wanted everything to go right this time. Maybe he wasn't the only one who had been a little too cautious; maybe she needed to encourage him more.

"Is sex all you want?" she asked, tension invading her as she waited for his answer.

"Hell, no!" he said explosively. "Honey, tell me what *you* need. I can do something about it if you'll tell me, but don't leave me in the dark like this. What can I do to convince you of how I feel about you?"

She drew back in the hospital bed, giving him an incredulous look. "Convince me? Dane, you've never told me to begin with! I don't have any idea how you feel!"

It was his turn to stare incredulously. "What the hell do you mean, you don't have any idea how I feel?"

She rolled her eyes beseechingly toward the heavens.

"Lord help me, the man's as thick as a tree. How am I supposed to know if you don't tell me? I've told you time and again that I can't read you! Say it in plain English, Dane. Do you love me? That's what I need to know."

"Of course I love you!" he roared, his temper flashing.

"Then *say* so!"

"I love you, damn it!" He surged to his feet and stood over her bed, hands on hips. "What about you? Are we in this together, or am I soloing?"

She thought of punching him, but decided not to put that much strain on her stitches. She contented herself with saying, "No, you aren't soloing."

"Then *say* it!"

"I love you, damn it!" She said it just as belligerently as he had.

His chest heaved with the force of his breathing as they faced each other down in silence. Finally the tension eased out of his coiled muscles. "That's settled, then." He sat down again.

"What's settled?" she challenged.

"That I love you and you love me."

"So what do we do? Call a truce?"

He shook his head and picked up her hand again. "What we do is get married." He pressed a kiss to her fingertips. "We aren't going to wait six months, either, like some people I know. It'll probably be this weekend. No longer than a week."

Marlie's breath caught, and a luminous smile broke over her face like sunrise. "I'm sure we can manage it by this weekend," she said.

He wanted to fold her in his arms, but he was too afraid of hurting her. He looked at her, and was amazed at how calm she was. She had been stalked by a killer, had emptied a pistol into him, and she seemed so . . . peaceful. Not even getting engaged had shaken that serenity.

He began shaking, as he had several times that night. "I'm sorry," he blurted, for the fifteenth time, his expression telling her where his thoughts had gone. "God, baby, I messed up bad. I never intended for you to be in danger. I don't know how he found you."

Her blue eyes were even more bottomless than usual. "Maybe it was meant. Maybe it was my fault that he found me. I should have gone to a safe house. Maybe, at the end, he could sense me the way I could sense him. Maybe I was the only one who had a chance against him, because I could tell where he was, what he was doing. There are too many maybes; we'll never know for certain. But I'm *okay,* Dane, in every way."

"I love you. When I thought he had you—" His voice cracked. Suddenly he couldn't stand it. With exquisite care he gathered her up in his arms and lifted her from the bed, then sat down and cradled her on his lap, his face buried in her hair.

"I know. I love you too." She didn't protest that the action jarred her shoulder, or that he was holding her too tightly for comfort. She needed that contact, the security and warmth of his embrace. She nestled against him. "Dane?"

"Hmmm?"

"There is one thing."

He raised his head. "What?"

"Are you certain you want to marry me?"

"Damn right I am. What brought this on?"

"I know how uncomfortable it makes you that I am what I am. And I can't marry you without telling you everything. I've pretty much recovered all my abilities. In fact, I'm better at it than I was before, because now I can control it."

He didn't hesitate. The only way to have Marlie was to take her as she was, psychic abilities and all. "But you can't read *me* at all, right?"

"Nope. You're the most thickheaded man I've ever seen. It's *such* a relief."

He grinned, and brushed a kiss across her temple. "It

wouldn't make any difference anyway. I'm going to marry you, no matter what."

"But I *can* check up on you," she admitted. "If you have a bad day, you won't be able to hide it from me, the way cops usually do with their wives. There won't be any tucking it away in a corner of your mind, because I'll already know what happened."

"I can live with that." Easily, he realized. At this point he could probably live with her even if she were a card-carrying swami and rode a magic carpet. "If you can handle being a cop's wife, I can be a psychic's husband. What the hell; how rough can it be?"

Epilogue

DANE ROLLED OUT OF BED, LOOKED AT MARLIE, TURNED green, and dashed for the bathroom. She propped herself up on her elbow, considering the situation with mild disbelief. "I'm the one who's pregnant," she called. "Why are you having morning sickness?"

He came out of the bathroom several minutes later, still rather pale. "One of us has to," he said. He groaned and collapsed on the bed. "I don't think I can make it in to work today."

She nudged him with her foot. "Sure you can. Just eat some dry toast and you'll feel better. You know Trammell will tease you if you don't show up."

"He already does." Dane's voice was muffled in the pillow. "The only thing that keeps him from telling everyone else is that I know something just as bad about him. We have each other in a Mexican standoff."

She threw back the covers and got out of bed. She felt wonderful. She had been queasy a little at first, but never quite to the point of throwing up, and that had soon passed.

For her, that is. Dane was still throwing up regularly, every morning, though it was just past New Year's and she was now six months along. He was paying the price for getting her pregnant immediately after their wedding.

"I wonder how you're going to handle labor and delivery," she mused aloud, giving him a wicked look.

He groaned. "I don't want to think about it."

He didn't handle it at all well. As a labor coach, he was a complete washout. From the time her pains started, he was in agony. The nurses loved him. They installed him on a cot next to her, so he could hold her hand; it seemed to give him comfort. He was pale and sweating, and every time she had a contraction, he had one too.

"This is wonderful," one older nurse said, watching him with joy. "If only all the fathers could do this. There may be justice in this world, after all."

Marlie patted his hand. She was ready for this to be over, even if the price was these steadily increasing pains that were now threatening to become very serious indeed. She felt heavy and exhausted, and the pressure in her pelvis threatened to tear her apart, but a part of her was still able to marvel at her husband. And *she* was supposed to be empathic! Dane had suffered through every month, every pain, with her; she wondered just how labor pains felt in a man.

"Oh, God, here comes another one," he groaned, gripping her hand, and sure enough, her belly began to tighten. She fell back, gasping, trying to find the crest of the pain and ride it.

"This is going to be an only child," he panted. "There won't be another one, I swear. God, when is he going to get here?"

"Soon," she answered. She could feel the deep, heavy tightening within. Their son would arrive soon.

He did, within half an hour. Dane wasn't able to be there during delivery; the doctor had been forced to give him a sedative to ease his pain. But when Marlie woke up from an exhausted doze, he was sitting in the chair beside her bed, looking pale and exhausted himself, and he was holding the baby.

His rough face broke into a grin. "It was rough," he said, "but we did it. He's great. He's perfect. But he's still going to be an only child."

"AN EXTRAORDINARY TALENT."
—*Romantic Times*

LINDA HOWARD

❀

"Linda Howard writes such beautiful love stories. Her characters are always so compelling....She never disappoints."
—Julie Garwood

❀

- ☐ A LADY OF THE WEST .... 66080-2/$5.99
- ☐ ANGEL CREEK ....66081-0/$5.99
- ☐ THE TOUCH OF FIRE ....72858-X/$5.50
- ☐ HEART OF FIRE ....72859-8/$5.50
- ☐ DREAM MAN......................79935-5/$5.99

AVAILABLE FROM POCKET BOOKS

POCKET BOOKS

Simon & Schuster Mail Order
200 Old Tappan Rd., Old Tappan, N.J. 07675
Please send me the books I have checked above. I am enclosing $_____ (please add $0.75 to cover the postage and handling for each order. Please add appropriate sales tax). Send check or money order–no cash or C.O.D.'s please. Allow up to six weeks for delivery. For purchase over $10.00 you may use VISA: card number, expiration date and customer signature must be included.

Name _____

Address _____

City _____ State/Zip _____

VISA Card # _____ Exp.Date _____

Signature _____ 765-03

Pocket Books presents. . .

Everlasting Love

Sparkling new springtime romances from

Jayne Ann Krentz
Linda Lael Miller

Linda Howard

Kasey Michaels

Carla Neggers

52150-0/$5.99

Available from POCKET BOOKS

Simon & Schuster Mail Order

Please send me the audio I have checked above. I am enclosing $_____ (please add $3.95 to cover postage and handling plus your applicable local sales tax). Send check or money order — no cash or C.O.D.'s please. Allow up to six weeks for delivery. You may use VISA/MASTERCARD: card number, expiration date and customer signature must be included.

Name _____

Address _____

City _____ State/Zip _____

VISA/MASTERCARD Card # _____ Exp.Date _____

Signature _____

1059-02

<u>New York Times</u> Bestselling
Author of YANKEE WIFE

LINDA LAEL MILLER

*proudly presents her first
novel in Hardcover*

✤✤✤✤✤✤✤✤✤

PIRATES

✤✤✤✤✤✤✤✤✤

COMING SOON *from*
Pocket Books

Don't miss it!!

POCKET
B O O K S

1035

POCKET BOOKS
PROUDLY ANNOUNCES

AFTER THE NIGHT

LINDA HOWARD

**Coming soon from
Pocket Books
Fall 1995**

**The following is a preview of
*After the Night. . . .***

It was steaming hot as she walked along the narrow streets of the French Quarter, and she crossed over to the shady side. She visited New Orleans frequently, because of the agency office here, but she had never really taken the time to explore this old district. Horse-drawn carriages moved slowly through the streets, with the driver and guide pointing out attractions to the tourists in the carriage. Most people, though, depended on their own feet to take them through the Quarter. Later on, the main attraction would be the bars and clubs; this early in the day, shopping was the goal, and the myriad of boutiques, antiques shops, and specialty stores gave plenty of choice and opportunity to people who wanted to spend their money.

She went into a lingerie shop and bought a peach silk nightgown that looked like something one of the Hollywood movie queens would have worn back in the forties and fifties. After wearing almost nothing but hand-me-downs for the first fourteen years of her life, she felt sinfully self-indulgent about new clothes now. She could never bring herself to go on shopping binges now that she had a bit of cash, but every so often she allowed herself a luxury purchase: lace underwear, a sumptuous nightgown, a really good pair of shoes. Those small indulgences made her feel as if the bad times were truly in the past.

When she reached the restaurant, Margot was waiting for her inside. The tall blonde jumped up and hugged her enthusiastically, though it had been only a little over a week since Faith had left Dallas. "It's so good to see you! Well, are you settling down okay in your little burg? *I* don't think I'll ever settle down again! My first business trip, and it's to New Orleans. Isn't this a great place? I hope you don't mind sitting in the courtyard rather than inside. I know it's hot, but how often do you get to eat lunch in a courtyard in New Orleans?"

Faith smiled at the barrage of words. Yes, Margot was definitely excited by her new job. "Well, let's see. I'm twenty-six, and this is the first time I've eaten lunch or anything else in a courtyard, so I'd say it doesn't happen too often."

"Honey, I can give you ten years, so it's even rarer than you think, and I intend to enjoy every minute." They took their seats at one of the tables in the courtyard. Actually, it wasn't uncomfortably hot; there were umbrellas, and trees to give shade. Margot eyed the bag in Faith's hand. "I see you've been shopping. What did you buy?"

"A nightgown. I would show it to you, but I don't want to drag it out here in the middle of the restaurant."

Margot's eyes twinkled. "That kind of nightgown, huh?"

"Let's just say it isn't a Mother Hubbard," Faith replied delicately, and they laughed. A smiling waiter poured water for them, the light tinkle of the ice cubes making her suddenly aware of her thirst, and how hot she had become on the walk to the restaurant. She glanced around at the other diners as she sipped the cold water, and looked straight at Gray Rouillard.

Her heart gave that immediate, betraying little jump. He was sitting, with another man whose back was to her, two tables over from her and Margot. His dark eyes gleamed as he lifted his glass of wine to her in a silent toast. She lifted the water glass in a return salute, inclining her head in a mock gracious nod.

"Do you know someone here?" Margot asked, turning in her seat. Gray smiled at her. Margot smiled in return, a rather weak effort, then turned back to Faith with a poleaxed expression on her face. "Holy cow," she said in a dazed voice.

Faith understood perfectly. The flamboyance of New Orleans suited Gray. He was wearing a lightweight, Italian-cut suit, and a pale blue shirt that flattered the olive tones of his skin. His thick black hair was brushed back from his face and secured with a bronze clasp at the nape of his neck. The tiny diamond stud glittered in his left earlobe. With the breadth of his linebacker's shoulders and the feline grace with which he lounged at the small table, he drew the eye of every woman in the courtyard. He wasn't pretty-boy handsome; his French ancestors had bequeathed him a thin, high-bridged Gallic nose, slightly too long, and a heavy beard that left him with a five-o'clock shadow even at lunchtime. His jaw looked as solid as a rock. No, there was nothing pretty about Gray. What he was, was striking, and dangerously exciting, with his bold, dark eyes and the lazy, sensual curve of his mouth. He looked like a man who was adventurous and confident, both in bed and out.

"Who is he?" Margot breathed. "And do you know him, or are you flirting with a stranger?"

"I'm not flirting," Faith said, startled, and deliberately turned her gaze to the other side of the courtyard, away from Gray.

Margot laughed. "Honey, that little toast you gave him said, 'Come and get me, big boy, if you think you're man enough.' Do you think a pirate like that is going to ignore the challenge?"

Faith's eyes widened. "It did not! He raised his wineglass to me, so I did the same with my water glass. Why would he think anything about it when he started it?"

"Have you looked in the mirror lately?" Margot asked, sneaking another look over her shoulder at Gray, and a smile spread across her face.

Faith made a dismissive gesture. "That has nothing to do with it. He wouldn't—"

"He is," Margot said with satisfaction, and Faith couldn't control a little jump as she looked around and saw Gray almost upon them.

"Ladies," he drawled, lifting Faith's hand from the table and bowing over it with an Old World gesture that seemed entirely natural to him. Her startled eyes met his, and she saw deviltry, as well as something hot and dangerous, in those dark depths before he shielded them as he touched his lips to her fingers. His lips were soft and warm, very warm. Her heart banged painfully against her ribs and she tried to withdraw her hand, but his grip tightened and she felt the tip of his tongue probe delicately into the sensitive hollow between her last two fingers. Startled, she jumped again, and his awareness of that betraying little movement was in his eyes as he straightened and finally released her hand.

He turned to Margot, bending low over the hand she had extended with a dazed expression, but Faith noticed that he didn't kiss Margot's fingers. It didn't matter. Margot couldn't have looked more bedazzled if he had presented her with diamonds. Wondering if that same weak, yielding expression was on her face, Faith quickly looked down to disguise it, though of course it was too late. Gray was too experienced to miss any of the nuances. Her fingers tingled, and the skin between her fingers throbbed where his tongue had touched. The tiny damp spot felt both hot and cold, and she clenched her hand to dispel the sensation. Her face was burning. His action had been a subtle parody of sex, a mock penetration that her body recognized, and responded to with a pooling of heat in her lower body, a growing moistness. She could feel her nipples tighten and thrust against the lace of her bra. *Damn* him!

"Gray Rouillard," he was murmuring to Margot. "Faith and I are old acquaintances."

At least he hadn't lied and said they were friends, Faith thought, watching tautly as Margot introduced herself, and, to her horror, asked Gray to join them. Too late, she gave Margot a warning nudge with her foot.

"Thank you," Gray said, smiling down at Margot with such charm that she didn't react at all to Faith's kick. "But I'm here on business, and I have to get back to my own table.

I just wanted to come over and speak to Faith for a moment. Have you known each other long?"

"Four years," Margot replied, and proudly added, "I'm her district manager."

Faith nudged her ankle again, harder this time, and when Margot gave her a surprised look, she glared a warning.

"Really," Gray said, sounding interested. His gaze was sharper. "What business are you in?"

Finally having gotten the message, Margot gave Faith a swift, questioning glance.

"Nothing on your scale," Faith said, smiling at him so coolly that he shrugged, realizing he wasn't going to gain any more information.

She exhaled with relief, but tensed again when he squatted by the table, a gracefully masculine action that brought his face more on a level with hers. It was more difficult to hide her expression now than when he had been standing. This close, she could see the bottomless black pupils of his eyes, the glitter in them as he looked at her. "I wish I'd known you were coming to New Orleans, sweetheart. We could have driven down together."

If he thought she would dissemble in front of Margot, he had sadly mistaken her. If he thought his charm had turned her brain into mush, he was wrong there, too. How she would like to rub his nose in the fact that she was a successful businesswoman, but the past week had made her wary of giving him any information about herself. Respectability wouldn't make any difference to either him or the town of Prescott; until—and if—she could prove that her mother hadn't run away with his father, nothing would change his attitude. Lifting her chin, a sure sign of temper, she said, "I'd rather have walked all the way than get in a car with you."

Margot made a choking sound, but Faith didn't spare a look for her; she kept her gaze locked with Gray's, the battle visually joined. He grinned with a buccaneer's reckless enjoyment of a fight.

"But we could have had a lot of fun, and shared . . . expenses."

"I'm sorry you're having money problems," she said sweetly. "Perhaps your business associate will put you up if you can't afford your own hotel room."

"I don't have to worry about hotel expenses." The grin broadened. "I own the hotel."

Damn, she thought. She'd have to find out which one he owned, and make sure she didn't book any tour groups into it.

"Why don't we have dinner together tonight?" he suggested. "We have a lot to talk about."

"I can't imagine what. Thank you, but no." She was driving back to Prescott this afternoon, but she would much rather he think she was refusing the invitation purely because she didn't want his company.

"It would be to your advantage," he said, and the dangerous look was back in his eyes.

"I doubt that anything a Rouillard suggested would be to my advantage."

"You haven't listened to my . . . suggestions yet."

"I don't intend to, either. Go back to your table and leave me alone."

"I'd planned on doing the first." He stood and trailed a long forefinger down her cheek. "There's no way in hell I'll do the last." He nodded to Margot and strolled back to his own table.

Margot blinked, her eyes owlish. "Shouldn't I check him for wounds? You really had the knife out for him. What on earth has that dark-eyed piece of work done to make you so mad at him?"

Faith took refuge in her water glass again, sipping from it until she had her expression under control. When she lowered it, she said, "It goes back a long way. He's a Hatfield and I'm a McCoy."

"A family feud? C'mon."

"He's trying to run me out of Prescott," Faith said baldly. "If he found out about the travel agency, it's possible he could cause trouble by ruining some of the tours we arrange. That would hurt our reputation, and we'd lose money. You heard him: He owns a hotel here. Not only is he filthy rich, so he has the money to bribe people to do what he wanted, but he has contacts in the business. I wouldn't put anything past him."

"Wow. This sounds serious. What started this feud, and has there ever been actual bloodshed?"

"I don't know." Faith fiddled with her silverware, not wanting to mention her suspicion that Guy had been killed. "My mother used to be his father's mistress. Needless to say, his family hates anyone with the name of Devlin." That would do for an explanation; she couldn't go into the full tale, couldn't trot out her memories of that night even for a sympathetic audience.

"What did you say is the name of this town?" Margot demanded. "Prescott? Are you sure it isn't Peyton Place?"

They both laughed, and the waiter approached then to ask their preference for lunch. They both chose the buffet, and went inside to make their selections. Faith was acutely aware of a dark gaze following her every move, and wished Margot hadn't been so set on eating in the courtyard. She would much rather have been shielded from his view. Who could have guessed that he would be in New Orleans today, though, or that in a city of this size they would immediately run into each other? True, the Court of Two Sisters was a popular restaurant, but New Orleans was larded with popular restaurants.

Gray and his business associate left the restaurant not long after Faith and Margot returned to the table with their loaded plates. He paused beside Faith. "I do want to talk to you," he said. "Come to my suite tonight at six. I'm at the Beauville Courtyard."

She hid her dismay. The Beauville was a lovely, mid-size hotel with a great atmosphere, built around an open courtyard. She had booked tour groups and vacationers in there many times. If Gray owned it, she would have to find another lovely, mid-size hotel with a great atmosphere, because she didn't dare use his again. In answer to his command, for that was what it was, she shook her head. "No. I won't be there."

His eyes gleamed. "Then take your chances," he said, and walked away.

"Take your chances?" Margot echoed indignantly, staring at his broad back. "What the hell did he mean by that? Was he *threatening* you?"

"Probably," Faith said, lifting a bite of pasta salad to her mouth. She closed her eyes in delight. "Mmmm, taste this. It's wonderful."

"Are you out of your mind? How can you eat when Mr. Macho just threatened to . . . do something, I guess." Frustrated, Margot picked up her fork and tasted the pasta salad. She paused. "This *is* good. You're right, worrying about him can wait until after we eat."

Faith chuckled. "I'm used to his threats."

"Does he ever carry through with them?"

"Always. One thing about Gray, he means what he says, and he isn't shy about throwing his weight around."

Margot's fork clattered to the table. "Then what are you going to do?"

"Nothing. After all, he didn't actually threaten anything specific."

"That means you have to be on your guard against everything."

"I am anyway, where he's concerned." Pain pierced her at her own words, and she looked down at her plate to hide it. How wonderful it would be to feel safe and relaxed with Gray, to feel she could trust that all his ruthless determination, his vital intensity, would be used in defense of her rather than against her. Did Noelle and Monica know how lucky they were, to have someone like him standing ready to go to battle on their behalf? She loved him, but he was her enemy. She could never let herself forget that, not let wishful thinking cloud her common sense.

Deliberately she steered the conversation into safer waters, namely the few problems that had developed with her in Prescott rather than on the scene in Dallas. She was relieved that the problems *were* few, and relatively minor. Some difficulties had been expected, but Margot was a good business manager and got on well with the travel agents in the other offices. The only real difference was that now Margot was the one traveling around, instead of Faith, though there would be times when Faith's presence was required. For the most part, everything had worked out. They decided that, since Faith was so close to Baton Rouge and New Orleans anyway, she would continue overseeing those offices, because it would be foolish for Margot to fly or drive all that way. Margot was a little disappointed, because she was entranced with New Orleans, but she was also extremely practical, and the change was her suggestion. There would be times when it wouldn't be convenient for Faith to get to either city, so she would content herself with the occasional visit.

After lunch, they parted company outside the restaurant, for Margot's hotel was in the opposite direction from where Faith had left her car. It was even hotter now than it had been before, the mugginess making the air feel thick, hard to breathe. The smell of the river was stronger, and black clouds were looming on the horizon, promising a spring thunderstorm that would temporarily relieve the heat, then turn the streets into a steam bath. Faith speeded up her steps, wanting to be on her way home before the storm broke.

As she drew even with a recessed doorway that led into a darkened, deserted shop, a strong hand seized her arm from behind and dragged her into the doorway. *Mugged!* she thought, and anger flashed through her, red-hot and reckless. She had struggled too hard for what she had to give it up without protest, the way the police advised. Instead she jabbed her elbow backward, slamming it into a hard belly and eliciting a very satisfactory grunt from her assailant. She turned, her fist drawn back and belatedly opening her mouth to yell for help. She had a blurred impression of height and wide shoulders, then she was jerked hard against him and her voice was muffled against an expensive, oatmeal-colored Italian suit.

"God Almighty," Gray said, amusement rich in his deep voice. "You little redheaded wildcat, if you're as wild as this in bed, it must be a hell of a ride."

Shock at his comment mingled with relief at his identity, and neither diluted her anger. Breathing hard, she shoved at his chest, freeing herself. "Damn you! I thought I was being mugged!"

His eyebrows drew together. "And you started slinging that sharp little elbow?" he asked in disbelief, rubbing his stomach. "What if I *had* been a mugger, and had a knife or a gun? Don't you know you're supposed to give up your purse rather than chance getting hurt?"

"Like hell," she snapped, pushing her hair out of her face.

His face cleared, and he laughed. "No, I guess you wouldn't." He reached out and tucked a fiery strand behind her ear. "Attack first and think about it later, hm?"

She jerked her head away from his touch. "Why did you grab me like that?"

"I've been following you since you left the restaurant, and thought this would be as good a place as any for our little chat. You really should pay more attention to who's behind you."

"Skip the lecture, if you don't mind." She glanced at the sky. "I want to get to my car before that storm gets here."

"We can go to my hotel—or yours—if you don't want to talk here."

"No. I'm not going anywhere with you." Especially to a hotel room. He kept making those sexually loaded remarks, alarming her. She didn't trust his motives, and she didn't trust herself to resist him. All in all, it was best to stay as far away from him as she could.

"Then here it is." Gray looked down at her, standing so close to her in the narrow space of the doorway that her breasts were almost brushing his suit. When he had jerked her against him to muffle her scream, he had felt them, firm and round and luscious. He wanted to see them, wanted to touch them, taste them. He was so physically aware of her that he felt as if he were standing in the middle of an electrical field, with the air snapping and sizzling around them, sparks flying. Fighting with her was more exhilarating than making love to other women. Maybe as a young girl she had been as shy as a fawn, but she had grown into a woman who wasn't afraid of anger, hers or anyone else's.

"I'll buy the house from you," he said abruptly, reminding himself why he had wanted to talk to her. "I'll give you double what you paid for it."

Her green eyes narrowed, making them look even more catlike. "That isn't a good business decision," she said, her tone light, but with temper still seething just below the surface.

He shrugged. "I can afford it. Can you afford to turn it down?"

"Yes," she said, and smiled.

The satisfaction in that smile almost made him laugh again. So she had made something of herself, had she? More than had been obvious at first; if she had a district manager, then obviously she had other employees, in several locations. He felt unwilling pride at what she had accomplished swell in his chest. He knew in intimate detail how little she had possessed when he'd had the Devlins thrown out, because he had watched her frantically picking her things up out of the dirt. Most people had a backup system of friends and relatives, pooled resources; Faith had had nothing, making her accomplishments all the more remarkable. If she'd had *his* assets, Gray thought, she might own the whole state by now. It wouldn't be easy to get rid of a woman with that kind of grit.

Lust coiled and tightened in his guts. He'd never been attracted to weak, helpless women who needed protecting; he had enough of that with his family. There was nothing weak about Faith.

He studied her face, seeing both the resemblance to Renee and the differences. Her mouth was wider, more mobile, her lips red and lush and as velvety as rose petals. Her skin was perfect, with a porcelain texture that would show the imprint of a touch, a kiss. He thought of marking her with his mouth, kissing his way down her body until he reached the soft folds between her legs, folds that protected places even more tender. The image brought him to full, painful erection. Standing this close to her, he could smell the sweet, delicious scent of her skin, and he wondered if that sweetness would be more intense between her legs. He had always loved the way women smelled, but Faith's scent was so enticing that every muscle in his body tightened with need, making it difficult for him to think of anything else.

He knew he shouldn't do it, even as he reached for her. The last thing he wanted was to follow his father's example; he still couldn't think of his father's leaving without feeling the hurt and anger, the betrayal, as fresh as if it had just happened. He didn't want to hurt Noelle and Monica, didn't want to revive that old scandal.

There were a hundred reasons, all of them good, why he shouldn't want Faith Devlin in his arms, but in that instant none of them mattered a rat's ass. His hands closed on her waist, and the feel of her, warm and soft, so vibrant that his palms tingled where he touched her, went to his head like a potent wine. He saw her eyes widen, the black pupils expanding until only a thin rim of green remained. Her hands lifted and flattened against his chest, the placement covering his own nipples, and a shiver of response rippled his skin. Inexorably, his gaze fastened on her mouth, he drew her closer until her slim body rested against him. He felt her legs tangle with his, her firm breasts push against his stomach, saw those soft, full lips part as she drew in a startled breath. Then he lifted her on tiptoe and bent his head, and fed that particular hunger.

Her lips felt like rose petals, too, soft and velvety. He slanted his head and increased the pressure of his mouth, forcing them to open, a flower blooming at his command. Blood thundered through his veins and he pulled her tighter, sliding his arms around her and holding her welded to his body, letting her feel the swollen ridge of his erection against the softness of her belly. He felt her shudder, felt the convulsive movement of her hips, arching into him, and fierce male triumph flooded him. Her arms slid upward over his shoulders, to twine around his neck, and her teeth parted to allow him deeper access. A low growl sounded deep in his throat, and he took it, plundering her mouth with his tongue. Her taste was sweet and hot, flavored with the strong coffee she had drunk with her dessert. Her tongue curled around his in heated welcome, then she sucked daintily, holding him within her mouth.

He drove her backward, forcing her against the locked and boarded door. Dimly he could hear the voices of the people passing on the sidewalk behind them, hear the sullen rumble of thunder, but they meant nothing. She was live fire in his arms, not struggling against his kiss, not just accepting it, but responding wildly to his touch. Her lips trembled and clung and caressed. He wanted more, wanted everything. Deliberately he cupped her buttocks and lifted her, drawing her hips inward so that his erection was nestled in the soft notch of her legs. He rubbed her back and forth against him, groaning aloud at the exquisite pressure.

Rain pattered on the street, signaling the arrival of the storm, and there was a scurry of movement as people darted for cover. A clap of thunder made him lift his head and look around, a little irritated by this intrusion into the sensual haze that clouded his mind.

Whether it was the thunder or his own reaction to it that broke the spell on Faith, she suddenly stiffened in his arms and began shoving against him. He caught a glimpse of her furious face and quickly set her on her feet, releasing her and stepping back before she began screaming bloody murder.

She wriggled past him, onto the sidewalk, where the rain immediately soaked her, and turned to face him. Her eyes were yellowish with turbulence. "Don't touch me again," she said, her voice rough and low. Then she turned and began walking as fast as she could, her head lowered against the rain that swept down the narrow street like a gray curtain. He started after her, intending to drag her to shelter, but forced himself to stop and step back into the doorway. She would fight him like a wildcat if he went after her now. He watched her until she turned the corner two blocks down, and disappeared from sight. She was almost running by then . . . escaping. From him.

For now.

Look for
After the Night
Wherever Paperback Books
Are Sold
Fall 1995